THE
DAMNED
PLACE

Chris Miller

BLACK BED
SHEET

The Damned Place
A Black Bed Sheet/Diverse Media Book
July 2019

ISBN-10: 1-946874-14-0
ISBN-13: 978-1-946874-14-6

The Damned Place

A Black Bed Sheet/Diverse Media Book
Antelope, CA

Praise for Chris Miller

On THE HARD GOODBYE:

"Brutal, driving suspense, with an opening that'll grab you by the throat — but keep in mind it's only the beginning."
—Ray Garton, author of LIVE GIRLS and RAVENOUS

On A MURDER OF SAINTS:

"Evoking emotional attachment for a diverse cast of compelling characters and inducive villain, author Chris Miller impeccably manages to place well thought out flashbacks through the narrative to heighten the tension of the enthralling thriller. This read is highly recommended to those looking for an extraordinary work of talent."
—Enas Reviews, enasreviews.com

This one is for my wife, Aliana. Here's a mean machine, baby.

The Damned Place

Chris Miller

Prologue:

November 19, 1989

Chester Laughton paid no attention to the smell.

It was there, and it wasn't as though he *couldn't* smell it, it was simply not registering in his mind as odd. It *should* have been registering, though. It was a subtle kind of awful. Underneath the smell of the rotting leaves and damp earth. The carcasses of innumerable insects and small animals. Even the trees themselves seemed to be more rotten here than the rest of the woods.

Sure, you could always find dead trees in the woods. You didn't even have to look that hard. They'd be scattered about, here and there, limbs broken off and hanging at forty-five-degree angles from the splintered joint, the fingers of branches in a frozen, eternal grip of the dirt.

But here it was different. Almost *all* of the trees, dead. Or at least dying. Well on their way to joining their wooded brethren in stoic afterlife.

Chester glanced around. He still wasn't paying any attention to that smell. Beneath the surface of the rest, but only just.

After assuring himself his buddy Mike wasn't around, he produced a small stainless steel flask out of the inside pocket of his hunting vest. He twisted the top and flipped it over on its hinge. He glanced once more all around to see if Mike had wandered back into his area.

He hadn't.

Chester grinned to himself, an involuntary reaction to the excitement of ingesting whiskey. He turned the flask up and arched his back as he guzzled down two big gulps of the amber drink. His eyes watered slightly as the evening sun pierced through the treetops and landed on his gaze. Also from the whiskey.

It was stout stuff.

He brought his head back down after the gulps and issued a satisfied sigh, replete with smacking lips and a weathered tongue that lapped any excess alcohol off his shaggy gray facial hair.

He recapped his flask and replaced it in his pocket. He gave his vest a pat over the area the flask rested, like thanking an old friend for being there for you when you really needed someone to listen. Then he pulled his rifle off of his shoulder and swung it around to a more ready position. Muzzle down. Loose grip. Safety on.

Chester was fifty years old. He stood at five feet and ten inches, and the girth of his ever-expanding belly rounded him out to appear to make that measurement seem almost spherical. His beard, which hung from his face in a scattered, mad-scientist abandon, hung from his chin to just above his ample male bosom. He was wearing camouflage overalls and an orange hunting vest and cap. He was carrying his favorite hunting rifle that day, the Winchester .30-.30, with a large, black Bushnell scope mounted to the top.

He and Mike had risen early that morning and spent the pre-dawn hours making their way into the woods.

The Damned Place

It was only about two miles outside of their little town of Winnsboro, Texas. But the hunting was typically damn good here. Deer and rabbits especially seemed to like to call the place home. They'd parked their trucks on the side of an old dirt-top road, half in the ditch, half out, and made their way into the darkened forest.

They'd made out OK, too, that morning. Mike had bagged a six-point buck, and Chester had shot a couple of rabbits. The .30-.30 was *way* overkill for the rabbits, so he had aimed for the head. The first one he'd hit a little below the target and turned what could have been a nice stew into nothing more than a pink mist and a furry red spot. The second had been on target, though. Head gone, body intact.

Dinner.

On the first rabbit, his hands had been shaking. He hadn't had a drink yet that day to really get him going. He remedied that promptly, his hands steadied off, and his aim had become more true.

They'd cleaned their morning kills back at Mike's house and packed the meat into a couple of large coolers with ice. Then they'd headed back out after a few afternoon beers before the evening hunt. Chester hadn't called his wife to let her know where he was or when to expect him. There was no reason to. *He* was the man of the house. And he'd had to remind her and their boy of that again the night before.

He had put about eighteen beers in his gut after three heavy glasses of Kentucky Deluxe whiskey. It was cheap stuff, but it was strong and it got the job done. His wife was watching some shit on the television in their single-wide trailer home that he'd cared nothing about. He had wanted to watch the evening football scores. He had a few bets down with the guys at The Whet Whistle, the bar on the edge of town. She hadn't wanted to change the channel. She'd been very interested in the show she had on. Some cooking nonsense with fancy spices and some faggot in a white hat with a sissy voice.

"Can't you check them tomorrow in the paper?" Cheryl Laughton had asked him. "I don't wanna miss this."

"I'll check it tonight on the TV," Chester barked at her as he snatched the remote off the arm of the couch where she was sitting. "Nobody gives a shit about these faggot dinners."

Cheryl frowned and looked to the floor in deep frustration.

"They ain't faggot dinners, Chester, they're fine meals," she said, her Southern drawl flattening out her I's and further simplifying her contractions. "I bet you'd like them if you try them sometime!"

"Bet you'd like my cock in your asshole if you tried it sometime, but you ain't doing that neither, so shut the fuck up."

Cheryl stood from her position on the couch. Her teeth were clenched. "You're such a bastard, Chester Laughton!" she yelled at him. "I can't never do nothing I want!"

Chester grinned. His chest rose and fell in quick succession as he quietly chuckled, never looking at her. He was staring at the television.

"Can't never my ass," he said as the laugh died off. He was still staring at the TV. "Can't never make a real dinner 'round here, neither. Can't never pick up the goddamn clothes. Can't never pick my whiskey up at

4

the store. Just what in the hell do you do around here all day, anyhow?"

He still hadn't been looking at her.

She shook her head and clenched her fists closed and opened them again and again.

"You go fuck yourself, Chester. You sure as shit ain't fuckin' me tonight, you fat drunk!"

She'd moved to go around him and back into the kitchen. He *still* wasn't looking at her. Wasn't even seeming to acknowledge her.

As she'd gone past him, she knocked the beer in his hand out of his grasp and it tumbled to the floor. Foam and piss-colored liquid splashed out onto the carpet.

Her eyes went wide suddenly.

"I'm sorry, Chester!" she'd said quickly. "I'll clean it up!"

Now Chester was looking at her.

"You damn right you will, you bitch!" he screamed. "You're gonna clean it up, alright!"

He'd grabbed her at the base of her neck, squeezing tightly on the soft area beneath her skull. Then he'd swung her around and threw her to the floor. Her face was right over where the beer had spilled.

"Clean it up, bitch!" he screamed.

He grabbed a wad of her hair and started rubbing it into the floor, mopping the beer with it as he did.

"You clean it up, good!"

Cheryl had begun crying at that point.

He shoved her hair around in the beer a few more times then stood up and kicked her in the ribcage. All the air in her lungs blew out in a pitiful gasp. Tears were streaming down her face now, and snot and phlegm dripped from her nose and mouth in strings. She had begun to cough.

"Goddamn whore," Chester had said and spit on her. He'd turned from her and headed to the kitchen. Down the hall past the kitchen, their son's bedroom door opened. Ryan Laughton stood in the doorway, staring at his father. There'd been a mixture of fear and fury in his boy's eyes. Chester could see the faint twinkle of tears in the corners of his son's eyes.

"Get back to bed, boy," Chester had snapped at him and pointed to the door beyond him. "You ain't supposed to be up."

"I heard Momma scream, Daddy," Ryan had said.

"You mind your business, son!" Chester barked at him. "Now get your ass in bed!"

But Ryan hadn't.

To Chester's bewilderment, his son had defied him and stepped into the hallway and marched right past him and went to his mother, completely ignoring his father.

Chester had watched him go, his mouth agape and eyes wide in furious wonder.

"You OK, Momma?" Ryan had asked as he reached her and knelt beside her. "Are you hurt?"

"Get the fuck back in bed, I told ya!" Chester screamed.

Ryan's mother raised herself up on an elbow and wiped the snot and tears from her face. Then she put a hand on Ryan's arm.

"Do what your father says, baby," she'd said to him. "Go get in bed. I'm alright."

But Ryan had shook his head.

"You don't look alright," he said, and glared at his father.

Ryan was eleven years old, and already was as tall as his mother's five feet and four inches. He was big too. Not like his father, with slabs of fat hanging and bloating every which way. Ryan was strong. He played outside most days after school and enjoyed physical education at school. His young body was muscular and one day he would be someone to be reckoned with.

Unfortunately, he thought he already was.

Ryan had stood quickly, his hands clenching into fists. His eyes bore into his father's.

"Don't you touch her again!" he'd shouted.

Chester had laughed out loud at this. He'd turned from his son and opened the refrigerator and fetched himself a beer to replace the one in the carpet and Cheryl's hair. As he turned back towards them, however, grasping the twist top to open his brew, Ryan was suddenly there. He'd swung a fist at his father and caught him across his left cheek. Wasn't a bad hit either, Chester remembered. It had hurt.

But it also had pissed him off.

Chester proceeded to smack the bottle in his hand across his son's face, bloodying his nose and mouth. When Ryan had hit the floor, Chester kicked him in the stomach three times.

One.

Two.

Three.

Then he opened his beer. Cheryl had been screaming and crying again, her arm reaching towards her son. Some foam from the disturbed beer spewed up from the lip of the bottle as he opened it. He had held the beer over his son and let it rain on his gasping and bloody face.

"Be sure you clean that up, you little son of a whore," he'd said in a measured and calm tone.

Then he'd gone to bed.

When he rose that morning, Cheryl had been lying next to him and Ryan had been in his bed. Both had cleaned up the spills and themselves. They'd been right where they were supposed to be, and he knew they always would be. Sometimes wives and kids needed lessons, and he considered himself a pretty good teacher.

Now, he and Mike were out in the woods for their afternoon hunt. The sun was dipping low on the horizon and daylight would be gone before long. They had less than an hour before they would need to be back at the truck to get going at last light.

Chester looked around again, knowing Mike didn't mind drinking but didn't appreciate being in the woods with someone carrying a loaded deer-rifle and drinking alcohol. But he didn't see Mike anywhere, so he repeated his moves from earlier.

Rifle slung onto shoulder.

Dig out flask.

Open top.

Drink liberally.

Reverse.

He issued another sigh of satisfaction and took a deep breath. He could smell the whiskey coming off his breath and his beard. He could smell the leaves, the trees, the smells of the woods. He could smell the...

What the hell is that? he thought.

The Damned Place

He finally noticed the smell. It was subtle. It almost seemed to blend in with the rest of the scent of the woods. Almost like it belonged. The dead leaves. The damp earth. The rotting branches and trunks. Dead insects and animals.

And this other thing.

He looked around, trying to identify where it was coming from. He sniffed at the air like a dog for nearly a minute before deciding it was coming from his left. He began to move that direction.

Twenty feet. Thirty. Fifty.

The smell was getting stronger. Whatever it was, he was on the right trail now.

He moved further into the woods in the direction of the smell. He was faintly aware of the fact that he was moving further and further away from the road, their trucks, and that the sun was going down faster now. He needed to find Mike and start heading back.

Soon.

He pushed the branches of a mostly dead dogwood tree out of his way and stepped around it. Ahead, he could make out the shape of...of a...

A house?

He stepped closer now, squinting his eyes in the diminishing light. It was definitely an old house. The woods had grown up around it, all the way up to it on all sides. It was an old, dilapidated place. He guessed it had been built in the late 1800s, possibly the early 1900s, but no sooner. Lots of rotting wood on the sides adorned the place, and the windows were mostly busted out, however, a few still had panes in them. Some were only half missing, their sharp, razor-like pieces standing there like threats.

Come on in. I dare you.

Chester was aware of the thought, *the words,* but had no idea where it had come from. He had no desire to go inside the house. He only wanted to find his friend and get the hell out of there before it got too dark to find their way back. But still, he'd heard it. It was there. In his head, but not *coming from* his head.

He shivered.

It was getting cold, and he needed some more whiskey to warm him. That was all.

He pulled his flask out again and took three huge gulps. Then he looked all around the side of the house. The stairs to the porch were splintered and smashed in places, but seemed sturdy enough near the edges. The porch itself led around to the right of the house and then turned and followed on to the back. To the left was a large column-shaped portion of the house that rose into the trees to a point which seemed to be a third level. Half-shattered windows and graying wood siding stood silently before him.

And that smell.

It was stronger here. *Much* stronger. A breeze was blowing through the trees and carried through the missing and busted windows of the columned area of the house. The smell was on it, coming from inside.

Probably a dead animal, he thought.

But this smell didn't really fit that. It seemed like something that belonged with death, but not death itself. It had a metallic scent to it. Almost a tang.

"Mike?" Chester shouted from the base of the stairs.

There was no answer. Only the breeze gliding through the pines and oaks and dogwoods.

10

And the smell.

"Mike, we gotta get going!" he shouted. "Where you at?"

He was met with more silence.

He raised his foot and took a step up on the stairs. He moved cautiously, putting his weight on it a little at a time until he was sure it would hold him. It seemed solid.

As he climbed the stairs, his eyes fell on the door. An ancient thing, hanging three-fourths open, its hinges rusted. There were the shattered remains of some old stained glass in the center, now just a few pieces remained, the intersecting and serpentine wire that separated the parts still standing defiantly.

Another gust of wind blew through the house and out the front door, hitting him in the face. The smell was on it, stronger than ever now. It was accompanied by something else. It took him a moment to place it, but once he did, he was sure it could be nothing else.

Shit and piss.

"Mike?!" he called again. His heart rate was rising steadily now. Another shiver went down his spine, but the thought of warming himself with the whiskey that still sloshed in the flask in his hand was the farthest thing from his mind.

Where the hell is Mike?

"Mike, quit fuckin' around, we gotta get!"

Silence.

Breeze.

Smell.

He reached the top of the stairs. He glanced around a few times before stepping onto the landing. There was nothing. Dead leaves and limbs littered the porch

11

in spite of the awning over it, but aside from that, there was nothing. He took a step toward the door.

"Mike, I'm gonna kick your a—"

His foot broke through the landing in front of the door. He tripped and his flask flew from his hand and into the house. It clanked and clattered loudly on the hollow floor within. He put his other foot out to catch himself, his hands beginning to flail in involuntary defense. His other foot crashed through the floor as well.

He was teetering forward now, his arms in full revolt. He managed to get his first foot out of the hole, but the second foot was also trying to free itself at the same time, as if operating on its own, completely independent of the other. He came crashing down into the door. It screeched and howled in protest as it swung inward the last quarter of the way and smacked into an eons-old wall inside.

Chester crashed down finally, half in and half out of the door to the house, the wind *whooshing* from him as he did. His rifle clattered to the porch behind him. He heard a sound of glass shattering and began to absently curse in frustration. The scope would be ruined.

"Son of a bitch!" he snarled through clenched teeth as he was getting his breath back.

He looked back through the door and saw the two wooden craters in the landing beyond where his feet had crashed through and shook his head.

Daring, are you?

It was that voice again. Inside his head, but not from it.

12

He swung his head around again to look into the house now. He squinted his eyes, the darkness of the house contrasting with the last vestiges of light outside.

The smell hit him again. And strong.

He took a moment, blinking to help his eyes adjust. The stench was so strong now it was covering up everything else.

Metal.

Piss.

Shit.

He started to push himself up and noticed his hands were on something wet. His brow furrowed as he looked down at his palms. A dark, viscous fluid covered them, and it took a moment before his mind registered what he was seeing.

His hands were covered in blood.

It was bright. Fresh. Still *moving* across the floor of the house.

"What the fuck?" he croaked as he looked into the house again. His eyes had adjusted, and God help him.

In front of him was an entryway about ten feet deep. At the end of that, the hallway separated to the left and right, leading to opposite areas of the house.

And sitting in the middle of it was Mike.

He was sprawled out, his right leg bent at an unnatural angle, the left jutting straight out towards Chester. His eyes were opened wide and his jaw was dangling wide and crooked. It was horribly out of alignment, like something had knocked it loose from the joints and tried to twist it around to the back of his head. His tongue flopped limply from behind several shattered teeth.

13

And his chest and stomach, all the way down to his crotch, were ripped open. Blood was everywhere. Mike's intestines were splashed in the blood in front of him and some were torn open, the somewhat digested waste spilling out from some of them. He could see his flask glint in the dim light just in front of the spattering of insides, partly coated in blood.

Chester screamed.

It was a shrill, maddened sound. Something you would expect to hear from a hysterical woman in one of those old movies from the thirties or forties. But here it was, screeching out of a fifty-year-old Texas man.

He began to scramble to his feet. His gut and chest were covered in Mike's blood. As he stood, he tried to paw at it and wipe it away. It went nowhere. It just smeared and soaked into his clothes with every batting motion.

He was on his feet now. His heart was thumping in his ears so loud he couldn't hear himself breathing, the frantic huffs like a galloping animal, nor could he hear himself screaming.

A shadow moved to the left of Mike's body.

I was hungry. Soooo hungry.

In his head again. That voice. It wasn't his.

Stick around, Chester. I'm making seconds!

Chester's last tenuous grasp on sanity snapped. He turned and ran for the stairs and the woods beyond, screaming like a dying hyena the whole way. He tripped over the holes in the landing and rolled painfully down the stairs, snapping several planks in the process. He hit the ground with a loud thump, but he could hear nothing but his thrumming heart, pounding in his ears.

And that voice.

Where do you think you're going?! it growled at him from somewhere deep within his mind. *I need meat!*

He howled another hissing, silent scream as he got to his feet and bolted as fast as a fat man could for the woods. It was by mere coincidence that he happened to be running straight for his truck, though that was still a good mile and a half or more through the trees. He was just running. Away. That was the only place he wanted to get to.

Away.

As he sprinted, he saw some faint movement behind him in his vision's periphery. Only a blur. A shadow. He pumped his fat legs as fast as he could. His rifle was gone. He had nothing to defend himself with.

And Mike...

Oh, God, what happened to you, Mike?

He recognized this voice. It was his. His internal talker. The one that reasoned with him. The one that reminded him of what he needed to do when the wife and boy got out of line.

But this voice was whimpering now, just as he had begun to do while running. He was crying. No, he was *sobbing.* Big strings of mucus were running from his nose and tears were streaming his cheeks and catching in his beard. Had he been more aware, he might have realized in this moment how much he resembled his family from the night before.

Yet, at this moment, however, the only thing Chester Laughton was aware of was running as fast as he could. To that special place. That place where there was safety and sanity.

Away.

He was heaving now. His fat frame hadn't exerted itself in such a manner since he was in high school, and it was vehemently protesting everything he was putting it through now. But he didn't stop.

Another shadow moved, slower this time, to his right and slightly behind him.

Don't you want some meat, Chester?

That voice was back.

Don't you want seconds?

He screamed again, snot strings flying from his mouth. He ran for what seemed like an age. He was heaving and panting and sobbing all at the same time.

The shadows quit moving. The voice was gone now. But still he ran. He ran all the way back to the dirt-top road and came out about thirty yards from their trucks, sitting silently in the moonlight. He turned and ran for them, night almost fully upon him.

He had made it. He'd managed to get away from that thing. From that *place*. He didn't know what he was going to do, but all that could be decided later. He needed to get home and get cleaned up. Then he needed to get some whiskey in him. A *lot* of whiskey. Yeah. That would do the trick. That would calm him down. Then he could decide what to do. Who to tell.

Or tell anyone?

He was almost to his truck when his foot slipped in the dirt. The last thing he saw before blacking out was the bumper of his truck rushing up to meet his face.

He had made it.

PART ⊕NE:

THE KIDS

Friday, June 8, 1990

CHAPTER I

Jimmy Dalton's mother would describe it as "*hotter'n hell's firebox!*" later that day, but for now she appeared cool and comfortable in front of the kitchen window-unit, smoking a Salem menthol cigarette and reading the morning paper. As she manipulated the pages in a fumbling manner, she sipped at her coffee from a mug reading 'Number One Mom', which Jimmy had personally witnessed her liberally garnish with bottom-shelf vodka. Jimmy ignored this. It was nothing new or shocking to him. In fact, he knew little different. He'd heard talk from others about the dangers of drinking, or drinking too early in the day, but his mom seemed to function okay, so he ignored it for the most part. He only hoped she could one day scale back her consumption so they could keep more essential things in the house, like milk and cereal.

He'd waved bye to her on his way out and she had given a half-hearted toss of the fingers back at him while never looking up from her paper. Then he was out into the heat and freedom of summer break, a wide grin donning his face.

Jimmy was riding his bike down the side of their street, called Mitchell, which connected to the main arteries of town via a few twisting and turning streets. Ahead would be Pine Street. Left from there would take you past the old cemetery and on to Highway 37, which doubled as Main Street while inside the city limits. Going right would take you down past one of Winnsboro's three—count 'em—Baptist churches and on to Highway 11, which doubled as Broadway Street. The only other main road was the farm road 515 on the South side of town, but Jimmy and his friends rarely went down that way. That was the *rich* area of Winnsboro, and they were far from wealthy, never mind they had no friends down that way. They did, in fact, have enemies there, however.

Jimmy took the right off of Mitchell onto Pine and headed West. He took his first left off Pine which happened to be the continuation of Mitchell and pedaled hard. The road swelled upward here in a steep incline and Jimmy had to stand on his pedals, chugging hard with his legs to get the bike up the hill. The bike teetered and tottered back and forth heavily as he did, but as he knew it would, it made it. Red could always make it.

He called his bike Red, or Ol' Red if he was feeling particularly southern that day, for the most obvious of reasons.

The bike was red.

His father had given it to him on his eighth birthday four years earlier. It was the last thing his father had ever given him. Two weeks later he'd gone out for a pack of smokes and never returned. Ever.

But Red was a fine parting gift. She got him all over town, wherever he needed to go, and though she wasn't much to look at, he really treasured the old bike. She was good to him and he was good to her right back. She kept him rolling and he kept her lubed and clean. It was a genuine love affair.

The Damned Place

After cresting the hill, the street leveled off and Jimmy was able to coast all the way to his friend's house a hundred yards further on, a fine summer breeze gently brushing his face and tousling his hair as he glided along.

Jimmy's friend was in the front yard of his parent's house. His name was Freddie James, and Freddie had his own bike, a silver and black thing with chrome handlebars, flipped over on its seat. He had a wrench in his hand and a spray can of WD-40 on the concrete driveway next to him. He was twisting some nuts with the wrench—which was obviously too big for him and dwarfed his small fingers—and spraying the lubricating oil here and there on the chain and sprocket. He didn't notice Jimmy for near a full twenty seconds after he had come to a stop at the curb in front of his parents' house.

"Is it falling apart on you already, Fred?" Jimmy asked to get his attention, a wry smile splitting his already sweating face.

Freddie looked up from his work, sweat beaded across the entirety of his reddish face. His matching red hair was matted with sweat across his brow and pushed to either side carelessly in sweeping arcs. He wore coke-bottle glasses which he pushed up on the lubricated bridge of his nose. His face was scrunched up, teeth pulled back across his braced teeth as he tried to transition himself from the maintenance on his bike to addressing his friend who had surprised him.

The transition complete, his face transformed to a broad smile.

"Jimmy!" he said, looking down to make one final adjustment on his bike, then tossing the wrench down to the driveway with a metallic clatter. "What's going on?"

Jimmy, who was still sitting astride Red, shrugged and looked down the street at nothing in particular.

"Nothin' really," he said. "Summer break already has me bored to tears. Figured I'd come harass you and your four eyes for a bit." He said this with a bit of a grin.

"All four, huh?" Freddie asked, chuckling. "Well I'm afraid you'll have to wait your turn on that, all four of my eyes have been busy checking your mom out in my dad's new Playboy."

Jimmy laughed and said, "Fuck you, Fred!"

"Naw, no thanks," Freddie replied. "Your mom's got me covered on that!"

At this, both boys doubled over laughing, nearly in howls. As they were cackling hysterically, Freddie's mother stepped out on the front porch. She was a handsome woman. She was slender and semi-tall, with flowing blond hair which was pulled back in a pony-tail. She was wearing a conservative, but very attractive, flower dress and some high heels.

Jimmy waved at her.

"Hi, Mrs. James," he said, unable to contain a hormonal smile.

"Hi there, Jimmy," she said, smiling warmly at him, her own fingers twittering a small wave. "Y'all kicking off the summer vacation today?"

He nodded. "Yes, ma'am, I suppose. Not much else for us to do. Is it OK if Freddie comes with me?"

Freddie looked from Jimmy to his mother. "We'll be back before dinner, mom. I promise!"

Mrs. James smiled but squinted her blue eyes at them in a mock form of suspicion.

"Y'all gonna be up to no good, I presume? Young men like yourselves, nothin' much to do, tearin' up the streets with your bicycles *always* tend to get into trouble."

"No, ma'am," Jimmy promised. "Just run around town, maybe go to the woods for a bit."

"We won't get in no trouble, mom," Freddie assured her. "When do I ever get in trouble?"

Mrs. James glanced down at him and cocked her head to the side.

"Won't get into *any* trouble, Freddie-baby," she corrected his grammar, "and I'm just teasing. Y'all have fun, but be sure you're home for supper. Your daddy is gonna grill some burgers tonight."

"Yes, ma'am," Freddie assured her.

"I'll make sure he gets back on time, Mrs. James!" Jimmy said, smiling at her broadly. She really was a pretty lady.

"Y'all have fun!" she said and stepped back through the door, vanishing into the house.

When the door was securely shut behind her, Freddie flipped his bike over on its wheels and set the kick-stand. Then he looked up at Jimmy, who was still staring at the closed door to the front of the house where Mrs. James had disappeared.

"Pick your jaw up off the ground, sicko!" Freddie said, a disgusted smile on his face.

"Oh, shut up," Jimmy said, his blushing face blessedly disguised by the heat. "You're just jealous you can't have her 'cause she's your mom!"

"What?" Freddie protested, shock on his face.

"Oh, wait, that's right, I forgot," Jimmy continued, putting his hand to his chin as if to ponder. "You guys are from Arkansas. I guess you can!"

"My dad's from Arkansas, you asshole!" Freddie barked, sounding angry even though he wasn't. "Mom and me are from right here in the great state of Texas!"

They stared at each other a moment more, then they both burst into laughter all over again. When it finally died down, Jimmy waved his arm over his shoulder.

"Come on," he said. "Let's get."

CHAPTER 2

As Jimmy and Freddie were discussing who really wanted to jump in the sack with Mrs. James, Honey Bascom was brushing her teeth. She was standing in the hallway bathroom—the only one in her house—scrubbing furiously at her teeth. The motion had an almost hypnotic effect on her. As she cleaned her molars and bicuspids, her mind drifted. She floated through memories and fantasies, some of her family, some of boys from school whom she had noticed she was starting to like, others she wanted to punch in the balls the first time she got a chance. It was purely random where her mind would land.

When it *did* finally land on something, it was a memory of her family. A fond memory, one from two years earlier. She had been ten years old then, and her mother and father were taking her to see a new movie that had come out in the theaters. It was a movie called 'Big', starring Tom Hanks. In the movie, according to the previews she had seen, Hanks played a young boy who, by making a wish on a fortune machine at a local fair, is turned into a grown man overnight and has to make his way in a grownup's world in a grownup's body with the help of his best friend, another young boy. It was being hyped as a huge hit, and she'd begged her parents to take her to see it. They had finally decided to take her, and she had been ecstatic.

In her memory, they were in her parents Oldsmobile '88, driving West towards the movie theater. The only theater relatively close by for residents of Winnsboro to go see a movie in was a small two-screener about twenty-five miles west in the town of Sulphur Springs. The theater was showing the movie in question and another feature called 'Bull Durham'. The second movie was rated R, so she wouldn't be allowed to go see that one, but she didn't care. She had no interest in that movie at all. She was just excited to be going to see Tom Hanks try to act like a young kid and show a bunch of grumpy old adults how to recapture the magic of childhood.

"You excited, Honey-bunny?" her mother asked from the front seat.

Honey looked up at her mother, who had turned in her seat to face her, and smiled.

"Yes, ma'am!" she said, beaming with joy.

"I hear Mr. Hanks may get an Oscar nod for this one," Honey's father Tom had said. "Real good performance from what I hear."

Honey had no idea who Oscar was or what the big fuss was about him nodding at you, but she smiled at her parents all the same.

"I bet it's gonna be funny!" she had said in reply to her father.

Tom Bascom smiled. "Yeah, that Hanks guy can be pretty funny."

"Daddy," Honey said, her tone changing from one of excitement to one of inquiry.

"Yes, Honey-bunny?"

"Can we get popcorn before we go into the movie?"

Her mother had looked from Honey to her husband and grinned broadly. Tom glanced over at his wife and smiled back at her. Then he half-turned to his daughter, glancing back over his shoulder.

"I think we can manage, baby-girl," he had said. "And maybe we can even get some malt-balls too!"

He turned back to the road.

"And some Twizzlers?" Honey had asked, unable to contain her excitement.

Tom laughed a short chuckle and glanced back.

"And some Twizzlers, ba—"

Her mother's scream had cut him off.

Tom had turned back to the road, both hands clenching in instantaneous white-knuckled terror. His butt rose out of the seat as he stomped on the brakes.

From her low position in the back seat, Honey could see bright lights fill the windshield, turning her mother's skin completely white like a notebook page. Tires squealed and howled, and Honey could feel the back of the car drift around to the passenger side.

Her mother was still screaming.

Then there had been a monumental impact. Glass shattered out of all four doors of the car, and Honey was vaguely aware of something wet spraying her face as she blacked out.

Sometime later, when she awoke, she had seen her mother's face. Her head was huge, almost seeming to be bloated like the Puffer Fish she'd learned about at school less than a week before. It even looked like she had the little spikes all over her face like the fish had in the pictures.

As her had head cleared, she realized that she wasn't seeing spikes on her mother's face, but hundreds of tiny cuts with blood streaming out of all of them at once.

Honey had started screaming then. When she did, her mother's eyes popped open all at once. Her normally beautiful hazel eyes were streaked with burst blood vessels and looked nightmarishly horrid. Her mother groaned, trying to say something, but Honey couldn't make out what she had said. Blood was pouring out of her mother's eyes and ears and mouth and out of all the hundreds of cuts on her face. She began to shake and convulse.

Tom, who had to this point been slumped over the steering wheel, finally began to stir. He brought his head up slowly, wincing in pain.

"What the—" he began to say as he touched his face and pulled back a bloody hand. "What in God's name?"

Honey was beginning to sob along with her screams. Her mother's jerking and bloody face spitting blood on her as she tried to speak.

"Janie?!" Tom screamed as he looked over at her. "Janie, can you hear me?!"

But her mother just kept staring at the ten-year-old Honey, spitting and oozing blood in huge gobs as she convulsed.

Then she had gone still.

Her eyes fell vacant on Honey all at once and there was a wheezing sound as her final breath found its way out through swollen pipes.

Honey spat the remainder of her toothpaste out in the sink as she cancelled the replay of the memory. She grabbed a few handfuls of water and rinsed her mouth out, swished, and spat again. Then she shut the water off and put her toothbrush in the plastic cup next to her father's toothbrush.

"Daddy?" she asked loudly as she wiped her mouth off with a towel. "Daddy, are you awake?"

She waited a moment and went into the hallway. She first turned left, which went to the two bedrooms in the small house. The one to the left at the end of the hall was hers, the one to the right was her father's.

"Daddy?" she repeated as she neared the door to his room.

It was standing about a quarter of the way open, and she pushed it in the rest of the way. She looked inside.

He wasn't there. In fact, there was no evidence that he had been there at all the previous night.

She stood in the doorway, her hand still resting on the flaked, gold-plated knob, and sighed. Her eyes drifted around the room a moment, looking for nothing in particular. Her father wasn't in here, that was obvious, but still she glanced around. It had been kept exactly the same since her mother had died. Her father still had all her clothes in the closet and bureau, and had never swapped the bedding that she had liked. Bright flowers and green grass were all over the bedspread and the pillows—most of which were merely decorative—and were still arranged just as she had always done them.

Her eyes fell to the nightstand.

On it stood a wood-framed photograph of her parents and her, taken just a few weeks before the accident. They were at the park, smiling brightly, Honey on her father's shoulders. She smiled for a moment as she let this new memory cascade over the one she'd recalled while brushing her teeth. She smiled remembering the PB and J sandwiches they'd shared and her mother pushing her on the swing. Her father staying under her as she grappled with the monkey bars.

Then she saw her mother's blood-soaked face squirming and shaking and spitting blood all over her.

Her eyes blinked back open and she saw the picture from the park again.

Keep your eyes open, Honey-bunny, and you can choose what you see.

She sighed again as she turned back to the hallway. She followed it past the bathroom and on into the living room.

"There you are," she said as she rounded the corner.

Her father was sitting in his recliner. His head was slumped down, chin resting on his chest. There was a good four days of stubble on his face. At *least* four days. His legs were sprawled out in front of him revealing a pair of dirty white underwear beneath his rolling belly. The only other thing he had on was a light blue robe which hung open, hiding literally nothing but his arms. Next to him was an end table with a lamp and a half-glass of whiskey. Honey deduced that it had probably started life with a couple of ice cubes in it because there was a wet puddle of condensation all around the base of the glass. In his other hand was a cigarette tucked between his index and middle fingers. It had burned all the way down to the filter, leaving a ghostly tail of ash that miraculously still hung in the air.

It was apparent the cigarette had singed his fingers, but it was *also* apparent he hadn't noticed. He had been too drunk to realize it or had already passed out by that point.

You're gonna burn the whole goddamn house down, she thought. *Thank God your fingers took the cherry instead of the carpet.*

She turned away from him with mixed feelings of embarrassment, resentment, and sadness. Tears stung her eyes as she marched down to her room to get dressed.

I'm sad too, you know! she thought as she stomped down the hall. *I miss her too! Why can't I just drown that away like you? Why do I have to live with it? Why can't I escape?*

She reached her room and pulled out a pair of blue jeans and a gray Texas Rangers t-shirt. She put them on and ran her fingers through her longish brown hair while she looked at herself in the mirror. Her dark eyes met her with sadness, and her young face was strikingly mature with the lines of pain and sadness.

She noticed her shirt was just a little on the tight side around her chest area. She had noticed some small amounts of pain behind her nipples a few months back and only that morning after getting out of the shower realized that she was getting the slightest swells of bosom.

Little mosquito bites, she mused.

Yes, she was becoming a woman, and she had no woman in her life to guide her through the changes her body was going through. No mother had been there to help her with her first menstrual period.

Boy, that was a gas, huh?

Her father had called a neighbor lady over to show Honey what was to be done to deal with that and explain all of it to her. Then the neighbor had gone and bought some tampons and given them to her father so he would know what to buy for his daughter. It had been absolutely, without doubt, the single most embarrassing moment of her life.

She pushed the memory away, the second unpleasant one of the morning, and grabbed her backpack. She went back to the living room and regarded her father for a moment before leaving.

Should she wake him up? Should she get him some water? Make breakfast for him?

She grunted.

Fuck him.

Honey went out the front door and into the summer air.

CHAPTER 3

Ryan Laughton stopped his bike on the old dirt road and let it topple to the ground. It made a metallic clanking sound as it dumped itself into the dirt and grass.

Ryan pulled his backpack onto his shoulder and started making his way into the woods toward the fort. It was mid-morning now and already the temperature was in the upper eighties.

It was going to be a hot day.

As he stepped into the woods, his feet crunching over the corpses of fallen leaves, pine needles and cones, Ryan noted that he wasn't terribly far from where his father had been found back in November. A couple of teenagers had made their way down the old dirt road—that was all but abandoned on most days— with mildly differing plans. The young girl with plans of her first kiss and falling in love with the boy, the young man with plans of his first penile wetting.

Neither had gotten what they wanted.

They had come upon the fat man leaning against the bumper of his pickup. His face was streaked in blood and his nose looked like he was pressing it up against a pane of glass. His front teeth were missing as well.

Good, thought Ryan, reveling in the memory. *You deserve to have your fucking teeth knocked in. Bastard.*

33

The teenagers had gotten out of the car—a late-seventies Camaro from what Ryan remembered hearing—and rushed to the man. He was ranting and raving about moving shadows that had torn his friend open. The front of his clothes were completely covered in black blood which had looked like ink in the night.

He'd been out of his mind.

They'd rushed him back to town, which had proved no easy task. Chester was a very fat man. The young girl had been forced to get in the mostly aesthetic back seat, and the raving fat-man had been screaming and crying the whole way.

But made it they had to the local emergency room. From there, the police had been called.

Cheryl Laughton and Diane Barton had already called the police station, reporting that their husbands were missing. Nothing had been done about it because they were grown men only missing for a few hours as of then, and the cops hadn't thought it important to go looking for them yet. They hadn't really cared either. Chester and Mike were two men the Winnsboro PD were all too familiar with. Dozens and dozens of calls about domestic violence and general assholery over the years had cast them in a poor light with Winnsboro's finest, and the department had quite honestly not given a damn what might have happened to them.

But now, here they were at the hospital with a raving madman, speaking of disembowelment and deadly shadows.

Chester Laughton had been deemed insane.

Ryan thought of his father, rotting away in an eight by eight padded cell at the Wood County Mental Hospital. He imagined him in a straight-jacket, smashing his face into the walls and screaming about the killer shadow that was coming for them all. This led to the memory Ryan had of the only time he'd gone to see his father with his mother at the mental facility. He'd been just as he was imagining him, wild-eyed and begging that neither of them go to the woods North of town.

"You stay away, boy!" Chester had screamed at his son. "You stay the fuck away from there, you hear me?"

Ryan had been too stunned to respond. He had simply stood there with wide eyes and mouth hung agape.

Chester had tried to put his hands on his son's shoulders, but couldn't move them because of the straight-jacket. The result was his shoulders and elbows simply dancing beneath the fabric in a comical waltz as he raved.

It was complete madness.

Not that Ryan minded much. He was glad to be rid of his father. He was glad that he'd never have to live in a house with him again, watch him beat his mother again, or kick his own ass again.

The police had gone into the woods and never found anything. The house was there, but no body, nothing aside from the strange house. Just an ancient, abandoned home in the middle of the woods. No blood inside it anywhere, no evidence of any kind. But the blood on Chester's clothes had been a match to Mike Barton's blood-type. He had been charged with murder, even without a body, but it had been decided he was not fit to stand trial because of the state of his mental faculties.

So, off to the nut house he'd gone.

Ryan was further into the woods now. He and his friends Jimmy and Freddie had been working on a fort. They had come across the perfect spot for it one day while playing guns. The woods had opened up just a bit and the ground became very sandy. Down the hill about fifty yards was a small creek, barely more than three feet across, and there were two large pine trees fallen over across the top of a washout. The fallen trees had created a makeshift roof structure, and the washout was a great start for making a really cool fort.

They had gathered limbs and brought a tarpaulin from Freddie's dad's garage out and covered the top of the fort successfully, then built up the sand in the front of the washout and reinforced it with sticks and pine-cones to make a front to it. They had sharpened many of the sticks, and they had laid them in a manner where they protruded from the front like a bunch of sharp impaling instruments, giving their hideout a menacing and diverting quality.

It really was a great fort.

Jimmy and Freddie were supposed to be meeting him at the fort that morning, but he'd wanted to get there first and get a start on digging out some shelving spaces in the back of the sandy wall where they could store things like their magazines and comic books, canned goods and can openers, and some toy guns and flashlights. Freddie was against this, arguing that the structural integrity of the fort would be compromised, but Ryan knew better than that. Freddie was smart, but he was overly cautious too. Jimmy had seemed indifferent to the idea at first, but Freddie had persuaded him.

Fucking asshole.

But that was fine. Ryan would make the shelf and prove them both wrong when they arrived. Then they would all have a place they could store their toy guns and flashlights and magazines. He could line the bottom of the shelves with pine needles and sticks to help keep moisture off of their stuff. They would see it was a good idea.

He stepped into the not-quite-a-clearing and saw their fort. It was just as they had left it, tarpaulin still in place, the be-sticked front wall in place. He clambered up the hill to their sanctuary and climbed in. He set down his backpack and pulled out a couple of toy revolvers, a flashlight, and three Playboy magazines he'd found in his father's stash after he'd been put away. He'd had to use some alcohol-soaked rags to get some substance off a few of the fold out pages. He wasn't sure what it had been, not exactly, but it had been sticky. He and Jimmy and Freddie had checked them out a few times while playing out here and Ryan had noticed that his thing would start to grow stiff. And large.

He didn't have a full understanding yet as to why this happened, but he did know that he liked how it felt and he liked how the girls in the magazines looked.

Titties were nice.

He also liked the hairy area beneath their bellies. Something about that drew him. From what he'd gathered at school from some of the older kids, a boy was supposed to put his thing in there. He had no idea what you were supposed to do once it was in there, just that that's where it went.

Wiggle it around, maybe?

He set the items on the floor of the fort and pulled out a half-gone pack of Winstons as well. He pulled one out, stuck it between his lips, and then dug out a lighter from his pack. Lit the cigarette. Inhaled.

Coughed.

There was an absolute fit of coughing, as a matter of fact. His body heaved and roared, and snot came from his nose and tears from his eyes. He even managed a completely involuntary fart in the midst of his convulsions, loud enough to echo off the trees.

Oh, my God! he thought. *Thank God their ain't no girls around to see this.*

That's when he heard a giggle and his thankfulness to God was replaced with bitter curses.

He spun around, the cigarette clamped between his first and middle fingers in a lobster hold, and saw the girl. He thought he recognized her, but couldn't place her name. In his class at school, though. He was sure of that.

Ryan's face was pale, streaked with tears and snot, and he'd just noticed that there was a formidable stench hanging in the air inside the fort from his runaway fart.

Oh, God...

"Hi," the girl said, still smiling and trying to hold back laughter. "I didn't mean to scare you."

Ryan took a few deep breaths, trying to draw in as much of the rotten stench from his ass as he could before she got any nearer. It was really horrible.

Fuck, what did I eat?

Still saying nothing, but visibly taking in deep breaths of vaporized shit, Ryan tried a smile. It was a goofy thing, all crooked and forced.

The girl giggled again.

Pull yourself together, fuck-nut! he told himself.

As he did so, he realized the girl was quite pretty. Long hair pulled back in a pony-tail, a gray Rangers tee, and jeans that seemed to fit her very well. He thought he noticed a hint of what he enjoyed so much from the magazines beneath her shirt.

Finally, most of the sulphuric stench now in his lungs, he managed to speak.

"Hi. Didn't know anyone was out here."

The girl smiled again. "I didn't figure you would, I was surprised to find anyone myself. I was just wandering around looking for the creek."

"It's just down there," Ryan said, pointing with the cigarette. He noticed now that he still had it and decided it was time to save face for the coughing and farting he'd just done. Nothing was cooler than a boy smoking a cigarette, after all, and it might help cover the residual smell from his ass.

She turned and looked over her shoulder, her pony-tail swinging as she did. Then she looked back at him, eyeing the cigarette.

"Could I have one?" she asked.

It took Ryan a moment to register what she was talking about. When he realized she wanted a cigarette, his cheeks flushed red.

"Oh, yeah, sure."

He bent to grab the pack and white-hot fear shot through him as he noticed the Playboys. Three issues were sprawled out on the floor of the fort, only just hidden by the sticks at the front of the structure.

Oh shit! he thought. *She's gonna see them!*

He grabbed up the pack of cigarettes and reached for his backpack. He heard her taking steps up the hill towards him. Sweat beaded on his brow as he frantically snatched up the magazines and started to stuff them into his pack in a furious panic.

They didn't want to go.

His backpack was stubbornly refusing to open its mouth to swallow the pornography. It seemed as if it were laughing at him, chuckling away like a bastard at his predicament.

Come on!

The pack finally relented and opened wide and allowed the magazines refuge.

He exhaled in relief and came up from behind the front of the fort pulling a Winston free as he did. She approached the front of the fort as he got it out and handed it to her.

"Thanks," she said.

She was really quite something.

Ryan stood there, his goofy smile smearing his face again. After a moment of twirling the cigarette in her fingers she finally raised her eyebrows and held it up in front of her face.

"A light?" she asked.

"Oh, right," he said, and dug in his pocket for the lighter.

He produced it and flicked it on. She leaned over the sticks and drew in on the cigarette to light it. As she exhaled the smoke—much more professionally than he'd done himself, this girl seemed to know what she was doing—her eyes fell behind Ryan to the floor of the fort.

"A reader, I see?" she said with a grin on her face.

Ryan, befuddled and confused, turned his gaze in the direction she'd been looking.

On the floor of the fort, his backpack sat with its mouth wide and gaping, exposing the magazines within.

Oh, Jesus Christ! he thought.

She burst out laughing again and he snapped his head around.

"They're not for me," he started, his voice wavering, "they're for my friends. I don't look at that stuff!"

She continued laughing and began to nod. "If you say so," she said, "but I really don't care."

"Well," he said, shrugging himself into some form of dignity, "I don't."

She took another drag on her cigarette and he did the same. She looked around at the fort.

"You build this?"

"My friends and me did," he said. "Been working on it for a couple weeks."

"Since school let out?" she asked.

"Pretty much."

"It's cool. I like it."

Ryan smiled at her again. This time it was more genuine, less forced. The goof-quotient was minimized this time.

"Thanks," he said.

She winked at him and he felt his face flush all over again.

"Well, I guess I should head on down to the creek," she said to him, looking back down the incline towards the stream.

"Yeah, OK," he said, his voice cracking.

"Thanks for the cigarette," she said as she turned to head down the hill.

41

"You're welcome!"

She marched a few paces away before Ryan's courage finally rose up inside of him.

"Hey!" he shouted to her back.

She stopped and turned around, looking him in the eye. She was radiant.

"I, uh," he started and looked to the ground as he took another drag on his cigarette, "I was just gonna say, if you want you can hang out. My friends will be here any time. You know, I don't know if you like to play guns or anything, but I've got an extra one if you'd like to."

She smiled at him and considered it.

"Sure," she said, "that would be fun."

"I'm Ryan, by the way," he said.

"Honey," she replied. "Honey Bascom."

Ryan smiled at her again. The goof was back in full form.

PART TWO:

THE BULLIES

Thursday, June 21, 1990

CHAPTER 4

Jimmy Dalton lay silently on a bed of leaves. His eyes darted this way and that, wildly alert. Looking for any movement. Anything at all, as a matter of fact. Sweat gathered on his forehead in giant beads and it streaked his cheeks. Swelling drops formed in his eyebrows, and more than a few found escape into his ocular sockets.

He blinked away the sting.

Jimmy and Freddie, along with Ryan Laughton and the newest member of their circle, Honey Bascom—*a girl,* but a pretty cool one, they all seemed to agree—were deep in the woods, not very far from their fort. They'd come out to the fort that day to play, smoke cigarettes, talk shit about their folks. Be kids.

The Playboy mags that Ryan had smuggled to them were pretty much a thing reserved for days when Honey couldn't join them. Not that she seemed to care much one way or another if they looked at them—she really was like one of the guys—but they just felt entirely too awkward looking at them with a girl around. Jimmy in particular started noticing that place on Honey's chest about eight inches below her neck all the more the last time they'd busted out the jerk-off books, as Honey called them. It had made him feel weird and strangely ashamed, though he didn't understand why. So they resided at Ryan's house.

After sharing half a pack of Marlboros that morning around the fort, they'd all decided it was a perfect day and a perfect place for them to play guns. All three boys had their gats of choice with them, but Honey hadn't. Ryan, who always seemed to be eager to do things for Honey as often as the opportunity presented itself, had leaped into action. He had some duct tape in his bag, something he'd used to make repairs on the front of the fort with that morning, and went to work looking for just the right sticks. He found a couple that were the right size and shape and went to work fashioning quite the nice little firearm for Honey to use against them all.

They didn't do teams. No, every time they'd tried, they found themselves arguing more about who got who, and a two on two verbal assault was not nearly as easily sorted as a one on three. Thus, every man for himself.

Or *her*self.

Jimmy lay frozen on the ground, his hand clutching his toy revolver in a white-knuckled death-grip. It was a substantial thing, really. Made for shooting caps, but doubled in childhood war-fantasy nicely. The barrel and molded chamber area were all metal, as were the trigger and hammer. The white hand grips were plastic, but looked real enough to Jimmy that he referred to them as ivory handles. They were no such thing, of course, but young men often took pride in deceit. It was even double *and* single action. He could pull the trigger straight through and the hammer would cock itself and then fall, or he could cock the hammer first and have a hair trigger. Not that hair triggers did you much good when you were shooting imaginary bullets,

46

never mind its utter uselessness when shooting caps. But the feature was there and he was glad of it. Sometimes, when the right situation offered itself, it even lent well to adding drama and suspense to the fantasy.

The sound of a limb snapping brought his focus dead ahead.

Where he lay was just on the other side of the apex—from where he heard the limb snap a moment ago—of a small hill. He peered over the top cautiously. His eyes were slits. His breathing had ceased, though not voluntarily. The air had hissed into his lungs when he heard the sound and then all pulmonary functions paused.

Another bead of sweat sprinted into his eye. He blinked it away and continued to peer stealthily.

There was another sound of feet on dead leaves and twigs snapping. It was coming from the same direction of the first noise. His breath began to slowly slip from his lungs again and onto the leafed earth beneath him. He was suddenly aware, to his horror, that he had to pee. And he needed to do it badly. None of those sensations had been present just a moment before, but now he felt like he had just drunk two gallons of iced tea within twenty minutes and desperately needed to evacuate his bladder.

Another snap.

He pushed thoughts of his throbbing bladder away and focused his attention towards the sounds. There was no time for pissing now, and moaning about it, mentally or otherwise, simply wouldn't do.

It was killing time.

He craned his neck up again, higher this time, but only just. He needed to get a bead on whoever it was that was coming so he could get a clear shot. A clear shot was the only thing that would go uncontested when playing a serious game of guns in the woods, especially when you refereed yourself. It simply wouldn't do to make a precarious shot only to be followed by five minutes—or even *ten* minutes—of barking argument back and forth about whether or not the shot had been true. Worse, when he jumped up and pulled the trigger, making his obligatory *shpewf* sound-effect with his mouth, the other person would inevitably spin around returning fire from their weapons—which never seemed to require reloading, as evidenced from the fact that their revolvers could fire up to fifteen times straight without ceasing when a really violent shootout erupted—and there would be a hail of clicks from their pistols (not Honey's, of course) and spitting *shpewfs* from their mouths.

Click-Shpewf-click-shpewf-click-shpewf!

No, he wouldn't allow any of that. He would wait. He would time it just right so that no one could argue that he'd indeed gotten them. He would be victorious.

More snaps and crunching. He followed the sounds with his eyes. A moment later, a shape emerged just for a moment and then was gone again, appearing from behind one tree and disappearing behind another. It was only the briefest of moments, but he was sure it had been Honey. Hard to mistake, really. Her hair was longer than all of theirs, she was slightly shorter. He saw the stick-pistol Ryan had put together for her. And, of course, his eyes had sneaked down in the fleeting moment. Involuntary. It always was.

It was her, alright.

He decided to use the sound of her movement to mask his own. As she was crunching and snapping and shuffling through the forest, he began a shuffle of his own. Army-style. On his belly, moving like a snake having spasms, he inched his way to an oak that was in marriage with a dogwood tree in full bloom. The dogwood was low hanging and if he could get inside its sphere of plumage, he would have the perfect spot to lie in wait for her to come by.

His plan to mask his sounds with hers worked. Jimmy managed to get into the dogwood and hug himself up against the oak and peer through an opening in the blooms.

Then he saw her.

The sounds had become louder as she moved closer to him, and now he could see her, just outside the protective wall of dogwood. She had no idea he was there. Exhilaration coursed through him and the need to piss like a fucking racehorse suddenly returned with a fury. His eyes were burning from sweat. He began to wonder if piss could back up in a person to the point of their eyeballs. Could it be? Could it be urine burning his eyes from inside his sockets? Hadn't he heard an old-timer say once that his piss was backed up to his eyeballs? He thought so. At the time, he'd assumed it was just a 'saying', but now he wasn't so sure.

He pinched his eyes shut and willed the gnawing sensation from his bladder to recede. It did.

When he opened his eyes again and peered through the opening in the leaves, he saw the back of Honey's head. Her pony-tail bouncing softly as she moved slowly, her stick-gun raised and ready.

He cocked the hammer of his gun.

It made a series of small clicks and he was immediately sure that Honey had heard it. She halted all at once, her head cocked around slightly, exposing her right ear to him. He could see sweat in her hair as well. It was hot. So goddamned hot in Texas. The woods provided lots of shade, which was nice, but they also quelled breeze to a great degree, which was not.

He froze. Waiting. If he were to jump out now and start clicking and *shpewfing* at her, she would likely have enough time to spin and get him before he got her. They would argue, sure, but there would be no definitive winner here, and he wasn't about to lose to a girl, not in front of his friends.

His heart began to pound in his chest and in his ears. All sound ceased aside from the incessant *thump-thump* of his heart, which had relocated itself from his chest to his head. His whole body throbbed with its every beat.

He refused to lose.

Then there was the return of the need to piss, but this time it brought along a friend. He was suddenly and quite surprisingly assaulted in the lower gut with a massive—and, quite frankly, *awful*—need to fart!

Oh, God, he thought. *Oh, Jesus Christ, not now!*

But his gut was hearing none of it. As if in open rebellion to his pleas, the sickening feeling in his gut began to descend. Jimmy imagined a floating ball of green gas squirming out of his stomach and diving into his intestines, making a beeline for his sphincter where, upon arrival, it would burst free from his body in odorous triumph with his butt-cheeks applauding the escape with deafening claps.

50

Not now!

He seemed to manage the discomfort in his bladder, but now he heard his gut audibly groan. Again, he saw the little green cloud with a smiley ghost face in the center, laughing at him, *sneering* at him.

Hold on to your ass-hams, Jimmy-boy! I'm coming!

His teeth clenched as fresh sweat erupted from his pours like lava from a volcano.

Don't worry, Jimmy! This'll be great! It's gonna be a gas!

The green cloud was laughing at him maniacally now inside his head. His thoughts were racing. Honey's head was turning more and more towards him now. If he didn't do something soon, she would have him. He couldn't allow that. Couldn't allow himself to be bested by a girl! Not even if she had a bastardly little son-of-a-bitch gas-clapper inside of him helping her out.

He leaped from the dogwood, firing like a madman.

"Shpewf-shpewf-shpewf!" he cried as he came out, pointing the gun at her.

Well, pointing it *sort of* at her.

He was off target. He had to admit it to himself. His aim had been wide by at least a foot. When he'd leaped out and begun firing, she'd heard him coming and moved the other way, clearing her of his intent.

And things were getting worse for him.

As he was leaping out in a maniacal frenzy, *shpewfing* away at her, he didn't see the broken limb on the ground. His left foot caught it and he was sent tumbling downwards to the earth, his arms flailing, his ass thundering with the traitorous fart, which was now finally breaking free.

I'm free, motherfucker! the evil, green ghost cloud screamed to him as it dissipated, still smiling, into the wooded air.

His cheeks—the ones on his face—flushed crimson as he toppled over. Honey was twirling around, a wide grin of coming laughter already spreading across her face, and drew her makeshift stick-gun down on him.

Jimmy thudded hard on the ground, the wind whooshing out of him, and a moment later he heard his doom.

"Shpewf!" Honey cried.

He turned his head back towards her and saw there was simply no argument to be made about whether or not she had gotten him. She had. She had him good. No doubt about it.

Now she burst into tearful laughter and dropped her stick-gun as she did. She fell to her knees, cackling, tears streaking her face now. It took Jimmy a few moments, but humor got the better of him, and he began laughing as well. He couldn't help it. It tore through his embarrassment and melted his damaged pride as his red face began to contort into a shape conducive to hysterical laughter.

That really *was* some funny shit.

He rose up to his knees, laughing but also wincing at the pain from his freshly skinned knee. A moment later, Ryan and Freddie jumped out from behind the trees as if from nowhere and opened *shpewfing* on them.

Jimmy was gotten again, and now Honey joined him in the afterlife of guns. Ryan and Freddie turned on each other, but what followed was the painful argument about who got who.

"You're dead!" Ryan bellowed.

"No way, dude, I totally got you!" Freddie fired back, his voice cracking.

This went on for several moments until a new voice cracked through the woods. This voice was older. It was meaner. There was none of the good humor these four kids exhibited towards each other in this new voice.

"Looky here, boys," the voice said. "We got ourselves a foursome of faggots!"

They all turned to look in the direction from whence the voice had come. Freddie and Ryan forgot all about who'd gotten who, Honey forgot all about Jimmy's fabulous failure, and Jimmy quit wondering if he'd left any marks in his pants from the dubious gas cloud.

Their eyes fell on Jake Reese. He was the one who'd broken their enjoyment. On either side of him were two more boys, about Jake's age of fourteen. They were Chris Higgins and Bart Dyer.

Chills went up all four of their spines.

Bart Dyer spoke next.

"I think it's three faggots and a dyke, Jake," he said, laughing and snorting like a pig in shit.

Jake backhanded Bart across the chest lightly, but firmly. "A faggot's a faggot, dick or twat."

Jimmy rose to his feet and began to back away. Freddie, Ryan, and Honey were already doing the same.

Jake's eyes narrowed.

"Get 'em!"

CHAPTER 5

All seven kids broke into a run. The three older boys began sprinting for the others. Jimmy, Freddie, Ryan, and Honey bolted in a panicked run directly the other way. Away from these older boys. Boys they were all too familiar with.

Jake's eyes had focused in on Jimmy. It wasn't for any particular reason other than he was the closest one to him, really. A deeper part of him also thought it was because he perceived Jimmy as their leader. Or at least a leader of sorts.

Of the four meat-bags before them, Jimmy was the only one who'd dared to stand up to him and his pals that last day of school nearly a whole month back. Because of this, and of course because of his relatively closer distance from Jake, he focused in on him.

"Run!" he heard one of the kids scream as their feet crunched and snapped through the forest's dead cells at their feet. He thought it was that little faggot Freddie. The one with the goggle-glasses on. Those self-righteous fucking spectacles.

On the last day of school, Jake and his pals Chris and Bart were walking up Walnut Street. It was a solid half-mile from the High School in town where they had cut out early from Mrs. Dorning's class. It was the last class of the year, and Mrs. Dorning had been thoroughly checked out since third period. They had slipped out while the rest of the school had simply been waiting for the bell to ring, signaling their release from adolescent prison for the summer sabbatical.

They walked down Coke Road into town, stopping in at the corner gas station and buying a Pepsi each and successfully stealing three Snickers bars in the process. Then they continued on past the grocery store and took a left onto Walnut. Here, Chris had pulled out a battered soft-pack of Camels and they'd each lit up. Their faces beamed pink with the pride of their rebellion and the onset of the summer heat. They took a right on a dog-leg section of Chestnut Street that led up to the Middle School, dragging on their Turkish tobacco and looking all-around super fucking cool.

Jake was a well-developed young man, tall for his age at five feet and nine inches. He was a good three years older than his little brother Norman, but Norman was coming along. His younger brother was taking after his mother who was an astonishing—for a woman, anyway—six feet. He suspected one day Norman would surpass him vertically. But he didn't care about that. Norman was his momma's boy to the core. *That* he cared about.

Jake and Norman's mother, Cherry, was what Jake had come to call a thunder-cunt. She was the absolute embodiment of it. She and her husband George had started their own little church in town a couple of years back after a nasty split with Faith Creek, the church they'd attended for most of Jake's life. But that wasn't what made her worthy of thunder-cuntdom. No, not that at all. What made her Queen Twat of Winnsboro-shire was the fact that she poured all her attention into

Norman. Scrawny, worthless Norman. Norman, who'd recently started jangling the strings on that cheap excuse for a guitar, whose tunes sounded to everyone like the dying wails of a rabid cougar.

Well, to everyone except Cherry Reese.

She swayed and smiled when Norman played, her enraptured lips a curl of sweet bliss as he chugged away on the strings in a timing that could honestly not be called timing at all. There was simply no sense to be made of it. Jake was no musician—he was more into sports himself—but he understood mathematics fairly well. And music was, ultimately, at its most base level, a mathematical equation. Three-four timing. Four-four timing. Hell, if you could count you could see the patterns to virtually every song, every piece of music out there. It was simple.

But nothing Norman played even *approached* anything mathematical. It was garbled noise at best, and everyone seemed to know it except his mother.

And apparently Norman, too.

So, his mother had come to worship Norman. Jake thought it was a little bit sick himself. She seemed to have absolutely no interest whatsoever in anything Jake was doing. Sure, she came to his games, most of them, anyway. She'd smile and greet people like a good preacher's wife is supposed to do, grabbing outstretched hands in both of hers while she stooped ever so slightly and cocked her head with her lips peeled back over her oversized chiclet teeth. She almost had to stoop to speak to anyone, even most men. She was so goddamn tall.

But nary a word of encouragement had been spoken to him at any point about his performance in games, or even an "attaboy!" once in a while. Nothing. Nada.

Fucking zip.

Even after he'd sacked a quarterback on the opposing team—from their *rival* team from Mt. Vernon, no less—absolutely stopping what would have been a game-winning play. The crowd had cheered and roared, not an ass in a seat anywhere in the stadium. His coaches had grabbed his facemask and shook his head violently in approval and he'd endured roughly thirty-six slaps on his ass to the jubilant exclamations of his teammates.

Not an ass in a seat. Except for two.

He remembered looking up and seeing his mother and Norman sitting in the bleachers. Sitting. Not on their feet. Not cheering. Not clapping. There were no hoots and certainly no hollers coming from their throats. Oh, no. No, they were sitting there, clutching each other in what had looked to Jake as almost a lover's embrace. His brother's face rested on his mother's breast, his arms around her waist. She had one arm around his shoulder, clenching and unclenching on the fleeting muscles of his bicep. The other hand was stroking his face. Their eyes were closed and both were smiling. Oblivious.

Norman was her boy. And that was fine. He got plenty of attention at school. He didn't need hers. Didn't even need his father's, though he at least seemed to try. He just wasn't very good at it. All he seemed to put his focus into was what he was going to preach about on the next Sunday morning.

So, fuck them.

Jake had pushed his dark brown hair back on his scalp while dragging deeply on the cigarette. He slipped his hand down and removed the stogie from his lips and exhaled the smoke from his nostrils as he had set his hazel eyes on the Middle School playground.

And that had been when he saw Jimmy, Freddie, and Ryan.

"Hey," he said, slapping Chris and Bart on the arms to get their attention. "Some little faggots!"

They had looked. And they had seen the little faggots.

"Look at 'em go!" Bart had said. He was pointing at the kids as they were swinging from the monkey bars. One of the kids had fallen and knocked his coke-bottle glasses off his face.

"Four-eyes looks like a fuckin' bug!" he exclaimed.

"And that's the kid whose dad wasted Mr. Barton, I think!" Chris said.

Jake peered through the haze of the cigarette smoke to focus in.

It was him. He'd read about it in the paper and, of course, the whole school had been talking about it.

"Ryan Laughton," Jake said. "That's him, alright."

"Yeah," Bart said, "yeah, that's his name. Dad's a fuckin' psycho!"

He burst out laughing in a cackle which could only be likened to a donkey's bray. Chris Higgins joined him in a similar falsetto of the chorus. The only thing missing were loud, coughing honks.

"I wonder if they're holding any cash," Jake had said.

"Them kids?" Chris said, reining in his stubborn animal chortles. "Naw, dude, they live over on the

North side. They ain't got enough money to buy toilet paper."

"Yeah," Bart agreed. "They're more broke than the niggers by the creamery!"

Jake assessed their retorts and decided they were probably correct. But that hadn't mattered. What mattered was attention. He craved it. Had to have it. *Would* have, by Christ. And if fucking with a threesome of little faggots would get him some attention, so be it.

They strode onward toward the kids. Along the way, they took a few more ultra-cool drags and releases on their smokes and tossed them on the grassy yard of the Middle School. Now they were only thirty or forty feet from the playground where the faggots rumbled.

Jake smiled.

"Hey, queers!" he howled at them.

The three kids had stopped what they were doing. Their joyful smiles began to vanish and their cheeks began to flush pink as they turned to face them.

"Yeah, I'm talking to you!" Jake continued. "What the fuck you doin' on my playground?"

At first the kids said nothing. Jake and his goons continued onto the lawn that mated with the playground, closing the distance to only ten feet from the younger kids.

"Huh?" he said, cupping a hand over his ear. "Didn't hear ya. Maybe you didn't understand the question. Or don't they teach you punks English anymore?"

Now it was Jake's turn to laugh, though his was less animal-like, if only just. Chris and Bart joined him, the braying in full effect now. This time, there had actually been a couple of honks from Bart, filling out the Opera of the Ass quite nicely.

"We understood you," one of the boys had said resolutely.

Immediately, the laughing had stopped. Jake and his friends looked at the boy, their eyes squinting and mild anger beginning to spread across their faces.

"We didn't realize teenagers liked playing on swing sets is all. Most Freshmen I know say playgrounds are for babies."

Now, fully realized fury was settling on Jake's face. Chris and Bart weren't far behind, but they were slower at getting the point of much of anything people said to them. This was evidenced by their grades in school, which were frequently doctored upwards to a cool seventy by teachers under pressure from coaches that required the boys on their starting line.

But they caught up eventually.

"The fuck you say to him?" Chris Higgins spat indignantly. "You know who the fuck you're talking to?"

"Shut up!" Jake said furiously. His lips were quivering now. Red rage was clouding his vision. "You'd better watch your mouth if you know what's good for you, faggot!"

Jake's finger was pointing at the kid now. The tip of it wavered slightly. He couldn't believe this little shit had said anything to him. To *him!* Who did he think he was?

I'll kill this little faggot! he thought. *I'll cut his fuckin' throat like a pig and fuck the wound!*

"Watch yours, asshole!" the kid said back to him.

60

Now Jake was utterly stunned. Stunned into wide-eyed silence for more than a couple of moments. More time than he'd wished, at that. He saw the kid realize that he'd gotten to him. The little fucker was smiling now. And, was he laughing?

No. He wasn't laughing. The four-eyed fuck-stick was the one laughing.

Jake turned his gaze to the kid in the coke-goggles, his lips in full quiver now. Chris and Bart were saying nothing. They just stood there like idiot calves staring at a new gate.

The kid was starting to laugh so hard there were tears coming out from behind his glasses and he'd begun to snort with his chuckles.

Little bastards think this is a joke? I'll show 'em. By God, I'll show 'em good!

Jake reached into the front pocket of his jeans and produced a knife. It was a foldable type with a faux pearl handle. He reached over with his off hand and flicked the blade out with expert precision.

The laughs stopped. Fear replaced the kids' courage in an instant.

"Yeah, that's right," Jake started when he had their full attention. "Shut your cock-holes, all of you!"

"Whoa, hey, Jake, cool it," Chris said. "This is getting too ser—"

"You shut your fucking mouth!" Jake screamed at him as he spun on him. *"Or I'll gut your ass right here!"*

Chris had stepped back and held up his hands in surrender.

"OK, Jake, it's cool, man," he said, backing up another step. "It's cool."

Jake whirled back on the kids and focused on the Laughton boy. He smiled, his confidence returning.

"Maybe I'll cut y'all's smart mouths off your faces like Ryan's daddy did Mr. Barton, huh?"

Jake saw Ryan's face immediately cloud over and tears well into his eyes. This pleased Jake. It pleased him deeply. It was better than the first orgasm he'd had when he had gotten carried away rubbing his pecker on the toilet that time when he realized it felt good to do so. Oh, yes. This pleased him good.

"What the hell is going on here?" a voice thundered behind them.

Jake had immediately returned his knife to the folded position and stuffed it back in his pocket. They all turned and saw Coach Bowden coming at them, his gray hair stuffed neatly into a red Winnsboro Red Raiders cap, his grizzled face scrunched together in a frustrated "Why the hell do I always end up having to deal with this shit" look. He stormed over to the three older boys.

"I said what's going on?" his voice boomed as he repeated the question.

"Nothing, sir," Jake said. "We were just talking to our new friends here."

Coach Bowden looked at him quizzically for a moment. Jake had no doubt the coach saw through to the full depths of his shit, but he didn't care. He wanted to get rid of him as fast as possible and get back to dealing with the little shits who'd bowed up to him.

"They're not our friends," the kid who'd defied him said.

Jake's eyes widened and he turned his head slowly from the coach to the kid, his lips peeling back over his teeth in a snarl of pure, unadulterated hate.

"You leave these boys alone," Coach Bowden said to Jake. "And get the hell out of here, or I'm calling all of your parents!"

Jake just continued staring at the kid. Furiously.

The kid smiled back at him.

"Jimmy," Coach Bowden said, referring to Jake's new nemesis. "You, Freddie, and Ryan get on home now. Get out of here!"

They did as they were told, sprinting to the edge of the street, jumping on their bikes, and pedaling away.

Jake took a few steps towards them, ignoring the coach, and yelled after them as they'd escaped.

"We'll see ya around, buddy! It's a long summer! I'm sure we'll see ya around!"

The coach had grabbed him, spun him around, and kicked him softly in the ass.

"You shits get the hell out of here!"

And they had.

Now, as Jake's feet pounded the leafed earth beneath him, his lips spread again over his pronounced chompers. He reached into his jeans as he ran and fumbled for his knife. He got it out and flicked open the blade. It glinted in the light.

"I told ya I'd see ya around, Jimmy! It's a long summer! It's such a LOOOONNG SUMMER!"

CHAPTER 6

Freddie's feet stamped briskly through the woods. He could hear Jake and his buddies laughing and yelling at them. Not far back, either.

He had to move faster. Had to get away. Oh, *Jesus,* why hadn't he stayed home today? His mother had asked him if he wanted to spend the day with her. Go shopping in Sulphur Springs, have lunch. Maybe even go catch a movie at the two-plex cinema.

But ooooh, no, not him! No, he just *had* to go to the woods with his friends. Had to work on the fort, which—admittedly—was coming along nicely. Especially after Honey had come along in the past weeks and added that feminine touch to the grungy hole.

I'd just had to, hadn't I?!

Yep.

Now, he was running for what may very well be his *life* in a place he had no real chance of getting out of. He wasn't fast. Not like Ryan and Jimmy. Hell, even Honey for that matter. He was shorter and skinnier and all-around less athletic. When Jimmy and Ryan were playing football after school, he was sitting in front of his Nintendo racking up new high scores on Donkey Kong and Super Mario Brothers. It was his fingers that were conditioned, not his legs and lungs. Not what he needed now to get away from the crazy assholes running them down even as his mind raced.

Up ahead and to his right, he thought he saw the outline of a house. For an insane moment, his mind started to ponder on just what the hell a house was doing way out here in the middle of the woods, but the immediacy of his situation overrode the mundane and irrelevant and screamed at him from within.

Go there! Get inside and hide!

For a moment, he started turning toward the house, not thinking, not caring, just wanting to get *away*. But then the wheels started turning in his head. They always did. He could count on that. When everyone else flew by the seat of their pants, Freddie was the one who could actually think. Sometimes he thought too damn much, he had to admit to himself, but by God at least he could do it.

No, no. You go in there and you're really *trapped. Even if you find a good spot and hole up, they might still find you. And what then? Huh, smart guy? Just what the fuck then?*

He began drifting back to his left and looked down a declining hill. It ran to the creek and he knew down by the creek there were plenty of places to hide. There were more bushes and even some hollows under the trees where the creek passed right next to them.

And those will be full of snakes, fuck-shit! Great idea!

But then he had to weigh the positives and negatives of this. He could hole up in the house and likely get found and pummeled. He could just stop and turn around, try to fight the bullying bastards. But that wasn't a very good idea. It's not like he'd even get a hit in. One good crack on their jaw or a good crushing of one of their ball-sacks. No. No, he knew it wouldn't happen. They'd be on him like flies on shit in no time, and he knew he was no fighter. He didn't stand a chance against them.

And Jake had that knife.

He hadn't seen Jake pull it out but, somehow, he just *knew* he would have it. Like he'd had it on the last day of school at the playground. There was no logical chance that he wouldn't be carrying it today.

And Jake was crazy.

They all knew it. Crazy like a fucking fox. Would they carve his calf muscles off, what little of them there were? Would they slice his throat open while laughing at his gurgling screams? Or would they carve their initials into his chest and belly like he'd read in that book his father had in his room, the one his parents didn't know he'd read?

All these possibilities seemed as likely as the next. Jake was nuts. His whole *family* was nuts, for that matter. His little brother Norman was the creepiest son-of-a-bitch he'd ever seen, and the bitch he was the son *of* was possibly the scariest of them all.

His decision made, he shuddered and sprinted left.

He ran down the hill toward the creek, all other options being cast from his consciousness as he fled. He had to get down to the creek and find a bush—he hoped to Christ there *was* a bush—or a tree-trunk hollow to crawl into. The snakes be damned. They were merely a possibility. Jake and his goons were a known commodity.

His chest heaved. Foam and phlegm slicked from his mouth while his legs pumped him as fast as they were able. He slipped on some leaves and fell to his ass, sliding several feet as he dropped over the top of the hill and began to descend towards the creek. He made a loud grunt as he did and began to tumble.

"Shit!" he barked as he rolled.

He managed to roll back onto his feet and make his way down the hill upright again. His eyes were scanning back and forth. He thought of The Terminator, the way his red robot vision scanned and beeped, the little white circle looking for something to lock onto, to assess.

There were no bushes.

"Jesus, Mary, and Joseph!" he whimpered under his heaving breath. *"I need a break here!"*

Then his scanning eyes fell on a tree butted up next to the creek. There was a large, mossy hollow underneath it, with bark and roots stretching out like tentacles from some horrible sea creature, the ends of which were digging into the bed of the creek.

It looked like a den of slithering monstrosities, but he had to take the chance.

"We're coming for you, faggots!" he heard one of the boys scream behind him. He didn't know who had said it, but it didn't sound like Jake. Chris or Bart, but he couldn't tell which.

He lumbered down the hill, splashed furiously into the water, and dived under the tree, into the hollow.

He curled up into a fetal position beneath the tree, peering out frantically through the fingers of the roots standing before him like the bars of a jail cell.

Freddie became aware after a few moments, as he was trying desperately to calm his breathing and slow his heart rate, trying to become silent and invisible, that there were water-droplets all over his glasses. He debated briefly on whether or not to dare risking taking them off and wiping them clear, and decided it had to be done. He had to be able to see. Had to be able to know if the bullies were close.

He pulled them off and wiped them on the only dry part of his clothes now, which was the few inches just below the neck of his tee-shirt. He saw nothing but blurred nonsense for a few moments as he worked at clearing the spectacles.

"You little fuckers are DEAD!" he heard one of them scream.

This time he was sure it was Jake. The others were bad. *Really* bad, as a matter of fact, but Jake was the only one who was a full-on crazy person. He was the only one he thought might actually take things well beyond an ass-kicking and into something more sinister.

Like murder.

He fumbled his glasses back onto his eyes and peered through the mossy, wet tentacles of the roots. He was fairly certain they hadn't seen him run down the hill and hide. To his relief, he saw that the disturbance in the mud at the bottom of the creek bed was gone already, carried away by the swift stream, so at least they wouldn't zero in on that.

Thank God for small favors, he thought.

He was also aware of movement under his armpit.

Just the water, he thought. *Just the current moving past you. It's nothing. Stay still. Don't move. Don't even fucking breathe! They'll never find you. Just pray they don't get the others.*

Then Freddie heard a hiss.

CHAPTER 7

Honey had seen the house too, but her logic didn't work like Freddie's. Her logic screamed *safety!*

She sprinted straight to the house. When she neared it, she saw a huge hole in the underpinning, smashed from years of disrepair and rot and disturbance from animals and creatures. She went straight for it, not thinking, not even *caring* what she might encounter under there, only knowing in her gut that she had to get away from these monsters that were chasing them.

"We're coming for you, faggots!" she heard one of the boys scream.

She literally dived into the hole and scrambled under the house. There wasn't much light, but there was enough from other punctures around the underpinning of the house, allowing beams of light to stream through the air like lasers to see the ancient beams holding the structure upright. She could see dust and pollen particles dancing through the air around the shafts of light like little worlds in orbit about their respective suns.

She crawled army-style for about fifteen feet and curled up behind one of the beams, panting for breath. Her hair was sticking to her forehead from the sweat standing on her brow.

She felt fear.

Fear like the night her mother had died. Fear like when she saw her father, drunk on whiskey, weeping and pawing at pictures of his dead wife. Like when she wondered how her dad would pull things together and provide for her. Keep a roof over her head. Keep food in the pantry.

Relentless, gnawing *fear*.

But this was somehow worse.

It was worse because those things she was thinking about were either over with or unknown. This was something else. This was fear of the *known*. She knew enough about Jake Reese to know he was capable of anything. Capable of causing real pain. *Physical* pain. Maybe even worse than pain.

Is he capable of killing? she wondered.

Her gut told her yes. Yes, he was capable of killing a person. One look into those dead eyes and you could see the incapability of empathy for another person. The coldness and fury of a sociopath. She wasn't entirely sure just what a sociopath was, even though she had read about it in a crime book her father had in his bedroom. But she knew enough to understand it was someone completely devoid of empathy for another human being, and an inability to feel for anything other than what *they* desired. What *they* wanted. That was all that mattered.

And Jake Reese's eyes were screaming that very thing.

She curled up behind the beam and began to sob. She desperately tried to control herself as she did, trying to not make a sound. Still, the snot and tears came out of her in fat strings. She began to wonder if her mother could see her. If she was in Heaven, looking down on her in that moment, and seeing what her little girl had gotten trapped in.

Is there a Heaven?

She began to question that. To question everything she'd ever been taught. Her mother and father had taken her to church as a girl, but since her mother's passing, her father had given up on spirituality and God and church. They hadn't been in nearly a year. He'd tried for a while after she had died, but seemed to have found more solace in his alcohol than in any greater deity. They'd stopped going to the First Baptist Church. Stopped seeing the pastor when he'd come by to check on them. Stopped having anything to do with them.

And now she felt completely alone.

It wasn't as though her father could do anything for her. Not now. It wasn't even noon, and she was certain he would already be stumbling drunk in their living room, smoking cigarettes and crying to himself, cursing that God he'd so loved and worshipped all her childhood before He'd taken his precious Janie away to Glory. Pawing at her picture. Throwing up.

No. Her father was useless to her. He wasn't even a father anymore. He was just a sack of meat, fermenting in his juices, sitting in his chair in his underwear and robe, rotting away his pathetic life. He couldn't help her now. Wouldn't help her. Couldn't even if he *wanted* to.

She was completely alone now, in the woods with some crazy boys, one of which she had seen was holding a knife. The *really* crazy one. That preacher's kid, Jake Reese.

71

That's what comes from the churches, she thought cynically. *Psychos and bastards. Preaching the love of Jesus and issuing the fear and pain of the Devil.*

"You little fuckers are DEAD!" she heard one scream.

She wasn't sure who it was, and it didn't matter. He was right. She *was* dead. As dead as her mother. As dead as her father's faith. Her worthless, drunk father. The one who was supposed to protect her. To lead her. To guide her. The one who was supposed to be there for her when no one else was.

Her fucking father.

Honey Bascom wept silently and fearfully beneath the ancient, dead house.

CHAPTER 8

Ryan saw the house and nearly vomited. He knew all at once what it was. The place his father had railed on about. The place where shadows moved with intelligence and malice and had torn Mike Barton apart. The place his father had gone completely insane.

The place his father had butchered a man.

The wave of nausea passed as quickly as it had come on and he turned right and sprinted for the road. The old, dirt road. Where his bike was. Where escape was waiting.

His legs pumped and he heaved breaths. He was a big, strong young man, but in spite of his physical appearance and capability, he was terrified. Terrified of the boys that were pursuing him and his friends.

Jake reminded him of his father. Ryan remembered the night before his father had murdered Mike Barton, how he'd finally rustled up the courage to stand up to him. To tell him to get away from his mother as she lay on the floor, her hair soaked in his spilled beer, sobbing. He'd felt righteous indignation well up within him unlike he'd ever felt before. He'd done very well on the Middle School football team. He'd grown strong and tall. He'd found strength and purpose on the field.

But all of that strength, that *resolve*, had vanished in an instant when he'd tried standing up to his father. He had been able to move people twice his size on the football field, simply push them out of the way. To go after the ball. Stop the opposing team. But when it came to his father, he'd ended up on the floor, his face throbbing and spattered with beer-foam. He was nothing more than a son-of-a-whore to his dad. His dad could throw him down in one fell swoop. None of his strength or height or resolve had been able to stop him. Nothing.

He felt like a coward.

Then Ryan's thoughts went to Honey. She was quickly becoming his best friend, even after their meeting in the woods a few weeks ago when he'd coughed and farted in front of her and tried failingly to hide the pornography in his backpack. Even after all of that, she had wanted to be his friend. To spend time with him.

With him!

That was what he couldn't wrap his mind around. She was beautiful and sweet and funny. She was able to be one hundred percent girl and still be able to play boys' games like guns in the woods with him. Able to just be a *person*. A *real* person. Most of the girls in school were preoccupied with what they were wearing and what particular backpack they carried. They were preoccupied with pink and purple and the latest Madonna album.

Girly shit.

But not Honey Bascom. Honey was *real*. Honey was someone he found he could be comfortable around. Be himself. She made him feel unlike anything he'd ever felt before.

She was like home. A home he'd never had. Even with his father locked away now, he and his mother didn't have the ability to connect. She was working double-shifts at the café seven days a week just to maintain their disheveled single-wide trailer and make ends meet. He hardly saw her. When he *did* see her, she was too tired to do anything but go to bed. He'd learned to fend for himself. To feed himself. To clean the house. Lord knew his mother wasn't going to do it. She *couldn't* do it. She could hardly stand on her feet when she was home because of the exhaustion of her job. Losing his father to madness and murder had created quite a serious problem for them financially, and his mother was doing all she could. But it still wasn't enough.

But Honey was. *She* was enough. She was able to fill something in him that his mother wasn't able to do. Make him feel appreciated. Make him feel wanted and cared for and loved and—

"We're coming for you, faggots!"

He heard the scream from the psychos chasing them. He pumped his legs harder and harder. Much the same way his father had described running from the made-up shadow thing that had chased him through these very woods. All he wanted was to get away. Away from the monsters chasing them.

New waves of guilt and shame fell over him as he ran away from his friends. Away from the bullies chasing them all. He knew they were after all of them, but all his young mind could focus on was saving his own ass. That's what was weighing on him.

He was his father.

His fat, wife and child-beating father. That worthless asshole, Chester Laughton, reincarnated. He was no better than him. He was running away while his friends were being chased down by a crazy jackass and his friends. He couldn't even stand up for Honey. The girl he was starting to fall for, even though he'd never really cared about girls before. All because he was a coward. A worthless Laughton boy who couldn't even stand up for his own mother against his fat-ass, abusive dad.

Tears streaked his face.

He saw the dirt road up ahead and pumped his legs harder and harder. The sharp, piercing pain in his chest seemed miles away now. Nothing mattered but getting away. Nothing mattered but his own hide. That was what he was telling himself anyway. Outwardly he was big and strong, but inside he was weak and worthless.

He got to the road, jumped on his bike, and peddled away, crying like a three-year-old baby.

"You little fuckers are DEAD!" he heard Jake Reese scream distantly.

Not me, he thought. *Not today. One thing you can say for cowards, they tend to live.*

He rode away, crying and ashamed. But he didn't look back.

CHAPTER 9

When Jimmy saw the house, he made a beeline for the front steps. A thousand voices were screaming in his head. Voices telling him to get home. To go after Ryan. To follow Freddie. Voices telling him things like, *Don't you know where you are? Don't you remember Ryan's dad? Mr. Barton? This is where he did it, don't go in there! Are you fucking nuts?*

But he was ignoring all of them. He knew, somewhere in his subconscious, that going into the house was cornering himself. It was deliberately putting his back against the wall. But he didn't care. Something was calling him to it. Something was drawing him in.

His eyes focused on the front door.

He leaped up the front steps, careful to stay near the edges of the stairs where the wood would have more strength. He bounded up onto the landing in front of the front door, which was hanging open slightly, and jumped over two smashed spots on the deck. He had a vague thought that these holes seemed to be relatively fresh in comparison to the dilapidation of the rest of the house.

But his mind wasn't focusing on that. All it was focusing on was getting inside. He knew he *had* to get inside. To hide.

He burst through the door and into an ancient foyer. There was a staircase just to his right and a hallway dead ahead of him past the staircase that would take him to the left or the right. He darted for the hallway and rounded the corner to the right, his shoulder smashing into the corner of the wall as he did.

He stopped dead in the hall as soon as he entered it. His chest was heaving. His cheeks were flushed. His eyes were wild and panicked.

Ahead of him were several doors. There were three on his right, two to his left, and another at the end of the hall. The floorboards creaked and moaned as he finally began to move, more slowly now. His eyes were darting this way and that, checking all the doors. He wanted something he could get in and hole up. Not a big open room, but something smaller. He didn't like the idea of a tight enclosed space, but his gut was telling him he'd have a better chance of holding someone back in a tighter quarter.

He looked again to the door at the end of the hall. He noticed it was slightly narrower than the others, and he moved toward it.

A closet.

Then he knew that was where he needed to go.

"We're coming for you, faggots!" he heard someone outside scream. His head jerked around in the direction of the front door.

They were close.

He took a few more steps down the hallway, his feet betraying him every step of the way. The boards seemed to howl and moan in shrieking ecstasy as he moved. Calling out to any who would hear them.

He's here! Right here! That little faggot Jimmy Dalton is right the fuck here! Standing right on top of us! Come and get him, please! He's RIGHT HERE!

78

His breathing was becoming more and more labored. He was desperately trying to get it under control, but his respiratory system would have none of it. It defied him, demanding deeper, faster inhales of sweet air. His blood screamed through his veins and he was faintly aware of the sound of his heart beating away in his ears and throat. Like it had moved from his chest and taken up residence right next to his eardrums.

Pull it together, Jimmy! he screamed at his brain. *Pull your shit together now!*

"You little fuckers are DEAD!"

Right outside the front door now. Probably ascending the steps at this very moment.

Jimmy could see in his mind's eye Jake, his lips peeled back over his wretchedly large teeth, that knife glimmering in his hand. Something else glimmering in his eyes. Something close to madness and utterly sinister.

Jimmy stepped as silently as he could manage to the edge of the hallway. He was not a carpenter, but he understood that the joints of the floorboards would be more stout there and less likely to creak. He got to the wall and began shimming his way down, his back dragging against the molded wallpaper. His vision was in a dead lock on the door. He was only a few feet away now.

Footsteps.

There was a sound from the front of the house like something dragging. He thought it was probably the front door being pushed open. The eons-old hinges sighed and hung, causing the bottom of the door to scrape across the entryway floor. Feet were clumping into the house. Jake's feet.

Move your ass!

Jimmy slid his way more quickly the last few feet to the door. His hand leaped out and grasped the handle. He was already turning it when he remembered that he should be more cautious of the noise the door would make when he did. But then he decided fuck all that, it didn't matter at this point. There were six doorways that would have to be checked in this hallway, and so long as Jake didn't see him when he slipped into this one, he would have a little time to think and figure out his next move.

Maybe there's a crawlspace or something. A lot of old houses have those, he thought as he swung the door open. It moaned a bit, but nowhere near the way he had expected it to.

Small mercies.

He threw himself into the closet and pulled the door closed behind him as quietly as he could manage. There were a fantastically long series of mechanical clicks and tinks as the door latched itself back into place, and for a terrible moment he thought it may never end. But finally, it did.

Then he let out his breath. He hadn't realized he had been holding it since midway down the hallway when he could hear Jake and his buddies coming up the stairs into the house. He let go of the handle and stole a quick glance around. It was dark in here, save for a small beam of light coming from around the door frame and through a keyhole beneath the knob. There were shelves on either side and then dark blackness towards the back. He assumed the back wall of the closet must be right there, just out of reach from the light coming from around the door and the key—

A keyhole!

In his panic, he hadn't thought about a lock. Assumed there wouldn't be one here. Most closets didn't lock. But this house was old. Older than any he knew, as a matter of fact. Sometimes they would have key locks on their doors instead of buttons or twist-knobs on the handles to lock up valuables in closets. He hadn't seen a key outside. Would there be one? Would it be sitting there, perched up high on the frame of the door, patiently waiting all these decades for someone to snatch?

He listened again, pressing his ear against the heavy wooden door. This door, he noticed, seemed to be holding up to age much better than the rest of the place. No direct access to the sun and weather. And old doors were made heavy and strong. They could stand up to a beating. They were designed to outlive people. But it would be useless if Jake or one of the others could just swing it open.

He didn't hear anything. He began to consider risking throwing the door open and reaching up on the doorframe, praying a key would be there, and snatching it. Pulling the door closed. Locking it from the inside.

It might have worked too. But that was when he heard Jake.

More footsteps. Jake wasn't bothering to be quiet. Wasn't bothering to keep to the edges of the hall to minimize the moaning of the boards. Jake didn't care. He didn't give one ripe fuck about how much sound he was making.

Jimmy knelt down and peered through the keyhole. He could see Jake in the gray light, standing in the center of the hallway, at the far end. His head was cocked forward and his eyes were blazing. Gooseflesh broke out all up and down Jimmy's spine.

"I know you're in here, Dalton!" Jake barked into the gloom. "I saw your faggot-ass run in here. And we both know I'm gonna find you. Your friends all bailed on you, by the way. Not sure if you knew that or not. But they're gone. Ran off like a bunch of yellow-bellied queers!"

Jake began moving down the hallway. The floorboards seemed to have no allegiance one way or another as to who was walking upon them. They ached and groaned audibly, announcing Jake's presence and whereabouts. But, unlike Jimmy, Jake paid it no mind.

"We need to have a talk about your attitude at the playground that last day of school," Jake said, giggling as he did so. "You apparently didn't know who you were talking to. *No one* talks to me that way! No one talks to a *Reese* that way! If I say jump, you say how high. If I say give me your money, you fork it over. If I say suck my dick, *you choke on it!*"

He shouted this last part. Jimmy's breaths were coming in short, shallow gasps. Jake was holding his right hand out now, towards the wall of the hallway. Jimmy could see the knife in it, glinting in the gloomy light. Jake pressed the edge into the wallpaper and let it drag along the wall as he continued walking, his eyes a pair of maddened black holes.

Jimmy slid backwards away from the door.

"Maybe that's what we need to do, huh?" Jake continued as he menaced down the hallway. "Maybe sucking my dick will teach you a lesson. If my big hard cock starts choking off your airway, maybe then you'll think about how you talk to me from now on! What do you think? You're a little faggot, anyway, so you should know all about sucking dick!"

Sweat was beading all over Jimmy's brow now. It was soaking through his shirt and making it cling to his chest. If only he'd thought about looking for the key! The goddamned key! If he would have just taken a moment to *think*, to look around! Be fucking aware of something in his life!

But he hadn't. And now he was trapped.

He looked up, the thought reoccurring to him about a possible crawlspace from the closet.

He saw a gray, dusty ceiling. No crawlspace. No attic door.

Then he remembered about the staircase and the fact that he was on the first floor. If there was an attic, the entrance to it would be on the upper floor, not down here.

Dumbass! You idiot, shit-head!

His foot moved out with an involuntary jolt and bumped the door.

It wasn't violent. It wasn't even all that forceful. Just a little *bump*.

But it was enough.

"I hear you, Jimmy!" Jake's voice boomed through the door. "Took the door at the end of the hall!"

Fuck! Fuck! FUCK! Jimmy thought. *Now what?*

Horrid thoughts of Jake reeling the door open and holding the knife to his throat while he thrust his penis into his mouth flashed through his mind. Tears stung his eyes. His already rapid breathing sped up even more. He thrust his hands against his mouth, one over the other, desperately trying to be quiet.

83

Quiet for what, dumb-shit? He knows exactly where you are and you know exactly what's going to happen now.

The footsteps started again. The moans and creaks from the floor started up their chorus again. Jimmy saw shadows dance across the light spilling around the doorway.

He looked again at the keyhole, crying, wishing to Christ he'd looked for a key. If only he'd looked! Even if he hadn't found one, this haunting feeling that his fear had retarded his senses wouldn't be here, taunting him, *mocking* him!

If only I'd had a key!

The light in the keyhole vanished.

Jimmy was staring at the spots on his vision from where the keyhole had been a moment before, on the ragged edge of a wild, terrified scream, when he heard a mechanical *snick*. A second later, Jake's hand was on the doorknob, twisting and rattling it violently.

But the door wasn't opening.

"You locked the door, huh, gay-boy?" he heard Jake's snarling voice through the door. "You think that's going to save you?"

Then there was a violent *boom* on the door and it shook in its frame. Then there was another *boom* and another shake.

The door held.

Jimmy, eyes wild and unbelieving, started to crawl backwards on his butt. Scrambling for the wall. A place to crawl up in the fetal position before Jake inevitably broke through. Jimmy hoped his assumptions about the old internal doors being much stronger were true, but he had his doubts.

And what about the lock?

The Damned Place

He'd heard it snick home, but he hadn't believed it. He didn't even believe it now as he was seeing the door hold against bat-shit crazy Jake and his knife on the other side. But it had happened. He was thinking about it, thinking about a key, desperately wanting it to lock, *willing* it to lock, and...

And then it had.

He didn't have time to dwell on that now. All he could think to do was to keep crawling backwards to the wall, to press himself against it, and pray the door held.

Oh, sweet Jesus, if you're real, hold that door!

But where the fuck was the wall?

He looked forward to the door that was *booming* and shaking violently every few seconds and saw that it was at least a good fifteen feet away. This wasn't possible, was it? How deep are closets? Three, four feet maybe? Even a hundred years ago they couldn't have been this deep.

Then he noticed new light coming around him. It was coming from *behind* him.

He spun around, no longer mindful of Jake's efforts to break through to the closet, and froze.

There was another door.

It hadn't been there before. He was certain of that. There had been nothing but blackness at the back of the closet. But here it was. Loud and proud, right before his eyes. He turned and looked back the way he had come. The door he'd somehow locked with his mind was there, perhaps twenty feet away, still shaking and jolting. He jerked his head back around at this new door.

Is this a way out? he thought. *Does this lead to a different part of the house? Can I find a way out through here?*

He didn't know. Didn't even really care at this point. All he wanted was to get away. As far away from Jake and his friends as possible. As *fast* as possible. He didn't know where this door had come from, or how he'd missed seeing it when he first entered the closet, but he wasn't going to argue with fate. If this door led to escape, he meant to go through it. No matter where it led.

"You open this motherfucking door right now, you little faggot cocksucker! You open it right now! I'm gonna cut you open from groin to gullet, you hear me? From your balls to your throat! That's right, I'm gonna cut you open, then we'll see who wants to talk shit to Jake Reese!"

Jake was screaming maniacally now. He had completely lost it. The door being locked seemed to have driven him over the edge into a full-on, child-like tantrum of pure rage and fury.

Jimmy looked back at the new door. There was either this and who knew what on the other side, or Jake Reese, with murder and God only knew what else in his eyes, behind the other.

There was no question.

Jimmy Dalton opened the door and his life changed forever.

Chapter 10

Bart Dyer had just watched the girl go under the house.

Jake was after the Dalton kid, who was running into the house, and Chris had gone left after the four-eyed freak down by the creek. That one had been fast.

But Bart's eyes were on the girl.

She had scrambled up under the house with surprising speed, the jeans covering her butt the main focus. Well, the main focus for Bart, anyway.

Bart wasn't a terribly smart individual. He managed to keep moving through grade school because his father was on the school board, and nobody fucked with Andrew Dyer or his kid. Nobody. If Andy said 'fix it', you'd better believe whatever it was got fixed.

In stark contrast to his boy, Andy Dyer was a very smart man. He'd graduated from the University of Texas at Austin with honors and a degree in business and marketing. He'd come back to Winnsboro after his years in college to go to work at his father's business. It was a successful manufacturing company on the edge of town that made wiring harnesses for all sorts of industries: automotive, aircraft, marine transport, and the like. The business was booming, and Andy had helped take the company to the next level.

A year after coming to work for his father, he had more than doubled the amount of clients the company retained. The money began to flow in like a cascading tsunami, and they had expanded their operations to two new buildings in Winnsboro, and had even set up some new manufacturing sites in Mexico and Japan.

And the clients just kept rolling in.

Soon, what Johnathan Dyer had built into a five million dollar a year company skyrocketed to a five-*hundred* million dollar a year empire under Andy's watch.

In 1975, Andy's girlfriend Amanda became pregnant. They'd married that fall, and a few months later their first son had been born.

Andy had a liking for unusual names, and had insisted—against vigorous objections from Amanda—that they name the boy Bartholomew. He'd won the negotiation much the same way he won clients for the family harness company. He was relentless. He was merciless. He just wouldn't stop until the opposition was raising the white flag of surrender and signing on the dotted line. He used tactical negotiation techniques coupled with intimidation and fear. Andy Dyer wasn't above blackmail, either.

Not that he'd had to *blackmail* Amanda. She simply knew her husband too well. Knew that his way would be had in the end no matter what, and thus she had relented.

Bartholomew.

It became obvious all too soon of little Bart's limited mental capacity, however, when he'd begun grade school. Andy had already writhed his way onto the board, and as soon as he started seeing grades, he started seeing teachers. Little was known about exactly what transpired in those meetings with Bart's teachers, but suffice it to say that overnight Bart's grades had instantly leaped from a D-average to straight A's. More than one of Bart's teachers had resigned in the months following their meetings with the senior Dyer, moving off to other school-districts and finding new jobs, but the grades remained. No matter how many meetings and insinuations and threats it took, Andy Dyer was ready, willing, and able.

Amanda had called her husband one day in a panic the summer of the prior year. She had come in from the grocery store to their home on the south end of town, the place where all the people with money lived on Coke Road. She had laid her bags of groceries down on the counter, calling for Bart to come help her. Upon getting no response, she went about her business of putting the produce away and throwing the bags in the trash can. As she threw the bags away, she happened to glance out the window in the laundry room.

There was Bart, outside on his knees.

She had been concerned about his demeanor, she had told her husband, and went to check on him. As she stepped out onto the back deck that overlooked their vast yard, perfectly trimmed and landscaped, she again began to call to her son as she had when she'd come in with the groceries.

He didn't respond.

As she moved in closer, she noticed the bronze fur of a dog's paw in front of her son's knee. She immediately calmed, assuming he was playing with the family pet, Rosie, and called to him once more.

When he finally turned to her, his chubby face a twisted gnarl of sadistic pleasure, chills ran up her spine and her skin erupted in gooseflesh.

Rosie's throat had been cut open. Blood was everywhere on the otherwise immaculate green grass. She saw too that it was all over her son's hands. In one of those hands he was holding a razor knife from the garage.

Her hands clasped her mouth to stifle a scream. As she continued to near Bart and their dead dog, her knees weakening, she saw he had also opened up her chest and stomach, and apparently had been pulling her insides out.

"My God, Bart! What have you done?"

Bart merely gazed up at her and smiled. There was nothing in his eyes. The *smile* wasn't even in his eyes, as much as she couldn't believe it. It was just blank. Vacant.

Nobody home.

"Last week in science class," Bart started, his voice steady and cool, "we dissected some frogs. They're amphibians, you know. At least that's what Mr. Blaire says. I didn't read the book..."

He had trailed off for a moment, and in that moment Amanda's knees finally gave up the ghost and buckled. She sank to her knees in the grass, still clutching her face in both hands. Horror and confusion had spread across her face. She didn't even know who the little monster before her was. Didn't know how this, this *thing* had come out of her. But here it was. All the evidence she would ever need to know that her womb had produced an idiot mad scientist, experimenting on helpless beings.

"Anyway," Bart continued, still blank and empty, "I didn't know if amphibians were different inside from dogs. I asked Mr. Blair if we could do a dog next and he said that was cruel, you know, 'cause dogs are pets. So I said to him, 'I know folks who have frogs as pets', and he just shook his head and quit talking to me. I was just curious."

Amanda's hands began to fall from her mouth as her monster son told her the story. She was unable to speak. Unable to respond in any way other than to sit there, tears streaming her face, and stare into the soulless void behind those blank eyes.

"But you know what?" Bart asked, a spark of something finally gleaming for just a moment in his eyes before dimming back to nothingness.

She tried to form words, but all her mouth could do was contort into a strained *oh*.

He continued. "They're not really that different! All the same stuff is in there. Rosie's stuff was bigger and there were more guts than the frog had, but basically they're the same! Isn't that neat, mom?"

At that point, she had leaped to her feet and run back into the house, hot tears stinging her eyes. A low guttural sound had finally found its way to her lips as she ran and it rose to an awful moan as she entered the house and locked the door.

"Ooohhhhh!" her groan issued.

It grew louder until it peaked at an all-out scream.

"Fix it," Andy had told her on the phone. "Wash him up, bury the dog in the flower bed. Just fix it. I don't have time for this."

She had been amazed at her husband's indifference to this horror.

"What do you mean, *fix it?*" she had hissed into the phone. "Do you have any idea what this means? Our son is a psychopath, Andrew! He needs help!"

Andy had sighed over the phone, annoyance prevalent in his tone. "Look, Amanda, he's fine. He's just a boy. Boys do crazy things sometimes. It's just a phase, he'll come out of it. Besides, telling anyone about this would just cause an overreaction and could cause him to have problems down the road. Problems getting into a good college. We don't need that kind of frustration in our lives. I go through enough to make sure his grades stay where they need to. Now do as I say and fix it, goddamnit!"

Then he'd hung up.

And so went virtually everything in Bart Dyer's young life. His father was determined that no boy of his could be as stupid as he obviously was, and he'd be damned if he was to be bothered with discipline. That was what he paid taxes for. For the schools to handle it. Hell, that was why he was on the fucking *board*, for Christ's sakes! They deal with the boy, but give him the results he needed so that Andy Dyer wouldn't be embarrassed and his boy would be successful just as he had been and his father before him.

Now, as Bart knelt before the opening in the underpinning where the girl had scrambled away, he thought about his parents. He loved them both, he supposed. At least he loved his dad. His mother was a total bitch, but what mom wasn't these days? Always drunk now, she would never touch him. Never let him near her. She had moved out of his dad's bedroom and into the guest room where she went to bed with the door locked every night. But his dad was OK. Bart didn't have to do much in school, and he never bothered with homework anymore. His dad had made sure he didn't have to. Oh, his dad would *say* he should do his work and work hard and all that, but Bart knew that was all bullshit. If he had to work hard and put in the time, then why did he always have A's in all his schoolwork? What's the point of working for something if it's handed to you like that?

Of course, occasionally there was something cool at school, like when they had to do bug collections and dissections. *That* was always awesome. He didn't bother with the alcohol in the jar to kill the bugs painlessly. He liked to pin them to his Styrofoam block while they were still moving. A hundred bugs, and close to half of them still squirming and trying to crawl, their jagged, barbed legs sprawling out over the thin air.

That *was* fun.

His dad *was* pretty cool, though. They hadn't let him get another pet after Rosie, but that was OK. There were always birds and squirrels in the back yard, and his BB gun packed enough punch to take them out good, so long as you got your shot in on their heads. And on the blessed days when a raccoon would wander into the yard, the .22 did the trick like a dream.

And his razor knife saw plenty of work.

He peeked his head under the house. Jake had already made his way in after Jimmy. He could hear him in there, screaming and beating away on a door or a wall or something.

Dalton, you little faggot, you don't know what you're in for! he thought and smiled to himself. *But neither does this little split-tail under here. Oh, man, she's gonna be something one of these days.*

He thought again of her butt jerking back and forth as she had crawled under the house in her panicked flight from them. She really *was* a cute little thing.

Maybe he would see what *she* looked like on the inside. Did people's insides look like the insides of squirrels and birds and dogs and frogs? He wasn't sure, but he was interested in finding out.

He got down on his considerable belly and looked in. It was dark down here, just a few shafts of light here and there. But it was enough to see alright. There were cobwebs all over and it smelled like dust and rot. It also seemed cooler down there too, by at least ten degrees or more.

He wiggled himself through the hole. He could hear her now, crying somewhere in the gloom.

"Hey, girly!" he shouted to her. "Why don't you come out and play with us, huh?"

He started laughing to himself again, a milder, more toned-down version of his donkey bray. He snorted this time rather than honked.

"We ain't really even after you," he said, continuing. "It was them other boys that back-talked Jake. He'll probably be glad for you to just go on. But if you ain't gonna listen to me and come outta here, well, who knows what he'll do?"

Who knows what I'll *do,* he thought, but didn't say. *I ain't seen a girl's titties up close before. Maybe I can see yours?*

He heard movement up ahead, behind one of the beams holding the house up. He squinted to see but only caught a shoe sucking back behind a beam.

Gotcha!

He writhed and wriggled and crawled some more in that direction, a grin spreading on his face, but not in his eyes.

"Hey, bitch!" he yelled now, his tone changing as violently as the crack of a gunshot. "I see you! And I'm gonna get you too! Maybe you can show me your little titties, what do you say? Maybe we can *all* get a look at them titties!"

He crawled deeper into the underbelly of the house towards where he'd seen her disappear. When he was about ten feet away, he heard something. It wasn't the shuffling he'd heard before when she'd tried to retreat from him. This was something different. Like a strange warbling sound, something similar to what he'd heard in old sci-fi movies he watched at night when people came close to some strange alien spacecraft or a time portal or something.

He even thought he saw the *air* waver. But then it stopped, just as suddenly as it had begun. Just beyond the beam he'd seen her shoe sneak behind.

Bart picked up speed and jerked himself around the beam, ready to reach out and grab her. Pull her near to him. Drag her out. Rip her shirt and pants off.

"I gotcha now, bi—" he started, then stopped short.

She was gone. She was nowhere to be seen. It was as if she had just vanished into thin air all at once.

He jerked his head around this way and that, but she was nowhere to be seen. The warbling sound and the sight he'd seen were gone as well. He made quick work of searching under the house for her, but she was gone. No doubt about it.

"Fuck!" he muttered under his breath.

He could still hear Jake above him hammering away at a door or a wall or something. Still screaming profanities and threats. He was seriously pissed off. Bart decided he'd make his way up to him and give him a hand with whatever he was doing and put off telling him the girl had gotten away from him as long as he could. But upon further reflection, he decided he'd go assist Chris in pummeling the four-eyed fuck-face down by the creek.

He made his way back to the opening in the underpinning and started to crawl back out to his feet. He was squinting his eyes against the brightness assaulting his ocular residents. The dark beneath the house had rendered him momentarily blind.

He stood to his feet, trying to shield his eyes and brush off the dirt and leaves clinging with strands of cobweb to his clothing.

Then he heard quick-moving steps crunching through the dead leaves. There was a loud *thunk*. He was aware of the sound of wood cracking.

Then he wasn't aware of anything for a long while.

CHAPTER 11

"Fuck! Oh, shit—shit—shit, FUCK!" Freddie whispered in a hiss.

He was looking down at a snake.

It was a nasty, scaly thing, moving upwards from beneath his armpit. It hadn't been the water moving at all that he'd felt. It was this slithering demon from hell, the serpent from the Garden he'd learned about in Sunday School. Lucifer in the flesh, right before him, his forked tongue leaping out at him like a pair of accusatory fingers.

Should've listened to that Jesus fellow, he could hear the snake say in his mind. *Should've listened for sure. Now you're in Hell and you're mine, motherfucker!*

But he wasn't in Hell. At least not the Hell from the Bible, anyway. He was in the hollow of a tree trunk in the creek, hiding from a posse of insane fourteen year-olds that were chasing them, at least one of which was a knife-wielding nutjob. And the snake wasn't Lucifer. Wasn't even a demon, for all its looks. It was just your standard water-moccasin, ready to pierce Freddie's flesh with poisonous fangs and pump certain death into him. If Reese and his boys didn't get him, the snake would. No doubt about it.

His eyes were fixed on the snake. Pure terror had frozen him into a statue, and that was probably what had saved his life. The snake just stared back at him, its black tongue slipping in and out like a knife in warm butter.

Then it looked away.

Someone was coming down the hill from the house toward him. He stole a quick glance, only moving his eyes, and saw Chris Higgins coming down the hill. Chris was the follower of the group. He never seemed to instigate anything, but always backed up Jake. And Jake was flat-out crazy, that was for damn sure. Just like his nut-job family in their nut-job church preaching their nut-job version of Christianity, which wasn't Christianity at all.

And there was Bart, too, somewhere out there. Bart gave him the chills. There was something off about him. Something *missing,* more than anything. But he seemed to be a follower of Jake as well. Whatever Jake said, they did.

But Chris was the least crazy of them from what Freddie could gather. Didn't much matter right then, however, because Jake was on a crusade against him and his friends and that meant Chris was going to act like a good soldier and do as he was told.

The snake was looking at Chris too.

Freddie's eyes blazed bright behind his glasses. Courage flamed up in him from a place he'd never known before as an idea struck him like a two-by-four over the head. He could almost *see* the animated light-bulb floating over his head blink on. Could almost hear the chiming *ding* as it lit.

Freddie reached out with his hand and snatched the snake just behind its head in a death grip.

CHAPTER 12

Chris descended the hill toward the creek. The younger boy he'd seen fleeing down there seemed like the least of Jake's concerns, so Chris had thought that would be the one for him to go after.

The truth was, Chris didn't really want any part of this. Sure, he enjoyed hanging out with Jake and Bart, they always seemed to have cigarettes, and even access to beer every once in a while. Plus, it didn't hurt that they always had money. Their parents were well off. Well, *Jake's* parents were well off. Bart's parents were filthy rich.

The Higgins family had money, too. Had more money than the Reeses, as a matter of fact. But unlike the parents of Jake and Bart, Chris's parents never let him have any of it. Not for nothing, anyway. He had to earn it the same way they had, or so they said. There would be no free handouts in the Higgins home. So, for Chris to get even twenty bucks to float on for a week, he'd have to mow the yard, pull weeds from the flower bed, do the dishes, vacuum the house, mop the floors, keep his room cleaned, go to the store on his bike and fetch milk or eggs or what have you. And this was five-plus days a week, mind you. This wasn't something he could do in a single day. Oh, no siree. No, for Chris Higgins to have his pittance, he had to slave day in and day out.

And it really *was* a pittance.

All his friends at school seemed to have a solid hundred bucks a week in their pockets to do with what they pleased, and their chores were laughable by comparison. Wash dad's car. Take the trash out twice a week. Make sure your laundry was in the hamper for mom to take care of. And on top of the hundred bucks they always had, they were driving brand new Mustangs and Silverado pickups! It was *nothing* compared to what he had to do for his mere pair of tens.

Now, of course, Chris was not *required* by his parents that he complete *any* of these chores. They had set it before him very clearly. He could live there, do as he pleased, live in a virtual pig-sty in his room, whatever. Didn't matter to them. But if he wanted money—*their* money, they never failed to remind him—he was going to have to earn it.

"You think money grows on trees, young man?" Walter Higgins had asked his son one day a few months before. "You think I get up every day to go out and pick it from the money bush all day long? No! I have to go out and bust my ass to provide for you and your sister and your mother. Nobody ever handed me a goddamned thing in this world, and no one's going to do that for you either. The sooner you get that through your head, the better! If you want something, you have to work for it."

And on and on the lecture would go.

So, they'd laid out all the things they wanted done each week, even made him a checklist on a dry erase board in the kitchen for him to mark away and them to inspect for quality. That was another thing. It wasn't enough that he merely *do* the chores, he had to do them *well*. Immaculate. His room had to be like the bunk of a soldier before inspection. The grass had to be at an even and consistent three-quarters of an inch off the ground over the entire lawn, and don't think for a second Walter Higgins wouldn't be out there on his knees with a tape measure to be certain. Where the weeds were pulled out of the flower bed there had to be fresh potting soil put in and smoothed to make it look as though no imposturous plants had ever been there. And so on and so on, ad infinitum.

But, like a good young lad, he'd started out well enough. He set to his chores and worked hard like his dad had demanded of him for his earnings, and really put the work in. Some days it took him until mid-afternoon, even after starting at eight in the morning, to get everything finished. The list of required chores also seemed to grow. If he caught up on everything they'd laid out for him by mid-week, there was always a fresh batch of new shit to be done. He could count on it.

When he'd finished his first week of chores after the agreement had been made, he was appalled at the infinitesimally small amount that his labors had reaped. His mouth hung agape after he realized that the two ten dollar bills were all his father was going to give him out of his wallet. The bill-fold was flipped closed and re-inserted back into his father's hip pocket.

Of course he'd wanted to say something. To protest the injustice of the amount he was being paid. Hell, *any* job he could get, even part time, would pay more than this in a day, never mind a week! He wanted to stamp his foot in righteous indignation and stand up for all the underappreciated kids the world over who did their chores for what almost *literally* amounted to peanuts.

But the stern look in his father's eyes had told him that no such protest would amount to more than another lecture about just how little he understood about how the world works.

"What do you think it costs us to raise you and your sister?" he heard his father lecturing away in his mind. "We feed you, we clothe you, we keep a roof over your head, we see to your education and your health! Do you think *any* of that is free?"

So he took his pittance and went about his business.

However, when he'd started hanging out with Jake and Bart, his money woes ceased. Full-stop, all at once. When Chris was out of cash—which was pretty quickly—Jake or Bart would pick up the tab. Every time. He didn't even have to ask. They wanted to hang, and they seemed to understand that if they wanted Chris around, they were going to have to pay his way from time to time. And it didn't seem to bother them.

So Chris had started slacking on his chores. He didn't get just a decrease in pay. His twenty dollars a week didn't drift down to fifteen or ten. It just stopped. All at once. To Walter Higgins, it was all or nothing.

"You want to do half your chores? Well, we agreed payment for *all* the chores, not half. So, no dough."

Thus, Chris didn't bother with *any* of the chores anymore.

He rather enjoyed having spoiled rotten friends, though he never realized even once that they were indeed spoiled rotten. No, to him they were merely treated with the respect and dignity they deserved. In his mind, his father was nothing more than an overbearing bore, and a spiteful son-of-a-bitch to boot. He was so tight with his money Chris wondered if his father's cash would suddenly turn into diamonds under the pressure.

Or was that coal?

Yet Chris took no joy in bullying. Not the way Jake and Bart did. He liked to see kids squirm, to give them a hard time now and then. Hell, Chris even thought they deserved it for the way he had to endure his own father. It was probably good for them. A rite of passage.

But Jake and Bart seemed to take things to a whole other level. Bart seemed to have no conscience at all on the matter, and Jake had an underlying well of fury that seemed to always be on the edge of eruption. Chris believed he really wanted to *hurt* these kids. And not just kick their ass either. No, Chris believed if Jake were left unchecked, he would make these kids *bleed*.

Bleed or not, though, Chris wasn't about to give up his meal ticket. So, when they had come across the bikes they recognized from that last day of school as belonging to the Dalton kid and his buddies, Chris had gone along with them to find them and make them pay.

But things were really getting out of hand now. Jake was screaming and beating on something inside the old house—and what an odd old house it was, just sitting out here in the middle of nowhere, not even a hint of trail or driveway to it—and Bart was going after the poor girl under the house. The big one had taken off, running away like a pussy at the first sign of trouble. He thought that was probably a good thing too, because if that kid ever realized he was as big as they were, he could prove to be real trouble for them.

That was why Chris had chosen to go after the little four-eyed punk. He was small and terrified. Chris wouldn't have to really do much to him. Didn't really *want* to do much to him. The kid hadn't done anything to him. All Chris wanted was his meal ticket to keep chugging along.

"Where'd you go, four-eyes?" Chris shouted down toward the creek-bed. "You can't get away, let's just get this over with! Take your beating and be done with it!"

His eyes scanned the creek and almost at once he saw the tree with the hollow under it, the creek streamed through the roots. And inside he thought he could make out a shape.

Got you, little man!

He made his way down the hill and stopped next to the creek. He was wearing blue jeans and a white tee-shirt, and none of that was a problem. The problem was he didn't want to get his brand new Nike sneakers soaked. The hollow was on the other side of the creek, and he'd have to cross it to pull the kid out.

Just get it over with, he thought. *Jake or Bart will get you a new pair.*

So he shrugged to himself and splashed into the creek. The clear stream immediately clouded as the mud was displaced by his feet. He could feel cool water soak straight through his shoes and socks. He grimaced as he moved, thinking of how he was ruining the brand new Nikes, but he trudged on anyway.

Now he could definitely see the kid under the hollow, curled up and pushing back against the rear-most part of the opening.

"I can see you kid, don't make me pull you out of there!" he said. "Come on, I've got you!"

But the kid didn't move.

Real annoyance started to build up within Chris now as he closed the last few feet to the tree. The little bastard wasn't going to come out on his own and now he was going to have to yank him out of there, probably getting himself completely soaked in the process, and then he was *really* going to be mad. Hell, he might actually *want* to hurt the kid at that point.

"Alright," Chris said, huffing loudly now, "you had your chance!"

He reached down, steadying himself on the base of the tree, and started to stick his hand into the hollow.

Then a snake leaped out at him.

Chris immediately shrieked, drawing to his mind comparisons to the sounds his sister and her friends would make when she had a sleepover and all the girls were running around with their dolls and toys, cackling and screaming as girls often do.

He recoiled simultaneously with his shriek and tumbled backwards onto his ass in the water. His right shoe had buried in the mud and the only garment on his right foot now was his white Hanes sock. There was a big splash as he collapsed down, and his fears of soaking all of his clothes were fully realized.

Chris looked up, wiping water from his face, and saw the snake rising up out of the hollow. It took him a moment to realize that it was in the hand of the four-eyed kid he'd been chasing and not simply rising up into the air on its own gargantuan body.

He scrambled backwards, sloshing through the creek, and got to his feet.

"You back the *fuck* up!" the kid holding the snake screamed.

Chris's hands instinctively shot up in a surrendering posture. His eyes were wide to the point of aching. What the hell was wrong with this kid? Did he have any idea what he had in his hands? That was a goddamned water moccasin, for Christ's sakes! Poisonous as all hell!

Nothing on the kid's face seemed to register that he was wielding a deadly poisonous snake in his hands, nor did anything in the kid's eyes seem to register that he would care even if he did. The kid's lips were pulled back in a snarl so over-the-top that Chris might have laughed under different circumstances.

But not now. Not with that slithering demon in front of him. If there was anything Chris Higgins hated, truly *despised* deep down in his soul, it was snakes. Not only did he hate them, he was mortified by them. He wanted no part of them, especially the sharp end.

"Take it easy, kid," Chris said, managing not to stutter. "Just take it easy! Do you know what that is?"

"Yes, I know what it is, you idiot!" the kid screamed at him. "It's a snake! And not just *any* snake, either! This here's a water moccasin, and they're poisonous as *FUCK!* So you just back the hell away from me and leave me and my friends alone."

Now Chris didn't care anything about his meal ticket. Didn't care anything about his new pair of Nikes, fifty percent of which were now being buried under the mud of the creek-bed. All he cared about was getting the fuck away from the snake and these kids and these damned woods altogether. He even thought it would be nice to go home and do some of those chores now. Chores never got snakes shoved in your face. They had that going for them.

Chris backed further away as the kid with the snake advanced. He came to edge of the creek and stepped up onto the bank, his hands in front of him, trying to make himself as unthreatening as possible.

"Okay, man, I hear ya," Chris said. "I hear ya. I'm sorry, okay? I don't know about the others, but I'll get the hell out of here! Just keep that thing away from me!"

"I'm not kidding around, fucker!"

"I believe you!"

"You—you *faggot!*"

The kid screamed this last part. Chris could see total fury in his eyes. They blazed behind his glasses, which were partially fogged now. He thought he looked a bit like Jake when he got really angry. But not exactly. There was justice behind these eyes. Righteous anger. In Jake's eyes, there was hate and torment. In this kid, there was something else.

"Okay," Chris said once again, retreating up the hill. "I'm out of here, alright?"

"Yeah you are, motherfucker!" a voice erupted from behind him.

A moment later, Chris Higgins's world went black.

CHAPTER 13

Ryan stood over Chris Higgins with a large tree branch in his hands. His knuckles were white over the bark and his chest heaved up and down.

He'd managed to get about a quarter mile down the dirt road before shame had overtaken him and resolve to be nothing like his father had gotten the better of him. He'd made his way back into the woods, ditching his bike and sprinting like never before back toward his friends. The main thing he was thinking of was Honey. Both Jimmy and Freddie were smaller than him, sure, but they were boys. They were partly why he came back, but Honey was the real thing. He liked Honey. Liked her a lot. Even when he'd farted in front of her the day they met, she hadn't made him feel bad about it or given him a hard time. Hadn't made fun of him.

And he would be damned if he allowed a boy to harm a girl again.

So, he'd snatched up a sturdy branch on his way and smashed it over that fuck Bart Dyer's skull when he saw him coming out of the hole in the underpinning of the house. He'd been about to crawl under and see who was there to help them out when he'd heard Chris Higgins on the other side of the hill going after Freddie.

Freddie actually seemed to be doing okay on his own, as it turned out. He was holding a snake—*a freaking snake*—and chasing the older boy with it!

Freddie had made eye-contact only once with Ryan, but it was enough. It had been while Higgins was climbing up onto the bank and backing up the hill. Freddie kept driving him back, and Ryan had clocked Higgins over the head.

Lights out.

"You okay?" Ryan asked Freddie, who was still holding the snake and soaked to bone.

"Yeah, I'm fine. Don't know what the hell I'm gonna do with this snake, though!"

"There's still one more, hang on to it."

They could hear Jake inside screaming and beating away on something. They made their way to the front of the house and stood before the front steps.

Ryan took a deep breath and clenched his branch tighter.

"Jake!" he screamed at the top of his lungs. "Jake Reese, get out here!"

All at once, the smashing sounds inside the house stopped. There were footsteps. They could hear boards moaning and creaking as the disturbed older boy made his way back to the front of the house.

Then he stepped out onto the porch, careful to avoid the broken boards on the landing. He was glaring at them, pure hate in his eyes. His face was scrunched into a wrinkled mess of fury and anger. Sweat was streaming down his face and his hair was matted with the stuff.

And the knife they'd seen that day at the playground was in his hand.

"What the fuck did you say to me, faggots?" Jake hissed.

The snake in Freddie's hand hissed back and Jake seemed to notice it for the first time. His eyes softened around the edges for a moment, not losing their fury, but allowing room for something else.

Fear, maybe?

"I said get out here!" Ryan barked, though his voice cracked. "And now that you're here, get the fuck out of these woods!"

Jake's eyes lingered on the snake for a moment more, then drifted to Ryan's hand, coming to rest on the limb. There were tiny spots of blood on the end of it from where he had clubbed Jake's buddies.

Then Jake's eyes drifted up and met Ryan's.

"Where are they?" he asked in a huffy voice.

"Over there," Ryan said nodding his head to the left.

Jake turned his head and saw Bart and Chris on the ground, laid out. His gaze returned to the two boys before him, that anger rising up again and driving out any fear that may have come before.

"You little faggots don't know how bad you just made it for yourselves."

"We'll be just fine," Freddie piped up. "It's you guys who are beat!"

Jake shook his head, his eyes darting back and forth between them.

"Nobody beats Jake Reese, cocksuckers," he said in a chillingly flat tone. "But I'll give you the day. Your pussy friend Jimmy is hiding inside. Seems he really *doesn't* have all the balls after all."

Ryan and Freddie said nothing. They just stood there, Freddie with his hissing snake and Ryan with his bloody limb. Inside they were trembling. Terrified. But outwardly they were holding their ground.

"These are *our* woods," Ryan stated firmly. "You guys stay out if you know what's good for you! Don't come back!"

Jake smiled and began to descend the steps. He folded his knife and put it back in his front pocket.

"Oh, we'll be seeing y'all again," Jake said. "Probably sooner than you think. I'm not stupid. You have the upper hand. Quite a feat for a couple faggots such as yourselves, but never mind all that. Like I said, we'll be seeing ya."

He stopped at the base of the steps and glared at them.

"And I'll fucking kill every one of you."

He made the statement flatly. He didn't scream. He didn't snarl. He didn't make it flamboyant, waving his arms in deranged anger. It was a simple statement. One of fact, Ryan and Freddie deduced. They believed he really meant it. And something in his eyes told them not only did he mean it, he was capable of it.

Ripples of gooseflesh stood out on their arms, but they didn't waver. They just returned the stare until Jake finally broke it.

Jake made his way over to Bart, who was now stirring, and snatched him up roughly to his feet, slapping him a few times and mumbling curses and rebukes to him as he did. Then the two of them moved on to Chris and did the same.

After that, the three boys, two defeated and one knowing when to fight another day, made their way back toward the way they had come. Bart and Chris hung their heads as they stumbled along. Jake didn't.

Just before they crested a hill and went out of sight, Jake paused and looked back at them.

"Remember what I said," he yelled to them. "When I'm done with y'all, they'll have to carry you out in a bucket."

No rage now. No screaming tantrum. Just cold, hard facts.

Then they were gone.

Ryan and Freddie waited a good ten minutes, listening hard to see if they would return. When they didn't, they went about the business of trying to find Jimmy and Honey.

Ryan first checked under the house and came up with nothing. Then they went inside the house and started to look around. Still nothing. No answer when they called for them. Nothing at all.

Where the hell are they? Ryan wondered.

They came back out of the house and Freddie realized, as though he'd forgotten, that he was still holding the snake. It writhed and squirmed around his arm, spitting its black tongue out like a whip every few seconds. He ran over to the crest of the hill that led to the creek and whipped the snake over his head like a lasso a few times, then slung it down to the creek. It landed with a splash and immediately slithered back into the sanctuary of its hollow.

Freddie came back to Ryan, who was still standing in front of the house scanning for their lost friends.

"Where do you think they went?" Freddie asked, looking about himself.

Ryan shook his head as he continued scanning the landscape.

"No idea. I don't know where they could have gone."

"Jake seemed like he was after them in there."

"Yeah," Ryan said, "and Bart was after someone under the house. But they're in neither place."

They stood there a few moments longer, looking around ponderously, when all of a sudden, they heard a strange warbling sound. A moment after that, there was the sound of a door slamming open and footsteps and creaking boards.

Ryan and Freddie turned to the house as a low din started to sound, seemingly from the house itself. It was like a growl and a moan all at the same time.

Then Jimmy burst through the front door, dragging Honey behind him by the hand. They were both filthy, covered in mud and some other horrible substance.

Slime?

Their eyes were wide and panicked. Ryan dropped his limb involuntarily.

"Guys, what the—" he started, but he was cut off by another sound.

A roar.

It came from inside the house. Jimmy and Honey looked back for only a moment and then darted down the steps in a full run. Jimmy's eyes were a thousand yards beyond them. Ryan started to ask them again just what in hell was going on, but the roar inside the house—somehow closer now—boomed again.

"RUN!" Honey screamed.

They needed no further instruction. All four kids bolted for the road.

Chris Miller

PART THREE

THE ⊕THER SIDE

Thursday, June 21, 1990

CHAPTER 14

Jimmy went through the door.

It opened into a hallway identical to the one he'd just come from. The decay of the house was the same, the creak of the boards, the howl of the old hinges as the door swung open. Gloomy light dimly lit the passage before him, dust particles dancing in the soft shafts of light.

Only, now he realized this hallway wasn't *identical*, as he'd first reckoned. Not exactly. There was no Jake Reese there in the hallway with his knife ready to cut him from his balls to his throat. This was a contrast he welcomed.

Jimmy looked back through the doorway and saw the door he'd entered the closet through. It was sort of like looking through heat-waves rising off the hood of a hot car, and he could hear a strange warbling sound. Faintly, on the other side of this warble, he could hear the banging on the door continue, and faint shouts of blood-lust from Jake.

He slammed the new door.

All at once the sounds ceased. No more banging door, no more Jake. No more warble.

He leaned his ear to the door and listened. Nothing. Then he opened the door again and saw nothing but a dark closet, just like the one he'd entered a few moments before. He walked up to the back wall and

117

put his hand against it. It was solid. Closed up like a wall should be.

What the hell? he thought.

Then he remembered willing the lock to shut. He stared at the wall and began to will it to open. Amazingly, the warbling sound returned all at once, and the wall started to shiver before him. A small hole appeared in the center of the wall and spread outward across the entirety of the structure. He could see the other door again, could see it rattling in its frame as Jake cursed and screamed from the other side.

He willed the wall back into place and an instant later the portal—*there wasn't really a better word for it*—closed.

Amazing! he thought. *What* is *this?*

He went back into the new hallway and began to make his way down it slowly. It was remarkable how *almost* identical everything seemed to be to where he had been moments before. All the same doors were there. The wallpaper was the same. The boards creaked and groaned, announcing his entrance to all that would hear, just as before.

But there were some differences as well.

He saw pictures on the walls here. There had been none before, from where he'd come, he was sure of that. He rewound the tape in his mind, playing over everything he'd seen in his panicked attempt to escape Jake and his fiendish friends. He was positive there had been no pictures littering the walls of the hall.

Jimmy walked up to one of the pictures and looked at it. What he saw sent chills up his spine.

It was a family portrait, at least he thought so. Only, in this portrait, the people in it looked all wrong. If you could even *call* them people, that was.

Four beings stood behind a chair. One of the beings sat *in* the chair. Their faces were very like normal people, but covered in a kind of fur. The noses were truncated and turned up, reminding him of a cross between the nose of a rabbit and that of a pig. At least that was the closest approximation he could muster. The hands of the creatures were sitting atop the back of the chair, but instead of eight hands, there were *sixteen*. That was when Jimmy realized there were two sets of arms on each of the beings. Their eyes were like cat-eyes, a vertical pupil slicing down through the center, and all the fingers of those sixteen hands had claws.

They looked sharp.

The creature in the chair seemed much older than the four behind it. Its two upper arms sat folded across the brim of what appeared to be the swells of breasts. The hands of the other two were clenching the two arms of the chair, gnarled and tense.

There were no smiles on any of the faces. The whole thing was steeped in a sepia tone. The picture looked very old, and the stances were eerily reminiscent of a family portrait from the turn of the century. All the furnishings in the picture seemed to be normal enough, certainly for the vintage of the photograph. Only the people-things stood out as different. They looked menacing, much like *all* people in photographs from that time period seemed to, but at the same time they seemed harmless.

Jimmy stumbled back a step from the picture, gasping and clutching his mouth with one hand, his mind reeling. He was still trying to make sense of how he'd *gotten* to this place, this *other* place, and now with the images of its beings in his mind, his brain was going into overload. It was too much to process, certainly for a twelve-year-old boy already frightened out of his mind.

He closed his eyes and tried to focus on something, *anything* else. He began to think of he and his friends, playing guns in the woods before Jake and his thugs had shown up. He replayed every image, every thought. He thought of trying to leap out to surprise Honey, determined to blast her to Kingdom Come with his imaginary bullets, and then tripping and farting and losing to her anyway.

He'd begun laughing quietly before he realized he was doing it, and then a horrible thought occurred to him.

Honey!

He remembered her diving under the house as he'd sprinted up into it. He also remembered that when Jake had come into the house after him, he'd been alone. Bart and Chris had stayed outside. Were they after the others? And what about Honey?

He didn't know where Ryan had gone, and he remembered Freddie racing down to the creek-bed, but where he'd gone from there was anyone's guess. The only one he knew where to find was Honey. If willing the wall to open for him worked in the hall closet, it just might work under the house too. It had seemed so easy to do.

He opened his eyes and made his way to the front of the house. He forgot all about the picture of the people-things he'd seen and focused on getting outside. Light was coming in from windows on either side of the door as he rounded into the foyer, but the light was different too. In his world the light had been bright and yellow. Here it was a dull, somewhat blue-gray tinge.

Jimmy opened the door to the porch and stepped out to a foggy re-creation of his own woods. It all seemed the same, but the trees here were dead. *All* of them. The ground was littered with fallen branches and swaths of leaves, much deeper than he'd seen in his woods, and all of it was bathed in an ominous fog. The porch didn't have any holes in it and the wood seemed a bit sturdier as well. It creaked a bit under his weight, but that was all.

He bounded down the steps into the gray light. The fog was almost thick enough to grasp, and he even reached out to try and do so. But his hands merely whispered through it, leaving a cool residue on his fingers. He was, however, able to push it aside with his hands it seemed, and as his arms paddled ahead of him, he could feel moisture collecting on his skin.

There was no hole in the underpinning here either, but he remembered about where it had been before and he reached down and pulled at the wooden panels. They gave easily enough and after a minute he had made an opening more than wide enough for him to crawl under. He paid no mind to the noise he was making as he worked.

Kneeling down on his haunches, Jimmy peered under the house. It was littered with cobwebs and smelled of mold and wet earth. He moved down onto his hands and knees and made his way under. There were piers of rock and wood spaced out evenly beneath the whole house, holding the structure up. They reminded him of gravestones. There were patches of black stuff on some of the wood that looked like the mold he was smelling, and swatches of green moss growing on many of the rocks.

Shaking off a building unease, he tunneled his way under the house, pushing strands of cobwebs out of his way as he went along. They were thick and clung to him as though with a thousand tiny, sticky hands, and he had to shake furiously and wipe them on his jeans to get the webs off his skin.

He had a faint sense of fear trying to rise up which he was still keeping successfully at bay, at least for the moment. The source of his fear was the thought of coming across any spiders. He *hated* spiders. Hated them more than anything he could think of, and the last thing he wanted to do was to come across one now. But the greater terror behind this fear was this shocking thought: *what if they—the spiders—were different here too?* If the people were so different, it stood to reason that *everything* would be. Or at least *could* be.

Shivers snaked down his spine, coiling around it, and gooseflesh cropped up all over his skin as he made his way along, pushing thoughts of horrible mutant spiders out of his mind.

Moving deliberately on his hands and knees, Jimmy made his way toward the back of the house, where he thought he might find Honey on the other side, and took a deep breath. He closed his eyes and willed the *air* this time—rather than any part of the structure—to open up into his world. A moment later, that now familiar warbling sound returned and he opened his eyes. Though he'd been trying to do this very thing, his astonishment was still not diminished one bit. The air before him spread open in a circular pattern just as the wall in the closet had done before. The dark, gray air turned a more golden color—though dark here beneath the house—and he could hear crying.

It was Honey.

She was about six feet in front of him, curled up behind one of the grave-like pillars. She was curled into a fetal position and tears streamed her face. She didn't seem to be aware of the warbling sound *or* his presence as he scooted along on his knees toward her. He clasped his hand around her mouth and stifled an instant scream from her. Her wide eyes darted around to him.

"Follow me!" he whispered harshly.

She nodded violently as he removed his hand and put one finger vertically across his lips to make sure she stayed quiet.

They crawled in unison back the six feet into the opening in the air, then six more. Honey was looking around in confusion and fear, also what Jimmy thought was awe, seeing all the same things he'd seen as he'd entered this other place. The difference in the light. The cobwebs, which seemed different here, too. They were thicker. Not in a more condensed sort of way, but the strands themselves seemed to have more girth.

They heard the voice of Bart Dyer from the other side come booming at them.

"Hey, bitch! I see you! And I'm gonna get you too! Maybe you can show me your little titties, what do you say? Maybe we can *all* get a look at them titties!"

The voice was close.

Jimmy closed his eyes at once and willed the air to close. It did immediately, and the sound vanished with it as though it were never there.

Bart's voice was gone as well, swallowed in another world.

Honey was looking around in shock and awe and terror, all rolled into one.

"What the hell *is happening, Jimmy?"* she hissed in a whisper.

Jimmy looked at her and shook his head, his mouth hanging agape, but with a hint of a grin at one corner.

"I have no clue."

CHAPTER 15

They crawled back out from under the house. They blessed and thanked all the gods that ever were—and a few who weren't—that they hadn't come across any of the spiders which had made those cobwebs, though they did so independently and to themselves.

Exiting the hole first, Jimmy quickly stood and helped Honey out of the opening. Then they dusted themselves off for a moment, but soon gave up on this activity as they considered their ruined clothes. Dark mud and dirt had burrowed into every fiber of their pants and shirts, and their efforts were utterly wasted.

Then they looked around in the fog. Honey's face had dropped the look of terror, but it maintained the wonder.

She turned to Jimmy.

"I don't understand what's happening," she said in a wavering voice. She was on the edge of tears. She could feel them stinging the corners of her eyes like tiny knives.

Jimmy nodded, looking around.

"I don't either," he said. "All I know is I got in a closet in the house. Jake was after me and I hadn't locked the door. He was getting close, you know, right outside the door, and I was looking at the keyhole, wishing to Christ it would lock..."

"And?" Honey prompted him after several seconds of silence.

"A-and then it did," he said, coming out of his momentary daze, his eyes blazing. "Just like that. It locked, all on its own, l-like it was *obeying* me or something."

This sounded utterly crazy to Honey, but no more so than Jimmy appearing out of a hazy hole under the house and pulling her into this other place.

"That still doesn't explain coming out of thin air, though, Jimmy!" she said.

"I can't really explain that either," he said, "but after the door locked and Jake was trying to beat it down, I kept moving back in the closet, trying to get as far back from the door as I could. I was wishing I could find a way out and then I look up and I had moved into this place."

He spread his hands out and motioned to the world they were standing in. This odd, similar, but very *different* world.

"There was another door," he continued, beginning to pace over the crunching leaves, his eyes distant and darting. "It was just like the one I'd gone into running from Jake. I opened it and came back out into the hallway. No Jake, no nothing. I remembered seeing you go under the house, so all I could think of was trying to see if I could get you out of there. Seems I got there just in time."

Honey's eyes spread wide and she felt a blush trying to flare up on her cheeks. It was sweet, him thinking of her that way. So...*sweet*.

"Do you know where the others are?" she asked, ignoring her blushing face. "Maybe we can get them too!"

Jimmy was shaking his head. "Freddie went down to the creek bed, but I have no idea where after that. And Ryan took off toward the road. They could be anywhere."

She nodded, her gaze shifting from his eyes to the foggy woods all around them.

"So, what now?" she asked after a full minute of silence.

Jimmy shrugged as though to say that was the question, wasn't it? What *did* you do when you found a portal to some strange new place? Especially when you knew that going back meant having to face down a menacing group of bullies. How long would they have to wait to go home? For that matter, would they be *able* to go home?

Honey had no idea if this crazy, wonderful thing Jimmy had discovered he could do would last. To hear him tell it, it had come out of nowhere. Would it vanish in like fashion?

There was a sound coming from the trees which pulled her from her thoughts. It wasn't far away, but through the misty fog, they couldn't see what it was.

Crunch-crunch-crunch.

Something was moving through the leaves just out of their sight. Jimmy had noticed it, too, and now both of them were walking in a semi-sideways fashion toward the trees, like crabs on a beach. Their eyes were peering through the mist, straining to see whatever it was that was coming along.

They wandered over a little way, now in front of the steps to the house. The sounds persisted. The two kids stopped moving and stared into the mist.

Crunch-crunch-crunch.

Then something materialized in the hazy fog.

There was a shape—somewhat familiar—emerging from the mist, but there were parts of it which didn't seem to match. And the size was all wrong as well. It was way too...*big.*

The thing that was crunching along moved further into their view. They could now see it more clearly, but they wished like hell they hadn't been able to.

The thing was a spider, or at least something very *like* a spider. Only, it was *all* wrong.

They could see eight legs protruding up and out from a furry ball at the thing's center before turning sharply back down to the earth. Two more legs, shorter than the others, came out from the front of it, under a face, feeling and prodding at the ground before it like nightmare fingers.

And the spider had a face.

A *real* face.

It wasn't like spiders they had seen and studied in science class. Nothing at all like any of those, in fact. There was an open hole which looked roughly like the hollow of a nose on a human skull. It had a large mouth with lips like a pair of green worms. The mouth opened and closed with wet sounds that slopped with the motion. There were bright red fangs inside the mouth and some sort of putrid, yellow pus oozed from the corners of the mouth.

And it had eyes.

Not compound eyes like most insects and arachnids tended to sport, but mammal-like eyes. With whites and irises and pupils. Only these pupils were diamond-shaped black things surrounded by purple irises. The eyes darted this way and that and it moved along with idiotic dullness. The two shorter legs jutting out beneath its chin—if you could call it a chin—wriggled and felt their way before it.

What they had taken for a furry bulb of abdomen initially, they could now see was actually something closer to *hair* than fur. Bright, orange hair. It moved like any spider they'd ever seen, but seeing it here, coming from the mist, it looked like the face of a diseased *man*, albeit a man coated in slime and pus. The orange hair on its back looked like a mad scientist's crazy hair, or like the hair of a man in the throes of electrocution in cartoons and parodies. What was even *more* horrifying was its size. It was at least two full *feet* in diameter, and that wasn't taking into account the spread of its legs.

Jimmy and Honey stood stock still, staring in awe of this creature. It didn't seem to notice them as it moved along. They followed the eyes and hair as it crunched its way over to the side of the house.

Then it did a peculiar thing.

When it neared the underpinning of the house, it jumped. It came a full foot in the air. As it leaped, straight up as if attached to wires, it turned approximately thirty degrees, facing them straight on. It landed down on all ten of its legs, the front two shorter ones now assisting in its stability.

"Fick-a-choo?" the thing uttered, as though asking a question.

And it had actually *sounded* like a question. The horrible green lips had moved and its eyes had widened in concern. The voice was phlegmy and high-pitched, but had a low, growling quality to it as well, like an undercurrent on a different frequency.

Honey and Jimmy maintained their statuesque poses, unable to move or breathe. Their hearts were racing, and though neither of them knew this of the other, they were both utterly terrified of spiders. *Regular* spiders, that was. Whatever this thing was, it wasn't terror that it invoked in them. Beneath the awe and wonder of what they were taking in, was something much more awful than mere terror. Terror didn't even *approach* what they were feeling in that moment. English had yet to develop a word for the depths of abysmal horror they were feeling in that moment.

Their hearts thudded in their chests, rattling their ribcages.

"Fad-a-chap!" the thing shrieked, louder now than its question before. *"Fad-a-chum! Fap-a-chap! Flap-a-dung!"*

The spider-thing was fidgeting around now, its legs working in perfect harmony to bring it about in small semi-circles as it cursed in its strange tongue.

Honey grabbed Jimmy's arm and took a step backwards toward the house. Her foot caught on the first step and she stumbled over onto the boards, pulling Jimmy along with her. He stumbled and caught his footing before spilling over himself, but as he gazed down at Honey, trying to help her up, he felt all his hair stand on end.

The spider-thing had stopped its barking tirade.

Jimmy and Honey looked slowly back toward the spider-thing, their heads turning in unison, eyes wide. Neither of them were breathing.

The spider-thing was facing them head on. The front, shorter legs were raised up in the air in some sort of shock, its diamond-shaped eyes were wide, exposing the whites at the edges, and its mouth was open, baring its bright red fangs.

The kids froze, perfectly still. An eternity passed as they faced down the spider-thing with its insane hairdo and maddening face. It didn't move, save for a rise and fall of its orange hair, as it sucked awful breaths in through its horrible mouth and nose. Slime and pus drew in and spat forth with every breath it made.

Sweat had formed on Honey's brow as she lay there on the steps, gazing in perfect horror at the terrible creature, even though the air had seemed significantly cooler here then it had in their world. Her lungs burned for fresh air, though she didn't dare take a breath.

She could feel Jimmy's trembling hand touching her arm where it had frozen when the thing had noticed their presence. He was as perfectly still as she was.

After another eon or so, the thing lowered its front two legs back to the ground slowly. It stood there, breathing in wet, burbling breaths for another minute more. Finally, it waddled back around to the opening in the underpinning and paused for a moment.

"Fick-a-choo?" it questioned again as it looked at the hole.

Then it crawled through and disappeared under the house.

Honey and Jimmy exhaled sharply when it as gone and took in gulps of much needed fresh air. Jimmy helped her up to her feet and they moved away from the house with some haste, far enough that it disappeared into the fog.

"What the fuck was that thing?" Honey asked in a gasp when the house was out of sight.

"It looked like a-a spider...sort of," Jimmy responded, his face pale.

"But its face was almost *human!*" she said to him in awe.

Jimmy nodded, his eyes distant again. Honey thought of a movie she had watched a couple years before. Her father had rented a videotape of a movie called 'The Fly', perhaps two months after the accident which had taken her mother from them. She remembered him being frustrated that it was apparently a remake of the movie he had wanted to watch, something he had seen as a kid way back in the fifties. He had turned it off when he realized the mistake.

But Honey had gone into the living room that night and put it in the tape player, the volume on the TV set very low. She had watched.

A fly had gotten inside this teleporting machine the main character had made, and their DNA had somehow fused. As the movie went on, the man had slowly changed into a human-fly hybrid monster.

The spider thing looked like some similar sort of abomination.

Honey and Jimmy moved further away from the house and its horrible arachnid-hybrid tenant, finding their way to the creek. It was there, just as it had been in their world. Though here it was masked in fog. They got closer and saw the water running through it. It was clear, much like water in their world, but here it had a reddish tinge. Jimmy knelt down and scooped up a handful of the water and smelled it.

It smelled like water. That was to say, it *had* no smell. None at all.

He decided not to experiment further with tasting, and let it run out from his fingers back into the stream. He wiped his hands on his filthy pants.

"You think Freddie is around here somewhere?" Honey asked, then added, "You know, on our side?"

Jimmy nodded and shrugged at the same time, looking up and down the bank.

"Probably so," he said, "but I have no idea exactly where."

"Could you try to do, you know, whatever it is you did back at the house and see if we're close?"

Jimmy considered this for a moment and then shook his head.

"If we come through and Jake and his boys are still there, we could be walking into a world of trouble. If they're close enough, they might be able to come over here."

"If they did, I'd feed them to that spider-thing," Honey added with spite rich in her voice.

Jimmy laughed. "Yeah," he said. "I'd like to see them shit their pants seeing that thing!"

They both laughed now, soothed by the humor. They hadn't realized how much they needed it until they were doing it.

But the laughter faded away when they heard new sounds.

There was a slurping sound that caught their attention and ceased their laughter. They turned and looked up the bank to see what had made the awful sound. Ahead of them, a giant slug was moving along, slow as slugs tended to move. It was at least three feet long, and looked like little more than a gelatinous mass trudging along its way.

Coming right towards them.

It seemed far less threatening than the spider-thing had, probably because all of its features seemed to be just like a slug in their world, save its massive size. They stood next to each other, staring in wonder at the monster slug as it moved along.

"Holy shit!" Honey said, a smile breaking across her face.

Her smile vanished in an instant when the slug sat upright on its rear third in a flash. The movement was incredibly fast and uncharacteristic for slugs back home, and it startled them both. It stood there, two fleshy prongs jutting up from what they guessed was its head, flopping around as though it were taking in information.

Then a mouth opened exposing a line of razor-like teeth.

The slug shrieked like a banshee and was suddenly coming at them with alarming speed. It strode upon its rear third, which was writhing along snake-like making its charge. Its teeth glared at them and Honey froze in fright where she stood.

Thankfully, Jimmy reacted.

He knelt down and picked up a large rock near the bank of the creek. It was heavy and big, and it took both hands to wield it. She saw his teeth exposed in a grimace as he struggled with its weight, and when he turned, raising the rock over his head, she saw his eyes peel wide. The monster-slug was only a few feet away now, screaming at them and baring its horrible teeth.

Jimmy swung the rock down at the last moment, smashing it into the slug. There was a loud *splatting* sound as he did, and slime erupted from the creature, showering them both in gelatinous ooze. They both seized up, spitting the slime from their mouths, taking deep breaths and coughing.

That was when they heard the voice. That horrible voice.

"Who comes to my world?!" it boomed.

It seemed to come from all around them instead of a singular direction. It was deep and full of fury and authority. They looked all around them, wiping sludge from their faces as they did, their confusion and panic reaching Everest heights.

Then they saw it.

It was across the stream, on the opposite bank. It was a hulking figure, insanely tall and broad in the shoulder. Its tiny waist sat atop legs that bent backwards like a goat, and its face was something out of a nightmare. The skin of the monster was a dark gray color and its eyes blazed from black sockets. Bones rose up from its back in sharp points, like the raised arms of a worshipping church-goer.

Jimmy didn't think. Honey *couldn't* think.

He grabbed her arm and wrenched her back up the hill. She followed without fuss or protest, and the two of them sprinted up the hill the way they had come.

"You won't leave here without giving me my MEAT!" the thing snarled at their backs.

Then they could hear it coming after them. Loud thumps and the crunching of dead leaves filled their ears as the beast came after them.

"Come on!" Jimmy screamed, pulling Honey along by the hand.

They were running with all they had. A few moments later, the house began to materialize in front of them. The thumping and crunching was getting louder and closer to them every second. There was some horrible breathing sound as the thing chased them down.

Honey stole a glance back as she ran hand in hand with Jimmy. She saw the thing coming at them, black eyes blazing like dark fire. It was on all fours now, running like a tiger in pursuit of its prey.

Fear gripped her from every angle, but she found it also fueled her retreat.

The house was fully visible now, and she saw with horror the spider-thing had come back out from under the house. It was standing directly in front of them, just in front of the stairs leading up to the house.

"Fick-a-choo?" it asked in its high-pitched growl, the alarmed eyes and front legs praising some deity.

There was a roar from behind them as the monster chased them relentlessly, getting closer with every step. With every millisecond.

"Fuck-a-dis!" the spider-thing shrieked and scurried away from them and back under the house.

Jimmy and Honey pounded forth, pumping their legs as fast as they could. They bounded up the steps to the porch and burst forth into the foyer in a full sprint.

Jimmy was as panicked as she was, but still seemed to be thinking. He looked directly ahead at the wall of the hallway that teed off from the foyer and focused his eyes. He was willing it to open for them, to lead them back to his world. The bullies be damned. What was after them now was infinitely worse.

As if on demand, Jimmy's gift caused the warbling sound to come up to pitch, and a portal appeared before them.

"Keep moving!" Jimmy screamed as they raced for the opening to their world.

They heard wood splintering and glass shattering behind them, right on their heels as they pressed onward. The thing was coming through the door and smashing it to bits in its bloodthirsty pursuit.

They moved through the portal and back into their world. Jimmy screaming at her to keep moving, and she didn't argue.

Their feet thumped down on the ancient boards of the house in their world and the brighter, more golden rays of sunshine berated their eyes. They thundered down the foyer to the door and burst through it and onto the porch.

A roar screamed from behind them, chilling them to the bone.

They saw Ryan and Freddie standing there, in front of the house, staring up at them in confusion and fear.

Jimmy and Honey descended the steps in a full sprint.

"RUN!" Honey screamed.

CHAPTER 16

They all ran.

Shadows seemed to be moving at them, all around them. The roars continued. The hot feeling of being chased. It was all there. But any time Jimmy looked back, he never saw the thing again. Not in solid form, anyway. Only shadows. *Moving* shadows, to be sure, but only shadows just the same.

Yet, he wasn't taking chances with even that. Whatever the thing was that had come after them, it was powerful. It was strong. It was a physical form in the other place, but here it seemed only to be darkness.

That by no means convinced Jimmy that it was *harmless*, though. He ran on, his three friends all right there with him. The sound of swooshing wind filled their ears from behind, and leaves seemed to billow all about in a whirlwind. Once, Jimmy could feel hot breath on the back of his neck. It served as a great encourager to his flight.

And then, quite suddenly, the sounds stopped. The billowing leaves settled. The shadows were gentle and still.

Whatever the thing was, it was gone.

They ran on, anyway, all the way to the road where their bikes were. They picked them up out of the grass, each one's chest heaving for breath and sanity. They were all covered in sweat now, and dirty. None more so than Jimmy and Honey. Streaks of dirt lined their face, held to them in a sticky mask of perspiration.

Bikes were mounted, peddles were pumped, and speed was gained. Jimmy wobbled Red back and forth, standing on his peddles, desperate to get away from whatever it was that had chased them. He thought of the portal he'd made as they fled and wondered if it was still open. Would the spider-thing be able to cross through? What if another of those horrible slugs came along and happened right through it?

He didn't know about that, but he knew the thing by the bank had chased them. Had come through. Though—as he thought vigorously, peddling harder and harder, his friends falling behind, unable to keep up—while it had come through, not *all* of it had come through. That he was sure of. It had still been dangerous, that was definite, but it was more like a *projection* of the thing had come into their world, not the physical form itself.

None of this made any sense to him, but he wondered again about the spider and the slug. He was relatively sure that his mere distance from the house would be sufficient to close the doorway to the other world and contain the horrible creatures that inhabited it, but several questions gnawed at him.

Why didn't the monster come all the way through?

That was bugging him more than all the other questions. He and Honey had gone through. Had *really* been there. They even got covered in slime from the slug. It stood to reason that if they could cross through, then things from that world should be able to do the same. That strange, horrible place contained horrors unknown. Everything seemed to be the same, but so awfully different as well. There had been nothing he saw that he couldn't identify with from his own world, yet it was so out of order with what he'd come to understand about nature it caused his mind to ache.

Spiders didn't have a face like a man. Slugs didn't have razor-lined vagina-mouths, and they *certainly* couldn't move so fast. Never mind the fact that the creatures were so big!

And a talking spider. *"Fuck-a-dis!"*

Yeah, fuck that.

The kids came to the intersection of Mitchell Street and Pine, and they hung a left back towards town and their homes. After they got a little way further, they finally came to a stop. There was a full minute of deep breathing and scared, terrified looks shared between them as they glanced around. They'd survived something, though Jimmy knew Ryan and Freddie still didn't fully grasp the gravity of what they'd just come through. They *couldn't*. They hadn't seen what he and Honey had. Jimmy wanted to tell them, to explain the whole thing, and he started to do just that.

However, Ryan was the first to speak.

"Shit, man, maybe my dad wasn't crazy after all!"

He was still breathing fast and deep, catching his breath, and his eyes were bright and moist, like he was on the edge of crying. His body was trembling.

"He always swore it was the shadows! *The shadows done it,'* he's always said. We all thought he was crazy, but...what I just saw..."

Jimmy was nodding.

"You may be right," he said, gulping deeply after his voice cracked, "but guys, that's not even the tip of the iceberg."

140

Freddie looked up through his thick glasses.

"Yeah, speaking of, where the *hell* did you and Honey vanish to? Ryan and I singlehandedly manage to get Jake and his goons to buzz the *fuck* off, and y'all are nowhere to be found! What gives?"

Honey looked back and forth between Ryan and Freddie.

"You wouldn't believe us. You *won't* believe us. But maybe Jimmy can show you?"

She turned back to Jimmy as she spoke. He was staring at her, his eyes still scared and distant, but he began to nod. Then he looked to the others.

Freddie said, "Show us *what?* For fuck's sake, somebody start making some goddamn sense!"

"Come on," Jimmy said to them all. "I know a place. I'll explain everything when we get there."

Jimmy began to pedal away again, and the others followed.

CHAPTER 17

Jake got home later that afternoon. He hadn't been so angry in all his life that he could remember. *Humiliated* by those little faggots in the woods. And right when he'd had them. *Really* had them.

He had planned to make an example of Jimmy. The one with the smart fucking mouth and the stupid, faggot face. Even the goddamn niggers were smarter than this punk. At least they knew when to shut their pie-holes and take their beating. They would take anything Jake Reese gave them, and they would thank him for the opportunity after.

But Jimmy Dalton was the one who'd gotten away. Saved by the coach on the last day of school. Managing to lock himself in a closet at the house in the woods.

Boy, wasn't that fitting? Little faggot boy Jimmy locked himself in the closet. What a little bitch.

Jake walked in through the kitchen and went to go back to his room at the other end of the house.

"Jake?" his father's voice stopped him.

Jake stopped at the mouth of the hallway and grimaced. He managed to stifle his curse to inaudibility, but not the grimace. It stayed, making a stunning performance. He didn't turn around, only turned his head slightly.

"Yeah, dad?" he said. The disgust dripped from his words.

"What have you been up to today?" George Reese asked.

Now Jake shoved off the wall and turned around to face his father. He saw him sitting at the kitchen table, reading over a newspaper. Jake was surprised he hadn't seen him when he'd come in, but he had totally missed him. Walked right past him. His old man had been so immobilized by the riveting local paper with stories of the mayor cutting a ribbon at the new foundry construction at the edge of town and the Little Miss Winnsboro Pageant that Jake had utterly missed him.

"Not much," Jake said, answering his father, keeping his tone even. "Hanging with my friends."

"You been out with that Dyer boy? And Higgins?"

Jake shrugged. "Yeah, so?"

"Your mother, well, your mother and *I* don't much care for those two. They aren't a good influence for a young Christian man such as yourself. You know the Dyers don't even go to church, right?"

George Reese was peeking over the top of the paper, his glasses perched at the tip of his nose, his eyebrows flexed to full height. Jake hated him.

"So what?" Jake started. "And no one influences me, okay? If anything, I influence *them*, so quit worrying about who I'm hanging with, okay, dad?"

George slammed down the newspaper and stood suddenly. His face was red and his eyes were taut.

"You listen to *me*, boy!" he shouted, pointing his finger across the room. "You sit right down here and listen to your father! You will show me respect and you will—"

"Fuck you, pop!" Jake said, cutting him off. "How's that for respect? Huh? Take that respect and shove it up your ass!"

George Reese had a bewildered look on his face now, sitting atop the anger of the moment before. It looked like he was trying to form the word 'what' over and over again, his mouth moving silently, but his voice wouldn't join the party.

Jake crossed the room towards him, glaring coldly at his father as he moved. He slid the knife out of his pocket and flicked the blade out.

"Mom used to try that shit with me, you remember?" Jake said in a low tone. "She used to scream at me and tell me what to do. Yeah, you remember, don't you? Then she'd get that belt, the one that had the metal tab on the end, and she'd wrap that buckle up in her hand and swing the belt like a fucking whip! Over and over and over again! You remember *that*, Daddy?!"

Jake slammed his fist—the one holding the knife— on the table where his father had been sitting as he spoke. George was staring at the knife intently now. His eyes flicked up to his son's.

"I-I know you've gotten some harsh punishment before, son, but spare the rod, spoil the child, you know, l-like the Bible says!" His father's voice was quivering.

Jake smiled.

"You can shove your Bible up your ass too," Jake said. "I'm not asking if you remember those whippings I got just so we can reminisce, I'm asking if you know why they *stopped?*"

"Well, you-you got t-too old, and—"

144

"No," Jake said, once again cutting his father off. He was standing next to him now. Jake was big for such a young man. He was already taller than his father at only fourteen, and he was stronger too. And his father knew it.

The knife was three inches from George's face.

"No," Jake went on. "No, the reason she stopped is because *I* put a stop to it. I took that fucking belt out of her hands and I tied her hands behind her back with it. You weren't home, you and Norman were somewhere together. But I did it. I threw her down on the bed."

George's eyes were widening as Jake went on. His lips began to tremble.

"And I told her I was a *man*, goddamnit! And *men* don't get spankings from their mother! They don't get spankings from *any* bitch!"

Jake started laughing, holding the knife in his father's face, its tip gleaming.

"Then I proved to her I was a man, Daddy," Jake said, leaning in closer to his father and touching the blade to his father's cheek. "Oh, I proved it to her. Twice. She screamed and she begged for me to stop, but you know what?" He leaned in close, his spittle spattering his father's terrified face. "I think she *liked* it, the twisted cunt. I think she liked it real good, actually. She got all...*wet* down there."

Jake's smile vanished suddenly and his face went hard. The tip of the knife pressed harder against his father's cheek, pulling the skin in on itself.

"So why am I telling you all of this?" Jake asked, rhetorically. "Why, I'm telling you this because you seem to not understand that you're talking to a *man* here, and you seem to have forgotten that you treat a *man* with respect. Ask your cunt wife why she never told you about that day. I dare you. It was probably because she doesn't respect you. No one does, of course. Because you're not a man, not really. *I* showed her what a man was, and she's backed off of me ever since. She doesn't give me shit, I don't pay her any mind."

Jake leaned his face closer and pressed his lips against his father's ear. The knife blade had made a small puncture and blood now trickled onto the blade and down his father's cheek. George was trembling now, his eyes wide and breaths coming in hitching gasps.

"Next time you talk to me like I'm some little boy," Jake said, bringing his voice down to a harsh whisper, "I'm gonna hold you down, and prove to you I'm a man, just like I did to your cunt wife. And remember..."

Jake moved to lock eyes with his father.

"...she *liked* it."

George stepped back suddenly from his son and the knife. His face was bleeding from the tip of the blade and he was shaking all over. Confusion and fear mixed on his face in perfect balance, and his eyes were welled with tears, though they didn't look like tears of sadness. Maybe anger or humiliation. Certainly of fear.

"You *monster!*" George said, pointing at him with a pitiful, shaking finger.

"No," Jake said, folding the blade of the knife and placing it back into his pocket. "*She's* the monster. And you're the monster's bitch. I'm the one in charge now. Don't ever ask me what I'm doing again...*bitch*."

146

Jake turned and went back to the hallway. George said nothing. George *did* nothing. Jake had known he wouldn't. His father was a pussy. His mother, on the other hand, had been made of sterner stuff. That's why he'd had to go so far to show her who was boss. And she'd never said a word about it after. Jake assumed it was because of a deep sense of respect. Of *awe*. Women liked it when a man took charge. Even liked it when a man showed them they were wrong. It was hardwired into them.

With his father, though, just the threat of it would do. His spine was made of oatmeal, and the thought of his son holding him down and fucking him had turned the oatmeal to water. Just as Jake had known it would.

Jake entered his room and shut the door. Locked it. Laid back on his bed.

He stared at the ceiling, satisfaction flooding him from the inside, and fantasized about peeling the skin off Jimmy Dalton.

Jake Reese smiled.

CHAPTER 18

Jimmy had just finished telling the story. He'd had some help from Honey along the way, filling in some parts after she had been pulled into the other place by Jimmy, lending credibility to his story with her impassioned account of the ordeal.

Yet, the looks from Freddie and Ryan were precisely what he had predicted they would be. It was obvious they didn't believe them. Jimmy could tell they *wanted* to believe the story, but their minds simply wouldn't wrap around it. Even in spite of their admission that some horrible shadow creature had chased them out of the woods, even feeling its breath on their necks as they fled, they still just couldn't believe it.

Freddie started shaking his head after a full minute had passed, one filled with odd looks and silence.

"You're right," he said, his eyes falling to Honey. "I think it's bullshit."

"I mean, come on, guys," Ryan said, raising an upturned hand of reason. "We saw some weird shit, I'll give you that, but locking doors with your *mind?* That *alone* is impossible to believe, never mind opening portals to other worlds!"

"Not other *worlds*," Jimmy jumped in. "Just one other world. I wouldn't believe it myself if I hadn't been there, if I hadn't *done* it. But seriously, you know me.

You *both* know me. I don't make stuff up! And Honey was there too!"

"It's the truth, guys," she offered with a shrug.

"Well, if I can't see it for myself, I can't swallow it," Freddie retorted. "Not calling you a liar—either of you—I'm just saying that, after the day I've had, my mind isn't willing to take anything for granted. I mean *shit*, dude! Jake and his goons were trying to *kill* us! And then whatever that was from the house...I..."

He trailed off, shaking his head again. Wrapping his mind around why some Freshman punks wanted to hurt them in the first place—to *really* hurt them—was hard enough to fathom, Jimmy reckoned, let alone stories about telekinetic abilities and other dimensions.

They were standing in an abandoned old garage on Richardson Street. It was about a mile and half from Jimmy and Freddie's homes, on the east side of Main Street. The old garage was an ancient thing, probably built in the thirties or forties, and looked to have been abandoned by the late sixties at the latest. There were old tools and workbenches about, rusted into uselessness, and wheel frames were scattered around, forgotten by whatever owner had left the place and the bank that had foreclosed on him. It had large sliding doors that refused to glide in their tracks, but there was enough pliability in the old corrugated metal of the doors to pull back enough to allow small children entrance.

Freddie was holding himself up on an old hoist that stood in the middle of the garage, a patina coated relic of some poor soul's long-lost American dream. Ryan leaned back cross-armed against one of the more robust workbenches, littered with ancient tools and bolts and trash of all kinds. Honey and Jimmy were standing before them in the center of the room.

"Maybe you can show them, Jimmy?" Honey offered, shifting her eyes to him as she spoke.

Jimmy snapped out of a short daze and looked up at her, worry now filling his eyes.

"I don't know," he said. "I mean, I can try, but, I'm not even sure how I did it before. It was like, I dunno, like *instinct*, you know? It sort of just *happened*."

"Just try," she said, placing a hand on his arm.

Ryan's stature visibly tensed when she did this, but only Jimmy seemed to notice. He took a step away from her, gently pulling his arm free from her grasp.

"Okay," Jimmy said, "I'll try something small."

He walked over to the workbench Ryan was leaning against, his eyes scanning the detritus upon it. Jimmy rummaged around for a moment through the junk, and finally came up with a bolt. It was a small thing, only a couple of inches long and no more than half an inch thick. He held it up to them.

"This," Jimmy said. "I'll try and move this. We'll start there."

Nods were issued all around and Jimmy placed the bolt on the floor in the middle of them all. All their eyes were pinned to it. Jimmy scanned the others, taking a deep breath, and watched as Freddie pushed his glasses up on his nose and then crossed his arms.

Please, Jimmy prayed silently. *Please work.*

Jimmy took two steps back, then knelt down on his knees in front of the small metal object as though he were going to genuflect. But he stayed down.

He stared at the bolt. They all stopped breathing as Jimmy's eyes narrowed to slits, his brow furrowing. His body began to tremble ever so faintly as he began this concentration. All three of the other kids began to lean in, so slowly it was almost imperceptible. The room had gone completely silent, save for the sound of leaves brushing on the rusted exterior of the old garage.

Nothing happened.

Jimmy focused with all his might over the next five minutes, begging whatever God there may be to please, oh *please*, let him show proof of these great claims he'd just made.

Still, *nothing* happened.

He relaxed all his muscles and exhaled loudly in frustration and defeat. His cheeks reddened with anger and embarrassment as he eased his butt back on his heels.

The others also exhaled and retreated back to more comfortable stances. No one said anything for a long moment, then Freddie finally voiced up.

"Don't be too hard on yourself," he said in a sympathetic voice. "We just had a really bad day, we were all scared. I've heard sometimes people can remember things that didn't really happen, even extraordinary things. Stress can do that. One time, I watched this crazy movie, Hellraiser—freaky shit—and that night I remember seeing one of the Cenobites, demon things *in* my closet. Like I *really* saw it! I can still remember it. But, you know...it wasn't—"

Honey was shaking her head. "No, Freddie, *I* was there! I saw it too! I didn't see him lock the door, but he did pull me out from under the house when that, that *lard ass* was crawling in after me! This wasn't some horror movie, it was real!"

"I believe you, Honey," Ryan said, standing up from the workbench. "I just, I don't know, maybe Freddie has a point, you know? When we're scared, sometimes we see things, our minds play tricks on us, like he said."

"You don't believe me, Ryan," Honey chirped sharply, "you just believe that *I* believe it. That's not the same thing at all, so don't give me that crap!"

Ryan re-crossed his arms and ducked his head a bit, thoroughly reproached.

"This is bullshit!" Jimmy cried from his position on the ground. "This is total bullshit! I know what happened out there, and I'm not making it up!"

"I didn't say you were making it up, Jimmy," Freddie started, but was unable to continue when Jimmy piped back at him.

"And my mind wasn't playing tricks on me either!" Jimmy yelled, his eyes blazing with anger. "That fucking door wasn't locked, and I *locked* it without touching it! And I *did* go through to somewhere else and pull Honey in with me! And that shadow thing that chased us, it wasn't a shadow in that other place, it was *real* over there, along with all the other things we saw!"

"Okay, okay!" Freddie yelled back at him, his arms waving in surrender, his own face reddening now. "But now you can't! Alright? No one wanted to see this more than me, I guarantee you that, but it didn't happen!"

Jimmy looked down at the bolt again, his face drawn back in a furious snarl, and screamed at it.

"Move, you fucker!"

He flung a hand through the air in the bolt's direction as he did this, animating his will for it to obey his command.

The bolt flew across the room and tinkered to the floor.

All four of them followed the flying piece of metal with wide, astonished eyes as it tumbled through the air and chattered across the floor. Saucer plates could have fit in their eye sockets.

And none were wider than Jimmy's.

No one said a word for a full minute. About thirty seconds in, Freddie pushed off the hoist in a sudden burst of movement, like a race horse released from the starting gate, and ran over to the bolt. He snatched it off the concrete floor delicately and held it up to his face with his fingers. His wide, amazed eyes regarded it like one might a fine diamond sparkling in the light.

Eventually, he wandered back to the other three, his astonishment never leaving his face, his eyes never releasing their hold on the bolt. Jimmy was standing to his feet now and Ryan and Honey had moved closer to him on either side. Freddie continued to gaze at the bolt until he was standing right before them. Then he looked at them, a broadening grin chiseling itself into his face, his braces gleaming in the light.

"I think I'm starting to reevaluate my position."

CHAPTER 19

The good fortune of figuring out how to harness his newfound power in a vacuum, and the subsequent glee which blossomed as a result of it, dissipated quickly when he'd tried to open a door to the other world.

With the bolt, he'd realized it wasn't so much about *thinking*, as though to move the object with his thoughts, but *willing* it to move. That came from somewhere deeper. He remembered this sensation when they'd been in the woods, but hadn't realized it until he stumbled across it here.

After the bolt, Jimmy moved several items around with his will. It didn't seem to matter what the size was or the weight or mass or anything. Once he got the hang of it, he was able to move pretty much anything he saw. He even moved a giant tractor tire that stood taller than any of them and had an extremely heavy steel wheel mounted to its center. He relocated it all the way from one side of the old garage to the other, to the continued astonishment of the others. Even Honey, who'd seen firsthand the other world, was completely enraptured.

But opening the door to the other world had proved to be an altogether different matter.

Jimmy had picked a spot on the wall that was relatively clear and would be easy enough to go through. He didn't like the idea of even trying this with the monster that loomed in that other place, but they'd convinced him that if locations lined up in the woods between the worlds, then the thing was far from where they were. Jimmy debated against this for a time, then eventually agreed.

But he couldn't make it happen.

The warbling sound manifested, and the air around the wall shimmered, but little else would happen. The portal wouldn't open. He strained with all his will, time and time again, but ultimately, he got nowhere with it.

"It's like it's… I dunno," Jimmy said, trailing off momentarily before finishing. "Like it's *thicker* here."

"Thicker?" Honey asked.

He nodded. "Yeah, in the woods it was effortless. I looked at a spot, wanted it open, and it just opened, you know? It was like wet paper or something. But here? It's like trying to pry open the trunk of an oak tree."

They all considered this for a few moments. After a time, Honey spoke up.

"That thing," she said.

All the boys' eyebrows perked up. She went on.

"Okay, hear me out," Honey continued, beginning to pace before them. "That thing that chased us over there. We only caught a glimpse of it, but you remember what it said Jimmy?"

Jimmy nodded. "Yeah, I think so. Something like *'Who comes into my world'*, or something to that effect, right?"

"Close enough," Honey said and went on. "It said it was *its* world. Like it belonged to him. Everything over there was the same, but it was totally different.

155

The air, the light, the spider and the slug. *Everything.* What I'm saying is, I think this thing is probably the cause of that. Like whatever happened to that place, that *thing* did it. Probably killed it, maybe the whole world. The only evidence of life were bugs and slugs!"

"Okay, but what does that have to do with breaking through there?" Freddie said as he pushed his glasses up on his nose.

"I'm not sure, this is all just a theory," she said. "But what if it came from yet another world before that? It was obviously able to break through into ours, but only partially. It wasn't fully physical. And did anyone else notice how it suddenly wasn't chasing us anymore? Like all at once, when we got closer to the road, it was just gone?"

They all nodded as it dawned on them for the first time. None of them had considered it at the time, they were too concerned with getting the hell out of there. But she was right.

"Well, if it *did* come from another world to that one, how was it physical there, but not here?"

Shrugs issued all around, but then Ryan spoke up.

"Maybe it has to feed!" he said. "You know, like babies have to have nourishment to grow when they're in the woman's stomach!"

Honey almost laughed at his choice of words, but suppressed it and went on.

"That's just what I was thinking!" she said. "I think it came into that world, fed, and grew there. Then maybe it has wasted everything there of value, so now it wants into our world. It just hasn't had the chance to feed enough here to do it yet!"

Freddie leaned in, crossing his arms like a college professor about to make a rebuttal.

"Decent theory, Honey-bunch, but it still doesn't answer why Jimmy can open the portal in the woods but not here."

They all looked back to her, but it was Jimmy who spoke this time.

"It's a thin spot," he said, his eyes distant in thought. "It has to be as simple as that. In school they talked about mass, how a solid block of wood can be denser in certain areas than others. Same principle here. I'm not sure what caused that place to be thin. Maybe it just *is*, like naturally, or maybe something *caused* it to be thin."

Freddie nodded, pursing his lips.

"Sound reasoning," he said. "In any case, if we have to go back there to try it out, I vote a big hell no on that!"

They all agreed. They didn't want to ever see that place again, or the shadows which haunted it.

"But," Freddie said, raising a finger into the air to drive home his words, "I'd sure like to know where that house came from."

CHAPTER 20

Jimmy arrived home just before dark.

He, Honey, Ryan, and Freddie had discussed trying to look up information on the house for some time after Jimmy's demonstration of moving objects and their hypotheses on the relative *thicknesses* of universal fabric. They had all agreed it was all hypothetical at best, but at the same time, even as they'd been saying the words, Jimmy and Honey somehow just *knew* they were right. Or at least very close to being right. They had absolutely no reason to believe this, and positively *no* evidence to support their claims, but all the same they just *knew*.

Jimmy had pondered this absolute confidence as he rode his bike home alone. He couldn't speak for the others, but he thought his experience in the other place had somehow endowed him with a certain knowledge. Probably Honey too, he mused. But at any rate, something *had* come back with them from the other world. Something more than the monster.

He'd come back wiser.

Coupled to his newfound wisdom, like flies to steaming shit, came courage. Not that he'd ever been a coward by any means. It *had*, after all, been he who'd stood up to Jake at the playground. But something new had risen up in him during the experience. The courage to face down the spider-thing, in spite of his numbing fear of *all* spiders. The presence of mind to fetch up the rock and destroy the giant slug.

But I was so scared of the monster...

True enough, he certainly had been. But that had been when wisdom kicked in. Bravery is a wonderful thing, but if left unlinked to the wisdom of when to stand and when to run, bravery could get you killed.

His thoughts had turned to Honey as he pulled into his mom's driveway. He thought of how brave she had been too. Scared, sure, but he had been scared too. Bravery wasn't the absence of fear, it was the ability to stand and fight *in spite of* that fear.

Jimmy marveled at all the things they had seen and experienced that day. How much their lives had been changed. Sure, they still lived in their crappy town, in their crappy houses, and they would certainly continue on living much the same way they had been before this day. Nonetheless, they had certainly been *changed.* In facing Jake and his thugs, and then the things from the other place, all four of them had found a courage they never knew they possessed. Self-preservation had played its role for sure, but there was more to it than that.

They all had discovered they loved each other.

Yes, *love* was what had brought that courage to fruition. Love for one another. Together, they had won the day and gotten out with their lives. Jimmy didn't know exactly *how* crazy Jake really was, but he was hesitant to find out. Most kids who were bullied just took it. They'd stand there, take the shame or the beating—*sometimes both*—but rarely did they stick up for themselves. He understood why, too. For the most part, people—especially kids like themselves—just felt powerless to do anything. Bullies typically chose people who were weaker and smaller than they, so a physical fight was pretty much out of the question, unless you wanted the beating to be even worse. There was also the option of *telling,* finding an adult, a teacher or a parent, and having *them* intervene on your behalf, but doing that was bound to make you the laughing stock of the entire town, never mind further escalating the situation. Only sissies *told* on people, everyone knew that. So most just took it and prayed for it to stop.

But on this day, Jimmy, Honey, Ryan, and Freddie had discovered that by standing together, they could win the day. And there was something about that to take pride in.

Jimmy dropped his bike on the grass in front of the house and went inside. There was little light coming from the darkened living room, only flashes from the television set as scenes changed and camera angles altered.

He slipped through the front door. His mother was sitting in her chair, smoking another menthol cigarette, and sipping at something. The stench of liquor was strong in the room. His mother's drink of choice was vodka with a splash of water. From the swimming look in her eyes as she looked up at his entrance, he thought she may well have forgone the pretense of the splash.

"Hey, Jimmy," she said, a somewhat sad smile spreading across her face.

"Hey mom," he said.

"Have fun today?" she asked and took a long drag on her cigarette.

Jimmy stifled a laugh. "Yeah, mom. Yeah we had fun."

"That's good dear," she said and looked back toward the TV. "There's some meatloaf in the fridge if you're hungry."

He hadn't realized it until that very moment just *how* hungry he really was. He was starving. He hadn't had anything since that morning, and he'd not even thought of it until now.

In spite of his hunger, the thought of cold meatloaf sounded about as appealing as sleeping naked with beetles.

"Naw, I'm alright," he said after a few moments. "I'm just gonna clean up."

His mother nodded, taking another drag on her cigarette and then smashing it out in an ashtray on the table next to her. He began crossing the room when she stopped him.

"What the *hell* is all over your clothes?" she asked in bewilderment.

Jimmy stopped and looked down at his soiled clothes. The filth and dirt caked into his clothing had escaped his conscious thoughts in all that had happened. As had the now crusted slime from the slug which laminated the filth in his clothes.

"Ah, we, uh," he started, unable to think.

"You look like you just walked out of a zombie picture!" she cried.

She was standing up now, swaying slightly on her feet. She took a moment and steadied herself on the wall. Jimmy didn't want her to get too close. Dirt and mud were one thing, but how would he explain the clear-white crust all over him. The room was dark enough now that she hadn't seemed to notice it, but if she got closer or—God help him—turned on the light, she'd see it for sure, vodka or not.

Jesus Christ, why didn't I think before coming in like this?

"It's nothing, mom," he said, waving at her to sit back down. "We were playing out by the creek and I just got dirty. I'll clean the clothes, I promise."

He hoped she hadn't heard the waver in his voice.

She stood there for a moment, her eyes swimming with the liquor, contemplating him. Her eyes were narrowed slightly and her brow was furrowed, but she seemed to be reconsidering coming over to him now. Hell, there were things to watch on television. There was more vodka to drink.

"You're damn right you're going to wash them!" she finally said. "And if they're stained, you can just forget me buying you any new ones! You can ride all over town as stained as my granddaddy's skivvies for all I care!"

She was sitting back into her chair, muttering and cursing about boys and their filthy games, always taking everything for granted, and pondering if perhaps they thought money grew on trees. Her butt settled back into the chair, and there was a hissing sound as the cushion deflated beneath her.

Her focus was already completely off of Jimmy now, looking back at the television and adjusting herself in the seat to get comfortable. There was a farting sound, and Jimmy wasn't sure if his mother had just let one rip or if her leg had just rubbed across the rubber fabric the wrong way.

He decided he didn't care and was just thankful she had abandoned coming over to him and inspecting his clothes. He retreated down the hall and went into the bathroom.

After stepping through the door, he locked it behind him and stripped to his bare ass. He looked over his clothes and decided that they would require a wash of their very own, independent of any other laundry. Then he turned to the shower and waved his hand. He hadn't thought about it, he'd just done it.

The curtain slinked back on the rod to one side, pictures of shells and conchs folding in on themselves as it went along.

Jimmy smiled.

This is fucking cool.

But cool or not, his night was bathed in nightmares.

CHAPTER 21

Jimmy's dream hadn't started out as a nightmare. It had started with Mrs. James—and rather pleasantly so.

He was at their fort out in the woods, by himself. He was checking out one of the Playboys Ryan had brought along and left out there. Jimmy very much liked the sight of naked women—what straight, pubescent boy didn't—but he was becoming bored with the pictures. Same thing, same ladies, never changing. And it being on paper was nothing all that special either.

He closed the magazine and tossed it up on one of their makeshift shelves which Ryan had dug out. Jimmy had decided it had been a pretty good idea after all to make the shelves, and the structure didn't seem to suffer from it at all. He was stepping over the lip of the front when a sound had caught his ear. And twisted it.

Crunch-crunch-crunch.

He froze. In his dream, he immediately thought of the horrible spider-thing, with its human-like face and bushy orange bulb of an abdomen. Its idiot eyes. Its insane questions. He wondered if it had managed to make its way into their world when he and Honey had fled that terrible other place. Was it now wandering around in this new environment, looking to perhaps lay eggs for thousands of new abominations to start cursing the woods? Did spiders even lay eggs?

164

He didn't know. Couldn't remember. But the thought of thousands of those monsters skittering about, spinning their massive webs, and asking their maddening questions terrified him to the bone.

Fick-a-choo?

Jimmy remained stock-still, only his eyes darting about the woods looking for the source of the sound.

Crunch-crunch-crunch.

His throat began to throb in tandem with his heart and thumping booms issued in his ears. His breaths were shallow remnants of what had until just recently been a vibrant and sound respiratory system. Sweat was now streaking his face, though he felt quite cool. Chilled, even.

Fear gripped him with icy fingers, refusing to let go, laughing at him. All the courage he'd found earlier that day seemed lost in that very instant, the last vestiges of bravery running for the hills with total abandon.

Crunch-crunch-crunch.

The sound was coming from his left.

He moved his head around as quickly as he dared, which translated to a speed akin to watching grass grow. He saw the pines and oaks and the random dogwoods scattered about through the wooded sanctuary. At any moment he would certainly see the spider-thing, and with this realization, any doubt that he might shit his pants vanished. He would fill them up all the way down to his shoes and would have steaming turds spilling over the top of his waistband.

Then—*finally*—he saw her.

It wasn't one of the spider-things at all. It was Mrs. James, Freddie's mother, walking through the woods. Just out for a leisurely stroll.

And, as he realized that she was not some crawling beast with diamond-shaped eyes, another realization came to him. Came to him like a warm—but not unpleasant—tidal wave. It almost knocked him over.

She was naked.

Here, right here, in the woods where he and his friends played, was Mrs. James, strolling around naked as the day she was born. She was so casual, it was like someone traversing a sidewalk. Her long, golden hair was pushed back behind her ears, and he fancied he saw a smile on her face. The twin swells of her breasts were both ample and exhilarating. All thoughts of the girls in the Playboy vanished at once, not even *beginning* to compare to what he beheld before him now.

She was absolutely beautiful. He'd teased Freddie from time to time about his mother, about banging her and such, but Freddie didn't realize just how much of what Jimmy said were not mere jokes, but actual, *real* desires.

Her head turned then, and her eyes met his. Locked *into* his. A hook was set in his jaw, and he didn't feel his feet moving beneath him. But he was moving towards her all the same, as though floating over the leaven earth.

Her smile broadened, exposing perfect white teeth which were not too small, not too big. Her pink lips stopped short of exposing her gum-line, making the expression all the more angelic.

She turned toward him as he glided to her through the warm summer air. She was head on with him now, and he could see the perfect curvature of her waist-line and the pool of her naval. Below he could see a golden triangle of hair, hair quite like that he'd himself only just begun to grow down there. Her thighs flexed and moved as she walked towards him.

As they neared each other, she stretched out a hand to him, upturned for him to accept. He did. She clasped his hand in hers and electricity shot through his body in a jolt. He was mesmerized with her.

"Jimmy," she said. "I was hoping I'd find you here."

Her smile never faded a single iota.

Hoping to find me *here?* he thought.

As if hearing what he thought, she nodded at him.

"Yes, Jimmy," she said, her voice husky and intoxicating, dripping with desire. "I've wanted you for a long time, you know? Such a *very* long time..."

He hadn't known at all, actually, but the knowledge thrilled him and brought bright red blossoms to his cheeks which stung his skin with their heat.

"I-I," he stuttered and stopped.

She had placed a finger on his lips to quiet him, and he had. His heart was beating harder now, even harder than when he'd thought she had been the spider-thing. It was pounding in his ears with audible booms, all but blurring out any other sound.

"Come with me, Jimmy," she said, and leaned in and kissed him on the lips.

Jimmy melted into nothingness, lost in the kiss. His free hand reached up and touched her left breast, squeezing it gently. It was incredible under his touch. The softness. The creamy texture of her skin. The rigid hardness of her nipple.

She pulled back from the kiss.

"I've got a place we can go, Jimmy. Will you come with me?"

Jimmy nodded furiously, his mind jelly at this point.

She led him away from the fort and through the woods. Jimmy studied every inch of her perfect body. Saw the sway of her buttocks in the gleaming light, taking in every curve and dimple and mole.

She's glorious!

By the time he realized where she'd taken him, he was already in it. He didn't remember arriving or entering, only remembered looking at her and following the rigid tent that preceded him in his pants.

They were in the house. The house in the woods.

"No, no!" Jimmy screamed at once, trying to pull her back towards the door. "We can't be here. You don't know what's here!"

But she was immovable. He was tugging on her arm, tugging hard, but he couldn't move her even an inch. It was like trying to move an oak tree by yanking on the branch.

"Come on, Mrs. James!" he cried at her again. "Come on, we have to go!"

She turned and looked at him, that smile now a permanent fixture on her face. She was shaking her head.

"No," she said, "we don't have to go. We have to stay. I want your *meat*, Jimmy! Didn't I tell you I want your meat *in me?*"

She said this last part with a vigor and vulgarity he'd never expected to hear from her in all his life. She was a fine and decent woman, always proper and upright. The fact that she was walking naked in the woods trying to lure a twelve-year-old boy away for sex *did* seem out of character for her, sure, but if he was to be the beneficiary of that, who was he to question it? So be it.

"And I'll give you my m-m-meat, Mrs. James!" he said, embarrassment cloaking his skin in scarlet. He was once again tugging at her arm. "I w-want nothing more in the world, but we can't s-stay here!"

Then she started laughing.

Unlike the look of her body and the sweet, sultry tone of her voice as she'd spoken to him before, this laugh was deep. Almost masculine. There were multiple octaves inside the laugh, layered tracks of insane cackling.

Jimmy watched in horror as the laugh rose in volume and pitch, and saw the beautiful skin start to peel back from her forehead. Thin, curling fragments pulling away from the skull beneath, which to his horror, was neither white nor red, but black. Her breasts started to curl inward on themselves, starting with the nipples and working back into the body. The nipples themselves simply fell off and tittered to the floor of the house. All over her, the skin was rotting away in hyper-speed and her maddening laugh continued to rise and expand. Her bright blue eyes had turned black now, and her perfect teeth were falling out of her mouth with every howling jump of laughter.

Jimmy began to scream. He pulled his hand to remove it from hers, but it wouldn't budge. She had him in a death grip, and the feeling in his fingers was vanishing under the pressure.

"Let me go!" he screamed at her. "Oh Jesus, *let me go!*"

All at once, the remainder of the skin on her body blew away violently and in a flash. No more than the blink of an eye. What was now standing before him was the thing. The monster from that terrible other place.

169

From that damned place!

"The next time you see the light of day," the thing boomed at him, *"will be when I shit you out my ass! I WILL HAVE MY MEAT!"*

Jimmy sat upright in his bed, a silent scream lodged in his throat. He was covered in sweat from head to toe, even though the room was rather cool. His sheets were soaked, as were his underwear. A strong tang of ammonia stung his nostrils, and he knew he'd wet himself.

He flung the sheets from the bed and stripped off his underwear, aware now that he was trembling.

I came back with something, alright, he thought as he shuddered, on the verge of tears. *Oh, God, we brought something back!*

CHAPTER 22

Ryan's dream started with no such pleasant pretenses.

He too was in the house in the woods. No explanation, no reason, simply was. He was standing in the foyer, staring out the open front door. His father was there, on his belly, cursing and trying to sit himself up. But he couldn't get off the floor. His hands kept slipping on something, something slick and viscous. It was dark, like oil almost, and it was getting all over him.

And there was an awful smell.

"Dad!" Ryan screamed at his father. "Dad what's happening?"

But his father didn't seem to hear him. He just kept struggling and slipping and cursing. His giant girth was making the task all the more difficult, but finally, after what seemed an age, he managed to get up on his knees.

Then he looked right at Ryan.

Ryan smiled broadly at him. Tears of sadness and joy. He hated his father, but the man was still his *dad*. He hadn't been totally bad, not all the time. Only really when he was drinking—which, he had to admit, was most of the time. Still, seeing him here and not in that padded cell with the white jacket wrapped around him softened his heart toward this man who'd caused so much pain and suffering in the Laughton home.

"Dad!" he exclaimed once more. "Dad, I know you weren't lying now! There really *is* something out here! You didn't kill Mr. Barton, that *thing* did! You were telling the truth!"

But Chester didn't look pleased. In fact, Ryan couldn't decipher what the look on his father's face *was,* exactly. His scraggly beard, dripping with that dark liquid, did little to disguise the pursing lips and the wide, astonished eyes.

Then Chester Laughton screamed.

He screamed right at his son, looking almost into his eyes, still seeming as though he weren't seeing him at all, even though he was there—right *fucking* there— right in front of him.

But there was no recognition in his face. None at all. Only soul-shaking terror in his eyes and screams of abject horror tearing from his gaping mouth.

Ryan whirled around, looking behind him for the first time, and saw Mr. Barton at the other end of the foyer. His chest and stomach were opened up in a jagged severing of flesh, and intestines spilled out all around his corpse. Blood soaked the floor and walls, and there were clumps of feces which had escaped his guts during whatever trauma had opened him up.

Then all of this vanished in an instant, and Ryan was left standing alone in the foyer of the house. Mr. Barton and his insides were gone. He spun back to the front door and saw his father was gone as well. All the blood was gone. Everything he'd just seen was gone.

"I will have my meat!" a horrible voice said.

Ryan spun back to face the interior of the house. A giant, black shadow there stood before him, though there was nothing Ryan could see which could have cast such a shape. Yet, it *was* there. It seemed *malevolent* somehow. It was something he just knew, from deep down in the marrow of his soul. And was the shadow...*breathing?*

No time was afforded to answer this question. In the next moment, the shadow moved in with ferocious speed and grabbed him, slamming him against the wall next to the front door. His feet dangled above the rotting floorboards.

He couldn't breathe. Whatever was holding him had his throat in a stranglehold. He writhed under it, kicking his legs out, but doing nothing of any benefit. He just kept hearing that same, horrible sentence over and over, and over again.

"I will have my meat!"

Ryan awoke in the recliner which had been his father's before that day in the woods. He was shaking and his clothes were soaked through with sweat, the pungent odor immediately assaulting his nasal passages. His breaths came in sharp, hitching gasps. His entire body seemed to be covered in gooseflesh.

And he trembled all over.

Ryan Laughton got no further sleep that night. None at all.

CHAPTER 23

Freddie—the only one of his friends to have both a mother and a father in the home—said his prayers with his parents before going to bed. They all knelt next to his bed, their elbows resting on the mattress, their hands folded together before them. They bowed their heads and closed their eyes, then prayed that God would bless them as they slept, protect them and their home from the works of the enemy, and grant them peaceful rest to carry them into another day, should the Good Lord grant them one.

Freddie always played along with this routine, and happily enough. Unlike his friends, he did genuinely believe in the Big Man upstairs, and assumed, like most children in their pre-teen years, that their parents were right in their presumption of a higher power. What his parents didn't know—and he'd be damned if he were ever to verbalize it to them—was that Freddie didn't buy into the whole living holy thing.

Both his parents were devout Baptists, and they attended church as regular pigs attended to their slop. Freddie had been in church since nine months before he'd been born, and he really knew nothing else. You went to church, you were nice to people and helped those less fortunate when you could, and at some point you went down to the stage—though the Baptists always seemed to call it an altar, something Freddie found an interesting misunderstanding of terms—during a service when the pastor told you that you needed to accept Jesus into your heart. You said a prayer and boom: you were *saved!*

But Freddie couldn't ever find this model in the Bible his parents' congregation regularly thumped. His parents had given him a teen study Bible when he was younger and, since he enjoyed reading, he'd read the thing. More than once, too. He really enjoyed all the gory parts in the first part of the Bible, the Old Testament, and while the New Testament had less action going on, he did find a lot to agree with from that Jesus fellow. He seemed like a solid dude.

But at no point could he find a place where one of the Apostles had a meeting where they were calling people down to a stage/altar to say a sinner's prayer for salvation from Hell. Just wasn't there. He'd asked his parents about the subject, but all they'd been able to explain was that even though it wasn't written in there, in plain black and white, that was just how it was done. You prayed—after all, you have to pray to God if you want to talk to Him—and asked Jesus to come into your heart and save you. Then at some point you would get baptized at a church service so you could make a public proclamation of your secret decision to follow Jesus. None of that part was all that important, not really, it was merely symbolic.

However, none of that had ever sat well with Freddie. If the Bible was supposed to be the infallible Word of God, would the Big Man upstairs not have specifically laid out the way for salvation? And if He did, and if it was by saying a prayer at an altar *(stage, it's a damn stage)*, wouldn't that have been included in the

175

text? And what about baptism? The guys in the Bible seemed to make a very big deal out of this, but at his church it was just something you did at some point, with no real consequences either way.

His parents just never had good enough answers for him. They *did* have answers, just not ones that satisfied his curiosity for what he considered to be inconsistencies between their denominational doctrine and what the Bible actually said. But his parents were good Baptists, and good Baptists just didn't go to other denominations. They had some things wrong, so why would you go to hear the wrong things taught, right?

So, Freddie believed in God, even believed in the Bible. But he wasn't too sure about all these churches. There were so many, and even in a town the size of Winnsboro—population thirty-five hundred—there were more churches than Freddie could think of to count out at one time. At *least* twenty, maybe even more. But, it was like that in pretty much every town he'd been in in rural East Texas.

They finished saying their prayers, said their amens, and his mother kissed and hugged him goodnight. His father tousled his hair and told the kiddo to have a good night, and they left his room, shutting the door as they did. When they were gone, Freddie laid there on his back, fingers locked together behind his head, thinking of all the events of the day. So much had happened and so much that he would never have thought possible had been presented to him in an absolutely undeniable fashion.

He and Ryan had staved off Jake Reese and his punk-ass friends. Of that he was rather proud, though he was at the same time terrified of coming across Jake and his pals again, even if it were just one of them, by himself. Then there was everything that happened at the house.

The *roar*.

The chasing shadows.

Jimmy moving the bolt. Honey and Jimmy's telling of the other world they had been in.

It was all so magical and horrible at the same time. And how about that house? Where in the green *fuck* had that thing come from, anyway? It was so odd, sitting out there in the middle of the woods, with no trail or even a hint that one had ever been there to get to it. Who would build such a structure in such a remote place? A place like that should have some sort of local legend surrounding it, a place everyone would know about. But he'd never heard about it before, and he suspected most everyone in town had no idea it was there at all.

He was contemplating these things when heard a door creak. The sound didn't terrify him or anything, didn't even really startle him. Doors creaked sometimes. Certainly, they did in this house. He'd long given up on the idea that he might be able to sneak out of his house at any time unnoticed. His parents would be alerted to his activities the second he took a step, let alone opened a door. There wasn't a single board in their home which didn't protest when it was tread upon or disturbed in any manner.

Yet, all the same, this door *did* catch his attention.

His eyes drifted around his dark room, playing across his poster of Batman from the movie the year before—it was his absolute favorite movie, and he was a *huge* fan of The Joker—and past a model airplane which hung on a string secured to the ceiling. Eventually, his eyes settled on the door to his room.

It was closed up tight.

Probably one of the other doors, he thought. *Mom or dad going to bed, maybe.*

It was certainly plausible. Their room was just down the hall from his, and it wasn't as though the walls in their house were anything more than glorified papyrus.

But this didn't sit right either. No, the door he'd heard had sounded closer. Sounded like it had been right there in his room with him, as a matter of fact. But it wasn't possible. He'd just located the door to his bedroom and found it closed up and out of service for the time being. He was in his bed, so no boards were creaking on the floor and no—

He heard the creaking door again.

It was louder this time, and more defined. There was no chance it could have been his imagination playing tricks on him. And there was also zero chance that the sound was coming from anywhere else in the house. It was in the room with him, right there.

Now the fear started to set in. His fingers slipped apart, and he brought his hands around to his chest, clutching the covers. The hairs on the back of his neck became electric, dancing there and tingling his skin. The James's had no dog, no cat. They had nothing in the house that could be strolling about, perhaps caught in the room with him after his parents closed the door. Nothing at all.

He shivered beneath his warm covers. His hands involuntarily grabbed the edge of his comforter and pulled it up to his face. His eyes—now wide—were moving on from his bedroom door to his closet, slowly and reluctantly.

The door was moving.

The moaning, aching, grinding sound of the hinges, unoiled in ages, was getting louder now. Louder than he'd ever heard them get. The door kept swinging open, and the pitch of the screeching hinges continued to rise, the bark of the howling steel repeating like a machine gun.

Freddie now had the comforter up so high on his face that the only things sticking out were his saucer-sized eyes and the top of his head. If not for the absolute *need* he had to see what was coming from his closet, he'd have gone completely under his covers and swam to the bottom of his bed, the only place of true and absolute security against boogeymen in the night.

Of course, he envisioned a nightmare creature leaping on top of his bed after he would have done this. It would tear his bed and his body to tiny red ribbons with massive claws and gigantic, dripping fangs.

So, no dice on the security there.

His breath caught in his throat as the door swung its final arc outward and stopped suddenly a few inches from the wall. Silence filled the room. Silence, that is, aside from the echoing heartbeat thrumming through his head and his shallow gasps when his lungs began to burn and demand a fresh supply of air.

Freddie peered hard into the darkness of his closet. He could see nothing beyond the frame of the door, even though there was substantial moonlight filtering in through his windows to create an ominous glow in his bedroom proper. Yet, the closet stood in stark

179

pitch, a black hole swallowing the light which seemed unable to penetrate the abyss.

His shivers increased in the minutes that followed. He had no idea just how long he laid there, staring into the abyss, breathing only when absolutely necessary and trying to ignore the booming opera in his head as his blood rushed and swirled through every beat of his agonized heart.

Several minutes passed.

Nothing seemed to be happening. After some time, Freddie tentatively began to lower the comforter from his face, first exposing his mouth, then his chin, finally his throat and chest. He began to sit up in the bed, his eyes never faltering from the inky blackness in his closet. He was squinting, *willing* himself to see, but it was only a black blur.

Your glasses, ass-munch!

Of course! He'd forgotten all about his glasses. He had taken them off when he went to bed, and they sat perched on his nightstand like a forgotten relic.

He peeled his eyes away from the closet for just a moment, looked over to his nightstand, and fetched his glasses. Put them on. Blinked.

Looked back to the closet.

His vision was clearer now. Not much, the room was still dark, and the closet was darker still. But now he could see just a little bit better.

Someone was standing in his closet.

Breathing once again ceased and the thrumming in his eardrums recommenced.

The figure was tall. Of course to a twelve-year-old, *everyone* was tall, even if they were only a little bit older than you. But this guy seemed *really* tall. His outline, dark as it was, reminded Freddie of a coffin, like the ones he'd seen in the old Dracula movies. And it seemed the guy was wearing a hat.

He couldn't think of the name for the hat right away. It wasn't a ball cap, or a chef hat or anything like that. No, it was something that had faded with another era, like the hats gangsters and private eyes wore in the old crime movies and film noir that his dad loved so much.

A fedora!

He further realized that the shape of the man's outline was much like that of the old gagsters and private eyes from those same movies he'd watched. They sort of looked like the old coffins. He could remember a movie with Humphrey Bogart, his dad's absolute favorite actor, moving out of some dark shadows wearing the—

The figure began to step forward.

Freddie slammed himself down on his bed and snatched his covers up to his nose again. He was breathing now, but it was really more akin to hyperventilation. He was suddenly aware of a completely full bladder that had given rise to his attention, demanding relief.

But he couldn't move. He couldn't flinch. All the bravery he'd exhibited early in the day was gone from him now. All that was left was a scared little boy with a gangster in his room, hiding in his closet, finally coming out.

"Did you ever dance with the devil in the pale moonlight?" a voice issued from the figure as it continued moving forward.

181

Freddie knew the voice. Knew the line the figure had just delivered too, but he couldn't place from where. His brain was running in circles, trying to define in his mind just what was happening before him, but it was moving too fast to lock on to anything approaching reason or structure.

"Wh-what?" Freddie managed to mumble.

The figure moved forward more and a small shaft of moonlight gleamed across his hand. It was wearing a glove. A *purple* glove.

Something started to click in his mind, but Freddie still couldn't grasp hold of it.

"I said," the figure went on in a deep, chilling tone, *"did you ever dance with the devil in the pale moonlight, kid?"*

"I-I don't know what you—" Freddie started, and then it hit him.

The figure stepped out of the closet now, revealing not only a purple glove, but a purple suit. There was a green button-down shirt under a blue vest and a purple tie with little white diamonds on it. The fedora—it *had* been a fedora—which sat atop the figure's pasty white face with bright red lips was purple as well.

His face was grinning so broadly it looked as though his face might split open from the strain. There was a low, cackling laugh coming from the man as he moved further into the room and his eyes blazed with pure, delighted madness.

"He-he-he-he-he!" the man laughed.

It was The Joker.

Right here, in his room, The Joker stood before him. He looked as though he'd been ripped right from the celluloid of the Batman film Freddie was so fond of and placed right here in this place.

182

Freddie's heart froze.

There was no more thrumming in his ears. It was as if his blood had frozen solid in the blink of an eye.

"I'm sorry, kid," The Joker said, hints of his maniacal laughter still haunting his voice, *"did I scare ya?"*

Freddie wanted to nod, to boisterously implore that yes, yes indeed he had scared him and there was likely going to be a stinking patty awaiting him in his underwear, to scream for his parents—*where were his parents after all?*—and make the psychotic supervillain disappear from his room. He also wished to Christ he'd never watched Batman, no matter how fucking cool it was, and that Jack Nicholson would haunt him no longer.

But he could do none of this. Not one part of it. His entire body had seized upon itself, refusing the electrical impulses from his brain, demanding motion and voice, and defiantly standing firm against it.

"I suppose I did," The Joker said. *"Well, I'll take your silence as a no to my question."*

The *he-he-he* laughter started again and the dark, crazy eyes descended into something deeper than mere madness, to a place Freddie couldn't comprehend at all.

The Joker stepped closer and stopped at the foot of Freddie's bed. His purple-gloved hands snapped out in a flash and clamped the wooden frame a foot from his feet.

The Joker leaned in over the bed.

"You will *dance with the devil, Freddie-boy,"* he said, the face-cracking smile now *literally* cracking the white face. Freddie could see what appeared to be porcelain fissures all across the insane, smiling face.

"You'll dance with the devil! And soon, too! And when you do, he'll open up your meat shirt and eat your heart right from your chest!"

The Joker burst out into a maddeningly loud cackle of psychotic, wheezing laughter, his mouth opened wide and yellow teeth chomping up and down with the hilarity.

Then The Joker's face—and everything else on him, for that matter—burst into a thousand pieces, like tiny particles of dust. What was left was a giant shadow, not unlike the one which had chased Freddie and his friends through the woods earlier that day.

The shadow leaped at him.

Freddie sat up in his bed, a choked scream on his lips.

Nothing was there. His room was completely empty. He checked his closet door. It was shut and unmoved. He noticed he was coated in sweat and he made a great effort to swallow his heart back down into his chest.

He had dreamed the whole thing. Or *nightmared* the whole thing, he supposed.

Freddie pulled the soaked sheet off the bed and laid back down on his moist pillow. He was starting to get his breathing under control once more with a deliberate effort, and his racing heart was beginning to fall into a more reasonable rhythm. It had been nothing more than a dream, a really *bad* fucking dream, but a dream all the same. He had to keep telling himself this over and over again, trying to calm himself, to reassure himself.

But every time his eyes fell back on the closet door, fear began tingling him again.

184

The Damned Place

You will *dance with the devil, Freddie-boy!*

It wasn't long before he realized that the sleep ship had sailed on for the night. He tossed and turned for a while and finally gave up. He went across his room and flipped on an old TV and fired up his Nintendo. The Super Mario Brothers would be his companions for the rest of the night.

As he waited for the game console to boot up, he looked up to his wall and saw the poster of Batman. Michael Keaton stood stoically in the Batman costume, and Jack Nicholson glared down from above him in a frozen laugh as The Joker. It was the same image he'd seen in his dream just before it became the shadow-thing.

He tore the poster off the wall.

CHAPTER 24

Honey dreamt of her mother. But that was only part of her nightmare. And not even the worst part.

When she'd come home, her father was passed out in his chair, wearing only his robe and a pair of soiled underwear. There was no cigarette in his hand this time—she was thankful for that—but the half-drunk amber whiskey was present at its post on the end table next to him.

She'd muttered some angry curses under her breath at him and then gone to her room. She changed out of her filthy clothes and showered, then put a load of laundry on. After that, she had headed back to her room.

Before stepping into her room, however, she had glanced over at her father's room. She thought of her mother, missing her dearly in that moment, and gone to the room. She went in and looked at the picture on the nightstand. She smiled as a single tear lined her cheek, and she played her fingers across the image. Remembering, longing, mourning.

At some point she'd fallen asleep there on her parents' bed, holding the photo. She had managed to turn the light off before slipping into slumber, but once she was fully down into the dream world, Honey saw her mother. In her dream, Honey was walking down their street. It was dark, marked here and there with sodium-arc street lamps glowing eerily above the street. She moved slowly, unsure of why she was out here or where she was going, yet moving along just the same.

Movement caught her eye somewhere in the distance, and when she squinted her eyes to focus, she saw a horribly disfigured person shambling jerkily down the road toward her. The person was coming towards her, but Honey realized after a moment they were actually walking backward. Yet, in spite of this, the face—bloody and shockingly mangled—was faced in her direction. Like the head had been put on backwards.

The back was leaned over at an impossible angle, and one arm hung straight out at the shoulder, jutting down in a sharp right angle, the elbow bent in the wrong direction to dangle like a hypnotic talisman. The person made terrible gagging sounds as they relentlessly continued toward her in nightmarish movements.

As the person drew nearer, Honey's breath caught in her throat as she drew in a gasp and covered her mouth as she realized who the person was.

It was her mother.

Blood was puking out of her mother's mouth and wide eyes seemed to be ready to pop from her skull. Honey was frozen in fear as her butchered mother stumbled toward her, seeming to move in such jerking motions that it was like she was watching a film with missing frames, or as though seeing it by the light of a flashing strobe light, just pieces but not the whole thing. Gurgling sounds were issued as her mother neared, and gouts of blood spouted from her mouth and ears. Tears of crimson flowed from her bulging eye-sockets.

"Oh, mom!" she cried.

"It will have your meat!" her mother burbled to her through thick, flowing blood. *"You'll give it your meat, you will!"*

The voice wasn't her mother's. She knew that in an instant. Even though it was filtered through the blood and torn flesh, it was still not that of her mother, Janie. There was something deeper to it, something more layered.

And she'd heard that voice before. Recently.

"You take it your meat, or the meat is coming to you, Honeybunny!"

Her mother's body exploded then.

Chunks of flesh and showers of scarlet rained down in all directions, coating her in warm sheets. Coils of intestine draped over her neck in loud slaps, and she could smell the stench of decay and shit and blood. There were several splatting sounds as various bits of flesh and organs smacked to the ground wetly all around her.

Her eyes opened wide and suddenly. She was sweating and breathing hard, clutching the picture of her family before it had been destroyed in that single, terrible instant on the highway.

And she heard breathing.

The room was dark, and her eyes had not fully adjusted to the gloom. Though she'd awakened in a shock, she hadn't moved from her position. She was still lying perfectly still on her parent's bed, right in the spot her mother used to sleep before her body had been battered and shredded into a corpse that night on the way to see 'Big'.

The breathing continued. It sounded shallow and wheezy, like a smoker's breathing. And she was certain she could smell the stench of whiskey as it stung her nostrils.

She didn't know how long she had been asleep. It had been dark when she laid down and it was still dark now, so there was little reference from which to draw.

Her eyes glanced up and saw the night clock on the stand. Big red numbers told her it was three o'clock in the morning.

She noticed her eyes were better adjusted now and she could make out shapes around the room. The nightstand was visible and the dim light from the clock illuminated just enough to see the bureau against the wall.

She also saw her father standing next to the bed.

He was down at the foot of the bed, swaying slightly where he was. He was still in his robe and underwear, and there seemed to be a film of sweat on his body as well. He was holding a glass in his hand and she watched as he lifted it to his lips and drank down the remainder of its contents, a rattle of melting ice jingling as he did.

She lay frozen, staring at him, not knowing if he would be able to see her eyes upon him or not. She gambled that he wouldn't in the dark and the blur of the alcohol.

He finished the drink, then turned the glass up to peer into it, making damn sure he'd gotten the last drop. Satisfied that he had, he stumbled over to the bureau and laid the glass upon it with a loud *thwack*.

The sound made Honey jump slightly, but she continued to lay perfectly still, though her every muscle was tense now.

"Oh, Janie," she heard her father say through slurred lips. "I've missed you so much."

He began to stumble toward the bed, the side Honey was laying upon. As he made his way, he shrugged off the robe and let it fall to the floor. There was a whispering sound of fabric crumpling onto carpet and the sound of slick thighs gliding against each other as he moved in closer to her.

"Janie, baby," he continued to slur, a sobbing tone invading his voice. "I've missed you so bad. I've needed you so bad!"

To her horror, he stopped right next to her. Her father's soiled underwear was right in front of her face and she could see something bulging from within it. She knew what it was of course, but couldn't bear to think of it, to name it, to *identify* it. Not from her father. And he was so drunk he was thinking he was talking to her mother, *wanting* her mother, and the evidence of that desire was literally staring her in the face.

You take it your meat, or the meat is coming to you, Honey-bunny! her mother's gargling voice shouted in her mind in a maddening, abominable parody.

Or, *was it* her mother's voice?

"I'm so glad you're home, Janie!" he said, slurring his words to the point it was hard to pick out what they were. "I need you *so* bad..."

He reached his hand out towards her. She glanced up and saw a glazed look of desire and heat in his eyes in the dim red light from the clock. His hand was reaching for her butt, sweat-glazed fingers wriggling through the air, coming for their purchase.

His breathing quickened still, and the wheeze became more pronounced. Honey's heart was thudding in her chest and throat and ears and head so hard it caused her teeth to rattle. Her eyes grew wider and wider as his hand neared her, neared a part of her that was off limits, off limits to *everyone*, but certainly to her father. Before her face, the tent of her father's underwear drew nearer as he reached, like a sheathed sword preparing to be drawn.

The meat is coming to you, Honey-bunny!

His mouth grinned and drool came from his bottom lip in a thin line of saliva. It was more than she could handle. Every muscle in her body had tensed, frozen in place, and the deafening beating of her god-forsaken heart pounded at her very soul.

"I *need* you, baby!" he said.

The bulge next to her face had reached a fever-pitch and she did the only thing she was able to do in her terrified state.

"Daddy?" she asked in a croaked and tearful voice.

His hand froze, inches away from her butt. The look in his eyes had changed to one of confusion and fear and shame all rolled into one. His fingers trembled now, no longer reaching out for pleasure. He snatched his hand back as though it had been stung by an insect and curled it to his chest.

Tom Bascom took a few steps back and stumbled into the bureau. Honey was openly crying now, her sobs audible. Tom looked around a moment and snatched his robe off the floor, almost tumbling into a summersault in the process. But he managed to get it and, with some effort and perhaps some divine providence, somehow got it back on. Unlike his normal donning of the garment, this time he closed the flaps over the front of him, concealing his now receding excitement, and tied the strap in front.

Honey continued to sob, covering her mouth now to keep from screaming out in both terror and relief. Her father had been intoxicated enough to believe that his dead wife was in the bed and wanting him intimately, but the second he'd heard his daughter's voice, he'd retracted. She supposed that was to be commended, even appreciated, but it didn't stifle the horrifying sensation of feeling her father's heat permeating off of him and on to her, his affections reaching for her through lustful fingers.

"I'm so sorry, Honey-bunny!" he croaked in a slur. "I-I..."

It was all he could say.

A second later, he stumbled out of the room and knocked a few pictures off the wall in the hallway as he made his way back to the living room.

She thought she heard him crying.

Honey jumped up from the bed, leaving the picture upon the comforter, and raced into her room. She shut the door loudly and locked it, her fingers trembling as she backed away from it a few steps. Then she dived onto her bed. Her whole body was shaking and images of her exploding mother and her dad's erect excitement filled her mind and shook her to her core.

She buried her face in the pillows and screamed.

PART FOUR:

ECHOES OF

THE PAST

**Monday, June 25, to
Wednsday, June 27, 1990**

CHAPTER 25

Freddie James arrived at the Library on North Main Street at ten o'clock in the morning. He and his friends had gotten together on both Saturday and Sunday over the weekend to play, and the subject of their dreams had come up. None of them had been very surprised to find that the thing from the woods had come to them all that night—it *had* been a traumatic day, after all—and yet, all four of them were astonished to find that in each dream, the reference from the thing about wanting their meat was concurrent across the board.

"The Joker?" Honey had asked Freddie after he had told of his encounter with the thing. "The fucking Joker?"

"Yes ma'am, indeed!" Freddie had replied, his already pink face reddening a deeper crimson. "Fucking Jack Nicholson was right there in my room, all done up in costume and makeup! Laughing a-and taunting me. It was *horrible!*"

Jimmy had told his story about the lady in the woods—he of course left out any mention of her nudity, as well as the fact that the naked broad he'd nearly relinquished his virginity to in the dream had been Freddie's own mother. Though Freddie had no knowledge of this, its omission was a kindness on Jimmy's part. Ryan had followed suit with the dream about his father in the house when his turn came about.

195

But it was Honey's dream, somehow, which seemed the most horrible of all to Freddie. Her mother, mangled and bloody, demanding she surrender her meat. She had shuddered after finishing, as if something had walked over her grave in some other world and some other life. And, for all Freddie knew, perhaps it had. The new knowledge they all possessed about reality posed many questions. And though the look on Honey's face had been curious to Freddie, he'd not inquired anything of her. She had such a sad look. Sad, horrified, and...something else.

He decided it was disgust.

Yes, it was disgust which put the cherry on top of Honey's sundae of misery. Utter, gut-wrenching disgust.

Freddie didn't have any idea what had spurred such a dreadful feeling in her, and he didn't know her well enough yet to really pry. Besides, she was a girl, and while she was a cool chick and fun to hang around, you just didn't talk all that deep with girls. What would he say if she were to break down crying? Forget what to say, what would he *do?* He didn't know how to handle an emotional girl, and he was pretty sure Jimmy and Ryan didn't either. That was stuff you learned in high school, like in health class or something. The older kids seemed better able to do that kind of thing, so he supposed it *must* be something they were taught. Maybe there was a chart with the outline of a girl on it, showing all the scientific names for all their parts and glands, and somewhere, either in the stomach or the brain maybe, there was an area that was labelled something like *Female Emotional Generator*, only he was sure it would sound more scientific than that.

196

The Damned Place

He brushed off the thoughts and decided he'd just wait for high school to learn how girls were wired and what to do when they got upset. The textbook probably had some good, practical techniques to employ.

The four of them had played at Ryan's house one day, then at Freddie's the next. The notion of going back to the woods, even to go to their fort, was completely off the table. *None* of them wanted to be anywhere near those woods, nowhere near that *house,* never mind the possibility of running into Jake and his gang again. Freddie had thought long and hard about the thing of shadows that had chased them, and about their theories that, if indeed Honey and Jimmy were correct, the thing had a real body in the other place, but only a projection in this world. And that projection seemed to have a limited reach, at least in physical terms. He didn't know exactly how far that was, but he did remember the moment when the presence was quite suddenly no longer upon them. He judged the distance and had decided that their fort was well outside of that reach, but still had decided to absolutely stay well the hell away from it. And now, with the knowledge that they had all dreamed of the thing that night, he was forced to consider that perhaps it had sent the dreams to them. Its physical reach into their world may have been limited, but its mental reach might be a great deal further. If that were true, even going out to the fort could be dangerous. If it could invade their dreams, it was reasonable that it could invade their conscious minds as well. If it was sending beautiful women to lure them close enough—like it had with Jimmy—their meat might get minced.

And there had been a lot of talk about that house. They all wanted to know just where the hell it came from, and more to it, who had lived there. Why—again assuming the validity of Jimmy's theory—was the fabric of the two worlds so much thinner there?

Freddie had decided to start looking in the only place he knew to try—the local Library.

He dropped the kickstand on his bike, threw his leg over the seat, and dismounted. His backpack hung over his shoulder, containing a sack lunch and a large bottle of water. He pushed his thick spectacles up on his nose and walked into the Library, clearing his throat and sniffing as he entered.

Fucking allergies.

The cool air inside confronted his perspiring skin and sent a chill through his body. Ripples of goosebumps rose all over him in chilled mounds. His nipples hardened and began to scrape against the cotton of his tee-shirt in an irritating manner and, God as his witness, his balls shriveled. He felt them collapsing in on themselves like crumpled paper and he found in that moment that he would not have been surprised had his genitals literally imploded on themselves and vanished altogether.

Thank Christ they didn't. He wouldn't know what to do without his pecker—*how would he piss?* After another moment, the sensations all began to pass. He coughed and sniffed again—*fucking allergies*—and was met with harsh shushing from a wrinkly old shrew of a woman behind the front desk.

He threw his hands up in surrender and whispered, "Sorry!"

There was a *'humph'* from the woman and she turned from him in disdain. She pulled up a newspaper and fiddled with it for a few moments as she inspected it. It made a great deal more noise than his cough and sniff had, and further, he'd now realized that there was no one else in the library to be disturbed, anyway.

He let all that go, however. He wasn't here to get into a battle of wills with an elderly woman, he was here to acquire information, and he meant to do just that. He made his way around the front desk and came up to speak with the old stickler.

Several long seconds went by where she was either not noticing him standing there or was ignoring him entirely. Freddie was pretty sure it was the latter. She was, after all, from the time when adults believed children should be seen but not heard. Perhaps neither seen *nor* heard, for that matter.

He finally cleared his throat, not too loudly, but enough to mark his presence. The old bitch's eyes snapped up from the paper and looked over both it and her grandmotherly glasses at him sharply. Freddie tried on his best smile, but he could tell right away she wasn't impressed with it.

"May I help you?" the old woman asked, a thick Texan drawl and frustrated intolerance dripping from her words like chilled molasses.

Freddie ignored her rudeness.

"Yeah, I'm looking for newspapers," he said, his voice surprisingly cracking in a nervous manner as he spoke. Puberty could be a real asshole.

"The newspaper machine's outside, you passed it on the way in, youngster."

He was shaking his head now. "No, no, sorry. I mean like really *old* newspapers. I'm not sure just how old but probably close to a hundred years or so. Maybe more recent than that, but I'm just not sure."

The old woman was spreading her paper down on the counter-top, loud crackles of smoothing paper littering the quiet room with noise. Her hypocrisy knowing no bounds, she then laughed a few choppy *HA!*s at him at what any reasonable person would find to be incongruent with Library etiquette.

Freddie just stared at her, suffering her condescension masterfully, though he could feel heat high in his cheeks.

"Old newspapers, huh?" she finally said when her laughter subsided. "Just what are you looking for, anyway, young man?"

"I'm trying to find information," he said. "My friends and I were playing the other day—playing in the woods, that is—and we found this old house. No trail to it, nothing like that. But it was there. I was curious if I could find out anything about it, if there was a story or anything. It's a..." he trailed off and his eyes darted around the room, searching for the right term.

"It's a weird place?" she finally added for him.

He nodded. "Yes, ma'am. Y-you ever heard of it?"

She stood straighter now, looking down at him with thoughtful eyes.

"Where exactly was it?" she asked.

He told her.

"Oh dear," she groaned, nodding slightly. "Yeah, I've heard of it. 'Course I'm too young to have been around when everything happened, not that you'd believe that, but it's the truth. And there was a story about it. But..."

"But what?" he asked, prodding her on. That 'but' had sounded loaded.

"But," she continued, "the newspaper's only got a small part of the story."

"Oh," he said, feeling a little dismayed. "Well, is there anything else I could get the rest of the story from?"

"How old are you, anyway?" she asked as if she hadn't heard his question.

"I'm, uh, I'm twelve."

She regarded him a moment, apparently deciding if the preteen age was sufficient vintage to hear the tale.

His curiosity heightened, almost unbearably.

"Pretty nasty story," she said. "Young man like you, your parents may not want you hearing that sort of thing, if they're good Christians, that is."

"Good Christians we are," he said, barely masking his rising frustration with the woman, "but I can take a story, no matter how nasty it is. I bet I've seen movies that are worse."

That sharp laugh reemerged, stinging his ears.

"Oh, youngster," she said through her guffaws. "I can tell you right now you haven't. No sir, you can take *that* to the bank."

She turned and came around the front of the counter, motioning for him to come with her.

"Follow me, son," she said. "We'll grab you the paper. The other part isn't out. Keep it in the back, and no, you can't check it out. It's considered a part of town history, no matter how foul it may be. But I'll let you look at it to satisfy your curiosity. But don't you come crying to me when you have to use a night-light for the next month."

He almost laughed at her insolence, but didn't. Something in her voice, the *certainty* in it, haunted him.

She waddled away towards the back of the library, and Freddie followed.

CHAPTER 26

Jake Reese was leaning against the brick wall of the gas station just North of the Winnsboro Public Library. He was smoking a cigarette, slowly drawing in through the filter, watching the embers glow as he drew in the smoke.

He exhaled slowly through his nostrils. This was cool as shit. He never got tired of how it looked and how it felt when smoke was exiting his young lungs through his nostrils in twin plumes of white cloud.

Bart was with him. They had met in town earlier and began riding their bikes around, looking for a way to score some smokes. Find someone old enough willing to buy it for them, or hope to find someone young enough working the counter to not give a damn and sell them a pack in spite of the rules and laws. They had finally found just such a person at this convenience store, after three separate failed attempts around town.

The first two places had been total busts. The clerks had both been middle-aged men from India—which made them sand-niggers in Jake's mind—and were extreme sticklers for rules. Having found no cooperation from other customers in and around the store to purchase them a pack, Jake had made the attempt himself. He was very tall for his age, and well built, and it wouldn't be *entirely* unreasonable to believe that he may indeed be eighteen years old if you didn't know better. Jake would have liked to have some facial hair—*that would really seal the deal*—but as yet, nature had denied him more than a thin shadow on his upper lip and a single lone hair which curled out from his chin now and then, when it found occasion to do so.

Neither the curl or the shadow were present this day, however. He'd shaved them off over the weekend, not thinking they would do much for him anyway and hoping that the act of shaving them off would help them grow back faster and fuller. He wasn't sure if this theory was actual science, but he'd heard it enough to believe it was plausible.

The sand-nigger hadn't been biting, though.

As soon as Jake asked for a pack of Marlboros, the man demanded ID.

"Must see i-den-cay-shun," the man said flatly.

His English was choppy and missing modifiers and was generally full of holes, but Jake could make it out. It *did*, however, piss him off that such a sub-species as this brownie were allowed to lord over him in so many stores around town. It was almost a fucking spectacle to look around in such a heavily Caucasian place such as East Texas, *especially* Winnsboro, and yet see so many sand-niggers, darkies, and faggots running the town's businesses. It infuriated him.

Jake had feigned digging through his pockets for a wallet (he didn't carry one), trying to produce an ID, and coming up with nothing but a faux look of *'awe, man, I forgot it'* on his face.

"Ah, crap," he had said to the clerk, "I must've forgot it at home! I've got a little cash, though, I promise I'm old enough."

The man stared at him through dark, distrusting eyes, his face displaying virtually zero emotion.

"Must have i-den-cay-shun or no cig-rette!" he said sharply, his voice betraying his blank face.

They had argued and Jake had considered pulling his knife out of his pocket and putting it to the guy's throat and *demanding* the cigarettes, but thought better of it even as his hand clenched the knife in his jeans. It was broad daylight and too many people were around. Someone would call the pigs right away and that wouldn't put him any closer to the cigarettes than he was now, and there would be a whole other world of problems to deal with to boot.

He and Bart left the store, throwing the door open wide and informing the man that he would be well-served to go and have relations with himself before moving on to the next store. As the door swung closed behind him, Jake could hear the clerk yelling harshly back to him in some sand-nigger language—he didn't know which one—and Jake flipped him the bird.

The next store contained yet another sandy, this one a woman. She didn't even let him get the question out before she was tapping on the sign which informed that the staff here obeyed the law and didn't sell tobacco products to minors. And she was having none of his bullshit either. Their encounter had ended much like the first.

The third had actually *almost* been successful. It was a white guy at this one, and he was probably in his early twenties. He'd actually been in the process of getting the pack for them when a cop walked in and looked over to the counter. The clerk had immediately dropped the pack behind the counter and started speaking loudly to Jake and Bart about how he doesn't sell to minors, so no ID, no smokes.

Jake had made a point to find this guy sometime in the future and cut his penis off.

But finally, the universe had granted them favor. They had made their way all the way to the Northern edge of town, just past the Library, and found a young girl working the counter, no other customers, no managers around, and no fucking cops.

Smokes acquired.

Now they leaned against the wall of the place getting their nicotine fix. They were only fourteen—Jake would be fifteen in another month—but they had managed to develop a nice addiction to cigarettes already. Bart fumbled around with the lighter in his fat fingers for a few moments before dropping it to the ground like the obese idiot he was. The shell of the lighter shattered and lighter fluid spilled out onto the asphalt lot.

"Goddamnit, Bart!" Jake said in a hissing voice, smoke spilling out around his face.

Bart looked up stupidly with the cigarette hanging out of his mouth from one corner and made the surrender motion with his hands.

"Sorry, man!" he said, the cigarette bobbing up and down as he spoke. "It was an accident!"

"You were the fucking accident, Dyer," Jake said. "Your daddy didn't pull his cock out your mommy's cunt fast enough and hear you are."

A faint smile threatened to curl up at the corner of Bart's mouth, but never quite reached full realization. Jake wondered if the fat fuck was thinking about his parents boffing and getting a hard on from it. Probably was, but fuck it.

Jake dug a second lighter out of his pocket. Bart reached out for it as Jake brought it up, but Jake swatted his hand away with his free one.

"*I'll* light it, retard!" he said, his eyes slits behind a film of rising smoke. "It's the last one I've got because of your butterfingered fat-ass!"

Again, the threat of a smile, then it was gone.

Jake lit the cigarette for him and then returned the lighter to the safety of his pocket. Then he leaned back again to the wall and drew in a long, satisfying drag. Held it in. Blew it out slowly.

Through his nostrils, of course.

Bart had leaned back next to him, making a valiant effort to imitate the cool-factor Jake was exuding, but failing miserably at it. He could hardly blow the smoke out from his nose without trickles of snot accompanying it, and he also managed, as if by design, to always get upwind of Jake. The smoke and vaporized snot—Jake assumed at least *some* of the snot vaporized and rode the cloud—always drifted into his face. Red anger welled inside him when this happened *(and it happened often)*, and Jake would always slap his arm, telling him to move.

"Get the fuck out of my face with that shit, jackass!"

Bart lumbered up from the wall and took a few steps out to get the smoke away from him.

"Sorry, man, lighten up!"

"Keep talking and I'll light *you* up," Jake replied in an eerie, cold tone.

"What's Chris up to?" Bart asked as if he hadn't heard.

Jake shrugged, taking another drag.

"I don't know, chores or some shit. You know how his dad is."

"Yeah, I guess. So, what are we gonna do? Wanna see if we can score some nudie mags?"

Bart's face finally bulged out into a fat and excited grin, the cheeks on his face turned pink with the strain. But Jake was shaking his head.

"Naw, you jerk off on your own time," Jake said. "I got other plans."

"Fine," Bart said, deflated. "Like what?"

Jake drew in another drag, the last this cigarette would allow. The embers were all the way down to the filter now, and he could taste an acrid bite in the smoke. He threw the cigarette down on the ground directly in front of a sign which posted 'NO LITTERING' and smashed it out with the heel of his shoe. He blew the smoke out, this time through his mouth, and stood up from the wall.

"I wanna find those little faggots and finish what we started," he said. There was something cold in his eyes, and Jake could see it didn't sit well with Bart, even though Bart was arguably as crazy as he was. This made Jake grin inwardly.

Bart was nuts, and he enjoyed inflicting pain on things, especially *weak* things, but there was usually no real malice in it. He just did it because he thought it was cool. Because it made him feel good. But Jake was different. Jake enjoyed causing harm, but it wasn't because it made him feel good. No, with Jake Reese, his desire to cause pain came from somewhere deeper. Somewhere hotter.

"Who knows where they even are?" Bart asked. "I don't even know where they live, and they haven't been back to the woods since the other day, I checked. Found their little fort and everything. You know they got Playboys stashed out there?"

Bart's eyes lit up when he mentioned the gentlemen's magazines he had come across and told Jake how he had ultimately stole the mags after sufficient masturbation all over the fort.

"I told you I don't give a shit about nudie mags, Bart," he said flatly, disgust in his eyes. He flipped open the pack of cigarettes and dug another out. "I don't know where they live either, but this isn't a big town. We can find them."

Bart dragged on his cigarette again and dropped it to the ground. He stamped it out. There had been at least half of the cigarette left to go, and this pissed Jake off, though he said nothing about it.

Bart reached out for the pack.

"Can I have another one?" he asked.

Now Jake *did* say something.

"The fuck, man?" he barked. "You just wasted a half of one!"

"Yeah, but I don't like 'em when they get down that far. They taste funny."

"Because you're a jackass! Get your own pack if you're not gonna smoke them right!"

Jake glared hard at him, but eventually handed the pack over anyway. Bart did the fat-fingered fumbling jive again and miraculously came out with a fresh smoke. Jake repeated all the motions with the lighter, including swatting Bart's hand away when he reached for it, and lit the tip for him.

"Thanks, man," Bart said taking a drag and coughing. "I'll smoke the whole thing this time, I promise."

"Fuckin'—A right, you will," Jake replied as he raised the lighter to his face.

As he did, his eyes flicked up towards the Library. It wasn't because he'd seen anything, he had been focusing on the lighter, but his eyes had just decided that they needed to glance up and look around. Take in the surroundings.

And there was the coke-bottle bespectacled faggot from the woods. Right there. Right in front of them. Carrying a backpack into the Library. He saw the kid cough and sniff and push his thick glasses up on the bridge of his nose.

Jake couldn't believe it. He stood there, staring over the flame of the lighter—which had still not come in contact with his cigarette—at the little faggot who'd held the snake to fight them off the other day. Jake had been brooding all weekend long about finding them and hurting them. Hurting them really, *really* bad. Jimmy Dalton mostly, but he wanted them all. He wanted to hurt them, make them bleed, and to fuck that little girl while they all watched.

And one of them had just fallen right into his lap.

"Use the payphone," Jake said, pulling some change out of his pocket. "Call Chris, get him here. No arguments, tell him to get the fuck up here as fast as he can."

Bart took the change, a confused look on his face. Then he followed Jake's eyes and saw the kid going into the Library just before he was out of sight.

Bart smiled broadly and took another drag on his cigarette, jangling the change in his fat hand.

"You got it, Jake!" he said.

Bart threw the cigarette down on the ground and stamped it as he trotted around the front of the store to the payphone. Jake had a moment of red fury rise up as he saw that, once again, Bart had only smoked half. But as his eyes drew back to the Library and his thoughts returned to who was in there—unknowingly trapped—his anger subsided and a smile filled his maddened face.

Jake lit his cigarette and started to laugh.

CHAPTER 27

Freddie couldn't believe what he'd found.

The old battleax had been right about the newspaper story. There had indeed been one, and it *was* incredible. But it was mostly aftermath. What had been found when the townspeople had finally come to the house, determined to run the family out of town.

And of the dread which had settled in on the community afterward.

The family's name was Brogan, and the newspaper containing the story had been dated at October 31, 1906.

Freddie read the story feverishly, then read it again. He was almost through it for the third time over when the old bitch returned with a book in her hands.

"I still don't think a youngster like you ought to be filling your mind with this stuff, history or not. Ain't proper. But, I ain't your momma neither, so have at it."

She let the book fall to the table before Freddie. It landed on top of the newspaper with a loud *thump*, and he could see dust-bunnies plume out all around it. It was an ancient tome, not terribly thick, but not a Dr. Seuss book either. The edges were worn with age and mildew, several swatches of the cloth cover torn here and there around its perimeter. The paper inside the book was thick and yellowed, though it probably began life in a shade much closer to white.

The Damned Place

Freddie delicately ran his fingers over the book, almost reverencing its antiquity. He slid it in front of him, gently lifted the cover, and opened it. He could smell the paper and dust thickly in his nostrils and his eyes glanced over the first page.

The old bitch was waddling out of the room, mumbling something about these young whipper-snappers under her breath as she trudged along.

"Thank you, ma'am!" Freddie called to her back as she left.

She flipped a hand up over her shoulder in acknowledgement and continued on her course. Freddie returned to the book and read the first page. It was a title page of sorts, hand-written in black ink in a cursive which predated anything he'd seen in his years in school. It was actually quite beautifully written, almost artfully, but he managed to get a grasp on what the words said.

It was entitled 'The Diary of Johnathan Michael Brogan' and there was a date below stating the first entry was January 3, 1906. There was nothing else written on this first page.

Freddie lifted the edge of the old split paper and turned it over. Read the first entry. There wasn't anything very special about it, just the musings of someone recording what their day had entailed all those years ago. Working the garden with Mother and an incident with his Father. Something about fixing the wheel to their wagon.

He read on through the next several entries and found much the same sort of triviality. Boring day-to-day goings on of a family at the turn of the century making their way in old Winnsborough, as it had previously been spelled. He also began to notice as he went along that the entries would sometimes have several days between them, and a few times more than two weeks.

"You didn't keep a daily journal, did ya, John?" Freddie asked no one quietly.

He pressed on, deeper and deeper into the text. Time vanished from his thoughts as he went on, and he began to notice a sense of dread developing in him as he got deeper into the diary. The dread turned to downright horror towards the end, and the gaps between the entries began to tighten from weeks, to days, and finally to daily entries. Sometimes multiple daily entries. Especially over the final thirty-one days.

October, 1906.

He finished reading, his hands shaking as they held the page of the final entry, and Freddie realized he wasn't breathing.

My God, he thought. *Oh, my God...*this *is why it's so thin there! That* has *to be why!*

He was sure of it. Nothing else could possibly explain it. Of course, there was plenty of supernatural terror in the tale he'd just read, even other-worldly horror, but something in those artfully drawn words spoke to more than mere monsters and madness. Something purely evil was afoot in those pages, something darker than anything he could ever have imagined possible. And somehow—*astonishingly*—this wasn't even common knowledge.

Almost no one even *knew* about the house in the woods. The Brogan House. That place hadn't seen anyone come by it for years before Chester Laughton and Mike Barton had stumbled upon it. And something horrific had happened out there, perhaps much more than what the police suspected. Then he and his friends had been cornered up there and the amazing things that happened after...

Freddie's mind whirled. The place was thin, alright. The wearing of the fabric of space had allowed a door to be opened there. A door to another world. A world filled with monsters and death.

A damned place...

He slammed the book closed, much more forcefully than he'd intended to do, and gathered it and the newspaper up to carry them to the front. The old bitch was there, re-reading her newspaper again, the sour scowl ever-present upon her creviced face.

"Who brought this to the Library?" he asked, holding the journal up.

She glanced up at him with her distasteful eyes and exhaled loudly as she put her paper down.

"If I recall correctly—and that may be in question, mind ya—it was the mayor back then. You saw the story in the paper. The people went out there and found them like that. One of them happened upon that blasphemous thing and brought it to the Sherriff. Weren't no city police back then, not here anyhow, and so it was the Sherriff who handled the lawin' in these parts."

"Yeah, yeah, yeah," Freddie said rolling his finger in the air to keep her moving. "I got it."

She took a moment to purse her wrinkled lips in disdain at him, but she continued anyway.

"Like I said, Sherriff got hold of it, used it in evidence. 'Tween that journal there and what they found after they put the story together, they had all they

215

needed to close the case. Some years later when the Library was built, the director here—name of Sam Wiseman it was, at that time—he asked to keep it in the Library as a part of town history. Everybody agreed and people come from time to time to look at it. After a while, though, and I mean quite a few years, maybe's many as twenty or thirty years, folks just got plum bothered by the story. Didn't want to hear about it no more. This was back when I was still stopping traffic with my stockings, you see."

Freddie couldn't imagine a time this old raisin could have ever turned a head, and the thought of her varicose-veined legs in stockings threatened a swell of nausea, but he ignored it.

"So they put it away?" he asked.

She nodded. "Sure enough did. Put it away in the back. Time went by, people quit talking about it. Folks that was around when it happened started dying off, old age and such. Younger folks hadn't heard of it. Wasn't a trail or anything out there to that house as you've seen, and it just kinda vanished from the town's mind, as it were."

Freddie was amazed that such an incredible—even if horrible—story of town history, something which had happened right in their own back yard, could be forgotten in such a way. He supposed he could see why, but it was just so incredible. All over the country there were urban legends and tales of wicked things, and in some cases, there were historical markers to document the events and gift shops to commemorate them. But not here. Not in Winnsboro.

Winnsboro had made it vanish.

He pondered this for a few moments, unaware that he was simply staring off into space while the woman was looking at him.

"Anything else, young man?" she asked after a full minute.

He snapped out of it and looked back at her, smiling sheepishly.

"Do you have a photo-copy machine?" he asked excitedly.

"For what?" she asked.

"You said I can't check this out. I understand that. But could I make a copy of it? You know, something I could study? The newspaper article too?"

She regarded him a moment longer and nodded.

"Suppose so, they're all dead and gone now, anyhow," she said hollowly. "Nickel a page."

He dug in his pocket and laid down a crumpled wad of cash in front of her, several coins of varying monetary significance clinking and rolling about in the process.

"Will this be enough?" he asked wide eyed.

She dug through the currency for a moment and nodded.

"I suppose 'twill," she said. "Machine's over there."

She was pointing behind him to the opposite wall. He followed her direction and saw the giant machine sitting quietly and stoically.

"Thanks!" he said breathily and hurried over to the machine.

Nearly an hour later, he emerged into the early afternoon sun and its blistering heat, his own copy of the full and terrifying story of the Brogan house in his backpack.

217

CHAPTER 28

Freddie mounted his bike in a hurry, flinging his right leg over the seat, slowing and balancing himself carefully for a moment as his still-descending balls, freed of their frigid captivity, were nearly crushed as he hopped on. Once his testicles were out of danger, he flipped the kickstand up, adjusted his backpack with the horror of horror stories inside, and pulled around towards the road. He glanced across the side road—Jean Street—which cut between the Library and the gas station next to it, and then to Main Street. His fingers drummed anxiously on his handlebars as he decided which direction he should go.

He decided to take Jean down to Pine and roll back up that way. It was a little longer than just taking Main down to Pine, but Main Street doubled as Highway 37, and there was always more traffic on it, and next to none this other way. He would only need to cross Main when he looped around onto Pine to get back to his side of town, and this way wouldn't have to worry about getting splattered by a great big truck with loud exhaust in the process.

He pedaled onto Jean Street and went on his way. His mind was racing with everything he had just discovered about the house in the woods. It was so fantastically frightening that he would spontaneously shudder multiple times as he played the tale over in his head. If the key to stability—such as the fabric of space—was rooted in good structure, then the key to *in*stability must be rooted in the opposite. A poor foundation could bring down a home, no matter how well built the rest of it was. This had to be the reason Jimmy was able to cross over at the house in the woods but not here. The structure of the place—not the house itself, but the very ground it stood upon—was *not* stable. Its foundation was one of an evil so great, it staggered his young mind to comprehend.

He pondered this as he rode down the street, the thin tires on his bike hissing along the hot asphalt and the chain clinking occasionally. He wondered if space and time were subject to the same idea. It had to be.

Around town, Jimmy had been unable to open the door he and Honey had told the rest of them he'd opened at the house. Multiple times at the house, at that. Was it because this place was mostly rooted on goodness and virtue? There were plenty of problems in Winnsboro, and bad things happened in every town, certainly, but it was built upon goodness. The little history Freddie *did* know about the town was that the town fathers had been God-fearing, hard-working, and virtuous men, and they'd instilled in their offspring the same morals they all—for the most part—shared. But if what the journal and the newspaper had stated were true—and he had no reason to doubt it at this point—the same could not be said of the Brogan house.

If anything had ever been conceived in evil, it was that place. If anyone had ever been evil, evil right down in their core, it had been Susannah Brogan, the mother of the journal's author.

He shuddered again, remembering the story. He made a ninety-degree turn on Jean Street where it angled around and led to Pine. His mind was haunted with thoughts of the damned place in the woods, the place so thin that monsters could come through. Had they really been playing out there, so near the horrid place, all these weeks and months? What if they had stumbled into it at some other time, under different circumstances? What if that thing had sensed them from the other side?

They'd all likely be dead, that's what.

Freddie knew this, but also knew that it was useless to worry about things which hadn't happened. He shook off thoughts of 'what if' and focused on what was. What *was* going on was something very dangerous was hiding out there in those woods. There was also Jake and his gang, but they were secondary. Easy enough to avoid. The house was easy enough to avoid, too, for that matter, but there was a larger issue with that. The problem was that Freddie and his friends were the only ones who *knew* there was something dangerous out there. What if someone else went out there? What would happen to them? Would they end up like Mike Barton? Was there more than one way for the creature to cross over? Jimmy had opened the portal before, but could it come across another way?

And, of course, there was the bigger question: what happened if the monster *did* cross over and get its fangs into a person over here?

He pulled up to Pine, shuddered, checked both ways, and looped to his right again onto the street. He was coming around to the old school building, now used for administrative purposes. Only right now it was deserted for the summer.

He had to get home, right away, then get Jimmy and the others on the phone so they could meet. He had to tell them, to *show* them, what he had found. They had to know the story of the Brogan house. Then they needed to decide what to do about it.

And just what do you think the four of you can do about any of it?

This question stood out in his mind like an accusing finger. Just what the fuck did a bunch of twelve-year-old kids think they could do about an otherworldly demon? Splash Holy Water on the place and call it good? Burn it down?

He didn't think any of those things would work. Never mind the fact that burning it down would likely set all of the woods on fire. What then? Do *nothing*? Just stay away and hope no one goes out there?

None of that would do. Perhaps his friends would have an idea. Maybe Jimmy would come up with something.

Thinking of Jimmy brought his mind back to the amazing ability his friend had exhibited to them at the old garage. Actually *moving* things with his mind! Well, his *will*, as Jimmy had explained, but shit on the semantics. He was moving things around without touching them! *That* couldn't be denied anymore.

And it was amazing how it had come about. In a moment of dire need and desperation, with Jake right on Jimmy's heels, just *poof,* there it was. All at once, out of nowhere. Where did something like that come from? Had it been inside Jimmy all along and he just happened to stumble across it right when he needed it most? Or had it come from somewhere else?

And from who?

He was almost to the school administration building now, and he could just see the mouth of the tiny alley that ran beside it. The side closest to him was lined with tall pines and oak trees, and enough bushes to conceal it completely. The other side was the brick wall of the building itself. The alley had a fairly steep incline, and if one were to go up it, they would be unable to see what was beyond the top.

He saw the large, industrial garbage dumpster which stood against the side of the building and covered half the alley's throat.

Jimmy will know what to do, he thought. *He's got the gift, I've got the story, and Jimmy will—*

All at once a wild man leaped out of the bushes across the road from the alley. He was snarling and screaming, waving his arms around in the air. For a moment, Freddie thought it would be The Joker again, perhaps testing out dancing with the devil in the bright sunshine this time, but that thought vanished almost as soon as it had materialized.

It was Bart Dyer.

Shit! Freddie thought.

Bart was almost all the way across the road, nearly right on top of him. His eyes were wild like a rabid animal and his teeth were bared in an almost comic display. Freddie knew if he were to keep moving along the way he was, Bart would be on him, and he couldn't turn left because Bart was too close. He'd wreck into him and would be in no better a situation.

That left going right. Into the alley.

Freddie turned hard, the rubber on his tires squealing as he made the diversion. He leaned hard into the turn, trying to make it as fast as possible, and started pumping his legs on the pedals to gain momentum for the uphill climb he was going to have to make. He figured he could get away from Bart, he was a fat-ass with a small fuel-tank and would give out before long, but if Freddie didn't get some momentum going now, Bart might catch him on the incline.

Freddie rounded into the alley and righted the bike. He was going fast now, and he knew he would be able to outrun the fat-bastard.

But then, in the next moment, he knew he wouldn't.

Jake Reese stepped out from behind the dumpster and clothes-lined Freddie off the bike. The blow hit him square in the throat, and sharp pain struck him. He began to fly off the back of the bike. His hands had released their white-knuckle grip on the handle-bars of the bike, and they and his legs were splayed out in front of him as the bike cruised away beneath him. The bike went a few feet, wobbled unsurely, then crashed to the ground with a metallic rattle.

Freddie smashed into the ground with a loud *clump*, and all the air in his lungs evacuated at once. He was straining to catch his breath, and was reaching for his injured throat when Jake and Chris Higgins were suddenly on either side of him, yanking him up roughly. Bart caught up to them, then, heaving from his short run, and laughing piggishly through the wheezes.

Jake and Chris dragged Freddie behind the dumpster and slammed him against the brick wall so hard that the little gulps of air Freddie had been able to recover to his lungs departed once more.

"Grab the bike, Bart!" Jake said looking over his shoulder but holding Freddie firmly against the wall. "Drag it over here out of sight!"

Bart took to his task, still breathing hard. Jake turned back to Freddie, grinning frighteningly, and flipped his knife out. It gleamed in the trickles of sunlight that managed to find their way into the alley.

Freddie was held firm on both sides by Jake and Chris, and moving was an impossibility. His eyes gazed through his glasses, now crooked on his nose, at the knife in Jake's hand. He watched as the knife came closer to his face and he tensed as the blade pressed into his cheek beneath his left eye.

"Now," Jake said, leaning in close enough to kiss him, "I think we have some unfinished business!"

Freddie began to tremble and was unaware for some time that he had wet himself.

CHAPTER 29

The smell of piss was a pleasing incense to Jake, to rob a line from his parent's book of fairy tales.

It wasn't that Jake particularly *liked* the smell of piss. That wasn't it at all. For Jake, context was everything. Something could be revolting *or* wonderful, depending on the context of the situation.

And in *this* context, it was fucking wonderful.

The wonderful part about it was the fear. The *fear* that loosened the bladder of the four-eyed-faggot before him was absolutely exhilarating to Jake. No, *more* than exhilarating, it was *intoxicating.*

Jake thought the smell of fear, or the piss of fear, or the shit or the tears or the visible terror—*any* part of it—was something he could get drunk on. The pure joy of extracting that thing inside every person, that thing everyone dreaded, that place the mind and body run to when something more powerful than they has their balls—realistically or metaphorically—in a vise-grip was something that he savored.

He'd gotten his first real taste of this drink with his mother a year before. She had always viewed him as her black sheep, the non-conformer. His little brother, Norman, was nothing like Jake. Jake thought for himself, where Norman relied on his parents—*especially* their mother—to think for him. Jake liked to do things his own way, Norman always sought the approval of

Mother. Jake wanted to be left alone, Norman never wanted to get off her tit.

And the dumb bitch actually used to think she was going to force him into line. *Him!* As if she were going to make her elder son into another Norman, another weak, pathetic, sorry excuse for flesh.

She would take the belt to him. Not like most kids, though. No, Jake had heard the stories of other kids getting spankings. They always consisted of either a hand on the bottom, or in the case of belts, they would be folded over and laid across the bottom a couple of times. And never really that hard, either. Further, it seemed to Jake that in everyone else's case's, these spankings had ended years ago. The most recent one was from when the child had been perhaps eight-years-old, maybe nine at the oldest.

But not with Jake.

No, with Jake the spankings had continued. Continued all the way into puberty and into his first teen year. Anything and everything he did would earn him a *whoopin'* from dear old mom. His father hadn't spanked him in so long, Jake wasn't even sure that he ever had, but that wasn't surprising. His father was weak. His mother had always been the disciplinarian in the home, and Georgie had been all too willing to let her wear the hat.

Jake reminisced on that day again, just as he'd relayed to his trembling father a few days prior, about his first real taste of the fear whiskey.

He had groaned audibly when his mother had caught him putting dirty dishes in the dish-washer.

"You *never* put dirty dishes in the dishwasher, Jake Reese!" she had bellowed at him in their kitchen.

"Why?" he had pleaded, honestly confused at this ridiculous idea.

"Because you want them to come out *clean,* you heathen!" she had almost screamed at him.

"Isn't that why we put them in the dishwasher?" he had asked with sarcasm and disdain. "You know, so they get clean?"

She had slapped him across the face then. And hard. Red fingers of pain welted up on his face as his head jerked back and he almost cried out. *Almost* cried out. He would never give her the satisfaction of showing her pain when she was trying to inflict it. He couldn't stand that look she would get on her face, that hideous snarl of righteous indignation and triumph. He'd be damned if he let her have it.

"You don't sass your mother, do you understand me, Jake Reese?"

She always used his first *and* last name when she was upset. Which was often. There was little chance of him ever forgetting his full name.

He said nothing. He only stared at her.

"You wash the dishes *in* the sink, using soap, and *then* you put them in the dishwasher!" she screamed at him.

Now Jake spoke.

"That's the stupidest thing I've ever heard."

He said it flatly. No sarcasm this time. No malice. Just plain, hard fact. After all, it really *was* stupid. No sane person would argue that.

But sanity took no residence within Cherry Reese.

She stared at him, mouth agape in horror and shock at his insolent response. Her eyes were alight with blue fire and her chin bobbed slightly as it trembled beneath her mouth in rage.

So, he thought it would be a good time to go on.

"Norman doesn't wash them first either, you know," he said. "He never does! Neither does dad! And while we're at it, I've seen *you* put them straight in the dishwasher too!"

A trembling hand was coming up to Cherry's mouth.

"That's right!" he went on, his eyes narrowing as he nodded. "It's only because it's *me* doing it that it's a problem! It's *me* you hate! It's *me* you want to punish, and I have no idea why!"

He had begun to shout at the end. Cherry had taken a step back as he'd gone on, fear beginning to etch on her face, but as soon as Jake had stopped, her fury returned in full force.

The hand lashed out again and slapped him a second time. He had been unable to contain a small wince this time, as she had landed on the already tender area she had slapped before. And before he could get his head back up to look at her, her hand had gripped the hair at the top of his neck and pulled up.

"You come with me, Jake Reese!" she hissed at him through clenched teeth.

She had nearly dragged him back into her bedroom, his hands trying to pry her claws from the hair on his neck, but finding every attempt to remove them only increased the pain.

She finally got him to her large walk-in closet—her personal torture chamber—and threw him down. He landed with a thud amidst a flurry of shoes and other miscellaneous items.

As he had looked up, she was placing the buckle of one of her belts in the palm of her hand. She wrapped the strap of the belt around the back of her hand once, and the rest of the belt dangled like a whip from her hand. Jake could see the gleaming metal which adorned the tip of the belt, the part that would be coming down on him in mere moments.

He'd been through this a thousand times. It was another area where his spankings—or *whoopins*, as his mother called them—differed from the norm. His mother didn't give a good god-damn *where* the belt landed. If it happened to be your ass, fine, but she didn't care. In fact, Jake had reasoned that she did it this way in hopes that he would willingly surrender his ass to her just to avoid being hit elsewhere.

"You're going to learn how to talk to me, *boy!*" she growled.

Boy.

That was what had really done it. Sure, he was fed up with the whole thing, he was much too old for spankings or *whoopins* or what have you, too old by far, but it had been that one word which had been the real clencher for him.

She called him *boy*.

He snatched her hand in the air on her first swing.

Total shock and awe exploded on her face like mortar rounds as he did so, indignation rising up beneath it like a tidal-wave. Jake had pushed her back into the wall and grabbed her throat in his other hand. Leaned in close to her face.

"Don't you ever call me a boy again, *mom*," he whispered coldly. "You're about to see how big of a *man* I really am."

Her eyes had washed over with fear all at once. What had been anger and self-righteousness had been replaced with dread.

He'd spun her around roughly, ripping the belt from her hand. Then he used it to tie her hands behind her back, cinching it tight. This particular belt had holes all the way around it, so he was able to secure her surely. She moaned and wept and snarled at him, but he paid her no mind. He shoved her into the bedroom proper and threw her down on her own bed. His parents' bed. The one he and Norman had been conceived in.

Springs groaned in concert with his mother as she bounced once and looked to him, pleading.

"Please," she begged, tears now coming into her horrified eyes. "Please, I'm your *mother*! Stop!"

Jake looked up at her and smiled coldly.

"Fuck you, mom."

And Jake knew she had seen he really meant it. She *really* got the picture when he tore her pants and underwear off of her. When he tore her shirt open and ripped her bra from her chest forcefully.

Yes, that day had been when Jake had first tasted the fear whiskey. And he was a fucking fan of it.

The four-eyed-faggot pissing himself wasn't on par with fucking his mother into submission, but it was still nice. If that day had been a glass, this was only a nip.

But sometimes a nip is all you need.

"You and your pals fucked up the other day," Jake said mere centimeters from Freddie's trembling face. "You guys fucked up *big*-time."

He could smell the kid's breath as he leaned into him. It smelled rancid with pickles and mayonnaise. He could feel the sensation of the kid's skin pricking open as the blade pushed through the outer layer of skin. The trickle of blood that followed across his fingers was almost orgasmic.

"And now," he went on, "you're gonna pay for it. If you live—and let me tell ya, that's a *big* if—you can let your friends know what they're in for. It's a long summer, faggot! And I'll find every last one of ya!"

Freddie tried to struggle to get free. Jake pulled him back as Chris and Bart stepped out of his way. Bart was laughing his donkey bray again and Chris was wide-eyed and breathing hard.

Jake ripped the backpack from Freddie's shoulders and flung it across the alley into the bushes. Freddie had tried to grab at it, but Jake overpowered him and threw him back into the wall, once again evicting his breath.

As Freddie looked up at him—tears now in the kid's eyes, Jake could see—Jake slashed at him with the knife.

The skin on Freddie's forearm opened up like a pair of lips and blood speckled the ground a moment before it began to flow freely from the wound.

Freddie cried out in pain and was met with a hard kick in the balls. He doubled over and fell to his knees. A sick, retching sound welled up from the punk's stomach as he did and, a moment later, he puked all over the alley floor.

Bart was still whinnying, and Jake had started to laugh now, too. Chris finally stepped forward and put a hand Jake's arm, the one holding the knife.

"This is going too far, Jake!" he cried out. "He's got the picture! Shit, man, this is fucked up!"

Jake jerked his arm away and came back with an elbow squarely in Chris's face. There was a pop as the nose broke and blood flowed like a jetting fountain as Chris toppled over on his back, cradling his face and whining in pain.

"Don't you *ever* interfere with me, motherfucker!" Jake roared as he pointed the tip of the bloody knife at Chris, his eyes wild and feral.

Chris looked up, tears soaking his eyes and still whining, and managed a nod.

Jake turned back to Freddie. The kid was done puking now, and was trying to hold his slashed forearm in his hand. But the best part was he was openly crying now. Jake's system flooded with pleasure.

"Just leave me alone!" Freddie screamed at Jake. "I've never done anything to you! You're just a bully and a bastard!"

Not a good choice of words, given the situation.

"A bully and a bastard, huh?" Jake said as he walked over to stand directly in front of Freddie. "I'll give you bully, sure, a man should own what he is. But a bastard? No..."

Jake kneeled down in front of Freddie and grabbed his chin in his free hand. He jerked the kid's face up to look him directly in the eye.

"I was born in wedlock, cocksucker."

Jake swung the butt of the knife into the bridge of Freddie's nose. There was a loud crack as his glasses shattered into a thousand pieces and the cartilage shredded inside the nasal cavity.

Freddie cried out in pain as blood began to pour from his nose and his eyes. He fell to his back, hitting his head on the brick wall as he went down. This caused more pain and further disorientation.

Jake watched with pleasure as the kid pulled his hands from his face. The shattered glasses had shredded the skin around the eyes, and it looked like there was a shard of glass, small as it was, sticking out of the left eyeball. More pleasure coursed through him as the kid began to tremble.

Jake stood, walked over to the boy, and loomed over him, pointing the knife down at him. The bray of Bart's laugh and the whine of Chris's pain lent a certain beauty to the score of the moment.

Jake smiled as he spoke to the terrified boy.

"And we're just getting started."

CHAPTER 30

Bob Lawson switched the radio off with a bitter look of disgust on his face. The sound of the conservative talking head on the AM station he was listening to blipped away into silence at once. Wind hissed through the worn weather strips in the doors of his old pickup, filling the sudden auditory vacuum. Coupled with the alto squeaks and groans of myriad joints and hinges, the truck's music was rounded out by the low bass growl of the huge eight-cylinder engine droning beneath the hood.

He'd already had a bad enough Monday morning to listen to anymore of the political bullshit going on. He had had it with the left *and* the right, and couldn't stand to listen to the people on the radio going on and on in condescending tones to each other from opposite viewpoints as though whatever they spewed from their acidic tongues were Gospel gold.

His morning had started off promisingly enough. There had been coffee—*good* coffee, at that—brewed to the perfect strength. He was a man who considered himself a connoisseur of fine coffee, and he worked hard enough to feel entitled to order the best money could buy. Just like all the political talking points, he'd had it with all the standard brands people carried in the big-box stores around the county. May as well be ground horseshit for all it tasted like, and he'd no more sully his lips with that garbage than he'd piss on the Holy Bible.

He had ordered this coffee in special from a magazine advertising fine coffee from Jamaica. It had been pricey—*really* pricey—but in the end it had been worth every penny. The smell, the taste, the bite, it had it all. And he took it straight black. That was how you really knew if a coffee was good. If you didn't have to fill it up with a bunch of crap to make it taste good, you had a fine brew.

And it had been fine indeed.

After drinking an entire pot—and subsequently *filling* an altogether different kind of pot—he'd loaded his pickup with tools and equipment he would need for the day. He was basically a handyman, did a little of this, a little of that, and he stayed consistently busy. House remodels, painting, pressure-washing, a little tinkering with air-conditioning units and water-well pumps, some mild electrical work—just about anything. And he was able to get the work because he was reasonable in his prices and honest with people. Need a wire run through a wall? Probably half what an electrician would charge. Water-well work? As much as a third of what the local well-service guys charged.

This day, he had been going to work on just such a water-well. The customer indicated that it was a submersible pump and motor, meaning that unit was down in the water of the well itself rather than sitting on top, and that it was a half-horsepower model. Should be a simple job. No water was coming out and after quoting a price, he'd been hired. People tended to get desperate for water when it was gone.

But Murphey—mankind's greatest enemy—had been alive and well that day, out enforcing his law with impunity.

First of all, it had *not* been a submersible pump, but rather a jet-pump, the kind which sit on top of the well. Second, the customer had already started trying to fix it himself, and had only succeeded in making a bad situation worse.

With jet-pumps, you have to prime them to get the water flowing. Submersibles do not require this, as they sit under the water already, which is a huge advantage. Sometimes a jet-pump will lose its prime, and there is a plug on them to pull out which gives access to prime the thing. But this customer hadn't bothered with the plug. No sir, this genius had pulled the motor cover and gone to tinkering with the goddamn wires inside!

Twisted braids of red, blue, black, and yellow wires were pulled out of their posts left to hang there with reckless abandon.

It was a total mess.

"Sir?" Bob had started with the man. "Was there a problem with the motor?"

The grizzled old man spat a massive wad of what appeared to be phlegm and tar onto the ground, leaving a brownish line of the stuff on his unshaved chin.

He made no move to remove it.

"Naw," the old man drawled out. "The damn thing was making noise, but weren't no water comin' out. I'd heard 'bout these damn submersibles losin' prime and ya gotta tear into 'em and realign the shaft."

Bob stared at the man dumbfounded.

"Realign the shaft?" he asked. "Who told you that?"

"Oh, it was my brother-in-law," the old-timer replied. "Used to work on wells for a time some years back. Six months or so, believe it was. Anyhow, he told me about working on these things, what a damn pain in the ass the submersibles were."

"Sir, this *isn't* a submersible, it's a jet-pump," Bob stated, pushing down his frustration. "And you *never* have to realign the shaft. If the shaft gets out of line or bent, you've got much bigger problems and should just replace the whole thing."

The old man peered at Bob through slits over his eyes, hiding behind the shadow cast from the bill of his old trucker's hat. He was a shockingly thin man, short too, and wore a faded pearl-snap shirt covered in almost invisible paisleys that was tucked into a pair of Wrangler blue jeans, cinched with a large gold-buckled belt. His white sneakers seemed a bit out of place with his outfit, but fashion didn't seem to be much of a concern for this man at the moment.

"That ain't what my brother-in-law says," the man replied.

There was an urge to sigh and roll his eyes, but Bob managed to reel in his disdain.

"I understand, sir," Bob went on in an even tone, "but I'm telling you what you have. This isn't going to be easy to get back together, and I'm pretty sure all it needed was priming."

He pointed to the plug on the other end of the device.

"See this here?" Bob said. "All you needed to do was pull this and put some water into the pump until it got primed and then put the plug back. That would have gotten you going."

237

The man seemed unimpressed. The brown line of tobacco-laden mucus winked in the sunlight as his wrinkled jaw hung open.

"Huh," the old man said absently.

Bob nodded and looked back down at the mess. It was really going to be a nightmare. There was a diagram—*thank God*—on the inside of the motor's cover panel, but even that wasn't going to be a great deal of help. Most of it was faded or scraped away. He knew he could get it done, but it was going to take a lot more work than he'd expected. And he had other customers to get to as well, which also weighed on his mind.

"Well," the old man said, ratcheting his jaw up. "Can ya fix it?"

Bob looked over the work before him again and nodded while he sighed.

"Yeah," he said, "but it'll take me a little longer than I expected."

"Whatever it takes," the old man replied. "Gotta have my water. Can't do without it."

"Understand," Bob said with a curt nod, and got to work.

And a nightmare it had been.

It had taken him an entire three hours just to get the wiring back properly, pouring over the faded and scraped diagram and coupling it with common sense, but he'd finally managed. He got the thing put back together, turned the power on, and discovered that he had been right: it had only lost prime.

But priming it had proven to be no small feat either.

Another two hours had been spent trying to get the stupid thing primed and flowing. Sweat and muffled curses marked the event with sour smells and sound. But he finally overcame, flipping the bird to Murphey in the process and calling him a motherfucker.

"Gotcha!" Bob quipped in triumph once he got the pump going.

Water began flowing into the pressure tank and the needle on the gauge started to rise up from zero. It stopped just shy of fifty pounds of pressure and he opened up a nearby garden hose to cycle the pump. The pressure switch engaged at around thirty pounds and refilled the tank.

Success.

However, the old man had been rather displeased with the bill. He kept recalling what Bob had told him on the phone. The price had been a good deal less than what Lawson's Services invoice was reflecting. Bob explained that it had been a unique situation, having to rewire the motor and all had been an unforeseen issue, and it had taken extra time. Time was money, after all, he explained, and had he known just what he'd be walking into beforehand, his estimate—*it was NOT a fucking quote*—would have reflected the price he was forced to charge now.

"I ain't payin' it," the old man snarled.

Bob felt his jaw tighten when the man refused to pay for the work he'd done. He saw again the spattering of tobacco juice on the man's chin, crusted over to a dull brown now with the passage of time. Bob wondered if it would stay there forever.

"Sir," Bob started, but the man held up a hand.

"Don't *sir* me, pal," the old man said. "We agreed on a price over the telephone, and I'll pay that, but ain't gonna be swindled out my hard-earned money."

"Sir," Bob started again, shaking his head, "no one is swindling you! I didn't quote you a set price, I told you about what it would cost based on what you told me over the phone and that didn't turn out to be the case! It was an *estimate*, not a quote!"

"You can take it or leave it," the old man said. "I'm going inside and I'm gonna grab my checkbook and my shotgun. You can decide which one I use."

Bob's dumbfounded face followed the man as he went inside, and he suddenly knew that the man had been dead serious.

Ultimately, Bob decided *some* money was better than *no* money—especially if it were coupled with a bad case of lead poisoning—so he'd taken the pittance in exchange for all his work. He smiled bitterly at the tobacco-spit marred face of the old man, took his check, and got in his truck. More than half his day had been wasted—for almost no money at all—and because of all the time he'd spent working on the pump, he was sure that if he *did* get to all his customers for the day, he wouldn't be getting home until after nine that night, and that was if he was lucky.

"Fuck!" he bellowed into the cab of his truck and punched the roof.

Sharp pain shot through his fist and he winced loudly looking down at his knuckles. There was a fresh wound and a trickling of blood flowing from between the second and third knuckles on his right hand. He looked up and saw there was a bent piece of chrome metal which surrounded the cabin light, and a small piece of flesh hung from the sharp tip. The scene seemed to mock him.

Murphey missed no opportunities.

Bob glared at the jagged metal for a few moments and then brought his eyes back to the road with a grunting, frustrated sigh. Then his eyes went wide.

He stood on his brakes.

Tires began to howl and smoke as the old pickup yawed first left and then right before skidding to a stop in the middle of Pine Street. Bob's now white face stared slack-jawed out the window at the terrible thing before him.

He threw open his door and jumped out after a short battle with the seat-belt—*Murphey was really on his game today*—and ran to the spot in the road which had caused him to slam on his brakes.

There was a young boy, no more than twelve or thirteen, and he was covered in blood. He was lying on the road and a trail of crimson followed from him back to the alley. Bob was in front of the school administration building, he realized. He'd been so caught up in his thoughts and frustrations that he hadn't even realized where he was, only that he was coming back into town.

He looked back to the boy, wide-eyed horror the expression on his face. The kid was literally *covered* in blood. There were slash marks on his arm and his face. His shirt was torn and bloody, and there appeared to be yet another laceration across his belly. His nose had been smashed and there was a piece of something, perhaps glass, sticking out of his left eyeball.

Bob fell to his knees in front of the kid and leaned over him. There was a steady rise and fall of breathing evident in the kid's chest, but it was shallow and raspy.

"Kid!" Bob yelled, louder than he'd intended. "Kid, can you hear me?"

241

The kid seemed to stir a bit and try to look up at him. His swollen and battered face twitched and the right eye fluttered open.

"I'm gonna get help, kid!" Bob said, again much louder than intended.

Bob looked up and down the street, then to the connecting roads. The whole area was completely deserted. This time of day during the school year it would be crowded with people, but now it looked like the remnants of a ghost-town.

He screamed anyway.

"Help!" he bellowed. "Somebody help me!"

Nothing and no one responded.

The kid was moving his hand and clutching a backpack. Bob hadn't even noticed it before now.

"Okay, kid," he said, "I'm going to get you to the emergency room, alright? I'm gonna take care of you! You'll be okay, I promise!"

He had no idea if this was true, but there was really nothing else he could say.

Bob lifted the kid forward and got his hands beneath him. Then he lifted him up, carried him over to the truck, and slid him in. As he was climbing in himself, the kid started to mumble something in a panicked cadence.

"What's that?" Bob asked, fumbling the keys in the ignition.

"Backpack!" the kid almost screamed. "I need my backpack!"

Bob looked back at the spot on the road where the kid had been lying and saw the backpack. He jumped out and ran to it, snatched it up, then threw it in the floorboard of the pickup as he hauled himself back in.

242

He got the engine fired up and started driving to the emergency room as fast as he dared, blaring his horn and flashing his hazard lights the whole way.

Once, he looked over and saw the kid reaching for the backpack on the floor. Saw the pain of the effort in the young boy's face. The blood flowing over his cheeks and his lips and everything else.

That horrible jagged piece of glass jutting out of his eye.

"We'll be there soon, kid!" Bob said, just to be saying something.

The kid didn't respond. He just kept reaching for the backpack and straining through the effort. He finally got his hand on it, gripped it, and pulled it up to his chest.

Then the boy hugged it tightly.

CHAPTER 31

Two days later, Jimmy, Honey, and Ryan were led down a blank, white corridor lined with peach-colored railings on either side, interrupted only by brown, wooden doors with brushed metal handles. The rooms were numbered and there were slots on the room number plates with little white and black letters pressed together to make names.

Martha James, Freddie's mother, was leading them.

"How is he?" Honey asked from behind her.

The three had heard of what had happened to their friend the evening after it had gone down. It had been abundantly clear to them that he'd been attacked by someone, but with the surgeries and medication, Freddie had been unable—*or unwilling*—as yet to identify who had done the attacking. He was mostly resting in the past two days, and the doctor had only just signed off on allowing visitors that were not immediate family to come and see him.

Upon hearing this news from Mrs. James herself— she'd been faithful in keeping her son's friends informed in spite of her understandable grief, God bless her—had contacted their parents and the kids had gotten a ride to the Trinity Mother Frances hospital in Tyler from Ryan's mother. She trailed behind the kids quietly as they walked.

"He's sleeping a lot," Mrs. James said in a strained, but altogether pleasant tone. "He's been in and out mostly, but today he's been more alert."

They neared another door and Mrs. James arced toward it. She stopped outside the door, her hand resting on the handle.

"Now, kids," she said and paused. Her face was red and there were hints of streaks across her cheeks, indicating she'd been crying a good deal over the past forty-eight hours. Her bottom lip quivered for a moment and she drew it into her mouth to steady it. Her eyes shut, she took a deep breath, and sighed it out slowly.

"Kids," she continued. "He's hurt real bad. He knows what happened to him, but won't tell me who. If any of you know, I'll expect you to tell me if he won't. Y'all run around together all the time, so if anyone knows, it's you, but I won't press it just yet. I just wish poor Freddie would tell me. But, in any case, try not to react to his condition, that won't do him any good at all. He's been cut up pretty bad and bandaged, but his eye was hurt really bad and his nose was broken. It's all patched up, but don't mention the eye. He may lose it altogether, they just have to see how it heals. He was really upset when he heard that, so just try not to mention it, okay?"

"Yes, ma'am," they all said in unison.

Mrs. James took another breath and opened the door to lead them into the room.

"I'll just wait out here," Cheryl Laughton said as the kids moved in past Mrs. James. "I don't want to crowd the room."

Mrs. James smiled sadly and nodded. "Thank you, Cheryl. If Freddie is up to it, I may give the kids a little time with him. I'll come visit with you, then, if that's alright?"

"Of course it is, Martha," Cheryl replied, giving a warm smile of her own.

Martha James followed the kids into the hospital room.

CHAPTER 32

Freddie was up to it.

Martha had spent the first few minutes as the kids came in and said their hellos and gathered around the bed. Freddie's dad had been in there, his face unshaven and hair frazzled. There were dark circles under his eyes indicating he hadn't slept much in the past two days.

After a few minutes, Freddie's spirits had leaped up and his parents welcomed the opportunity to go out and visit with Cheryl and perhaps head down to the cafeteria.

"If you need anything—*anything at all*—you ring that bell, you hear me?" Martha said to her son. "They'll get us right away."

"Yes, mom," Freddie drawled out. "I'll be fine!"

She smiled again, leaned over the bed, and kissed her son on the forehead.

"Be back soon, baby," she whispered to him. "I love you!"

Freddie's visible facial skin blushed, but he tried to blow it off as an annoyance. His boyhood ego seemed to be perfectly intact.

"Geez, mom, okay, okay!"

Martha and her husband left the room.

"What the fuck happened to you?" Jimmy bolted out as soon as the door closed.

"Yeah, man," Ryan pitched in, "we've been worried sick!"

Freddie seemed to shrug beneath his bandages.

"I got cornered up by our boy Reese and his assholes," he said. "Knocked me off my bike and fucked me up. Fucked me up good."

His visible right eye dropped and seemed to withdraw, a sad and angry look filling the socket.

"Well, I'm glad you're going to be okay," Honey said after a few moments of silence. "We figured it was those guys, we've all been watching our backs."

"Yeah," Jimmy said, cutting in. "I don't get why you won't tell your mom, though. This could get Jake put away for sure!"

Freddie was shaking his head.

"First of all, no it wouldn't. At least not for long enough. He's a minor, best case scenario is he does some juvenile time, *maybe* a year, takes some anger management classes, then he's out. But I don't think even *that* will happen, not with how prevalent his parents are. So then he's out, and it would only be worse. And second..."

The word hung there in the air as his uncovered eye drifted to the window next to his bed.

"Second?" Jimmy prompted him.

Freddie's eye swung back to them, darker now. Harder.

"Second," he went on in a cold and flat voice, "*I* want him."

That eye peered into them, *through* them. There was no twinkle there. No jokes. No sarcasm. Only pure, red rage.

"*You* want him?" Honey came in.

248

He nodded. "Me. They've been fucking with us since school let out. Fucking with us for no good reason. And there is something off in Jake. Bart too, but not like Jake. Chris, I think, just goes along to get along. And Bart is cruel, but Jake, he's different. He gets off on it. People like him, they only understand one language, and that language is violence."

A chill slithered up Jimmy's spine when he heard this, and he suspected Honey and Ryan experienced something similar.

"So, you guys keep that to yourselves, you understand?" Freddie said, a weak finger now pointing at them in front of a bandaged arm. "I mean it! You don't tell my mom, you don't tell your parents, *nobody!*"

The three of them exchanged bewildered looks and then all began to nod as they looked back to their battered friend.

"Good," Freddie said, letting his arm drop back to the bed. "Now, on to other business."

Jimmy almost laughed at this, the way Freddie took charge. Freddie was no wimp, in spite of his small size and sheepish features. But it struck him funny just the same to see the resolve in his friend's eyes.

It inspired him.

"What business?" Ryan asked.

Freddie pointed to the corner of the room to a pile of clothes and a bloody backpack.

"Bring me that backpack," he said. "I don't know how long we have until my parents get back, and they can't know about any of this. Thank Christ they haven't gone digging through it yet."

Jimmy turned, following Freddie's pointing finger, and crossed over to the backpack. He picked it up and carried it over to the bed. Freddie's hands were outstretched, reaching for it while he was still ten feet away.

When he had it in his hand, he fumbled with the zipper with his bandaged hands, cursing a few times as he struggled to gain purchase. Honey finally stepped over, placing a comforting hand on his arm as she did, and took the backpack.

"I got it, Fred," she said.

He nodded, his face flushing again.

"Thank you," he said. "But don't call me Fred."

She smiled at him and unzipped the pack. Jimmy leaned over and saw the photocopied pages inside and instinctively knew these were what Freddie was after. Honey removed them and handed them over to him.

Freddie took a few more moments, straightening the pages satisfactorily, then looked up at them.

"Before fuck-tooth and his used-douche friends suckerpunched me, I was doing some research at the Library."

He looked at them, a mischievous grin spreading across his swollen and bruised face.

"Research?" Jimmy asked, even though he thought he already knew what this was about.

Freddie nodded. "Yep. On that god-forsaken house in the woods."

"What did you find?" Ryan said, leaning in closer now, his face drawn together with intrigue.

Freddie patted a bandaged hand on top of the stacks of photo-copied pages, his grin widening ever more.

"I know why the space between worlds is thinner there," he said.

"How?" Jimmy asked, fully intrigued now.

"Because that house was built on a *really* fucked up foundation."

PART FIVE:

THE BROGEN

HOUSE

Wednesday, January 3, to
Wednesday, October 31, 1906

The following are selected excerpts from the journal of Johnathan Michael Brogan, penned in the year 1906, as well as a newspaper article from the Winnsborough Press from that time. Narrative has been inserted in appropriate places so as to help us fully grasp the happenings of that damned year as our friends Jimmy, Freddie, Ryan, and Honey understand them.

CHAPTER 33

January 3rd, 1906

Finished construction on the house near three weeks ago, now. Daddy and I worked every bit of a full year on the place. Mother, of course, was rather impatient with the process, but that was to be expected. Can't be helped when there is only two people working on such a structure. Well, I say two people. Can't really say that, I suppose. Richard helped where he could. He's only thirteen years this past November, but he did lend a hand, I reckon. Evangeline too, though her femininity often won the day over her labors. She turned sixteen past summer. She really is beginning to bloom into a young woman. Noticed old man Roscoe at the General Store take notice of her Friday last. Didn't much care for that if I'm being honest. He's a hundred years old if he's a day, and he's looking at my little sister. Worse, I fear he was looking at her bosom. Evangeline always dresses proper and modest, but there is an unmistakable swell in her chest these days. Mother says she needs to take out her dresses to accommodate her budding, but she hasn't yet.

Mother seems agitated more these days, too. I'd have figured her for the happiest woman in the world since the house is finished now. Made it to her specifications and everything. Even the location. Daddy argued and argued with her, saying we needed to clear a trail, but Mother would hear nothing of it. In the end, peace won the day against Daddy's protests. There'd have been none at all had Mother not had her way, and he thusly—and rather wisely, in my estimation—relented.

"Happy wife, happy life," Daddy told me when the decision was made. He said it was better to let a woman, especially my mother, have her way and live in peace than to win the battle only to lose the war.

There seemed a lot of wisdom in that sentiment. Much as I could tell, anyhow. Only, the peace hadn't come. At first, we reckoned it was because she was so antsy about finishing the house. Living in the tents all that time was frightful miserable, especially through the winter. We managed alright, but heavens it was tough. Nothing like back East in the fine home we'd had there. Plenty of room, heat, and comfort. Lands, do I miss the place.

But the one thing about life I can say—what I've learned in my meager nineteen years—is it always changes. Here we are in East Texas, in a nothing and nowhere town, building a home with no trail or reasonable way to it at all in these nothing woods. And why? I haven't a clue. I suspect Daddy doesn't really know either. The whole thing had been Mother's idea. She'd been downright insistent on it, I tell ya true. Why, I'd never seen her so indignant.

"I tell you, Cloris demands it!" she'd cried time and again until Daddy relented. None of us knew who Cloris was. Still don't, matter of fact. But Mother can be a little crazy from time to time. I hate to speak ill of Mother, and I mean no malice in it. But the fact is, it simply isn't unheard of in her family. Grandmother

Josephine went straight off the rails yonder ten years ago, and though he doesn't say so, I think Daddy fears the same may befall Mother. But her impatience aside, she seems alright. Except, that is, for when she speaks of Cloris.

It wasn't as though we didn't have the money to move. Daddy had made near a fortune in the coal business back East. He was set to retire early and enjoy the mountains for the remainder of his life, but it just wasn't to be, I'm quite afraid.

But hell, here I am rambling, telling a story. I guess I've a tendency to do that. This is a journal, a gift from Evangeline. A fine gift it is, too. I do so love my sister. Precious, she is. Well, I'll stop the rambling for now, perhaps I'll have more to say in the coming days. I aim to make an entry every day, but I'm wise enough to my own weaknesses. I know better. But I do plan to enter as often as I'm capable. Lots going on, so there should be plenty to report. It will be fun to come back to this one day and take a gander at all the funny things that were running through my head at this time. Off to bed for me. Early morning tomorrow, and we've got to fetch supplies from the General Store.

I've got my eye on Roscoe.

January 7th, 1906

Wheel broke on the carriage today. Daddy was frightful mad about it. Happened close to the house, so thank Providence for that. Coming in through the woods is what did it, with no proper trail to traverse. Daddy cursed bitterly as we repaired it, going on and on about the lack of trail to the house. How none of this would have happened if Mother hadn't been so insistent on our seclusion out here.

"That Cloris bitch can be goddamned!" he said at one point.

It frightened me so to hear him in such a state. Real anger in his eyes. I pray that anger is never directed at me.

Thing is, I never heard Daddy speak that way before. Just not in his vocabulary. I have, however, heard Mother speak in such vulgarities. Never in the open, mind you, but I've heard it. Why, I remember just two days ago coming upon my parents' room. Daddy was out working in the garden, getting it ready for season, and I was gathering the laundry through the house. Mother hasn't been keeping up with it like she should of late, so I thought I'd help out. But I heard her in her room talking to somebody. I peeked in, making sure Mother didn't know I was there, but she was all alone. Nevertheless, she was carrying on something fierce, speaking to the wall. Terrible sight after knowing what happened to Grandmother Josephine and all, but that wasn't the worst part, not by a sight. What she was saying was awful. I hesitate even in writing the words, for they seem like utter blasphemies, but I suppose I'll share it here with myself so as not to forget in the coming years. Strange, some things you just want to forget, but dare not.

She said, *"From cunt to cunt comes the runt, seed of Devil's dew! Witch to bitch and bitch to witch, we'll make a Brogan new!"*

I regret even copying the words down, but they simply chilled my spine like I've never felt before. I know her mind is feeble—hell, all minds in her side of the family seem to be thus—but it tears my heart out to see Mother in such a way. I wonder who she thinks she was talking to in there? Cloris, perhaps?

I would assume so, as that is who she goes on and on about, Cloris demands this, or Cloris is pleased with that. It's madness, I tell you. Pure madness.

Anyway, Daddy and I got the wheel fixed, and he insists that we are going to start working on a proper trail from the road to our house. Says Mother will just have to live with it and Cloris can be damned for all he cares.

I agree with him, but daren't say so to Mother. She and her Cloris seem quite inseparable.

By the way, I am now wholly convinced of old man Roscoe's ill intentions toward Evangeline. I've not told my parents, and I wouldn't dare sully Evangeline's view of the decency of people by telling her such a frightful thing. But I saw him. He was most certainly undressing her with his eyes. Part of me has a hard time blaming him. She is a beautiful girl, my sister. But another part of me feels pure, ungodly rage at the man when I see him doing it. I will no longer arrange for Roscoe to make deliveries to our home if I can avoid it. I will make the trek into town to acquire what we need and bring it back.

If his ocular inquiries persist, I may well pluck his eyes from their sockets. The Bible says if thine right eye causes thou to sin, to pluck it out and cast it from thyself.

Unfortunately for Roscoe, it seems total blindness may be his only salvation.

January 24th, 1906

Well, I've not kept my promise of keeping up with my journal, have I? Seems the days and even weeks get away from me the more I am required to work. There's much to do around here. The garden preparation, for one, as we prepare it for the season. But also we have to hunt game near every day. It's cool enough still that if we catch enough it will keep for several days before turning sour, but it seems harder and harder to find game just lately. Having to travel further and further from the house to find anything. Strange occurrence, I tell you true. Time was—before the house was built, this was—we'd see deer and rabbits and squirrels and every other kind of creature on God's Earth skittering about all over. Yet now, they seem scattered.

Between preparing the garden—*and my, what a massive and glorious garden it shall be!*—and the hunting, never mind cleaning the clothes since Mother is no longer handling her duties there, I've simply not got the time nor energy most days to make my entries here.

I've also been spending more time with Evangeline and Richard, as much as I can I reckon. They need that. Mother seems to have little to nothing to do with them right now, and Daddy is just as worn and tired as I, hence the younglings suffer. So, like in so many other ways, I'm attempting to step up. I help them with their studies, and we even play games when occasion approves. Just the other day, after finishing studies for the afternoon, we played a delightful game of hide and seek. Evangeline would have won too, had it not been for Mother's fit.

I was hiding in the closet at the end of the hall where our rooms are downstairs, and she'd already found Richard. I could hear their laughing, a heart-warming cackle in the cold of the house. Evangeline was coming down the hall to me when I heard Mother begin speaking. It seemed she was just in the other room, but this time I actually heard a voice speaking back to hers. I'd be a liar if I told you it wasn't disturbing, because it was. The voice had a moist quality, and seemed to burble at times, but it was a definite and distinct voice indeed. I could still here Evangeline and Richard laughing down the hallway. I'd hoped they would quiet down soon so as to make my eavesdropping all the easier, but they didn't.

I leaned my head against the wall of the closet...

CHAPTER 34

...and he listened hard. There was no mistaking his mother was having a conversation in the room on the other side of the closet wall.

A chilling conversation.

"There's still time, but you must *begin soon!"* said a voice that iced Johnathan's heart.

"I know!" his mother hissed. "It's their daddy who's the problem, he's—"

A fresh burst of laughter exploded down the hallway from Evangeline and Richard, as though some god of laughter had infected them with a lethal dosage of the killing giggles.

"Gods *damn* those children!" he heard his mother spit.

There were clunking sounds of shoes on wood and an ear-splitting shriek as the hinges wailed on the door to the room next to the closet.

The laughing stopped immediately.

"You'll close your cock-traps this instant, sir and ma'am, or I'll pull the tongues from your very throats! Is that understood?"

It was his mother's voice, but the words were so vulgar that Johnathan was once again convinced of her descent into madness. His heart sank both for her and for his siblings.

"Oh, Mother..." he whispered in the dark of the closet.

That was when he heard a gasp.

Not his mother's either. It was a voice seeming to come from the other side of the wall.

"Who's there?" the voice hissed.

Johnathan held his breath. Though it was quite cold in the house, he felt his brow begin to sprout forth blossoms of sweat.

What voice is this?

He had determined to come out of the closet and see for himself just who it was his mother was visiting with in that room when he heard the voice again.

"Susan!" it whispered harshly. *"Susan, come back!"*

Johnathan heard the clomping heels of his mother's shoes again, the reverse shriek of the hinges of the door, and the *thunk* and *click* as it found home and purchase in its frame.

"I'm here," he heard his mother say calmly.

"Someone is here!" the voice proclaimed. *"Someone is near!"*

"It's only the children," his mother said, again, quite calmly. "I've sent them on their way. They won't be bothering us anymore."

"I thought I heard another as you were chastising the brats!"

There was a pause. A rather long pause.

"Well, I'm sure it was nothing," his mother finally said. "The kids are back to the outside, Butch is working in the garden. Not terribly sure *where* Johnathan is, but he wasn't with the children."

"I heard him!" the hissing serpent of a voice said. *"This must be completely in confidence, between us alone!"*

263

Then a sound which Johnathan had to this point not even realized he was hearing suddenly stopped.

As he thought of the now-missing sound, his mind began to reconstruct it. It was like a low warbling sound, the sound one imagines a hummingbird's wings might make if amplified.

But it was gone now.

More clumping and clonking of shoes on wooden floors. Another shrieking door. More steps.

They stopped.

The steps stopped right outside the door to the closet.

Johnathan was holding his breath now. The crop of sweat which had come to his brow out of season began to migrate down to his eyes. The last thing he wanted was his for his mother to find him in there and to know he'd been eavesdropping on her private conversation with...well, with *someone*.

The silence seemed to go on for an eternity as he waited for something to happen. Waited for the door to fly open and reveal him huddled in the corner of the closet, eyes wide and mouth agape. Perhaps his bladder would release then, and he would create a large crescent of dark moisture in his crotch.

He waited for all of this to happen, finally remembering to take a few shallow, quiet breaths.

Then the clumping and clonking started up again, and it was heading down the hallway away from him. He waited for a full two minutes to make sure she was gone, checking periodically through the keyhole to assure himself she wasn't coming back.

He never did hear his mother's visitor leave.

Finally, after a truncated eon, he slipped out of the closet. He peaked into the room his mother had been conversing in through the open door.

No one there. No trace, no sign, no nothing. Just a big, empty room.

Move it, Johnathan!

Right.

He scampered down the hallway and out of the house, shivering and sweating all at once.

CHAPTER 35

February 16th, 1906

Mother is getting worse. It weighs on my heart to see her so, but it cannot be denied. More and more I hear her speaking to that no-one friend of hers.

Cloris.

Seems Cloris is more than just a friend to her. I fear Mother believes her to be some sort of god, or the messenger of some god.

We've never been a terribly religious family. Back East, Daddy had come up in the Roman Church, but upon reaching manhood he left the tradition and never returned. Mother has never spoken of a faith in all the years of my living, at least never in my presence. And I do believe she would have. Mother loves to speak to me of things which are of great import to her. Well, at least she used to. Of late, she's done little talking to anyone but her dear Cloris.

Just who is Cloris, anyway, I wonder? I've not dared to ask her right out, though I suppose I should. Daddy seems to take no interest in this. Daddy spends his days hunting and gathering firewood and preparing the garden. I've no idea what else could be done to prepare the garden at this point, yet he can certainly make a day of it.

We never made a trail to the house, either, as Daddy had sworn we would. It's of little mind to me, but he'd been so adamant about it that it simply awes me that he has reneged so quickly. I recall he'd gone in to speak to Mother about the issue, and he'd interrupted one of her palavers with the phantom Cloris. Daddy ignores this part of Mother's madness outright in all cases, and so he did that day. He went right in to tell her of his intentions and to demand that she get on board with the idea.

That's when the screaming had started.

Several minutes of this went on, all the while my terror maturing into something I dare not wish to ever revisit. Then the door flew open and Daddy came clomping out in quite a state. His cheeks were so red I thought we might use them as embers to start a fire. His beard could not fully conceal the quivering of his lips.

It will be interesting to see if Daddy tries again. I suspect he shan't, but you never really know with him.

Funny thing, if I may change the subject—and of course I may, this is, after all, my journal.

Went to town two days ago to the General Store to fetch supplies. There was a preacher man there, name of Chambris Hart. The good reverend Hart began to speak of a revival he'd soon be leading. Invited my family, he did. Mother was with me when this happened, and she actually spat at the man's feet. Not quite on them, mind you, but she didn't miss by much, I tell ya true. Anyhow, after spitting her distaste she declared in wide-eyed fury, "May Cloris shit in your mouth that your lips can spread the truth!".

I tell you, I've never seen her in such a state. The old degenerate Roscoe's eyes were wide as saucers. The preacher didn't say another word after that. Folks around here are very religious, and more than mere frowning occurs when you're not in lock-step with their brand of worship.

It all keeps coming back to that goddamned Cloris. I suppose it really isn't all that funny after all.

February 23rd, 1906

Long day. Long several days.

Game, it seems, is harder and harder to come by as of late, and Mother's madness seems to be taking a turn for the worst. It has become my sole responsibility to teach Richard and Evangeline their studies and to launder the clothes.

Speaking of laundry, I noticed something odd when scrubbing Mother's things across the board. Seems a brown stain of some sort simply will not come fully out of her sleeve. I tried like hell, but I just couldn't get it. Not fully. Mother likely could have when in her right mind, but heavens, she can do little but have private meetings with her Cloris anymore. I mean to find out more about this. I mean to ask Mother just who this Cloris is. And perhaps it will help jar her back to some realm of sanity.

Or perhaps not. But that damned stain. Frustrating as hell, I tell you.

Oh, Daddy said we were going to make the trail after all. I'm not to tell Mother.

The Damned Place

March 1st, 1906

I've never been more afraid.

March 13th, 1906

Started the trail this morning with Daddy. Mother knows nothing of it. After I confronted her about Cloris, I've spoken next to nothing to her since. Such madness! Such horror!

I just flipped back a page and realized I didn't finish my last entry, and it was on the very matter weighing on my mind now. I suppose it was with good reason. Writing it down will force me to relive it, and that is the very last thing I desire to do. But I suppose I must. A record should be kept in the event we ever are able to get her help. As of now, that will not happen. But if she becomes as weak in body as she is in mind, perhaps then we may be able to get her to a doctor. Not that Daddy seems to have any interest in this whatever, but I do, and so do the children.

Mother's madness is indeed real, but so—as I have learned with great horror—is Cloris. I'd not believe it myself had I not witnessed it, but I did. I walked right in there, where Mother was, heard her speaking to her, or it, or...I don't rightly know just what to call what I was shown. I do recall hearing that strange sound. A sort of wavering, humming sound.

But I digress. I walked in and demanded of Mother to tell me who this Cloris was. It was my intention to wrench her back to sanity, when she realized she could not show me what she was claiming. And Mother did protest. At least at first.

"You mustn't meddle, child!" she bellowed at me.

But I was having none of it, and after stamping my foot and declaring that I'd not move from the spot until answers were given, she relented.

And oh, God, how I wish she never had.

As she resigned to show me, she turned to the wall she'd been speaking with and I saw...

CHAPTER 36

...a strange shimmering film over the wallpaper.

It was unlike anything he'd seen before. It was wholly surreal. At one point on the wall, the pattern of the wallpaper began to ripple, like water in a pond, and then the further in he looked, it became clearer and clearer, as though he were looking through glass. The shimmer never went fully, but instead danced over the image his mind was trying desperately to process and comprehend.

Awe turned to shock as he realized that what he was seeing in the wall seemed to be a mirror image of the very room he was standing in. Well, not *exactly* a mirror image, per say. The *room* was exactly the same. Its contents, however, were not.

He didn't see himself or his mother in this reflection. Nor did he see the wood-framed bed and vanity. There *was* a bed, and indeed even a vanity and bureau, but they weren't those contained in the room in which he stood. They were similar, but the colors were different. Shapes too. Where the mirror on the vanity in the room on this side of the wall had an oval shape, the one in the reflection—only not a reflection at all—was perfectly round. The bed in the room he occupied was small, made for a single person, but the one in the image before him was quite large and had tall posts on all its corners, as well as a canopy which sagged over the middle.

Johnathan's mouth hung agape.

"Wh-what is this, Mother?" said Johnathan after several moments of stupefied astonishment.

But his mother didn't answer him. Instead, she called a name. A name all too familiar to Johnathan's ears. One he associated with her madness and failing grasp on reality.

A name he came to associate with terror.

"Cloris," his mother said.

Then, as beckoned, the creature stepped into view.

And *creature* was the only thing one might call it. There were elements to the thing before him that he recognized. Elements that, on their own, the mind could register without issue or hesitation. There would be no problem processing the images coming into his ocular receptacles had they been on their own. Only they weren't. The elements were all put together in an amalgam of something that, for a few horrifying moments, his brain simply refused to accept. As though there were a maid in his mind, using a massive broom to shew the images from his brain because they simply could not be real.

But the power of sight, in the end, won the day. And Johnathan Michael Brogan thought he was losing his mind.

What he saw was a face that was very similar to that of normal people, yet radically different all the same. It was covered in fine, silky fur which seemed to whip faintly as if it were being tousled by some phantom breeze. The nose that the face possessed was truncated and turned up. It reminded him of a cross between a rabbit's nose and that of a pig. The hands which hung from the creature's sides were lined in the same fine fur he'd seen on the face, and long, feline-like claws extended from them.

Then, to his horror—his mind was still processing the images quite slowly—he saw there were *four* arms.

The tailored clothes the creature wore looked proper enough. It was a full-bodied dress, dark, with floral patterns which seemed to coil about the thing's body. It was a fitted dress, and it clasped tightly around the neck and extended to the ankles and all four elbows, where the sleeves stopped.

Then he saw the eyes.

They were cat's eyes. Vertical pupils sliced down through the center like vicious cuts. They were utterly out of place here on this thing, the whole of the parts an abomination. Yet, the eyes were beautiful at the same time. They were outlined in greens and golds, melded together in rapturous harmony. He'd never seen anything so amazing in all his life.

Nor anything so horrifying.

He began to scream, his mouth opening on its hinges and his tongue moving to the rear of his oral cavity. A groan—much too high-pitched for a lad of his age—began to rise out of him like an escaping prisoner.

His mother snatched his collar and slapped him across the face, once with the palm of her hand then again with the back of it.

It silenced him.

He stared into his mother's mad, hazel eyes. And though he'd just seen the creature who was called Cloris, he knew his mother *was* mad. She wore a

273

devious grin over her quivering chin, a look which spoke of urgency and discretion.

"Shut your mouth, Johnathan!" she hissed at him.

He did.

Then he looked back to the shimmering wall and took a second try at comprehending what he was seeing. The creature stood there, all four hands clasped, one pair above the other, the head cocked up in indignant pride.

"What is this, Mother?" he asked through a croaked and cracking voice. He'd been certain his pubescent age had passed, but his voice was betraying him now as it had in the awkward years when it had first begun to change.

His mother looked back to the thing for a moment, and he could see the edges of a smile on the corners of his mother's mouth as she did. Then she looked back at him and took a deep breath, all the frustration leaving her at once.

"This is Cloris, Johnathan," she said evenly. "And she is trying to bring us the good news of the Glutton."

The Glutton? he thought as his brain refused his vocal chords their normal operation.

"That's right," the creature said.

He recognized the voice. It was the same one he had heard call his mother's name that day he'd been hiding in the closet while playing with the children. It was quite normal. Well, *could* have been normal, were it to have come from a human being, that was. Johnathan could hardly accept anything coming from this thing's mouth to be *normal*, no matter how regular it might sound.

He managed to rummage around in his throat for a moment and found his voice again.

"Wh-what," he began and had to swallow hard. It was like swallowing dry sand. All the moisture in his mouth had evaporated along with his grasp on reality as he'd known it.

"What is the Glutton?" he finally managed in a wavering voice.

The warbling, shimmering sound came to the forefront of his mind again, and he was able to place it as the sound of the, the...well, he didn't know just what the Christ it was he was looking through. A door, maybe? Call it what you will, he was referring to the shimmering opening in the wall which was showing him Cloris.

The creature smiled. His mother smiled. He felt his bowels loosen.

"The Glutton," the creature named Cloris began, "is the eternal balancer of the worlds."

"Worlds?" he muttered, not quite under his breath.

Cloris nodded.

"Yes. He is ageless. He has always been. He has no creation. Much like your God in your world. Even in mine, for that matter. God is not a concept unique to your world, in case you thought He may be. All worlds are held to the same basic order. The same basic creator, if you will. But God also is quite willing to allow, shall we say, *too much*. The Glutton is the balance. We don't know his name, as he will not tell us, but that is what I have dubbed him."

Johnathan's mind was reeling, swimming through massive swells of impending, threatening madness.

"I-I don't understand," he mumbled, panic threatening to overwhelm him. "Mother, I thought you had no place for religion!"

His mother shook her head.

"I've no place for *God*," she spat bitterly. "But the great Glutton, aye, he is one whom I could serve!"

He looked from his mother to Cloris.

"Why us?" he said. "Why here?"

Cloris only smiled for several moments, but finally replied.

"Because my world is almost balanced," she said, her clawed hands unfolding and dropping to her sides. "And the Glutton must move on. He's not of creation, so he requires certain...*diets,* if you will, to move on to the next world. A place where the fabric of the worlds is thinner. A place where he may be served meals so that he may grow *into* your creation. To become incarnate on your side. He can do little more than peek into your world without the food necessary to enter. And the food *must* come from your world."

Everything he was hearing was absolute madness.

"What do you mean thin?" he asked in a bark.

"The fabric is already thin here," she said. "It was thin enough in your previous home to communicate. To inform Susan—your precious mother—of where to go. It's thinner here, but still not enough. We must tear down the walls between our worlds to bring forth the birth of The Great Glutton into yours!"

Now his mother spoke.

"Don't you see, Johnathan?" she said with wild fascination. "We've been chosen to balance the world! And I've been promised a child! A *new* Brogan, the one who will serve the Glutton at his right hand!"

Johnathan could take no more. He clutched the hair at either side of his head, and his lips peeled back over his teeth.

"This is madness, Mother!" he screamed. "You must see this! We've no idea what this, this *thing* is trying to do to us! Think of Daddy! Think of your children! Of me, Evangeline, Richard!"

With this last part, he grabbed his mother by the shoulders and shook her.

"Don't you see that, Mother?" he pleaded.

But he could see in her eyes that she did not. What she saw was glory. Prestige. A place at the table of unimaginable power.

And a new child.

Cloris was laughing now. A mean, spiteful chortle rumbling from her throat. Her laughing voice sounded not at all like the normalcy of her speaking voice. It sounded wet and gravely. Depraved.

It sounded like evil.

"From cunt to cunt comes the runt!" his mother said, joining Cloris in her maniacal laughter.

"Seed of Devil's dew!" Cloris chimed in. *"From witch to bitch and bitch to witch!"*

"We'll make a Brogan new!" his mother finished with a mad howl of laughter, her eyes wide and insane, her hair askew in all directions.

They were both soaked in the horrific laughter. Cloris's mouth was wide now, and Johnathan retreated a few steps as he saw sharp lines of fangs protruding from black gums, opening and closing with the riotous laughter of pure malice.

He stumbled back further, his hands grasping the sides of his head once more, desperately trying to block out the sounds of their voices and their laughter.

They laughed all the louder.

"Stop it!" he cried, tears now slipping from his eyes. *"Stop it! This is madness!"*

But they didn't stop. Instead, they began the chant again, in unison this time.

"From cunt to cunt comes the runt, seed of Devil's dew! From witch to bitch and bitch to witch, we'll make a Brogan new!"

It was all too much for him. He turned and ran from the room, sobbing and groaning with horror and white-hot fear as he shambled down the hall and out the front door where he fell to his knees and put his face on the leafed earth. He could still hear them in the house, laughing and chanting their psychotic mantra.

Johnathan screamed.

CHAPTER 37

March 24th, 1906

I believe Mother has discovered that Daddy and I are building the trail. She seems more agitated than normal and I dare not approach her again. Not after seeing Cloris and hearing of their mad plan.

I made one attempt to tell Daddy about what I know, but I couldn't bring myself to do it. What would Daddy think? He'd think me mad is what he would think. As mad as Mother. I couldn't do it. He speaks to no-one but me now, and then only when we are working. The children have said he's not spoken to them in many weeks now. This saddens my heart. They need their father and I am but a poor substitute for such a role. But Daddy seems so detached these days. I'm not sure why. Sometimes I think perhaps it is because of his great sadness at the loss of the woman he once knew—my mother—who now has little resemblance to what he married.

Ah, Mother. She has, in fact, spoken to the children, but there is no nurture in her voice when she does. She hasn't referred to them by name, only, only...well, such horrible names. Richard is now 'cock-licker' and Evangeline is 'little whore'. I've never raised my hand to a woman, and don't mean to, but I damn near struck Mother when she spoke to Evangeline that way. Such hate in her! Evangeline is a fine young woman, and she deserves Mother's respect and love.

But those days are over now, I presume. No surprise there. Normalcy has transformed into this strange nightmare now, and when I think of times past, back East, when things were good and we were happy, it's as though I'm looking at the memories of someone else.

I find myself thinking of Cloris and Mother often, despite the terror I felt that day in the bedroom. They still palaver. I hear them sometimes, when Daddy and the children are out working or playing. But I dare not go back in there. My sanity won't stand it.

Perhaps I've a deficient spine, and if so, so be it. Cloris is real. I must accept that. But the Glutton? Certainly, that is a fiction. It simply must be.

Right?

April 1st, 1906
Daddy is dead.

April 10th, 1906
I've attempted to make record of my pain and what happened several times these past days. How long has it been? A week? Longer?

I see it has been a full ten days after checking back to my last entry. It seems like it has been much longer than that, yet my sorrow is as fresh as if it had happened only this morning.

Something frightfully awful happened to Daddy. I know precisely what, as well, and at whose hand. I saw it. But what am I to do? I feel so trapped and alone, and the children are positively heartbroken. I'm doing my best to handle things as we move forward. Mother is of no help whatever. She seems positively pleased about the matter, point in fact. And why not? With what I know of the matter, it seems fitting she would, the mad bitch!

I shall attempt to make record of the event as soon as I am able, yet I am still weeping even as I write this, and I feel I must stop. I've not the fortitude to write more now. I am grieving so.

April 13th, 1906

I've planned this whole day to make record of Daddy's final day, but feel I must record something more peculiar now while it is fresh on my mind and before sanity and reason can fully dismiss it from my memory.

I found Richard this morning crying by the firewood stack. He was in an awful state, sitting on his bum, hugging his knees to his chest and rocking back and forth. I made several attempts to soothe him, to get him to speak to me, but it was as if I weren't there. His eyes never registered my presence. It seemed as though he were looking right through me, I tell ya true!

His face was red with tears and he had begun to shake and cough with the strain of his grief. I assumed outright that he must be grieving Daddy, just as I and Evangeline have done much of these past weeks. I tried to speak of that to him. To help him remember the good times with Daddy and even tried to coax him to go inside and lie down. No firewood was being cut anyhow, and since Spring has fully bloomed, we need far less of it to boot.

But nothing worked. Nothing I said calmed him in the slightest. He just kept right on sobbing and rocking and weeping.

After a time, I finally scooped him up in my arms and carried him to the house. He stunk of salt and...something else. The salt I attribute to his tears, as his face was just on my shoulder, but the other, well, I simply could not place it. It was coming from his shirt and pants. Well, not particularly from them, but beneath them. It was a strange scent, one with which I am not familiar. It was similar to body odor, like what I've smelled under my own arms after a hard and sweaty day of work, but it lacked the stench. It was a sort of musk. Perhaps that is the right word, though I am unsure. Whatever this scent was, this musk, it was almost...sweet.

Whatever it was that I smelled, Richard was in no state to explain it. I took him to his bed and tucked him in. At this point, he had begun to mutter something, but it was so quiet I could not place what it was he was saying. I leaned closer and asked him what he had said, but he kept on shivering and crying and staring at the wall, repeating it over and over again. I finally caught it.

"The snakes," he said. "The snakes will open the door, and then the runt will crawl the floor."

He said this over and over again in a hushed and desperate voice. None of it made sense to me, but at the harking of the word 'runt', my breath froze. It reminded me of Mother and Cloris and that awful, godless chant they sing together during their black palavers. The mantra was different, but it shared the recurrence of that one word. A word which has come to carry fear upon its utterance as often as I hear it repeated.

The shakes took Richard completely then and I rushed to heat up the bath for him. I made a fire and began heating pails of water, and once I got the tub full I took him in. I stripped his clothes from him as he continued to stand there, staring blankly at nothing and everything all at once. He didn't fight me. Didn't struggle.

Then that musky scent came back.

It was much stronger now, and I confirmed that it was coming from his lap. His genitals were filthy, with some sort of crust I could not identify upon them. It was mostly white, and flaked off as I pulled his skivvies free. I attributed it to sweat at first, though, I do not believe it to be that.

And that smell. It was....*sweet*.

I got Richard into the bath and scrubbed him thoroughly. He lay there, still seemingly unaware of my presence, the whole time. His shivers did finally abate, however, and for that I was thankful.

I toweled him off and dressed him and put him back to bed. As I finished tucking him in and went to leave, he grabbed my hand with a firmness I was hereunto unaware he possessed.

Then he spoke that same mantra to me, looking directly into my eyes, seeing me for the first time since finding him by the firewood pile.

"The snakes will open the door, and then the runt will crawl the floor!"

With that, he released my arm and fell back into his bed and seemed to instantly fall into a deep sleep.

My mind reeled as I left him, and I went to find Mother. And oh, God...I found her.

She was lying in her bed, nude as the day she was born. Her eyes were closed and, for a moment, I was thankful she'd not witnessed me seeing her in such undress. I turned at once to leave, but heard her call out that same sentence Richard had spoken to me. Then she led into her and Cloris's mantra, sending chills down my spine.

"The snakes will open the door, and then the runt will crawl the floor! From cunt to cunt comes the runt, seed of Devil's dew! From witch to bitch and bitch to witch, we'll make a Brogan new!"

I turned back, all at once forgetting of her nudity and shame, and saw her eyes, mad as a blind bat's, staring into mine. She was laughing so that my whole body burst forth with goose-flesh and I turned to run from the room.

I threw the door open to run and felt a scream rising within me that I struggled to contain. But I noticed something else as I fled. Something I almost missed. *Would* have missed if not for its peculiarness and it being at the forefront of my mind before I entered Mother's room.

That odd, sweet smell was on Mother.

The Damned Place

April 17th, 1906

Things are falling apart here. Richard seems worse every day, and Evangeline is becoming distant. Mother has lost all sense of reality, and her palavers with Cloris are becoming more frequent and more open. Richard continually vanishes for a time—Mother as well at these times, now that I think of it—and when I do find him, he is in that same catatonic state and reeking of that same strange smell. I must admit, I rather like the smell. I've no reason as to why, but it just...does something to me. It is rather arresting, not to put too mild a point on it.

I've abandoned the trail. Daddy and I made little progress before he met his end, and I've no wish to join him. Not in the way he went.

Before I go further, I must tell of this.

I went to his grave earlier today, and because of what I found, I mustn't wait another moment to tell of his demise. I dug his grave myself, and I'm quite sure that I put him plenty deep to avoid disturbance from the wildlife. But something had dug him up. The grave was open and destroyed. Desecrated! I don't know what could have taken him, but I've my suspicions.

My mad mother Susan. Perhaps in cahoots with that damned Cloris.

But this is of little import at this stage. I will tell of what I found the day Daddy died.

I was in my room, preparing to enter into this very journal, when I heard commotion by the wood pile. Daddy made the point of chopping wood daily, so that we had plenty at all times for cooking and the like, but also to be prepared for this fall and winter. He'd vowed to me after our winters in the tents building this monstrosity of a home that we'd never go cold in the night again if he could help it.

But the commotion rose and I...

CHAPTER 38

...went to his window and looked out.

He could see nothing from this vantage, save the edge of the wood pile. But still he could hear something. Some sort of struggle.

Johnathan turned from his window and rushed down the hall to the foyer and out into the open. The day was fading, and pink and purple hues danced and twirled through the wooded forest all around him as he descended the steps and stopped. He took a moment to look and to listen.

Quiet.

Then there was a strange sound. Like a crunch and a mumbled *'oomph'*. Then there was a thumping sound as something collapsed onto the leaved floor of the woods.

Johnathan took to running immediately around the side of the house. He was faintly aware of a strange scent in the air. It was metallic and acrid, and beneath it there was another smell beginning to bud. This one was a stench and had his mind not been racing, he would have identified it at once for what it was.

But he hadn't.

As he rounded the corner in a full sprint, his mind and body locked all at once. His feet skidded over leaves and loose dirt, and his arms flailed out as he struggled to maintain balance. As his eyes took in the information and began trying to feed it to his brain for processing, all the impulses telling his knees to stand firm ceased. He buckled and fell to the ground, his mouth open in a silent, moaning prelude to a scream.

His daddy was there, on his knees, looking up at a creature which Johnathan did not at first recognize. The creature before him stood on two legs and wore a dress that went from throat to ankles, and he noticed the sleeves reached down to meet all four elbows.

All *four* elbows.

Johnathan began to tremble. Random pulses of electricity fired out from his brain in spurts and stops, desperately trying to process and reject the images before him all at once.

The thing was covered in a fine, silky fur. The fur was white for the most part, but there were speckles of scarlet and crimson spattered all about in a random pattern on the thing's face and dress.

Then his mind finally relented and he saw the axe buried in his daddy's face.

Blood was spewing out in jets and spurts, sailing out of his father's face in unpredictable volumes and angles. His father was convulsing now, shaking all over, his hands flapping like the wings of a dying sparrow from limp wrists.

Then Cloris twisted the axe first left, then right. There were horrific sounds of cracking, shattering bone, of cartilage and sinew ripping and tearing and popping. More blood sprayed and her horrible, fur-covered face became awash in the life-liquid of his dying daddy.

Then she put her foot—Johnathan could now see it was not a foot at all, but a hoof—on his daddy's chest and wrenched the axe free as she pushed him back. His father fell back onto the ground and began to roll and flop and convulse. A brief—and all too comic—image of a fish pulled from its liquid paradise and thrown onto a sand-encrusted bank flashed into his mind.

Then Cloris seemed to notice him for the first time.

She turned to him then, her blood-slimed, fur-covered face finding his, the cat-eyes blazing at him and the rabbit/pig nose flexing up and down a thousand times a second. A smile tore through the gore on her face as her horrible eyes met his. Her teeth were sharp fangs, and all at once Johnathan's mind began to shatter.

That was when he found his voice.

The scream which erupted from him was a mixture of terror, grief, and madness. What he was seeing defied all reason, all logic. Nothing before him could possibly be real, not even in the imagination of the most imaginative story-teller, yet here it was. His mind was better than most, yet it was still struggling to accept the information it had just received. The mind is a strange thing, and often it works based on context. It understands things based on context and knowledge and reason. But all of that was lacking here. From the murder, the setting, the creature herself.

None of it had any real context in his mind, and thus his mind was breaking apart, desperately searching for something, *anything*, that it could use to make sense of what his traitorous eyes were telling it was happening.

Cloris turned to him, the axe swinging down by her side, dripping blood and brain and an assortment of other gore onto the ground in thick, audible clumps.

"There must be absolute seclusion," she said to him, even as his scream was only starting to abate. *"Your mother and I are agents of the Glutton, and he demands SECLUSION!"*

There was no more screaming after that.

Johnathan's voice caught in his throat and he found his legs were willing to work once again. He stumbled to his feet, swaying this way and that, his arms reaching out at the air for balance.

Cloris took a few steps towards him, her blazing eyes never leaving his, those horrible, vertical slits boring into him, *through* him, straight into his soul.

"This is the warning, elder Brogan," she began. *"If you aim to save the rest of your family, you'll stay out of our way. Out of the way of The Great and Mighty Glutton!"*

She began to laugh. It was a rather terrible sound, wet and bubbly, and it seemed to have the slightest hint of an animal howl lurking just beneath its surface.

"Perhaps he'll let you live when he brings his judgement into your world, but you must steer clear! And you must maintain seclusion! The people in this world will stop at nothing to keep their precious way of life! Just as those in my world did! But I— yes, I alone—was wise enough to see the inevitability of the Glutton's coming, and rather than be slain with the rest, he chose me—and my gift, to be sure—to usher in his coming!"

Johnathan, mouth and lips trembling with exhausting rapidity, turned and ran. He'd made no more than ten feet when he rounded the corner and saw his mother, standing there with her now familiar insane smile.

He nearly ran into her, but instinctively made to dodge around her at the last moment, only to succeed in sprawling out on the ground.

Her eyes never left his. Those hollow, blank, *mad* eyes.

"Prepare ye the way of the Glutton, my dear son!" she spat in an odd and curious movement of her mouth that was void of normal speech pattern. Her jaw simply moved down and up, down and up, not allowing for any of the fine nuances which accompanied normal speech in any way. Spittle flew from her mouth as she said this again and again.

"Prepare ye the way of the Glutton, my dear son! Prepare ye the way of the Glutton!"

Johnathan scrambled to his feet and ran for the house. He neared the stairs and thought better of it all at once. He turned and headed for the woods.

And he ran and ran and ran.

He ran through patches of Dogwood and brush and around pines and oaks. Finally, his feet slipped on leaves and he tumbled to the ground. Rather than get to his feet and keep moving, he simply buried his face in the earth and wept. He wept long and hard, giant heaves and groans escaping him as he lay there. He was trembling all over. Snot and tears were leaking from him like a broken dam, and on more than one occasion he inhaled dirt and broken particles of leaves into his mouth as he carried on.

But he noticed none of this. His mind was breaking. His soul was already broken.

And his will was shattered.

CHAPTER 39

Later, he stumbled back to the house. He'd lain there, on the floor of the woods—these foreign, horrible woods, so far from his home back East—and wept like Jesus.

Once, he'd picked up his head and peered back towards the house and seen Cloris, walking on all six of her appendages like a nightmare centipede, striding next to his mother as they reentered the house. As they entered the hall and drifted from his sight, he saw the thing rise up on its hind legs, its hooves clopping distantly.

Richard—though still distant, he was strangely not catatonic on this day—and Evangeline were out in the woods playing somewhere, and he'd had the gnawing thought that he could not allow them to see their daddy that way when they returned.

He'd gotten himself up, dusted off, and made his way back. There was no fear in him now, not for himself, anyway. But he did fear the fate of his siblings. They were precious in his sight, as though they were his own offspring, and he meant to do right by them. He would not allow them to find their daddy murdered and splattered on the forest floor, but he would break the news to them in his own way. The sun was falling fast now, and they would be back soon, so time was of the essence.

He moved quickly and fetched a shovel from the shed attached to the house, then picked up his gored father and carried him into the woods in a direction he knew his siblings would not return.

Then he set about the business of burying his father.

As he did so, he thought about what they would do now. What would they tell the townsfolk? Should he go to the Sherriff and tell him of the murder?

Tell him what?

That was precisely the problem. What exactly *could* he tell the Sherriff? It wasn't as though any of this were logical. None of it. So, what would they believe? The Brogan family were already the outcasts of the community, whispers of witchcraft and devil worship already hung over their heads like dark clouds when they went into town for supplies. They weren't from here. They weren't part of the local community. They kept to themselves. They didn't partake in Reverend Chambris Hart's brand of religion.

So what would they think?

He ignored these thoughts as he buried his father.

It took him some time to get the job done, but he dug the grave deep, making sure no animals would be able to come by and take him from his grave.

He patted the grave with the shovel to seal it with great deference and took a step back. He stared at the grave, thinking he should say something, *anything*, over his father. But nothing came to mind.

In the end, he wept once more. It was quieter this time and, when he'd shed his last tear—the last one he thought he had within him—he turned and made his way back to the house.

As he approached, he saw his siblings coming toward the house. They were skipping and laughing, oblivious to the horrors that had occurred here, and the horrors that seemed to live within their home. They were so happy. And Richard was in such better spirits than Johnathan had seen him for some time. He knew what he would tell them would destroy this happiness, and feared Richard may return to that awful state he'd been in so often of late. But it didn't matter. It had to be done. Only, he couldn't tell them what really happened. Not only would they never believe it, it may cause their own sanity to fail. With his own slipping away and their mother's already long gone, he could not risk that.

They saw him, and turned to him, smiling. Their smiles began to fade when they saw how filthy and sad he was. Eventually, they stopped coming towards him, so he went to them, fighting back fresh tears.

Johnathan dropped the shovel and lied to his siblings.

CHAPTER 40

May 23rd, 1906

I've not entered for some time, more than a month, I've noticed. This is because I simply cannot find the energy to do so most days. Oh, I started to on multiple occasions, but even as I brought my pencil to the paper, I simply could do nothing. I could not write a single paragraph. A single sentence.

A single word.

Things have devolved further. Summer is preparing to set in, and the air is growing hotter. Daddy's grave being emptied drove me to near madness for a time, but I believe I've my wits about me once again. Richard is becoming much like a, well, I don't rightly have the words to describe it. He stares at the walls mostly. He drools too. He had seemed to be coming back to his old self until the day Daddy was murdered, but now he's fully regressed. Much of his time is with Mother, and though it chills me to leave him with her, I've too much work to do to watch him all day. And speaking of Richard, I have to do everything for him now. He cannot bathe himself or even maintain continence. He's been reduced to wearing diapers again, and I have to wash them daily just to keep him sanitary. Evangeline has entered a deep depression. I tried to tell her of all that I knew some weeks back, but she refused to hear of it. Oh, the hurt on her face! It is more than I could bear.

Mother has brought Cloris into the house several times now, always when Evangeline is out. Richard is near catatonic at all times now, and Mother seems to have no mind whatever to care what I see. So long as I stay out of her way! She and her goddamned Cloris! They and their goddamned Glutton!

I've still seen no evidence of this Glutton they speak of, but I fear more and more that there may be something to it. The only sense I can make of Daddy's grave having been emptied is that Mother—or she and Cloris, more likely—must have dug him up in the night. My work to maintain the garden, to find game, and take care of Richard exhausts me so, that I fall into the deepest of sleeps in the nights, and I fear the Apocalypse itself would not wake me.

Evangeline refuses to have any part of caring for Richard. She doesn't understand what happened with Daddy, and she doesn't comprehend what is happening with Mother. And I cannot blame her, can I? I told her nothing but fiction in regards to Daddy's death. That he'd had an accident and fallen on his axe.

I suspect she doesn't believe me.

I also have been maintaining all the trips to town for supplies and the General Store. Roscoe and others I've encountered are full of questions about Daddy, but I've nothing I can tell them. What would I say? Should they hear it they would certainly call in the Sherriff and have us all put away in the asylum. And rightly so, I often muse.

Yet, there are questions looming over our family. Mother is completely mad with Cloris and her Glutton, but my affection for Evangeline and Richard is as steadfast as it ever was. No matter if Evangeline is approaching the outskirts of hate for me, and Richard has been reduced to the state of a toddler.

And to Richard...I suspect something terrible is going on with him. I cannot be present every hour, much less every second, and thus cannot be sure of his afflictions. But that musky smell is on him daily, and I have found Mother more than once in her state of shame and nudity, awash in the same scent.

If only I knew more of the world and its ways, perhaps I could understand what was happening! I am a man now, but I am not accustomed to the ways of men. I am but a boy trying to fulfill the role of a man, and I no longer have Daddy to teach me.

Mother rants on and on about making her Brogan new. A *new* Brogan? Is that what she means? A new child? But how will she accomplish this without Daddy? I admit my naiveté in the matters. Daddy never spoke of it with me, and neither did Mother. I was too young to remember the birth of my sister, but I do recall that of my brother. Yet, while I understand the basics of the mechanics of making a child, it seems impossible to do so without a husband. At least in the proper sense.

Nevertheless, I strive on. I tend the garden. I fetch game for dinner. I cook. I clean. I acquire goods from town. I do my best to fend off the suspicions of the townsfolk and their dreadful Reverend Hart. My family has been shattered, and though I see most of the pieces, I've no idea how to mend them together again. I feel much too young to bear this weight on my shoulders, but what else am I to do? It isn't as if I can simply lie down and let my siblings starve! Heavens, no. I must continue and do my very best to make sure to salvage as much of their childhood as I can. If not for my efforts, they would be as mad as Mother.

And of course, Richard may well be so. I fear going to anyone in the town to seek help. There is so much talk of witchcraft and satanic practice over my family, the gossiping, hypocritical horde of fools! They would leap at the opportunity to destroy us, I fear.

No, help is not a luxury I have at my disposal. All I have is myself, and I fear it is not enough.

Yet, I will carry on. I pray I am able, anyway.

July 7th, 1906

I have created an outright fiction. It was not an intended thing, merely something which sprang up in the heat of a moment.

What happened was this:

I was in town, there to fetch goods from the General Store and trade with some of our vegetables—which are coming in quite good now, I might add. I'd taken Evangeline with me. Richard is still far too feeble of body and mind to take on such ventures, but he seems to have improved a great deal all the same. He still isn't speaking much, mostly soft mutterings and rambles, but his spirits are up and I've even caught him smiling on more than one occasion. Because of these improvements, I elected to allow him to stay home with Mother while Evangeline and I made the trek into town for bartering. Evangeline has been in low spirits since Daddy's passing, but as with Richard, she has been improving as of late, and I thought a day out of the house—out of those damnable woods—would be good for her soul.

So off we went.

We first spent some time at the General Store, I having to keep sharp, keen eyes on Roscoe, whose own drifting eyes still dare to scour my sweet sister with sinister intent. Evangeline seems oblivious to the man's lusts and, for that at least, I am grateful.

While we were there, loading up on flour and grain, along with some household items we were in dire need of, a few townsfolk walked in. There were four of them, all told, and their ranks consisted of Willis Gaunt, Merrill Parton, Merrill's wife Claudia Parton, and the Reverend Hart.

All wore smiles and were freely allowing merriment and glee to pour from them as they laughed at some amusement that must have transpired just before they entered. Reverend Hart was wearing the most amusing hat, something I've not seen before. It differed from the typical 'western' hats I see many in Winnsborough wearing, but seemed to be a cousin of sorts to it. It was black, and had a bulbous top in the center, ringed in some form of white ribbon. The brim of the hat seemed to reach and bow out from the base in all directions for what I would wager was an entire twelve inches. It bobbed and quivered with his hearty laughter.

Then their eyes fell on my sister and I as we were loading the last of our purchases up to the counter for Roscoe to count up our debt.

"Well, well," Merrill said to us, the last remnants of his laughter retreating from his face and crawling back into the crevices which were institutions upon his hard face. "Seems we have some members of the Brogan tribe among us here!"

I noticed Evangeline's face tighten and lose its normal, lovely hue in favor of an absence of color I've not witnessed outside fresh snow.

After my glance at my sister, I looked to the foursome and nodded politely to them.

"Good day," I said.

"Is it?" the Reverend Hart questioned me as I finished my pleasantry.

I glanced around their faces for a moment and then to my sister, whose white face was now accented by twin blossoms of pink high on her cheeks, which caused me to think of a clown.

I looked back to them.

"I assume so, sir," I said. "Seems as fine a day as any."

The Reverend smiled at us and then to his companions.

"Well, I concede that to the untrained eye it may appear so," the Reverend began, "yet the Good Book tells us that the devil himself will appear as an angel of light. There's more to good days than bright sunshine and happy smiles! A good day must come from the joy of the Lord!"

"Here, here!" said Claudia Parton, as she folded her hands delicately across her midriff.

I nodded, feeling quite a lot of boiling hostility from these folks just beneath the façade of their smiling masks.

"If you say so, Reverend," I said, turning to Roscoe to pay the man. I very much wanted to get out of there, and in a right hurry, I tell ya true.

"Indeed I do," the Reverend replied to me in a flat and rather cold voice. "Say, young Brogan—forgive me, I've forgotten your name?"

"Johnathan, sir," I told him as I waited impatiently for Roscoe to make my change.

"Ah, yes," he said. "Johnathan. Well, Johnathan, I've noticed, or rather should I say, have *not* noticed any of your family at our church services since you all became a part of our community. I pray you, why?"

All I could do is shrug. All eight of the foursome's eyes were upon us, pressing into us, and the weight was positively physical. My family has never been of the religious sort, not in my years and at least until Mother's involvement with the demon Cloris. But of course, they could know nothing of this. No one could *ever* know anything about it whatever.

"I'm sorry, sir," I stated slowly. "My family has never been religious, I'm afraid. I assure you, no offense was intended."

"Not religious!" Claudia almost barked. "Why, I never!"

"Calm down, Claudia," the Reverend said, patting her on the shoulder. "A person can't be held to account for what he does not know."

Then he turned to me, his eyes seeming to darken to a shade of black I've never seen before, nor do I wish to see again or dwell on now.

"But now you know, don't you, son?" the Reverend said. His voice had taken on a hollow quality and caused me to shiver.

Evangeline shivered as well. I'm quite sure it was involuntary, but the shudder was so obvious that the foursome's eyes moved from me to her. A crack moved across the Reverend's face, exposing a smile.

"My dear child," he said, his smile widening as he leaned forward, as though speaking to a pre-pubescent runt. "No need to fear! The Good Lord seeks to save *all* the lost, and you can hope in that!"

Then he leaned back and spread his arms to us both in a manner of presentation.

"I tell you what," he said. "Why don't you and your whole family come to service this Sunday? Why, that would just bless the Lord's heart, and your good Reverend's Hart as well!"

He grinned mischievously, so as to make me believe he'd made a pun using his name, though I cannot be sure of this.

"Perhaps," I stated firmly, finally getting my change from the cold molasses that was Roscoe. "I'll discuss it with my family."

"Why don't I just come on by your place and speak with your father?" the Reverend said, and my spine locked.

This is where I created my fiction. I had not thought of the fact that no one in town, or anywhere for that matter, had the slightest clue of Daddy's fate. Of course, no one would ever believe my fantastic retelling of the demon Cloris burying the axe in Daddy's face—even my siblings do not know of this detail—but further, we'd made no announcement of it whatever to anyone at all. I'd buried him myself and simply taken over as the man of the house.

"I-I," I tried to start, but my words caught in my throat. What was I to tell them? Certainly, I could not allow them to come to our home. Mother's madness alone would be enough for them to tear us further apart than we've already been, but if there were any inkling that Daddy was gone or dead, the scrutiny would be more than I could bear, I reckon.

"You what?" the Reverend asked me.

Those eyes. That smile. That *goddamned* smile.

"I'm afraid that won't be possible," I finally croaked out. "Daddy has traveled back East for a time, handling some family matters at our former estate, and won't return for some time. I expect a letter any day now to update us on his plans of return, but I've just not received it yet."

He maintained that wretched smile, his dark eyes flicking back and forth between my sister and I. In the periphery of my vision, I saw Evangeline turn to me ever so slightly as I was lying through my teeth, and could feel—more so than see—her eyes growing.

"Your mother, then?" the Reverend pushed back.

I shook my head.

"Afraid Mother is quite ill just now. She is quarantined to her bed for the time being. And, speaking of which, we should really get back to her. But I assure you, we will discuss the matter of visiting your congregation as a family sometime."

The smile remained. My breath was caught in my throat and I dare say Evangeline plum forgot how to breathe altogether, and I feared for a moment she may pass out.

Finally, the Reverend broke and told us he was quite sorry to hear of our mother's illness and that he hoped to have us grace his congregation in the near future with our presence. I told him we would make every effort to do so.

We went about our business and, before returning home, I stopped in to the General Store once more—after making quite sure the Reverend and his crew were gone—and made arrangements for Roscoe to begin delivering goods to us every Monday evening.

I mean to cross paths with the Reverend Hart no more.

I shall make one more entry tonight. I woke up from a rather bad dream thinking of this, and since I've lit a candle, I may as well put it down.

Upon returning from town, what little progress Richard had made seemed to be lost once more. He reeked of that stink again. That stink that doesn't stink at all.

I do wish I knew what it was...

July 15th, 1906

I am baffled and appalled. I don't know what to make of things just yet, but I simply cannot understand it.

I have turned it over and over in my head, but to no avail. I thought I understood the mechanics well enough to know this could not be, yet it is. Mother's announcement has cemented it into reality.

She is pregnant. She is going to have her 'Brogan New' in the new year.

Richard seems worse than ever.

The Damned Place

August 2nd, 1906

Cloris was in our home today when I came in from hunting. She and Mother were chattering away like old pals in the sitting room, and to my shock and horror, Evangeline was with them!

My poor sister seems to be adopting the madness our mother has so egregiously embraced, and I can no longer ignore the matter after seeing her carrying on with Cloris as though she were just another person. That alien witch is no person at all!

Richard is completely reduced to diapers now, though the odd scent that seemed to permeate from his loins so often before is gone. I cannot recall precisely when the smell vanished, but it was some time after Mother's announcement of her pregnancy.

Or was it before?

I cannot be sure. My mind reels and sways, quite often on the very precipice of a madness of mine own, and it is all that I can do to maintain sanity in my crumbling world.

Oddest thing, however. Before bursting forth into the sitting room to find Mother and Evangeline congregating with the devil Cloris—laughing and carrying on like old chums—I heard Mother referring to a child nephew to Evangeline. She quickly corrected herself and called the child her new brother, apparently in the context of the new child growing within her. Yet she made the same mistake thrice more before I entered.

What a strange way to refer to the child...how does one mistake a nephew and a brother?

August 27th, 1906

Cloris is now a frequent visitor in our home. And the horror I stumbled upon today laid to rest all questions I held of what became of Daddy's body and of the reality of the Glutton himself.

I live in absolute fear and horror in my own home, and God help me, I often dream of ending my family with the very axe Cloris used to end Daddy. My mind seems to break more and more every day. It is impossible for me to make entries every day. I pray that this record will help me hold fast to my grasp on sanity, even if it proves of little other value. As I look back over these scattered recollections, it seems the ravings of a madman.

Perhaps they are.

September 13th, 1906

I must elaborate on my previous entry. I dread the very idea, as merely dwelling on it seems ready to thrust me into the abyss I am ever standing over. The very mouth of madness.

As I stated before, Cloris has become a frequent visitor in our home of late. I haven't the words to describe her arrivals, but suffice it to say that she possesses some psychic power to open doors between our worlds. She has been preparing Mother as a helper to bring their wretched Glutton into this world. It seems positively insane that anyone would ever agree to aid the transition of a thing that could rightly be described as the very eater of worlds or death himself into this place, but that is precisely what Mother is: insane.

The Damned Place

Evangeline is as well now. My poor, sweet, beautiful sister. But that is another matter.

I'd been laboring in the garden all morning and then out hunting in the afternoon. As I rested Daddy's rifle against the siding of the house on the porch and dusted off my pants with waves of my hat, I heard the familiar voices of Mother and Evangeline mixed with the now-horrifically constant voice of Cloris. My hand rested upon the door handle and I...

CHAPTER 41

...turned the knob.

There was a soft creak as the door fell inward on its hinges under its own weight. The voices became louder and Johnathan felt a marriage of fear and loathing sweep over him in nauseating quantities as his foot softly clopped upon the wooden floor of the entryway.

"The first meal is an amazing thing to witness!" the hideous voice of Cloris floated to his ears from down the hall. "Consider yourselves privileged to spectate this glorious event!"

That odd, warbling hum was in the air, and Johnathan had almost missed it entirely as he focused on the voices.

He stepped cautiously past the door and shut it as silently as he was able. It slinked home with a soft *shuck*.

"The runt is privilege enough!" his mother's voice danced off the walls. "But this is a treat!"

"Indeed it is, Mother!" Evangeline's sweet, soft voice croaked in an uncommon waver. "Prepare the way of the Glutton!"

Madness! Johnathan thought, his eyes wild and darting. *What hellish horror are they conjuring in my home?*

It wasn't long before he found out, and he would forever wish he had not.

He rounded the corner to the hallway. Before him stood the strange halls and doors, and the closet at the very end. The door just to the right of it hung open, and the voices seemed to be floating from that room.

He moved as briskly as he dared down the hall, cursing the boards beneath him every time they creaked and moaned, but it seemed of little interest to the ladies and that demon Cloris in the far bedroom.

As he reached the doorway, he slowed and pressed himself against the wall, sliding his back along the wallpaper until he'd brought his shoulder flush with the frame.

He peered around, ever so slowly, sweat beading and dropping in coin-sized plops onto his clothing, shoes, and floor. His left eye peered into the room first and finally, after all the time and talk, the horror was revealed to him.

He might have stopped there, turned screaming or running or both, but his mind refused to accept the information it was receiving from his left eye, and demanded confirmation from the right. So, with a tremendous force of will and an absolute need for reproach, for *something* to tell him what he was seeing wasn't *really* being seen at all, merely conjured from a splitting and tortured mind, he slid his head further into the frame of the doorway. His right eye came into view and saw the full scene, complete with full depth perception.

His left eye had been vindicated.

There in the room was a shimmering wall, one that looked into the same room in a world, somewhere else in the multi-verse, and there was a beast there. Its body was collapsed on the floor just inside its own world, yet there was a domineering shadow of the thing that was leering inward to Johnathan's world.

Great, black talons stretched out from the shadow fingers, reaching over the trio of women and there was a hint of a tooth-lined mouth which split vertically across the shadow's face, exposing black, shadowy fangs.

But none of this was what gripped Johnathan's heart with fingers of ice and locked his feet to the floor like the roots of a five-hundred-year-old tree. What did these things was what was laying on the floor between the women and the shadow beast.

The rotting, putrefied corpse of his father, face split and skin worm-eaten and gray, lay on the floor, the focus of this gathering of the damned.

Johnathan's voice had been caught in his throat, frozen in the grip of the same icy hands which gripped his heart and spine, but it found new strength now and wrenched itself free of their frozen grasp and tore forth from his mouth in a howl that succeeded not in halting the event or even drawing the interest of those involved, but only in shattering the silence that had fallen on the room and the last vestiges of reason and sanity that Johnathan Michael Brogan retained in his young mind.

The shadow beast's talon-equipped hands thrust downward and tore into the puss-infused flesh of his months-dead Daddy with a sickening splatting sound. A stench rose from the punctures that smelled of rancid meat and fresh shit. There was a soft and ever so brief *whoosh* and *hiss* as pent up gases escaped from the wounds, releasing the nasal horrors.

Then the thing lifted the body from the floor and the terrible mouth seemed to open.

A moment later, his daddy's head was torn loose from its body in a bone-crunching rip. Bones and rotten meat, skin, and tendons snapped and tore and split, and there was a sound like a massive egg cracking as the thing bit down on the skull.

Johnathan's scream continued to ring out in terror, still drawing no attention from the thing and its spectators.

And as he watched in placid, crippling terror, he saw the thing's shadow begin to take more form than a mere dark mist. Tiny strings began to slink and move about it, forming the rough and complex network of a circulatory system.

Little more than this happened as the thing devoured every aspect of his father. But it was there, and it was defined.

At some point, his screams abated as his throat betrayed him and refused to carry the sounds further. He protested this for a time with raspy hisses, but even these could not be maintained for long as exhaustion fell upon him.

Yet his eyes could not move from the sight.

The Glutton was real. It was right there, just before him, eating the rotting corpse of his daddy and materializing itself before his very eyes.

He slid slowly down the door-frame and collapsed to the floor, watching the hellish vision before him play out in terror-struck awe and nightmarish wonder.

When the thing finished, there was nothing left. Not a morsel. Not a bone. Not a tooth.

Absolutely nothing.

That was when he heard the thing speak, and the loose, wet sound of the thing's voice—which seemed to be layered in strange, almost musical chords—was what made Johnathan finally faint.

"I require more meat," it said. *"Something...fresher."*

Johnathan's eyes rolled back into his head, and he collapsed back on the hallway floor.

Still, no one in the room noticed.

CHAPTER 42

October 1st, 1906

So much meat. I have to hunt enough to feed our family and the wretched thing. Its body seems to grow more and more with every feeding, but the pace is incredibly slow. It demands more meat, the likes of Daddy's, but fresh. Yet it doesn't dare take any of us. It seems to *need* us to continue this birthing, if you will allow me to call it thus.

So far, I've refused.

Roscoe makes his deliveries like clockwork and I meet him out near the road to carry them back. Questions are arising something fierce in town according to him. Questions about Daddy, and about our continued absence from the religious community. At first, I tried to shrug these trivialities off with fictions and expounded additions to the fictions. But no more. I simply give no answer and Roscoe takes his money.

He tells me to be on guard, though. The talk of witchcraft in town has risen above a murmur, and he fears that little more will be required to break the back of the camel. The Reverend preaches quite hard against such things, and indeed quite hard against my family, I'm told.

If only they knew. If only they could understand!

But they cannot, and it is a fool's errand to set out to convince them.

I'm not sleeping much. Not at all, really. I do shut my eyes, but slumber eludes me through the nights and I rise with the dawn.

If I still believed there might be a God, perhaps I would ask Him to take me. But I'm no longer convinced such a being exists, and if so, I've no interest in meeting Him. Yet, despite this, I do pray.

I pray for death.

October 3rd, 1906

I am convinced that there is a rather severe snake infestation in our home. Even as the weather cools with the stride into autumn, I'm seeing them. Their kind escapes my knowledge. They are a solid, glossy black with the most striking crimson stripe down the length of their backs.

I first saw them yesterday and spent the afternoon trying to shew them from our home. The devils are elusive, however, and I accomplished nothing more than frustration.

Evangeline and Mother seem not to notice them. Of course, Richard is entirely aloof now, and I believe he sees nothing whatever. Only I seem to be aware of them, and I've no idea if they are poisonous. I am very much in loathing of the creatures in general, and their presence in the house will do nothing to assist my sleeping habits, which have all but vanished now, anyway.

While they are frighteningly abhorrent, they are, however, fascinating creatures. Especially this breed in particular. My ignorance of the breed aside, I'm rather sure snakes as a species cannot scale vertical walls, and certainly are not capable of slithering onto ceilings. Yet these are. I witnessed quite a lot of them do just that very thing: slink across the floor, straight up the wall, and go right over my head after transitioning to the ceiling.

Frightening and fascinating.

Their concentration seems most focused in two particular rooms of the house, though I have witnessed them all over. They seem most drawn to that damned—no, that *god*damned—bedroom where Cloris lurks and comes back and forth. Where the goddamned Glutton feeds.

Also, in Richard's bedroom.

October 7th, 1906

Mother is beginning to show in her belly. Seems much too soon, yet I cannot deny what my eyes behold. Though God knows I wish I could. The things I've seen, the things I *continue* to see...it is simply more than man was meant to bear.

I found Mother lying in her bed morning before last, and she was surrounded with snakes. My instincts tried to lurch to action at once and shew them away from her as they slithered over her swelling abdomen.

But then I stopped.

A rather malicious and honestly frightening thought occurred to me: let them have her!

Yet they did her no harm. Again, she seemed to be wholly unaware of their presence. Her eyes were wide open and she was silently mouthing that devilish, damnable chant she shares with the contemptable Cloris.

And they just slithered all around her. All *over* her.

Yet, my mind continued returning to that thought so full of malice, of outright hate of a breed I've never experienced before, and certainly not for my mother!

LET THEM HAVE HER!

But they will not take her. It was as if they were protecting her. Protecting whatever ungodly brood is growing within her.

I left her there with her snakes, snakes which I am now convinced only I can see. I found Richard in much the same way only moments later. Only Richard chose this one maddening moment to break his silence— which he has adhered to as though it were a vow—and speak to me. He wasn't seeing the snakes, I'm almost certain of this, yet he said the most peculiar thing, almost referencing them.

He said, "They will protect my runt!"

I turned this over and over in my mind the rest of the afternoon. His face had taken on a cheery sort of color that has been absent from him for some time now when he spoke. And it was only these five words which he spoke. Nothing more.

And his use of the word 'my'...at first I was sure I must have misheard him, that he likely had said 'the', or some other identifier in relation to the runt. But I cannot deceive myself, no matter how much I wish to be able to do so.

"My runt!"

I am finally starting to understand, no, starting to *accept* how this runt has come to being. It is Mother's. It is Richard's. It is the brother of Evangeline and I.

And it is our nephew.

October 8th, 1906
Goddamn, fucking snakes!

October 9th, 1906
Mother. Richard. Runt.
RUNT!

October 11th, 1906
Infestation. That is the only word for it. The snakes have tripled, possibly quadrupled in number in the last few days. I've fed the Glutton countless squirrels and rabbits and possums. It demands human flesh.

It *does* see the snakes. And it mocks me.

Richard has moved into Mother's room. They lie in the bed, *their* bed, their abominable bed! The snakes! Oh, God, the SNAKES!

Everywhere! As I write these words they slither into my room. They stare and kiss the air with their black tongues. Yet they are never still. Oh, no, never for a moment! Constantly moving, slithering, crawling, writhing!

Evangeline has begun the chant. The one Mother and Cloris cawed, still, *still* caw together! She moves toward me with mad smiles. Horrible intentions.

I am rambling. I...I don't know how to stop it. My dear, sweet Evangeline. My blessed sister. She comes to—

Oh, dear God! And I am weak. I am so god-damned weak! My exhaustion, my despair! It has all

317

made me so weak! We are alone here. We are heathens! Abominable! A family of moral abortions!

I now know from whence comes that odd, sweet, musky smell.

October 13th, 1906
I chopped wood today.

October 14th, 1906
I chopped wood today.

October 15th, 1906
Johnathan-Michael Brogan chopped the goddamned wood today! The wood! The fucking wood! I chopped it!

October 16th, 1906
I like chopping wood.

October 18th, 1906
Snakes and wood! Is there anything else? Oh, Evangeline! Why? Sweet sister, mother of runt! We've damned ourselves!

We are low on flour. Roscoe's visit on Monday will come in just the nick of time.

October 22nd, 1906

Roscoe came today. And what a day it has become!

I thought I might show him the snakes. Prayed he would see them. Though I am unsure why I desired this. I typically meet him at the road to make our transactions.

But not today! Ha!

No, today I did not meet him. I waited. I wanted to show him the snakes. But I also had to fetch dinner. Dinner for us, dinner for the Glutton.

Dinner for the Glutton. The Glutton. The Glut—

Everyone has to eat. Eat, eat, eat. Always eating and drinking and shitting and pissing and round and round she goes!

I fetched the rifle, it's really a shot-gun. Many say they are the same, but I disagree. *THEY'RE NOT! NOT THE SAME AT ALL!*

No, not the same.

I fetched the *shot-gun*, and went to get the dinner. The dinner, dinner, dinner.

As I returned, I saw...

CHAPTER 43

...the front door was hanging open. Johnathan hadn't run a bath for himself—or anyone else for that matter—in days now. He reeked of body odor and the stink of sweat. The stink of a poorly wiped ass.

The stink of his sister.

The rest of the family was in no better condition than he. And the snakes. The snakes were making a mess.

Slithering and crawling and writhing, shitting and pissing where they were, leaving streaks of filth and excrement behind them in stinking trails.

But the door was open. He was positive that he'd closed it on his way out. He'd closed it to prevent the flies from getting in. They were getting in anyway—how could he avoid them with the stench and filth they were living in?—but he meant to give them no quarter of his own will.

There were two dead squirrels in the pack which hung from his side. He'd shot them, planning to feed his family with one and the Glutton with the other. He'd hoped for more, but game was becoming scarce in the area, likely from the volume of hunting he'd been doing since the Glutton's arrival.

But, hoping—that last, damning bastion of the optimistic—that he might find more, he'd reloaded both barrels of the break-over double-barrel shot-gun with loads he'd purchased from Roscoe's General Store.

Now, he cocked the hammers on both barrels.

He crept towards the house, mindful to roll his feet from their outer edge inward, minimizing the noise of his footfalls on the leaf-blanketed forest floor. He went silently enough, and after a few moments, he was all the way to the base of the porch stairs.

He listened. Listened for what may have been a long time or only a moment. He couldn't be sure. His senses were so skewed now that the most fleeting of moments seemed to drag on like slivers of eternity. His neck craned outward, carrying his head and cocked left ear up and towards the house, the open door, straining to pick up on the vibrations inside.

All he could hear were the fleshy, scaly sounds of the snakes writhing all over the house.

Filthy serpents!

They really were becoming a bore. He'd found he could no more shew them from the house than he could pick the world up on his shoulders by standing on his hands. They were a nightmare of slinking demons, thinning the walls and the very air all over the house. Not even the Glutton, that persistent, threatening beast, would touch them. Wouldn't dine upon them. Wouldn't even brush one aside.

Johnathan had tried on more than one occasion to brush them away, but to his horror he'd found that he couldn't ever manage to touch one. His hands never passed through them or anything so otherworldly, but simply could never make contact. They weren't the ghosts of Luciferian descendants. Nothing so tangible as that. But it was as if his depth perception simply

321

could not gage their distance, and thus he could not make contact. It was like judging distance with a single eye instead of a pair.

Yet, this was not the case with anything else. He'd discovered that readily enough. He could reach out and accurately and efficiently fetch any other thing he desired. He could grab the old coffee can from the shelf with no difficulty. He could pull back the sheets to his bed with the efficiency of a cat. He could snatch up the bags of flour with the precision of a professional athlete.

But he could *not* touch the snakes. They were always just out of reach.

And they were fucking loud.

Oh, God, were they loud! Their slinking movements had been virtually silent at first, but in concert with his deteriorating mind, the volume of their movements had been ever rising.

Rising, rising, rising!

All he could hear were the snakes.

He took one tentative step up onto the first step of the porch and paused again, once more trying to hear something, *anything*, which wasn't that incessant, slithering orchestra of the goddamned snakes.

He could not.

Another step. Then another. Soon, he was standing on the porch, the butt of the shot-gun pressed tightly against the concave of his shoulder, the barrels pointing down at roughly forty-five degrees. Another four short steps and he was standing by the door, his head still craned out from his body like a snapshot of a rooster in mid-crow.

Then he *did* hear something else.

The Damned Place

It was faint, and ever so slight, but it *was* identifiable. A voice—no, a *pair* of voices—floated out to him from the belly of the slithers. He immediately recognized one of the voices as that of his dear, sweet sister, that beautiful young woman he'd loved, and loved so dearly. That he was now loving far too much. He knew it. Knew it was wrong. Knew it was abominable. He even knew that it was due to the madness which had befallen his entire family, including himself.

But he didn't care about that. Not now.

What he cared about was the other voice which slinked down the corridors of the house like a drawling whisper. A voice he also knew well, and identified only a moment after that of his sister's. It made sense, too. He'd been awaiting him all day, and he now realized that in his trek through the woods, hunting game for family and beast, he'd missed his meeting with him by the road. And now he'd come to check. The first visitor to the Brogan house.

It was Roscoe.

Johnathan stepped into the house through the open door, snakes slithering out of his way as he came, still unable to touch them even with his feet. They parted before him like the Red Sea in the old story he'd once heard of about a man named Moses. They spread before him, as if to make a trail, a path to follow.

And he did.

He crept down the path, the shot-gun pressed tight against his shoulder, his first and middle fingers hovering shakily over the pair of triggers in the guard of the gun.

The snakes continued to spread. Their path went through the foyer and slinked to the right down the hallway. The hallway that went toward the bedrooms.

Stink filled his nostrils, but he didn't notice. Hadn't noticed for some time now. He could see streaks of dried urine and feces all over the walls and floors, even the ceilings, from the damned snakes. But he didn't really *notice* these either. Hadn't for some time now. It was simply part of the house. Part of his reality. As was his filth-caked body, and those of his family.

He rounded the corner to the hallway and raised the gun. But no one was there. Only the snakes, their parting beckon splitting down the center of the narrow hall.

All the way to the last door on the right.

That room. The room of the witch Cloris. The room of the doorway. The room of the abominations.

A thin cut of a smile split Johnathan's dirty face. His red lips peeled back, just barely exposing the tips of his yellowed teeth.

He could hear the voices again. They were still quiet in the cacophony of the slithering snakes, but louder here than they'd been before.

"Come on, honey-girl!" the voice of Roscoe drifted to him. "Give old Roscoe a kiss!"

The smile on Johnathan's face collapsed upon itself at once.

"Sir, you cannot be here!" Evangeline said, a hint of panic in the back of her throat. "You've no business with me! My brother will be home soon!"

I'm home now, my dear, sweet sister, Johnathan thought as he raised the barrels of the gun level with his chin.

The Damned Place

Johnathan moved more swiftly now, but only just. The snakes continued to prepare the way for him, always just out of the reach of his softly falling feet. To his amazement, the boards of the floor didn't creak or groan at all as he moved. Even his boots managed to avoid their customary *clop* as they propelled him forward. A fleeting thought occurred to him that it was perhaps the layers of snake-shit beneath his feet that lent him stealth, but he did not dwell on the whys. There was no reason to question the whys.

Only to move forward and deal with Roscoe.

"Unhand me!" his sister was saying now, her voice rising to a sharp crack.

Johnathan wondered briefly where his mother and Richard might be, and why they were not reacting to this scuffle, when he heard another sound in the opera of slithers and struggle. A faint creaking from above.

Creak-creak-creak-creak!

Bedsprings. It was the bedsprings creaking and bending and releasing. Mother and Richard. Bedsprings.

Creak-creak-creak!

"You've been teasing me for months now, every time you come into my store, and it's time to pay up, little girl!" Roscoe was saying.

Johnathan was three-quarters of the way down the hall now, and their voices were getting louder as he approached. His fingers trembled over the triggers. His mouth was open again, but in a grimace rather than a smile.

Creak-creak-creak!

"Get your hands off me!"

Creak!

325

"You're gonna give me what I want!"
Creak-creak!
"Please!"
Creak!
"You're gonna milk my udder, bitch!"
Creak-creak-creak!

Johnathan rounded the corner of the doorway to the room—*the damned room*—the gun raised and level. He swept into the room sideways and saw Roscoe had Evangeline in the far corner, next to the wall where the Glutton fed on the pittances Johnathan would bring it, and she was struggling to break free of him. Roscoe had his hand underneath Evangeline's dress. It was pulled up past her waist, her long undergarments exposed and streaked in filth. His hand was bulging through the blouse of her dress, gripping her breasts and Johnathan could make out the edge of a grotesque smile on the side of Roscoe's face, brown teeth glistening with saliva and his pink tongue stretching out from his jowls with horrific intent.

Johnathan's eyes blazed with fury and hate, a hue of scarlet descending on his vision.

"Get your hands off her, you wretch!" he screamed.

Roscoe jumped, startled by the unknown presence of Johnathan, and his hand released her and slid out of her dress as he whirled around, eyes wide and mouth agape. He made a sound like *'eep!'* as his back slammed into the wall.

Evangeline ran from the corner and behind Johnathan, not wasting a moment to flee the advances of the old man.

The gun was leveled at Roscoe's head, fingers hovering just over the triggers, and shakily at that.

"What in hell do you think you're doing in my home?!" Johnathan screamed now.

Creak-creak-creak!

Now he could hear panting and laughing coming from the room upstairs. The snakes were crawling all over the walls and floor and ceiling and every single thing in the room like a moving network of roots.

Roscoe looked from Johnathan to Evangeline and back again. His lips were quivering and his jaw was shaking, moving up and down in rapid motion trying to form silent words from a voice that was on retreat.

"I-I-I..." Roscoe stammered.

Creak-creak!

Moans. Laughter. Snakes. Snakes *everywhere*.

"Damn you, Brogan!" Roscoe said, his voice coming back from retirement. "Damn your whole family! You can't do this!"

"Wrong," Johnathan said in an even, icy tone. "You're on *my* property!"

"You let me out of here, you hear me!" Roscoe spat, taking a step from the wall and clenching his hands into fists. "Everyone knows where I am! They know I deliver here every Monday! They'll know, I tell ya, and they'll come for you and your whole damned, witching family!"

The snakes writhed. Roscoe couldn't see them.

"You're right," Johnathan said, lowering the barrel ever so slightly.

Roscoe's stature seemed to deflate slightly, relief starting to wash over him like a tidal wave.

"I *am* right," he said. "Now I'll just be leaving, and we'll forget the whole thing!"

But Johnathan was shaking his head.

"No," he said. "You're right. We *are* damned. A damned family."

He raised the gun back level.

"And you came to the wrong damned place!"

He jerked both triggers back in tandem. There was a deafening roar as fire and pellets exploded from the twin barrels of the shot-gun, and Johnathan expelled great effort to keep from being thrown backwards on his ass.

Roscoe's wide-eyed, jaw-dropped face exploded like a stick of dynamite. Blood and bone spattered all over the room, and thick, foamy jelly followed it in yellowish-gray clumps.

The snakes somehow managed to separate, wholly avoiding getting their black and red backs covered in the stuff. Roscoe's headless body fell back against the wall and slid down, the gory stump of his neck fountaining blood around a crimson-soaked stick of bone and tubes.

The only thing Johnathan could hear was a high-pitched ringing in his ears. It was like a tuning fork was humming away inside his head, the vibrations seeming to intensify rather than dissipate. He couldn't hear the snakes. He couldn't hear the creaking of the bed upstairs. He couldn't hear the moans and laughter.

He couldn't hear his own screams.

He dropped the gun to the floor, it once again avoiding even the slightest touch of the snakes. He fell to his knees in a clearing made just for him amidst the serpents. His hands went to either side of his head and his fingers curled into his hair, pulling it tightly. He was trembling.

What have I done?

Then the ringing began to fade. He stared at the blood and brain-soaked wall. At the headless body of Roscoe, sitting neatly up against it. He had stopped screaming at some point, though he'd never heard the sounds. He could feel strain in his throat from the effort.

He looked up to Evangeline who was standing next to him, streaked in filth, and smiling down at him sweetly.

"You're a good brother," she said to him, a twinkle in her eyes as she gently patted her still flat belly. "And you're going to be a good father to the new runt. Such a good, *good* father!"

He began to tremble and goose-flesh burst forth over every inch of his body. His gaze shifted from her and back to the gore-soaked remains of the General Store's owner.

Then he heard the warble.

The snakes cleared the wall at once and the tiniest sliver opened in the wall, right in the middle of the splatter. A long, black, snakelike appendage slinked through and began to slurp up the brains and bone and blood.

Then the sliver opened wider and wider, exposing the thing, the wretched Glutton, as it sucked and slurped and slobbered, feasting on the sweet treat of human flesh.

Johnathan watched in abject horror as the thing came out and devoured every last ounce, every last *drop* of Roscoe.

Evangeline watched too, but in her eyes there was adoration and joy. Her wild, beautiful eyes twinkled with amazement and her smile spread to the point

Johnathan thought her face might shatter from the strain.

When it was done, the Glutton looked at him. Johnathan was still on his knees. The thing before him was *growing*. New muscles and sinew and tendons and skin were visibly spreading across its massive structure, moving in a way that reminded Johnathan of the way the snakes moved about the house.

Then it spoke.

"More meat."

It said nothing else. Only that, and nothing more, staring at Johnathan through empty sockets with throbbing veins twisting into existence within.

Then it stepped back and the wall closed. The warble disappeared and the snakes covered the place where it had fed. There was absolutely no evidence that a murder had just occurred here, and there wasn't a single drop of blood from the now digesting Roscoe.

"Praise be to the Glutton!" his sister exulted. "Praise be to the god of Cloris!"

Johnathan wanted to scream again, wanted to run from this place and be done with it all. Done with the abominations he was conducting with his sister. Done with caring for a family of mad-hatters. Done with the Glutton and its demands.

But he couldn't. All he could do was embrace the insanity that was welling within him.

He began to cackle in laughter as his sister sang the praises to the anti-god they had just fed.

Creak-creak-creak!

CHAPTER 44

October 23rd, 1906

I managed to fetch the supplies from Roscoe's cart. Took some doing, I tell ya true, but I also disposed of the wagon. Horses too. Two fine mares.

The Glutton ate them greedily. Strange, the horses and squirrels don't seem to cause nearly as much growth in the thing as Roscoe did. Or even Daddy's wormy corpse.

I have moments of horrifying sanity in the midst of my waking nightmare now. These moments have me thinking the most awful things. Things I could not bear to consider under normal circumstances.

Yet there is nothing normal in my life anymore. Nor shall there ever be again. I swim in the comfort of madness now, and happily so. It is only the slivers of sanity that wash forward from time to time which cause me sorrow. The moments when I realize just how awful our lives have become. How utterly evil we really are. The times I desperately want to fetch the axe by the woodpile.

The times like right now.

October 26th, 1906

The Reverend Hart. I saw him. I'm sure of it! He was out there, there in the woods, watching us, watching our home!

He never wandered close, but oh, I saw the man!

I was watching out the front window. I could feel eyes on us, on the house. Mother and Richard were sitting in the front room, reeking in their excrement and filth, Evangeline was doing likewise in the kitchen. I suppose I cannot, *should* not, pretend I was not doing the same in the parlor. I was! I stood there in my filth, grabbing at the snakes and never grasping one!

I will, though! I tell ya true, I shall have a snake!

I noticed something moving beyond the snakes, feeling those judging eyes upon me like lusty moths coming to a flame. The bastard was there, and he was watching us!

I know not his intent. Or do I? Methinks sometimes I know just his intentions. And what of them? Come, I say! Come, and behold we Brogans! Behold us and be cursed, I tell you! Cursed!

Cursed, as we are cursed. I am suffering in another moment of sanity, another godawful window of crystalline lucidity! I know this is a damned place, and I feel that we are damned likewise. Damned to that fiery eternity the devil Reverend Hart spits about from his pulpit. His brimstone-soaked sermons.

Ah, yes. I went to his service. I went, but no one knew! No one knew at all, you see, because I was clever! I snuck to town, knowing it was deserted, a place of ghosts, whenever the good Reverend was speaking.

Clever, I tell you! There was never one so sly as me!

I crept to the windows and peered within and saw him. Heard him! And I heard my family's name upon his blistering lips!

They are coming for us.

Well, come, come. Come, Revy, my good man! Come! Come and see what you all fear! My sanity hath returned, and God help me, I shall end it! I shall end my sanity and enter the eternal sleep of the damned! You think that Glutton won't come through and eat your soul from within your very carcass?

Think again, Reverend! Come!

October 29th, 1906

It is dark. So dark. But I can see them out there. They think I do not, but I do. I see them.

I caught a snake today. That was fun. Well, I cannot tell a lie. It *allowed* me to catch it. It beckoned me to it. Slithering and sliming its way out of the house, its black fork of a tongue calling me forth to it. And I came. Oh, yes, God help me, I came!

It led me from the house to the woodpile. The sanity was upon me once again. Oh, how I loathe it! The terrible, lucid clarity!

It coiled itself upon the axe handle, and I grabbed the thing. I hefted it. Caressed it. *Petted* it.

It was colder than I thought it would be. The snake, I mean, of course.

The rest haunts me, and I shall not retell it. Not all of it, anyhow. It is not as though I will be reading this back to myself in the future. There *is* no future. Not for me. Not for my family. Not for us damned Brogans. No. None for us. This is the end.

They are carrying torches. Little more than a glimmer in the dark, blinking in and out beyond the trees. Closer now than before. What time is it? It doesn't matter. It is late, and the Earth is dark. So very dark.

I shall sway above them. When the Reverend and his mob arrive, oh, what a sight they shall see! My only prayer, if I dare call it such a thing, is that the Glutton will not take us all before they come.

Methinks it will not. I managed to lure Cloris out of the place where it resides. Wretched, furry beast! Yes, I lured her out and put her to pieces!

I have never laughed so boisterously in all my days. The lucid sanity washing over me was a delight for the first time in an age. How I savored it!

I know not the details or the mechanics, but it seems she had some power within her to open the doorway. Something within her will that could tear the walls down between our worlds. The Glutton has this power too, but he is weak at the moment. Malnourished. It takes him great effort to open the door. That is why he needs meat. The meat of this world, of mankind, to draw strength. Cloris was his helper. He found her and she found Mother.

Mother has the power too, I have found. *Had* the power, forgive my joke, HA-HA! It was the pair of them, Mother and Cloris, working in tandem to bring the beast into this world. Without them, he'd have never been able to come through.

But Mother and Cloris were caught off guard! Oh, clever me, I caught them off guard! Mother screamed and wailed, begging for her life and the life of the Brogan new, that goddamned demon of incest growing within her stinking belly! My brother! My nephew! God, what have we become!

I am no better. I know that. I could never really deny it, even in the rapture of madness. Evangeline, my sweet, dear sister. She was taken with the fever that possessed Mother. That wretch Cloris infected them, I tell ya true! It was she! That rabbit-pig-insect-demon Cloris! I curse the day you were born, and all of your kind, demon!

I am of reasonable confidence that the door is closed. For now. I fear the day when it may be reopened. Should the Glutton regain the strength to open it himself, or should another possessed with the powers of Cloris or Mother come along and bring it here, the whole world will be done in.

Perhaps that would be for the best. This world, what good is there in it? What good there seems to be, what good I thought there was in my family, look at what it has become! So many bleeding chunks of flesh, *ha-ha-HA*!

No. There is no good in this world. That is why I have done what I have done. There is no salvation outside of death, and behold, that is what I have become! Death, that life may not destroy! It is life, that cold mistress, that icy beast, which is the source of all misery! No more, I say!

It shall be no more!

I write these final words with the noose about my neck. I can hear them now, coming through the woods. Their torches are brighter. Their footfalls are audible. I can hear their shouts.

Well, come then. Behold what horrors life brings, and what sweet release there is in death. May you find my words here and beware this damned place! May it be cursed and burned to the ground! May it be an altar of abomination, and a warning to all who venture nigh, that man should not treasure the things of this world but to purge himself from it! We are the scourge of the land and the rapist of nature!

Farewell, good Reverend. May your nights be haunted by what you find, and I beg you, destroy this damned place!

Destroy it, I tell you!

CHAPTER 45

From the Winnsborough Post, October 31ˢᵗ, 1906:

The Sherriff of Wood County, joined with Reverend Chambris Hart and members of his congregation, found what could only be described as a house of horrors late Monday night.

In the woods just North of town, the posse, led by Sherriff Joseph Harleton and Reverend Hart, marched on the secluded home of Byron and Susan Brogan, after it was reported that foul play and witchcraft was afoot on the estate. Roscoe B. Dyer went missing after he left for the day to deliver goods to the Brogan home last week and was not heard from again. The report of his disappearance from the Brogan place was delivered by the Reverend Hart, who approached Sherriff Harleton after his evening service this past Sunday.

According to the Reverend, Mr. Dyer informed the pastor of his weekly deliveries some time back and asked for prayer when going. Mr. Byron Brogan, who was known as "Butch", had been missing for some months, supposedly on a trip to their former home back East to handle family business. But Mr. Dyer was suspicious of the eldest Brogan boy, Johnathan Michael Brogan. The boy, he claimed, was rather odd, and he feared that inappropriate behavior may have been going on between he and his sister, Evangeline Brogan.

Mr. Dyer stated to the Reverend that he was going to confront the young man and his mother.

He was never seen again.

Upon hearing of this, Sherriff Harleton assembled a posse to approach the Brogan home in the woods. The approach could prove dangerous due to the peculiar lack of trail to the home in the woods. The seclusion lent to fears of ambush, thus the assembling of the posse, which was made up mostly of congregational members of Hart's church.

They let out late Monday night, hoping to take the young Brogan and his family from the home to investigate the disappearance of both Mr. Dyer and Mr. Brogan.

What they found was a scene fit for this All Hallows Eve.

Upon entering the home, they found the bodies of Susan, Evangeline, and Richard Brogan, apparently dismembered with an axe, lying about on the floor of the foyer. Johnathan Brogan was hung from the banister above the foyer, swaying neatly over his family. There was another body, some sort of animal which neither the Sherriff nor any of the others in attendance could identify. The local veterinarian, Dr. Paul Chambers, was also unable to identify the beast. It was also determined that Mrs. Brogan had been pregnant, and likely due in less than a month.

It appeared to be murder and suicide, the culprit of both being the elder Brogan boy.

Reports from all state that the home was in serious disarray, and filth was covering the floors, walls, and oddly, the ceilings as well. No one knows how the home was brought into such a state after only being built late last year.

A journal was found amongst the bodies, suspected to be penned in the hand of the elder Brogan child, and while the details are being withheld at the moment, what has been relayed is that the boy apparently suffered from a psychotic break, leading to the tragedy. Much can be pieced together from the pages, but much is still left to know, though we likely will never know the whole of the tale.

According to reports, it seems what happened was...

CHAPTER 46

...his mother stood in the kitchen.

Johnathan could not see her, but he knew she was in there. He could hear her in there, mumbling to herself and chanting some satanic filth about the Glutton, about Cloris, about her precious Brogan new.

He shuddered. It was getting colder. Rain had started outside, and a blinding streak of lightning ripped the sky apart outside in the downpour. The booming thunder which followed shook the walls and the windows rattled in their frames.

Johnathan was holding the axe.

He crept down the foyer and looked to his left at the hallway. The shadow of his mother danced in the candlelight in the kitchen as she made about her business.

"The baby will be, the snakes will see," she said in her low, mumbling voice. *"Praise to the Glutton, Cloris, and me!"*

He turned to his right. The hallway with all the rooms stood in the gloom, occasionally lighting up when the lightning tore holes in the sky, the bright, electric blue casting ominous shadows upon the walls which seemed to guide him, lead him toward the room.

The room at the end of the hall.

No more, he thought as he began down the hall, the chanting voice of his mother bouncing off the walls in maddening cackles. *It ends tonight.*

He walked, not being entirely quiet, the blade of the axe dragging listlessly beside and behind him on the wooden planks of the floor.

Richard and Evangeline were upstairs. He knew this too. He had checked to make sure they were in bed before he went to get the axe in the growing downpour of the rain.

He was soaked to the bone. He was cold, too, but he wasn't shivering. The heat of his resolve seemed to course through his veins, warming his flesh beneath the frigid raindrops covering him from head to toe.

"Baby boy from baby boy," his mother's voice carried to him. *"Gave my cunt a baby runt!"*

He grimaced, disgusted. With himself, with his mother, with his family. But more than all of that, disgust with his inability to stop it. His inability and his fear that kept him from going by his mother's room when she was in there with Richard.

Creak-creak-creak!

The memory of the sounds made his stomach turn.

He was disgusted with himself for allowing the fever that had infected his mother and his sister to infect him as well. The fever that led him to his sister's room night after night.

"Brogan new! Fuck the shrew! Give me that baby goo!"

Another shudder. Another crash of thunder.

The shadows. Beckoning him.

He drew further down the hall, nearing the door to the room where Cloris lurked. Where she always lurked. Her furry, repellant face, the nose that bounced

341

a thousand times a second, and the hooves that clonked, clonked, clonked as she walked about.

You're coming with me, Cloris, he thought silently.

Rain drummed on the roof. It was becoming louder now, so loud, in fact, that his mother's mad chants were drowned out by the incessant downpour. The scraping, dragging sound of the axe slogging along behind him became a distant scratch.

He reached the doorway and stopped, standing in the frame. The house was dark save for a few distant candles in the kitchen and front room. Shadows cast by the tiny flames licked and danced down the hallway to where he stood like gargantuan tentacles flailing for purchase on invisible prey.

He peered into the darkness of the room.

The snakes were here. They were all around him. The floors, the walls. Yet they spread before him, as they had done the day he'd dealt with Roscoe, in an inviting arc.

Not much further, he heard them say in hissing whispers. *Just a little further now! Come! Come and feed the one!*

Feed it with what, though? Were the damned creatures blind? He didn't have anything with him, only his axe, and no one was in the room except for the snakes themselves.

He needs meat! they shrieked through slinking tongues. *Meat for the Glutton! Fetch him meat!*

But Johnathan would do no such thing.

"No!" he hissed into the room at the snakes as they slimed and squirmed before him.

All at once they seemed to pause in place, a giant gnarled mess of black and red scales. A thousand eyes, maybe ten-thousand, seemed to stare back at him from the darkness. There was a hushed hum coming from the room, and for a moment, he thought it might be the snakes themselves.

"You black devils!" he once again hissed at the countless still snakes. "Be gone with you! Be gone to the pit from whence you came! I've no business with you, and I mean to end the madness once and for all!"

Lightning ripped the sky apart outside once again and it flashed in through the window. In that instant, that split second before the thunder came booming over the drumming rain, he saw the snakes flash into oblivion. All at once.

Gone.

Tears stung the corners of his eyes and an absentminded left hand came up and rubbed the left side of his face. His expression was a mix of relief and anguish, rolled into one horrible dish.

They're gone, he thought. *But were they ever here at all?*

He didn't know. More to the point, he didn't care.

He stepped into the room and turned to face the wall beyond which Cloris lived. Lived in her damned world filled with the horrors of hell itself. Lived with her maddening, manipulative, abomination of mind.

Where she lived with the Glutton.

"Cloris?" he whispered to the wall. "Can you hear me, Cloris?"

He fell silent, listening. He listened for a long time, straining to hear anything other than the rain and the occasional roll of thunder.

There was nothing.

He could still hear the faint sound of his mother, cackling to herself down the hall. Quieter now than she'd been before.

"Cloris?" he called again, allowing his voice to rise just a precious few decibels, praying the rain would continue to drown out the sound from his mother.

He waited again. This time he waited a full two minutes before daring to try once again. He peered into the darkness, trying, *willing* for Cloris to hear him, to respond to him.

To come to him.

He was drawing in his breath for another attempt, one that he was sure would this time be overheard by his mother, which would certainly be detrimental to his course.

The word was—no, no, that *name*, that horrible, poisonous *name*—was on the tip of his tongue, on the verge of spilling from his lips in a final attempt to call upon the alien witch from the other world, his lungs full of air to send the noun forth with frightening volume when he paused a hair's breadth shy.

He heard something.

It was low, and almost inaudible beneath the pounding rain, but it was there. A whisper of a sound, growing steadily louder. A sound he'd heard before, more times than he cared to know, rising from the wall before him.

The dark seemed to shiver before him as the warbling sound rose and rose. Then dimly, ever so dimly, he saw the darkness open before him. It was a similar darkness on the other side, but just noticeably brighter.

He slid the axe behind him, shielding it from view.

"Cloris?" he whispered again. The utterance of her name was punctuated by the flash of lightning and the growl of thunder in very fitting manner.

As he leaned forward, the axe behind him, he saw the repugnant, furry face that was a mixture of madness and abomination. The nose which bounced with feverish rapidity.

He heard the *clonk* of a hoof.

It was her. Leaning in around the corner of her world, peering into his. She'd heard him, alright. The worlds were thin here, worn down so thin by the weathering of evil.

One merely had to speak to be heard from the other side.

She stared at him, dark eyes intent behind dirty fur. Waiting eyes.

Suspicious eyes.

"Why do you call me, young Brogan?" she asked warily but still with an air of authority.

Johnathan's right hand instinctively gripped tighter on the axe handle.

"It's Mother," he said, deliberately putting a waver to his voice that sounded on the verge of panic. "She isn't moving! I—"

"You what?" Cloris asked, seemingly unconcerned.

This was a surprise to him. He'd expected that their times of palaver and meetings would have grown a kinship in them. He knew they were using one another, sure, he'd had no doubt about that, but still he'd expected there to be some sort of affection in there. But the eyes which bore into him now seemed to hold none of that. Had he been wrong about her? Should he change his plan? Now? This late in the game?

He did.

"I—uh," Johnathan began, "I think she's collapsed, and, well, perhaps she would be good feeding for the Glutton?"

Cloris stared at him for a long time. It was likely only a matter of seconds, but to him, in that moment, it seemed an eternity. *Two* eternities, if one could conjure such a thought.

Then, mercifully, she broke the silence.

"Your mother has been chosen for the Glutton," she said slowly, stepping more fully into view on her side of the worlds. "Yet you would have us feed her to the Glutton? To what end?"

To what end? Yes, to what fucking end? Think man, THINK!

His mind was reeling, eyes darting about as his mind sprinted frantically for something, *anything*, that would make sense. All he needed was to lure Cloris out of the wall, end her, and close the door. Lock the Glutton away. If not forever, then at least for a good long time.

Yet here he was, on the precipice of success, trying to come up with a reason why this thing should help him feed his pregnant Mother to the beast.

He rolled with it.

"Me," he said, droplets of rain falling from the ends of his hair and running down his face as he forced a smile to break his features.

"You?" she asked and cocked her abominable head to the left.

He nodded. "Me. *I* want to be the chosen one. *I* should be the one to bring the Glutton into this world and send it to reap the whirlwind!"

He was faintly aware that he could no longer hear his mother's chants in the other room. He supposed this was good, as he'd just told Cloris she'd collapsed. Yes, yes that was good. But what was she doing? Was she listening to them? Was she coming down the hall this very moment, waddling with his goddamned brother—*nephew*—in her belly, growing too fast, *much* too fast. Would she waddle on in here in another moment, revealing his fiction to the witch and spoiling everything? Would he become the next feast of the loathsome Glutton?

Johnathan's pulse quickened and he could feel a vein protruding out and in, out and in, out and in on his throat. There was a similar sensation on his forehead.

He could feel beads of sweat bursting forth from his pores, mixing with the cold rain which still clung to his skin, creating a sickening feeling of hot and cold upon him that made his flesh crawl. His hand tightened upon the axe handle, and though he could not see them, he knew with Gospel-like certainty that his knuckles were as white as fresh snow.

He forced his smile to remain, his gaze upon Cloris—and hers upon him—never breaking for even a moment.

Then, one hoofed foot stepped into his world.

Clonk.

"You're shaking," she said as she paused.

From somewhere deep behind all the other sounds, perhaps from her world, he heard a deep and distant growl. It was a wet and menacing sound, deeper than the lowest baritone, popping and burping every half-second.

347

"I'm cold," he lied. "I was caught in the rain."

Cloris stood stock still for a new eternity, one hoof in, one hoof out of this world. The warbling sound seemed to be at a fever-pitch, but he was barely hearing it now. The rain and thunder also seemed a million miles away.

He heard the growl again.

This time, Cloris turned and looked back into her world. He was certain now that it was coming from that alien land. He was also certain of what the beast emitting it was.

The Glutton.

Come on! he thought desperately. *One more step!*

Sweat stung his eyes as it slipped off his brow and rounded the inner corner of his eyebrow. He blinked it away, holding his gaze.

Gripping the axe.

Finally, she turned back to him, a curious look in her eyes. Her wretched, awful eyes.

"We'll just bring the Glutton to her, then!" she spat cheerily.

The forced smile on Johnathan's face retreated all at once. He could no longer hold it, and to try would have been an exercise in utter futility.

No! No, not him! I have to stop him!

There was another growl, closer now. Another flickering of lightning danced through the windows and his ears tuned back to the world around him as the thunder crashed and the drumming rain re-filled his ears.

She was smiling at him. The bitch was actually smiling at him with that terrible, furry, pig-rabbit face.

Boom-boom-boom!

Footsteps. *Massive* footsteps. Coming from the house behind Cloris. From *her* world.

The Glutton was coming.

Her cackle rose as she looked into his increasingly frightened eyes. Tears spilled from those frightened eyes now, and he felt a fearful, panicking shriek welling up from within him like a geyser.

Boom-boom-boom!

Laughing.

Growling.

Fear, gripping him by the balls.

Boom-boom-boom!

His fearful paralysis broke then. He went into a full sprint, raising the axe up from behind him, and darted towards her. She had just turned her head back towards the sound of the oncoming Glutton, still laughing maniacally, when he moved into action.

When she heard his footsteps, she whipped her head back towards him, the laugh ceasing at once, but the smeared smile of it still upon her face beneath widening, wet eyes.

He grabbed one of her four wrists and yanked her into the room in his world and spilling her to the floor. All four of her hands went out to break her fall, but she still hit hard and he heard a distinctive *"ooph!"* as the wind ejected from what passed for her lungs.

Another growl struck his ears then, this time louder than ever before. He stole what very likely might be his last glance back and saw the horrible, clawed hand of the thing coming through the door to the room in that other world. The side of its fanged face was just coming into view when he turned back to Cloris.

349

She had just rolled over on her back, glaring up and him and heaving for breath, teeth bared under snarling, fantastic lips. Her eyes blazed.

He was swinging the axe around in a wild arc, his mind certain both that if he were to miss, it would all be over, and that he was destined to do just that.

You can't!

The axe came down hard and fast. Cloris was hissing up at him, scrambling to get to her feet.

Boom-boom-boom!

The blade slashed through her throat, almost all the way through it. It went about nine-tenths of the way through, spraying blood in fascinating lines and sheets all over him and the room.

He dropped the handle of the axe and knelt to his knees and covered his head, awaiting the inevitable demise which was booming and growling and lusting after him.

But after several seconds, nothing happened.

Johnathan was shaking now, dripping with sweat and Cloris's blood, adrenaline pumping though his veins. He could hear nothing from her but faint gargles and the quiet *slish* of the blood squirting from her opened throat.

He stood and turned all at once, and saw the wall was back. The door was closed. He'd gotten her to turn it off, and though he had had no idea if doing so would work, it had.

He noticed he was right about something else too: the Glutton couldn't open it on its own.

At least it hasn't yet.

It would have, though, he knew that. If it could have, it *would* have.

The Damned Place

He turned back to the bleeding horror on the floor that had been the witch of the worlds. Cloris.

He began to laugh as he pulled the axe from her neck and began dragging her body down the hall, the dark tendrils of dancing fire-shadows pulling him along the way.

He still couldn't hear Mother.

CHAPTER 47

Johnathan dragged the corpse of Cloris down the hall, flashes of light spilling into the house from the windows and splashing across his blood-spattered face as he labored. Cloris was heavier than she appeared, that was for damn sure.

Rain pattered and thumped on the house causing a near maddening hum to reverberate through the home that, for a moment, reminded him of the warble of the portal which Cloris and his mother had made between their worlds so many times over the last several months.

He wondered how they had communicated before moving here from back east. Mother had been going mad even then, but she was only on the outskirts of insanity, not yet a bona fide resident. But she'd been speaking with Cloris even then, hadn't she? She *must* have been, he had concluded, because the location for them to come and build their home had been so specific. Right here, right on the place he was now dragging the creature from another world, who, in its own reality, had been known as a *person*.

His mind swirled with these thoughts and others, trying to grasp the reality that his world, what he knew, was only one small part of existence. There were perhaps a hundred other worlds, perhaps a thousand. Maybe more. For all he knew there were millions, or even an infinite number of unknown worlds which overlapped with similarities and contradictions. Worlds that were as alike and as odd to one another as his own and the world of the witch, Cloris.

And then there was the Glutton.

Yes, the beast that seemed to transcend *all* worlds. He remembered Cloris saying something about it being eternal, as eternal as God. Something uncreated, yet still existing.

He supposed he could grasp the outer edges of understanding of this idea when it came to God. He wasn't religious, his family never had been, much to the chagrin of the locals of this small haven. But putting that reality on something like the Glutton wasn't adding up.

Madness.

Yes, it was madness for sure. Madness of the first order, as a matter of fact. But it didn't help him to understand the realities his mind was being forced to accept these past months, and had finally been broken by.

God was all-knowing. All love. All goodness. At least that was what he'd heard the religious of various brands refer to Him as. But the Glutton was none of those things. Only something that existed in pure goodness and light could be uncreated. At least that's what he believed. Evil wasn't a *thing*, not tangibly speaking, anyway. Evil was the *absence* of a thing, namely goodness. And the Glutton was certainly void of goodness.

He supposed Mother would disagree. She'd been desperate for another child. So desperate that she'd followed the call of Cloris to this desolate, isolated place. Followed her every demand and manipulation. Brought her family to this god-forsaken pit where the witch could feed her Glutton, to bring it into a new world. And what did this thing bring when it entered a new world?

Death.

The thing was death incarnate, that was what Johnathan Michael Brogan believed. And it hungered for the flesh of people above all things. Of persons. It would eat animals, sure, but they couldn't sustain it. They didn't give it life. It needed persons, and he feared that the more persons it fed upon, the stronger it would become in that respective world. Strong enough to enter it fully, to don a flesh of its own which came from that world.

And then he would destroy it.

The fever may have found them all, ruining his mother, killing his daddy, stripping Richard and Evangeline of their innocence. It had done the same to him, he supposed. He'd been unable to resist his urges and he had succumbed to the temptations set before him like a raccoon who has found garbage.

It was as if he couldn't help it.

No more, he thought as he rounded the corner into the foyer.

He dragged the blood-soaked body of Cloris into the foyer and dropped her to the floor. She settled with a fleshy *clump,* and her head—which was now only attached to her neck by the thinnest of sinew—lolled to the side, opening her throat in a bizarre way which looked like a horrible, gaping mouth. Sweat stood on his body now, mixing with the already drying and congealing blood spattered all over him. Streaks of crimson ran down his cheeks in jagged lines and smeared on the soft flesh of his throat.

The rain continued to hum.

It was almost hypnotic, that sound. Taking a few breaths, he'd allowed himself to focus on it, and found himself entranced by its consistent, overlapping, and over*powering* drum.

He was faintly aware he was smiling, and fresh tears streamed from his face, further smearing the blood of the witch he wore. Tears of many conflicting emotions. Tears of loss. Tears of pain. Tears of joy as the end neared. Tears of—

"What have you done?" a voice hissed behind him.

It was angry, full of venom. A voice he knew very well. A voice he had loved. Once upon a time, anyway.

Mother.

He turned slowly, the trance brought on by the sound of the rain broken for the moment. His eyes trailed lazily around the foyer as he did until they settled on his filth-streaked Mother standing at the mouth of the hallway.

Her eyes were wide and her lips were drawn back over browning teeth in a snarl which almost looked inhuman. Her hair was matted and askew with some substance he didn't care to identify, and she wore only a dirty slip. Her belly swelled from beneath the slip, showing a pregnancy that was much further along than it had any right to be. Whatever was inside of her, Johnathan decided that it couldn't be his brother or his nephew. It couldn't be human. It was some demon, some monster from the other world, seeded by his little brother, perhaps, but only in mechanics. He knew this somehow without knowing why. But all the same, there it was. As crystal clear as the fresh stream water down the hill behind their house.

He also saw his mother was holding a knife.

"Hello, Mother," he said in a flat, emotionless voice that defied the tears which continued to fall from his eyes.

She stared at him, eyes full of hate and vitriol. He could see she was trembling.

The knife's blade wavered in the candlelight.

"What have you done?" she hissed again. Her voice reminded him of the snakes which had vanished with suddenness only a few minutes before. Snakes no one but he had seen.

He, and perhaps the Glutton.

"I'm fixing things, Mother," he said in that same, flat voice. "I'm going to set things right. You're mad. Perhaps you don't know that. I expect you wouldn't. But it doesn't change the fact."

"You have no idea what you've done!" she shouted this time. "We were so close! Close to the power of immortality! We were—"

"We're close to DEATH, Mother!" he shouted back at her. *"That thing is death! And that thing inside of you is a monster!"*

She gasped at this and her empty hand slapped up to her mouth with an audible *clap*.

"How dare you!" she wailed in a high and wavering voice. "You dare speak of your brother in such a way!"

"It isn't my brother!" he shouted back, now clouding out the sound of the rain with the boom of his voice.

He heard a door creak upstairs but ignored it.

356

"You bastard!" she shrieked to him. "I should have listened to Cloris! To the Glutton! You are just like your father and you should have been fed to something greater than yourself just as he was!"

That knocked the breath out of him. The thing before him was not his mother. Perhaps it had been, in some distant history, but no more. Whatever deal she had made with Cloris had robbed her of her humanity and stripped her of the motherly love so intrinsic in a woman towards her children. She had lost all traces of the woman she had been, the one who'd loved him and cared for him. Who had fed and bathed him. The only thing she cared about was the monster inside of her.

Her precious Brogan new.

"What happened to you, Mother?" he asked, his voice breaking into a sob as the words left his mouth. "We were happy once, all of us!"

She didn't answer. She only glared and snarled that inhuman snarl at him, as though she were looking at a pile of excrement on her kitchen floor rather than her firstborn son. And he supposed that was fitting. A fitting end to a madness which could never be explained. After all, could *any* madness ever be explained?

He thought not.

There were some audible footsteps coming from above and he looked up to the banister that overlooked the foyer. Evangeline came into view, looking over the banister and down at them. Her eyes were sleepy and one hand grasped the railing while the other drew her nightgown tight about her chest. She had a confused and disoriented look upon her face.

Johnathan smiled at her.

"Johnathan?" Evangeline said in a sleepy voice. "What's—"

Then her eyes fell on the body of Cloris beside him. They grew wide and awake all at once. Her mouth fell open, her jaw dipping almost to the top of her chest.

"My God!" Evangeline screamed. *"My God, why?"*

Johnathan's smile wavered and retreated. His resolve boiled within him again. It had faltered for just a moment when he saw his sister—his beautiful, sweet sister. The one who'd put the fever into him in all this mess.

But now it was gone. *She* was gone. They all were, and it was time to—

That was when his mother screamed like a banshee, rushed forward, and buried the knife into his upper chest, nearly to the hilt.

He was aware of liquid warmth pouring over his chest and his stomach before there was any pain. When the pain came just a moment later, it washed over him in sheets.

Lightning flashed.

In that moment, in that split-second of bright clarity, he looked into his mother's eyes for the last time. Everything had slowed down, as though reality itself had come to a crawl.

Everything but him.

Her eyes were wild, like an animal, the pupils dilated to the point they looked like wet, black balls protruding and bugging out from their sockets.

Then he looked up, the world still crawling, and saw his sister. What he saw chilled him to the marrow.

Her eyes were identical to those of his mother. And where his mother was snarling in acid hate, his sister's face was shattered with a broadening smile.

"*No more!*" he screamed.

Reality came back to full speed. Johnathan pushed his mother back and she stumbled to the floor, her giant belly wiggling to and fro as she reached out to break her fall.

"God damn you, Mother!" Johnathan snarled down at her, raising the axe which was still gripped in his hand all this time. "God damn this place, God damn your Glutton, and God damn us all!"

His mother's eyes looked up at him and the hate and revulsion left them at once, replaced by knowing horror.

She didn't even have time to raise her hands.

The blade of the axe buried into her swollen stomach, making a horrible sound like a bursting pumpkin and a wet splash. His mother was screaming now, almost howling. His ears picked up another shriek coming from the stairs. Evangeline was descending them now, shouting and screaming all the way down.

Johnathan grabbed the handle of the knife and wrenched it free from his chest. White-hot pain ripped through him and fresh streams of blood spewed from the wound.

He winced, tossing the knife to the floor beside the corpse of Cloris, her open neck grinning up at him like a circus clown. It clattered to a stop and was silent.

He looked back to his mother, lightning flashing once more through the door, filling the foyer with ominous blue light. He raised the axe and walked unevenly towards her, spitting blood from his mouth as he went. Blood was pumping out of her belly as she struggled to crawl backwards on her hindquarters. Desperation filled her face, and while fear had not completely abandoned her expression, the black hate was back now as well.

"No more, Mother!" he bellowed from deep in his gut, blood spitting from his mouth as he went. "No more!"

Then something stung his shoulder, and fresh pain bolted through him. He winced and arced his back, reaching around blindly with a free hand and grasping something protruding from his back.

He jerked it free and saw the knife in his hand, the one he'd only just tossed to the floor. More hot liquid streamed out of him, down his back into his pants.

He looked towards the front of the foyer and saw Evangeline standing there, heaving breaths and snarling at him.

The same look his mother wore.

He was seeing red at this point. Pure rage had taken him, fueled by the hate for the fever he'd been victim to with his sister.

He spun around, the axe swinging in a wide arc. It sliced into the side of his sister's skull with a crack and her eyes took on a bewildered quality. She began to convulse. He could feel her shaking up the handle of the axe as she collapsed to the floor.

He never took his hand off the weapon.

His mother was screaming again, but he paid her no attention. His attention had now been drawn to another shape, one he'd not noticed until this moment. One which had been silent all this time, and had descended to the foot of the stairs as lightly as a feather.

The Damned Place

It was Richard.

But Richard's face was not full of the hate that had poured from his mother and his sister. His face had a sad look of relief, of resignation. It cut bitterly to Johnathan's heart.

"Richard—" he started, but could say no more. What was there to say?

Richard looked to Evangeline's now-stilling body, the blade of the axe still situated in the side of her skull. Then they looked past him to their squalling Mother.

They stood there like that for a long time. Johnathan had no idea just how long, but it seemed to drag on forever. Hot pain was throbbing through him, and his chest was tickled with wet blood, which he coughed up every so often.

Finally, Johnathan jerked the axe free from Evangeline's head and stood straight with great effort. Richard's gaze was upon their mother, behind him. Johnathan turned slowly to look at her.

She had dragged herself to the wall under the stairs, and the wound in her stomach was torn open much larger than it had been originally. She was fidgeting with a wad of gore that contained some of her intestines— which were spilling out—and another, larger thing, something which seemed almost to be human. The head of the blood-covered little beast was split open and a yellowish substance was leaking out and clopping to the floor. His mother was wailing incoherently, holding the thing which was half in her, and half out of her.

"My baby!" she shrieked. It was the only thing she said that could be understood.

Johnathan felt no regret. None at all.

He began making his way towards her, using the axe like a crutch. Blood continued to spew from his mouth as he went. He was going to finish it, once and for all.

No more.

Then a hand fell on his arm.

He turned, startled, and realized he'd all but forgotten Richard was there. One of Richard's hands was on his arm, the other outstretched towards the axe.

His eyes communicated everything to Johnathan.

Johnathan propped an arm on the wall and extended the axe to Richard, who took it with a reverence and purpose which seemed almost religious.

Then Johnathan watched his little brother chop their mother to pieces.

After the wails had stopped—which had been after the second swing or so—Richard had continued with a cold efficiency that would have been chilling if had not been so triumphant. His flat expression never changed, and his eyes barely blinked, even as sheets of blood splashed upon him time and again.

Then he went to Evangeline.

She was already dead, but this didn't seem to matter to Richard. He made quick work of her, as he'd done with their mother, and Johnathan was frightened to discover that he was in awe rather than horror of what he was witnessing. Richard had been in a near vegetative state for months, being used by their mother in the most ungodly and unmotherly fashion, and now he was back. Perhaps not in his emotions, but his brain was back, lucid, and full of purpose.

He finished with Evangeline, then turned on Cloris. After a time, the foyer was littered with gore and blood and body parts. The smell was horrific, but they were long past being revolted by stench. The metallic tang in the air almost smelled of victory rather than utter defeat, and Johnathan relished it.

It was almost over.

Richard strode silently back to Johnathan, holding the axe out to him as he went. Johnathan took the handle, and felt a final tear fall from his eye. A single droplet, no larger than a seed, dripped from his socket and down his cheek.

Richard knelt to the floor and spoke one final time.

"End it, Johnathan," he said in a cold voice which matched that of his expression through the whole event. "God damn us Brogans."

And Johnathan did.

CHAPTER 48

Johnathan managed to fashion a noose out of a piece of rope and hang it over the rafters above the banister that overlooked the foyer. He grabbed his journal, making a final entry. The rain had stopped, and he could hear the posse coming. Could see their torches flickering through the trees outside.

Come on, then, he thought bitterly.

He was getting very weak. He had lost a lot of blood, but he supposed none of that mattered now. Nothing mattered anymore. He was making his final plea to the world, his final request, bequeathing his responsibility to destroy this place—this *damned* place—by whatever means necessary. Burn it, tear it down, it didn't matter. So long as they heeded his words. The words of a madman, to be sure, but that didn't make them any less true. Any less urgent.

Please, he thought as he penned the final lines, *do what I could not. End this place. Close the door forever. You've no idea the horrors which lurk just beyond these walls.*

He finished writing and tossed the journal down amongst the body parts and gore beneath him, laughing a little as he did. Blood spat from his mouth, and he winced. The pain was lessening now, and he was feeling cold. So very damned cold. He would be warm soon, he knew. Warm for eternity.

They were very close, and he could hear their angry shouts. Their angry accusations.

Hypocrites! he thought angrily. *If you only knew! If you only fucking knew!*

"Come on, then," he said to himself as he placed the noose about his neck and cinched it tight. "Come in here and behold the damned Brogans! Behold the damned place!"

He stepped over the railing, holding himself in place as he spoke a final time in this world.

"And heed my words! Heed them, you hear? Or be damned as we are damned!"

He let go of the banister.

Chris Miller

PART SIX:

TAKEN

Thursday, July 5, 1990

CHAPTER 49

Twenty-four hours after the celebration of his country's declaration of independence from Britain, Jimmy Dalton's belly was still so full that the very thought of food was sickening to him.

The previous day had been spent over at Freddie's parents' house. They—Freddie's parents—had invited plenty of their friends over, and Freddie had been able to invite his friends as well. They all came; Jimmy, Honey, and Ryan. Burgers and hot dogs were flying off the charcoal grill, aptly manned by Freddie's dad, who amiably smiled and nodded as he talked with a group of men huddled about the grill as though it were a campfire. He'd guffaw with them at a particularly funny joke, while flipping burgers and hot dogs, sliding them onto serving plates which had been piled obscenely high, and wiping grease and sweat off himself on his 'Kiss The Cook' apron.

Jimmy could still hear the sounds of sizzling meat and the crackling of burning fat as it dripped from the handmade patties to the hot coals beneath, flaming up angrily and searing the ground beef. The hot dogs charring and wheezing like slowly deflating balloons.

And then there were the smells. The meat, the burning charcoal, the tangy odor of dill pickles and the tear-inducing scent of sliced red onions. The hoppy aroma of beer in plastic cups and the sugary spark of various sodas.

It had been an absolute feast.

All of it had been utterly delicious, as well, and Jimmy and the other kids had eaten exactly how growing, pubescent kids do: to great excess.

Jimmy himself had managed to down four hotdogs, replete with mayonnaise, mustard, ketchup, and dill relish, along with a rather massive cheeseburger piled high with all the fixings, including four strips of sizzling bacon.

And, God as his witness, it had all been cooked perfectly.

They had run around in the back yard at Freddie's house, zigging and zagging between folding tables and chairs with thin plastic covers taped to them depicting exploding fireworks over American flags and slogans like 'Happy Fourth Of July!' and 'Independence Day!', along with pictures of crossed muskets.

Quite a few people had been there, thirty at least, if Jimmy's estimating skills were on target. Many were from Freddie's church, others were the parents of Freddie's friends, along with a few of his aunts, uncles, and cousins. The adults stood around, drinking iced tea and cold beer, eating their grilled meals in much more modest quantities than the children. The kids ate, ate some more, then ate yet again, and between these feasts they would play guns and toss horseshoes toward the back of the yard until their raging metabolisms demanded more fuel. Then back they'd tread to the stacks of burgers and hot dogs and fixings—a stack which, despite their rather frequent plundering, never seemed to diminish in height.

The Damned Place

Freddie had been donning a large white bandage over his eye, his coke-bottle glasses sitting atop this in a comical display. The doctors had done what they could with his eye, but it had been determined that it was beyond repair. They were giving it a couple of weeks to be sure the tissues were indeed dead, and then there would be another surgery done to amputate the eye from the socket and insert a glass replacement.

Jimmy couldn't imagine how he might feel if it had been him who would be losing his eye. After all, you only got two. That was something his mother had often reminded him of whenever he would be going out to play and she feared he might get too rambunctious. Now, that sentiment seemed to strike home with a new reality.

But Freddie seemed to take it all in stride. He was a tough kid, Jimmy knew, despite his smallish stature and pale skin. The events out at the house in the woods had shown that. Jimmy couldn't think of anyone else, including himself, who would ever dare to snatch up a poisonous snake and wield it as a weapon. That took balls. Balls and, perhaps, quite a bit of outright fear and rage—that was to be sure—but balls all the same.

Freddie's parents had not let up in the questioning of just what had happened, either. They had even gone so far as to call the police station, and an officer had come to their house and tried to gently pull the whole story out of Freddie. Told him there was another kid, Chris Higgins, who had come to the hospital that same day with a broken nose. Young Higgins wasn't saying much either, only that he'd walked into a door in a house that his mother swore he wasn't in at the time, but he stuck to his story all the same. The cop tried to encourage Freddie, assuring him that if someone had hurt him, they could make them stop, and he needn't fear repercussions.

But Freddie had never budged. Only he, Jake and his pals, and Freddie's own friends knew what had happened.

I want him.

Jimmy remembered his friend's words as he lay there in his hospital bed, beat to hell, cold resolve in his good eye. A sentiment he'd repeated after telling them about the visit from the police.

People like him only understand one language, and that language is violence.

Jimmy understood how Freddie felt. Hell, he felt the same way every time they crossed paths with Jake and his boys. But even he, with all the newfound power he possessed, hadn't any real interest in going after the little psychos. *Violence only begets more violence,* his mother had said to him often, and he believed she was right.

Yet, moving about in fear, hoping not to have to face a problem—or running from one when it found you—didn't seem like much of a solution either. Jake deserved something bad to happen to him. Something *really* bad. Not only for what he'd done to Freddie, but just for being a bullying asshole in general.

So they'd all kept their mouths shut in loyalty to Freddie and his wishes. None of the parents liked it much—which the foursome had expected—but it was what it was, and without any proof, neither the parents nor the cops could do anything about it.

In the times they had *not* been getting interrogated by parental units or police officers, they had been poring over the photocopied pages of the old journal

Freddie had found at the library. Studying it. Looking at it from every angle. Trying to grasp the gravity of it all.

They had come to the conclusion that Johnathan Michael Brogan had indeed been insane, at least in the last couple of months of his life. Certain things couldn't be counted on to have any validity or truth, such as the snake infestation of which he spoke so hauntingly. But quite a bit of what Brogan had written, they inferred, was purely lucid, in spite of how crazy the rantings had seemed.

For one thing, they knew the thing—what Brogan had referred to as the 'Glutton'—was real. Both Jimmy and Honey had seen it first hand in their trip to the other world. And, of course, because of that trip, they knew without a doubt the other world existed.

Then there was Cloris.

Jimmy remembered the picture he'd seen hanging on the wall of the house in the other world. Remembered the furry faces and the four arms. Cloris had almost certainly been one of them. The fact that no other part of the family had been mentioned in the journals led them to believe that Cloris had likely fed them to her Glutton, that horrible beast in the woods from the other world, and it had been using her to break through into their own.

The fact that it hadn't immediately opened up the portal when Cloris died—which they had inferred from the fact that her body was amongst the Brogans' when the posse had found them and the thing had not come through and eaten them—was rather telling. It seemed to *need* the help of someone else to get through, someone like Cloris or—God help him—even Jimmy. At least initially.

This seemed to conflict with what happened with Ryan's father and Mike Barton, however, as Ryan had aptly pointed out one afternoon when they were in the old station that now substituted for their fort after the events in the woods. Mike had been dead, torn apart according to Chester Laughton, when he'd found him. This begged the question...

How did it get through?

They didn't know. They theorized, sure, but they didn't know. Not for sure. Their best guess was that perhaps it could open the doorway periodically, perhaps only after much time and preparation. Or maybe it found another like Cloris who could do it. Maybe not *all* of Cloris's family had been dead, at least not then. After all, if Cloris was able to open doorways between worlds, maybe it ran in the family.

They further theorized that perhaps even Mike Barton himself had done it unintentionally, much like Jimmy had done. They thought this to be the least likely explanation, but it couldn't be tossed out altogether, either. Chester and Mike were notorious for drinking while they hunted, though both would chastise the other if they caught them doing it. It was possible that, in an inebriated state, perhaps Mike had inadvertently opened the doorway and the thing, the Glutton, took him.

But all of this was mere theory. They had no proof one way or another, and decided the only important thing was that it seemed the Brogan house was the only place—the only place they *knew of*, at least—where the doorway could be opened. And it would behoove them to steer clear of it.

They had discussed the rest as well, though it often made their stomachs sick to think about. There was a certain foundation of evil in that place, and it made sense that space itself would be *thinner* there than in other places.

Their young minds reeled over all this information. None of it fit in with anything they had ever learned, or even with myths they'd been told around campfires. No part of it seemed to jive with physics and reality, yet, there it was all the same. There was no denying what they had seen and experienced, and now they had leather-bound, eighty-four-year-old proof that they weren't the only ones to come across this thing.

Now, his belly protesting movement of any kind, Jimmy rolled himself off of his bed and stood. He belched and could actually still taste the burgers and hotdogs from the day before, even though he'd drank plenty of water since then and brushed his teeth that morning.

It was not *nearly* as pleasant a taste when it came across the palate in reverse, and he winced as he smacked his lips.

He half-walked, half-waddled out of his room and down the hall to the living room. His mother was there, sitting in her chair in front of the blaring TV. Her head was cocked over to one side, her temple resting on her shoulder, a thin line of drool slinking from the corner of her mouth and terminating in a small, spreading dark patch on the fabric of her shirt just above her breast.

Jimmy looked to the lampstand which sat next to her chair and saw the half-empty glass of vodka, mixed with little else than ice. He frowned, but not in disgust. This was the norm. What she did most every day when she wasn't working. He was used to it. Hell, he even thought she *deserved* this after the way his father had just up and left them in search of that ever-elusive pack of cigarettes.

He briefly wondered if his father was even alive. Was he out there somewhere, living and going about his life—his *new* life—working and eating and shitting? Did he have a new family? Had *that* been why he left them? And if so, why had he never made contact with his son?

Or maybe he was dead. Either way, it didn't make much difference to Jimmy. But he realized that, deep down, he *would* like to know. Just to know if the man was alive or dead. Just to know if he was okay. He wasn't angry with him, not really. Not anymore. He and mom had gotten along without him this long, and he supposed they would continue to do so if mom could keep from drinking herself to death.

Still, he wondered.

He turned the TV off and relished a seemingly deafening silence for a moment. Then he went and reclined his mother's chair and propped her head back at a more natural angle so that she wouldn't wake up with a crick in her neck. Then he kissed her on the forehead.

"I love you, mom," he whispered to her with a small smile.

She responded with a loud snort and then began to snore. She wriggled in her chair, an unconscious movement to get more comfortable, and farted in the process. He giggled to himself silently as he stood and, despite the humor he felt, a single tear slipped from his eye. He blinked and wiped it away quickly, though there was no one there who would have noticed him doing it.

He wiped his hand dry on his pants, then grasped his mother's hand with his. Squeezed it gently. Repeated himself.

"I love you."

Then he turned and left the house, off to meet his friends.

CHAPTER 5Ø

The knife stuck into the wall with a loud *thud*.

Jake Reese smiled, looking at the faux-pearl handle that protruded from the wall opposite him in his room. His cunt mother had come into his room once earlier, when he'd still been trying to master the skill, and sheepishly asked what the commotion was. But one look from her son, whom she knew all too well was in charge, had sent her scurrying the other way, shutting the door behind her.

He crossed the room, still smiling to himself, and pulled the knife from the wall. A small clump of drywall fell away and dusted the floor with a fine powder. He regarded it for a moment and decided he would send the bitch in to clean it up when he went out. And she would do it, too. He knew that. She did pretty much anything he wanted now, if for no other reason than to avoid another good fucking.

As he crossed the room to work on further honing his new skill, he looked at the knife in his hand. Regarded its weight. It was a good knife, faux handle or not. The blade was sharp, and he knew how to handle it well.

Practice makes perfect.

He smiled again as he noticed a single speck of dark brown on the hilt. It was tiny, and he'd missed it until now. After the business with the four-eyed-faggot he had had quite a time washing the knife. Blood had managed to get into every nook and cranny of the object, and by the time he'd gotten home and begun washing it, most of it had congealed into a hardened glue-like substance that was a son-of-a-bitch to get off. But, in the end, he'd managed well enough, he supposed.

He reached the other side of the room and turned, facing the wall he was using as his target. He had no pictures of the little shit-holes he so desperately wanted to divorce from their collective skins, but he had a pretty good imagination. He envisioned the four-eyed faggot with his bleeding eye—God he *hoped* the fucker would lose his eye!—and he began to laugh. Then he conjured up their little shithead leader, the one who had hid from him in the closet of the old house. He imagined slashing his throat open and splashing the gouts of blood onto the kid's face as he died, desperately trying—but failing—to scream. The bigger kid—*what was his name, Ryan? Yes, Ryan*—clawing at his spilling intestines from an opened belly.

And there was the girl.

Ah, yes. The girl. The little girly. The titty-sprouting little girly-girl, her mouth open in a wide *oh*, choking on his cock as he held the blade to her throbbing jugular.

His laugh intensified.

Jake's voice had almost settled into a deeper, more adult tone, but it still cracked occasionally, and it did now as he laughed in his room. The sound made his laugh cease at once.

Fucking puberty!

His smile had been abruptly replaced with an angry snarl. He looked back to the wall, a half-dozen stab marks in it now from his knife-throwing, and envisioned the Faggot King himself, Jimmy Dalton.

He threw the knife. It tumbled end over end, and for just a moment, Jake had the dreadful feeling that he'd released the knife a half a moment too soon. He could see in his mind the knife's handle bouncing off the wall and the blade clattering to the floor.

"Missed me, bitch!" wall-Jimmy would say, laughing hysterically in high-pitched cackles like the faggot he was. *"Why don't you try again? Or are ya too much of a pussy? I'll bet you are, aren't you? A little pussy boy! Pussy boy likes to fuck his mother! You know what that makes you, pussy boy? Huh? I'll tell ya what it makes you! A motherfucker!"*

Wall-Jimmy would burst out laughing and cackling, his voice cracking in far higher pitches and with greater frequency than his own, but that wouldn't help the matter at all. No, it was mocking him. *They* were mocking him.

Faggots!

But his fears were misplaced. The blade of the knife dug home into the drywall, burying in just where wall-Jimmy's puny little heart would have been.

Jake exhaled, relieved he hadn't miscalculated his throw. But his joy was short-lived. Now he had to cross the room, fetch the goddamned knife, come back, and do it all over again. It was maddening. It wasn't like darts, where you had several you could throw before having to go and retrieve them. He had only the one knife.

He wished he'd been able to buy more than just the one knife when he'd gotten this one, but he hadn't had the money. Later, when he'd begged for more money—this had been some years ago—his parents had refused.

They told him if he wanted more money that he needed to work for it, and there were a plethora of chores he could do, earning himself a quarter an hour.

They had smiled at him, seeming to be proud of their wretched parenting skills, as if a quarter an hour were some kind of a gift.

But that had all been before the motherfucking. *Since* the motherfucking, Jake Reese got whatever the hell he asked for. He thought, as he stood there across the room from his knife which hung jaggedly out of the wall, that he would go and demand some money from his parents. He wouldn't ask. He didn't need to. Not anymore. A simple demand would suffice, and they would pay up. Then he could go on his bike to the store and pick up a few more blades just like this one. He knew they were there. He had seen them the other day when he'd gone in and stolen two candy bars and a soda. They were displayed, right there, in a glass case right next to the cashier's counter.

Still, none of that helped his situation right now, and it pissed him off.

"Fucking stupid knife!" he hissed as he took a step towards the opposite wall and lifted his hand out to grab it when he got there.

Then the knife yanked itself free from the wall and flew into his hand.

Jake stood, motionless, eyes bugged in fascination. He watched the drywall powder fall from the hole and clump to the carpet in a soft whisper.

His hand was still outstretched, the flying knife now clutched in his grasp.

Did I just do that? he wondered to himself.

Finally, after forcing his muscles to relax and reasserting his will over them, he brought his arm back down and looked at the knife in his hand. It was the same old thing it had always been. Faux-pearl handle. Tiny dot of blood on the hilt.

He turned it over in his hands a few times, inspecting it to be sure.

Yep, he thought. *That's it, alright.*

He looked back to the wall, then to his hand again, then back to the wall.

A smile spread across his face. The smile was malicious. It was *delicious.* Whatever had just happened, it was changing his world.

Oh, little faggots, he thought. *Oh, the things I could do to you!*

But he was putting the cart before the horse, he realized. He had to make sure it wasn't a fluke, a one-time occurrence, a chance mishap.

He went back to the place he had been standing when he threw the knife and tossed it again, this time with more force than ever before. It flipped and vaulted end over end and thudded into the drywall, much deeper than before this time.

Blade first.

The handle jutted out from the wall, pointing back to him, back to the hand that had thrown it, like an outstretched hand begging for help. It *was* begging him, too, he saw. It reminded him of the horseshit story in that book his parents peddled to all the feebleminded sheep at their congregation about the guy trying to meet Jesus on the water and sinking. Reaching out to him.

Begging for help.

The Damned Place

He reached his hand out and willed the knife back to him. It came.

Jake Reese smiled.

CHAPTER 51

Honey Bascom rode her bike lazily in the afternoon heat. She weaved and yawed through the mostly empty streets, thinking about her time with her friends the day before. It had been lots of fun and, unlike the boys, she hadn't stuffed herself to the bursting point with dead cow and pork bits. She'd enjoyed a more modest helping, only eating a single hotdog and half of a cheeseburger. Then the foursome had run about with some other kids she hadn't met before and played guns and hide and seek, to what limited ability they'd been able to.

It had been a good day.

This was in stark contrast to her life in general, though, and she had been happy for the reprieve. She'd been spending as much time as she could with 'the boys', as she called them, for the simple fact that being in her home was like living inside of a nightmare.

Her father, since the drunken incident with his bulging manhood in her face, couldn't muster the strength to look her in the eyes. But he sure talked a lot, mostly aided by copious amounts of Jim Beam when he had the extra cash, but more often it was Kentucky Deluxe.

He would ramble on and on to her, asking her how her day had been, what she had been up to. It always started like that.

"Whachoo been up to, Honey-bunny?" would be his typical, slurred opening.

"Not much," she would exclusively respond.

"Been playing with those boys, have ya?"

"I guess."

Then he would nod for a few moments, again, never looking her in the eye. Often, he would reach over and snatch his tumbler from the lampstand and gulp down another heaping portion of his poison.

It always went this way, as if read from a script. However, lately, he had begun to add to the conversations.

"That kid with the glasses," he would say, "he healing up okay?"

"Like I said yesterday, Daddy," she would respond, both huffing out a sigh and rolling her eyes, "he's coming along. Probably gonna lose his eye, though."

Another nod from her father.

"Well, that's a shame."

Then came the most intolerable sequence of these miserable conversations.

"Honey," he would start in a deeper and more reserved tone, "you know I love you, don't you?"

The first few times he'd done this, her eyes had filled with stinging tears and she'd stormed off to her room, leaving him holding his glass and crying himself, but as time went on, she had begun to respond.

"I guess," she usually said.

"I do, baby-girl," he said. "I really do. I loved your mother, too. So much. God...I miss her."

"So do I, Daddy," she would respond in a quiet voice, now averting her own eyes from him.

Yet another nod from her father.

"I know you do, Honey-bunny. I know you do. I, well, I just want you to know, no matter what, I love you with all my heart. It may not seem like it sometimes, and I'm sorry for that, honest I am, but it's the God's-honest truth. You're all I got left. I don't know what I'd do without ya, Honey. I don't...I—"

Then came the tears.

He would break down, then, and blubber over his whiskey and take new gulps from the tumbler between sobs of anguish. And during this time, Honey would typically go on to her room and shut the door.

And lock it.

She'd been doing that ever since the incident. God knew she loved her father. She really did. There was no question in her mind or in her heart about that. No matter his flaws, no matter how much of a fuck-up he was, she loved the man.

But she was also terrified of him.

She had deduced that on the night of the incident, her father had had no intentions of raping his little girl. He was drunk. In outer-space drunk. And she had happened to fall asleep on her mother's side of the bed that night as she had been thinking of her and missing her and trying to grieve in her own way. He had become confused. Had called her by her mother's name.

He missed her. She knew that. It was his grief, and more to the point, his inability to *deal* with that grief, that had turned him into what he now was. A drunk. A drunk that missed his dead wife and still got horny for her.

All the same, the incident had scarred her. Seeing him like that, in that state, with his, well, his *thing* right there in her face, had cut her deep down to her soul.

The once strong, kind, wise man that had been her father was now reduced to a stumbling, weepy alcoholic with a hard-on for his dead wife and an inability to separate fantasy from reality once he got really loaded.

So she locked the door every time she got in her room. She didn't dare go back to her father's room again after that, for fear of a similar occurrence. She had her own pictures of her mother she could look at.

But it was that one in there, in what had been her parents' room, that meant the most to her. She often found that no matter how hard she tried, she sometimes could not conjure up any solid memories of her mother. There were fragments and blips of times past, but just trying to think of a specific time with her on her own without some sort of talisman like the picture in her dad's room to aid her was nearly impossible.

Once, she had even been completely unable to picture her mother's face, never mind a memory of her.

But that picture, that sweet picture of the three of them, together, happy, the sun shining on their smiling faces, *that* picture always conjured the memory and her mother's sweet, loving face.

It was her favorite picture. Her favorite memory.

She leaned her bike and coasted onto the street where their new clubhouse was. She was going to meet 'the boys' to talk about dealing with the bastard Jake and his son-of-a-bitch buddies. Freddie was livid with rage over the situation, and his flushed cheeks displayed his desire for revenge every time the subject came up. Honey had no idea what—*if anything*—they could do about it. She was with Jimmy and Ryan on that point:

Freddie should tell his parents and let them and the cops sort it out.

But Freddie wouldn't budge on the issue, and their sense of loyalty to him kept their lips sealed.

She saw the old garage up ahead and realized she was going to be the first one here. No matter. She had a picture in her backpack of her mother she could look at. One she had snatched off the nightstand in her father's room that morning. The one that filled her with blissful memories of a woman she would never see again. She wanted—no, *needed*—this time to reminisce. Doing so at home, where her father always was, was too distracting. Here, it was better. She'd have the time to herself to longingly pore over the picture and the memory, to really get her mind back to a time when her mother was alive and beautiful and her father was sober and happy. When they were *all* happy. She sometimes thought it was the last time any of them had truly been happy.

She needed this, and beating the boys here was the perfect opportunity for her. In fact, she had timed it so that she would be here well before the others. She had wanted the time alone, away from her house and her drunk father—he was getting blitzed earlier and earlier in the day lately—and just spend some time with her mommy.

She was so focused on these thoughts as she pulled up to the garage-turned-clubhouse that she didn't see the person up the street who watched her go in, and peddled quickly towards her, a fat, stupid smile on his face.

CHAPTER 52

Bart Dyer's slobbering face wiggled and danced with the effort he expended pedaling towards the abandoned garage. He almost couldn't believe his good luck. Finding one of the punks come riding right to him. And it was the girl punk on top of that!

What luck!

He knew this would be thrilling news to bring to Jake. Chris wouldn't care too much. In fact, he'd been kind of a sourpuss ever since his failed intervention with Jake and the four-eyed faggot—that was Jake's name for him, and *boy*, could Jake ever come up with a name!

Chris had ended up with a broken nose. He'd had to lie to his mom about what had happened, but that was no real trouble. They had been almost certain the four-eyed faggot, not Chris, would be what got them into real trouble. In fact, Bart believed that the only reason Jake hadn't cut the little fucker's throat that day had been because of Chris. Even though he was down for the count with his bleeding, busted nose, Jake didn't think Chris would go along with killing the little puke.

Bart didn't care. As a matter of fact, he relished the idea. He had often wondered if people's insides were anything like the insides of a dog. He knew all about those, and he assumed it wouldn't be too much different inside of a person, but all the parts and sacks would be bigger, that was for sure!

He had to admit, though, it had been wise on Jake's part to stop when he had. They had heard through the grape-vine that the kid was probably going to lose his eye, and that had made Bart laugh so hard his spleen felt like it was going to burst. And that had led him to wonder just what a spleen *looked* like.

He hoped sometime soon he and Jake could find out. That would be rad!

And, he thought, perhaps this could be just their chance. The little girly bitch was just ahead, slipping into the old garage, completely oblivious to him as he sped towards her. Or, at least what *passed* for speeding when it came to Bart Dyer and his gelatinous build.

He thought about how cool it would be to see her titties before they checked out her spleen, and the thought actually made him salivate more. They weren't much, smaller than his mom's—he'd seen hers a few times while peeking through a small hole he'd made into their bathroom when she was getting out of the shower and masturbating—but he figured they would still be cool to check out.

He skidded his bike to a stop—the rolling force of his ogre-like frame was no small thing to bring to rest—and stepped off the bike. He let it collapse to the ground as he made his first few tentative steps towards the garage where the girl had disappeared.

It was hot out, but despite this, he felt his skin pebble with goose-flesh all over. Even on his balls. He liked that feeling, and it got even better when a bead of sweat rolled across his scrotum. It was thrilling, and his adrenaline factory, located in some unknown location

390

inside his body, was pumping the stuff out at maximum volume.

He shivered.

Bart moved faster now, hunkering over slightly in a pathetic attempt to move with stealth. It didn't serve to hide him from discovery whatsoever, but when he reached the door the girl had slipped through—which was still standing slightly open—he saw it wouldn't have mattered anyway.

She was leaning up against an old work-table, looking at something she held in both hands, almost as though it were a sacred thing.

It was a picture, he determined after a few moments of inspection from his viewpoint. Some picture she was looking at. The girl was smiling and crying at the same time as she gazed upon it, unaware of anything or anyone else in the world.

Bart smiled.

This was going to be great. The goose-pimples on his balls seemed to excite and a tingling sensation filled his groin. Jake was gonna owe *him* one now, for the first time ever! Boy, oh, *boy*! He couldn't wait.

He peeked in a little further, being as quiet as he could, trying to control his panting breath from all the excitement. His eyes moved from the picture in her hands to the tiny twin bumps under her shirt.

You're gonna show us them titties! he thought lustfully. *And then we're gonna see your spleen!*

He had no plan. No real idea at all, actually, of just what he would do, never mind how he would transport her, make her do what he wanted. But none of this was going through his mind just then. All that was going through his twisted, adolescent mind were images of boobs and blood.

His two favorite things.

CHAPTER 53

Jimmy pulled up to Freddie's house on his bike.

He was thinking of his bicycle today as Ol' Red, because there was a particularly Southern feeling in him that day. The way he'd left his mother, in her stupor of a state, which had made him feel chivalrous and noble, and thus his mind had adopted the more south-of-the-Mason-Dixon proper terminology.

He was both excited and nervous about meeting with his friends this day, because they had decided to come up with a plan to get back at Jake and his fuck-rag pals. Something that would rectify them for what they had done to Freddie when they had brutalized him. Something that would make them pay.

But what?

He really didn't know. All he knew was they were going to meet at the clubhouse—the old garage across town—and discuss the matter. He had a feeling Freddie had some ideas, being the one who had been brutalized, but beyond that, he was basically along for the ride.

Ryan's bike was already there. He could see Ryan and Freddie in the yard, conversing and laughing as he braked the bike and dropped the kickstand.

"What's happening, guys?" he asked as he threw his leg over the bike and stepped off.

They turned to look at him as he spoke, until now unaware of his presence. They both smiled.

"Off to the clubhouse, man!" Freddie exclaimed. "We've got plans to make!"

Ryan didn't say anything, as was his norm, and just smiled stoically as Jimmy approached.

"Is Honey meeting us here?" Jimmy asked as he came to a stop in front of them in the front yard of Freddie's house.

Ryan shook his head.

"Not here," he said. "She's meeting us at the clubhouse. She called earlier and said she'd see us there."

Jimmy nodded and looked back and forth between them.

"So," he said, a small, almost imperceptible grin scarring his face. "You got a plan, Freddie?"

Freddie looked at him through one eye, the other shrouded in bandage, and grinned back at his friend.

"I've got a million ideas," he said, "but I'm not sure any of them are plausible."

Plausible, Jimmy thought. *Nice fucking word.*

Jimmy was always surprised by Freddie. He was the smallest of them all, including Honey, and seemed to be what one would refer to as weak, or passive. But the fact of the matter was that Freddie James was anything *but* weak and passive. Inside of this kid was a resolve and fight unlike anything Jimmy had ever seen in another person, and that included all the adults he'd ever known. Freddie never looked for a fight, but he would sure step up to the plate when the time came. Whether this was motivated out of pure fear or resolute rightness, Jimmy was never sure, but it was there all the same, and that was what mattered.

The kid had grit.

"Okay," Jimmy said, "Do we roll, then?"

Ryan and Freddie nodded, but Ryan responded.

"Let's go get our girl and figure out how to fuck these assholes up!"

As they were saddling up on their bikes, Freddie's mother stepped out. Jimmy was struck again with her beauty and with a memory of the wonderful and horrible dream he'd had about her in the woods. The one he was sure the Glutton had projected into his mind that night a few weeks back when they'd *all* been plagued with terrors in their sleep. His cheeks flushed and darkened to new shades of magenta which had as yet to be identified.

"Jimmy?" she called to him, causing his heart to skip a beat.

Or three.

"Y-yes, ma'am?" he choked a reply.

"Phone for you!" she said. "They say they're a friend of yours?"

Jimmy, his flushed cheeks calming to their default color, pondered just who in the hell would be calling him, and here of all places. He was with all of his friends here. Well, all but Honey, anyway. And she had already called to say she would meet them at the clubhouse.

So just who could it be? he wondered.

He got off his bike and made his way to the door Mrs. James—in all her glory that drove adolescent boys out of their minds—held open for him. Then she led him to the kitchen where the phone laid on the counter-top.

He grasped it in his hand and put it to his ear.

"Hello?"

Over the next sixty seconds, his breathing almost stopped completely, and then resumed forcefully, almost panting as his body kicked his mind aside to acquire the desperately needed air.

His knuckles became white on the receiver.

CHAPTER 54

Bart Dyer was *literally* beside himself.

He couldn't believe what he'd managed to accomplish. *Him!* Of all people, little old fat-boy Bart had managed to snag the cream of the crop, the prized hen. The itty-bitty-titty-kiddy herself. The bitch of the fags.

He was still in a stupor of disbelief that he'd pulled it off, though during the event he had never thought a single time. Not once, and that was no exaggeration. It had been pure, unadulterated action.

Bart had simply acted on instinct, and it had managed to work out in his favor, as few things in his life ever had. It happened often enough for Jake, even Chris sometimes, but rarely for him.

Yet, this day was different. He had seen an opportunity, and seized the day.

Carpe diem, baby!

He didn't know where he'd heard that phrase before, and it didn't matter. It fit the situation flawlessly, and made him grin, even though he was wholly unaware it was actually a correct use of language.

He was riding his bike, following behind the bitch—Honey was her name—and staring at little else than her ass as it flexed and bobbed on her own bike. She was in his control now, and the thought of this

397

made him grin so wide that, for a moment, he thought his face might burst.

He had stepped into the garage she had vanished within, while she was crying over some picture that had been in her hands, a picture which was now in his pocket. A picture he'd seen had been of her and what he presumed to be her parents.

He had heard a story once about a bad car accident a couple of years back between Winnsboro and Sulphur Springs on Highway 11, one where the occupants of the car were a man, a woman, and a young girl.

The mother had died.

It wasn't until he had snatched the picture from the tiny-tittied girl at the garage that he'd put together it had been *her* who had been in the crash. That it had been *her* who had lost her mother that day in the accident.

And then, in the rarest of forms, inspiration had struck him.

The girl, who he meant to open in both clothing and skin with his buddy Jake, had begun to tremble when he'd taken the picture away. As his feeble mind began piecing together just what this picture meant to her, he was struck with just how he could control her.

That was the thing he had needed, had *known* he needed, from the moment he'd walked into the garage. Sure, he could have hit her over the head with one of the myriad blunt objects lying about in the place, but this was better. This was a way that he could extract maximum damage on her, and maximum satisfaction on his own part, as well as that of Jake's.

And it had worked out flawlessly.

She had trembled and begged, begged for the picture to be returned, and had been reduced to tears when he'd held it in both hands as though he were going to rip it apart.

"Please!" she'd screamed at him. "Please, no! I'll do whatever you want, just don't do that!"

Bart had smiled viciously at this, and responded to her.

"Anything, huh?"

She had nodded, tears streaking her face, her eyes red and watery.

"Yes!" she wailed to him, reaching for the picture which he snatched away, laughing and hawing in his donkey bray.

"Well," he had said, "we'll just have to see about that!"

That had been when she succumbed to him completely. No longer was she trying to snatch things from him. She had resigned to his power over her, and was at his disposal.

He had made her get on her bike, and told her where to go. First, they had gone to the gas station by the library, the place he and Jake had been when they had seen the four-eyed faggot just before they beat the shit out of him. Well, before *Jake* had beaten the shit out of him, anyway. Bart had done more watching and laughing than anything else.

Then he made a phone call.

"Hello?" a woman's voice answered.

"Yes, ma'am," Bart had said. "Is Jake there?"

"Uh," the voice of Cherry Reese said and paused. "Well, yes, he's here, but I think he's busy at the moment."

There was a sound in the background of a plate smashing—at least that's what it sounded like to Bart—

and then he heard Mrs. Reese talking with the phone away from her ear.

"Norman!" she said. "Oh, sweet baby, are you okay? Did you cut yourself? It's fine, don't cry, mommy will make it all better! Just leave it there, sweetheart."

"Mrs. Reese?" Bart inquired to the receiver.

"Yes, dear, I'm here," she said. "Look, Jake is very..."

She trailed off, as though searching for the right words.

"...well, he's just tied up at the moment. I really hate to disturb him right—"

"He'll want to talk to me, Mrs. Reese," Bart had said. "I promise you that. Could you just get him for me?"

There was a pause, and then she said, "Okay, hold on just a moment."

There was a *thunk* sound as the receiver on her end was laid down. Then he heard her speaking to that weird little brother of Jake's once more.

"Norman?" she said in the softest and most loving motherly voice he'd ever heard. "Could you please tell your brother to come to the phone?"

"Yes, mama!" came a reply from what Bart assumed was Norman, the weird little shit the Reeses seemed to adore and glorify.

At least Mrs. Cherry Reese did, anyway.

Then he'd spoken to Jake. Jake was even more excited than Bart had hoped possible. This filled him with a joy he'd not felt since the last time he'd opened up a small animal with the knife his father had given him for his birthday and studied the thing's insides, turning them over and examining them with rapture.

He was ecstatic.

"You know where to go," Jake had said on the phone. "I'll get Higgins on the phone and we'll meet you there. And I'm gonna call the faggots too."

All cool with Bart, he'd said sure thing, and hung up.

Now, the girly bitch was rocking and swaying on her bike in front of him, going to the place Jake had told them to go, and crying the whole way.

"You don't know what's out there!" she exclaimed to him, looking over her shoulder. "You have no idea what you're dealing with! You should listen to me, Bart! We saw—"

"Shut the fuck up!" he barked at her from behind. "Just shut your cunt and ride!"

And she had.

She rode on, knowing the way almost better than Bart knew himself.

They rode as far as they could go on their bikes, then dismounted.

"Okay," Bart said, still stifling giggles of the ass variety and rubbing his hand over the pocket which contained the picture, the one that meant so much to the little girl. "Lead the way, bitch."

Then they set off into the woods.

CHAPTER 55

Ryan's face went ghost pale at the news.

It wasn't far from Freddie's house to get to their new clubhouse. Jimmy had come out from the phone call looking much the way Ryan did now. He had said little, only that they had to move. That he would tell them everything at the clubhouse.

"Just trust me," he had said, mounting up on his bike. "We've got to move, and fast!"

Freddie and Ryan had mounted up without another word, and they peddled off after Jimmy for the short ride to their abandoned garage turned clubhouse.

Jimmy told them everything.

"It was Jake," he had said.

"What?" Freddie retorted to this news with shock evident on his face and in his unconcealed eye. "How the fuck did he get my—"

"Never mind that now," Jimmy said, cutting him off. "They have Honey!"

Ryan felt as though his guts might actually spill out the back of him. It was an acutely separate sensation to that of feeling as though one might shit their pants. This felt as though the very structure of his bowels might turn themselves inside out and spew from him like a gory link of sausage.

He'd never felt so afraid. Never so sick.

And never so angry.

The mish-mash of feelings and emotions exploded within him with sickening fury. His mind spun and his vision blurred deliriously as he struggled to get hold of himself. The boy knew cowardice and he knew bravery. Hell, on their last encounter with the assholes in the woods he had exhibited both qualities in near totality, his bravery finally winning the day, but only by a thread.

A thread which he felt now might break.

And wasn't that just fucking jolly, too? Here they were with the girl who had made his heart skip a beat every time he saw her since they'd met in the woods, as he'd farted and struggled to hide pornography. She was in a dire situation, a situation far *more* dire than anyone but they could fully understand, and desperately needed their help. Yet, all the same, he could feel that sick, deep, awful stallion of fear and cowardice gripping him from within, braying and bucking, ready to break free at the slightest hint that he might let his inner barn door open.

Pull it together!

Yes, he had to pull it together. It wasn't as though he was the only one who cared about her. He knew they *all* did, though, in his mind at least, to varying degrees.

He also could see the fear on Jimmy's face as he laid the story out to them. He turned, willing himself not to break down and cry like the little puny baby his father had always told him he was, and could see quivering liquid in the one exposed eye on Freddie's face.

No, he wasn't the only one who cared. That was for damn sure. But Ryan cared *more*. He wasn't sure if the others knew that, and he was almost *positive* Honey didn't, but it was the truth all the same. He didn't just like their new friend, didn't just care about her. It was deeper than that. Something his young adolescent being had never yet experienced, and he feared never would again.

He *loved* her.

"They found her, somehow, at the clubhouse, I think," Jimmy was going on. "I guess she got there early. She was waiting for us! They—"

"Goddamnit!" Ryan suddenly erupted, raising his hands, clenched into white-knuckle fists, into the air like an angry Viking.

The others fell silent. Stared at him. Understanding.

"We'll figure this out," Freddie put forth weakly, his voice cracking dismally. "We just have to think!"

"While you guys *think*," Ryan spat as he turned to the door, beyond which their bikes rested, "I'm going after her. It's our fault she's with them anyway!"

"What do you mean it's our fault?" Jimmy quipped back at him, righteous indignation upon his face. "We didn't take her! She's *our* friend too, you know!"

Jimmy stood there in the middle of the old garage with frustrated anger painted on his face in magentas and pinks, and his hands comically displayed on his hips, one of which had cocked out to the side in what Ryan thought to be an almost laughable attempt to display such indignation.

"Maybe you forgot, but it was *me* who pulled her into that other place when Bart was crawling after her under that damned house!" Jimmy barked. "It was *me* who smashed that nasty slug thing out there in the—"

"I don't give a shit!" Ryan roared with surprising authority. It was enough to silence Jimmy, whose hip

popped back into alignment and hands dropped down flaccid to his sides.

"It's *our* fault," Ryan went on, more calmly now as he began to control his breathing. "Those jackasses were after *us* when school let out. Not her. And we *knew* that! But we still let her into our circle, into our club, into our fort! If we hadn't done that, she wouldn't have been there that day, and she wouldn't be there now!"

He stopped then, allowing the brief reverberating echoes of his speech to die out naturally. In short order, the only sound in the room was their labored breathing. Somewhere, probably a couple of streets over, they heard a horn blast and the distant, inarticulable voices of people arguing.

After roughly an eon, Freddie took a couple of steps forward, putting himself between Ryan and Jimmy, who had ceased to speak.

"Guys," Freddie said, spreading his arms out between them, trying to form a unifying bridge for the trio, "this isn't helping Honey at all, agreed?"

His good eye bulged wide and he looked from Ryan to Jimmy, then back again. They both lowered their gazes and nodded slowly.

"And no matter what the reason," Freddie went on, "no matter who's to blame, none of that matters right now. What matters is that we help Honey. Do you agree?"

Again, the others nodded, not looking up. Ryan could feel that stallion getting riled up again, even after the beating he'd been giving it while screaming at his friend across the room. Now it was kicking at the door again, whinnying loudly and violently, threatening to break free.

"Now," Freddie said more calmly and lowered his hands, "since we've reached that understanding, how about we listen to a little reason, huh? Because we have something Jake doesn't, and something he doesn't even *know* we have."

"What's that?" Jimmy said, breaking the silence between he and Ryan.

Ryan was looking confusedly to Freddie as well. Freddie smiled, looking now from Ryan to Jimmy.

"You," he said, winking with his one eye at Jimmy. "We have you, mister moves-shit-with-the-force-of-his-will!"

As he glanced back and forth between them, smiles began to break out between Ryan and Freddie. Jimmy's face remained flat.

All the same, Ryan felt the bucking stallion of cowardice inside of him fall silent.

CHAPTER 56

"Thnis is gohning doo far!" Chris Higgins exclaimed in a hushed and violent whisper, his words slurring into nasal obscurity behind a cotton-packed and spline-taped monstrosity which rested over the contours of his busted nose.

The resulting hospital visit after his ill-advised attempt at intervention on behalf of the bespectacled kid named Freddie had turned out to be almost worse than the actual breaking of his nose in the first place. There had been plenty of pain, to be sure, when Jake's elbow had slammed over the tender bridge of his nose, and the hideous *crack!* which had echoed in his ears for what seemed like hours was no walk in the park either. But none of it had compared to the moment—that terrible, spine-tingling moment—when the doctor had exhaled in an aggravated, *is-this-really-what-my-life-has-been-reduced-to* tone.

"Okay, here we go," the old doc had said.

His hands—one of which had been holding the back of Chris's head at the base of his skull, the other gripped in preparation about his misshapen nose—had tensed for one horrible, agonizingly suspenseful moment which had seemed to stretch on into some form of eternity.

Then there had been a hard yank.

Black comets streaming red haze had flashed across his eyes like racing semen in search of a fertile egg. There was another loud *crack!* in his head which echoed off his ear-drums like a heavy-metal soundtrack, the drummer using a double-kick on the bass drum at the speed of light.

Pain, a devilish monstrosity in comparison to the original break, exploded in his head, on his face, and behind his eyeballs.

"Yeeeoowwwww!" Chris had screamed in a pitch several octaves higher than he imagined even Freddie Mercury from Queen could have matched.

Then the tears began to flow from his eyes in rivers. It wasn't so much from the pain—though there was more than enough of it to justify some blubbering—but more from a simple involuntary release from the tear ducts. It was as if there were a reservoir, holding back a monumental tide of overflow, and someone had just released the dump-valve.

The doctor had sported an indifferent look when he'd asked what had happened and Chris had told him he'd had an accident on his bike. Chris didn't think the old doc believed him, but the old doc didn't seem to really care too much *how* it had occurred so long as his mother's insurance went through and he got a check in the mail for his troubles.

His mother, however, had bought the story easily enough. When he'd come stumbling in the door, his hands, face, and shirt covered in darkening blood—and fresh streams of the stuff still leaking from his butchered nose—she hadn't given much of a damn one way or another how it had happened. All she'd cared about was getting him to the doctor, and right quick.

408

The Damned Place

After the horrific resetting process at the hands of the indifferent old doc, they had fashioned a malleable metal spline over his injured nose and taped it in place, as well as stuffed what seemed to be a metric ton of cotton into his crusted nostrils.

The healing wasn't happening as fast as he'd hoped, or even as fast as it should have been. By now he should have at least had the cotton out of his nasal cavities, but he'd bumped it pretty good just a few days prior when his foot slipped in the shower and he'd broken his fall with his nose before his hands could fully engage. This incident inspired fresh eruptions of both pain *and* blood, soaking straight through his gauze-stuffed nostrils and dripping out in stringy cords. Again, he saw the scattering comets of fury as his consciousness toyed with fainting.

But he'd managed to stay on his feet and avoid collapsing altogether. This diversion had prompted a second trip to see the old doc, who had stared on with patient indifference. The swabs were extracted and discarded, and fresh truck-loads of the stuff had been mashed up into his skull as he restarted the healing process from ground zero once more.

Fuck you, Jake!

That was an almost constant mantra chanting through his head like a throbbing organ. Every time he thought of that asshole's elbow smashing into him and sending him down this trail of neverending misery—it really did seem to the young man that this horrific pain and misery would go on forever—his cheeks would flush a shade of crimson which seemed hot to the touch and his fists would clench until the knuckles turned white and all circulation ceased to his fingers and they began to ache.

But none of this seemed to stop him from continuing to submit to the will of Jake Reese.

Every time he called, Chris was there. He went with him and Bart wherever he was beckoned and did so with minimal grumbling. Not that grumbling would do much good, anyway. Bart and Jake were still his bread and butter, so to speak, even though Chris's mother seemed to find a shred of heart within her since he'd busted his nose in the phantom bicycle accident.

Chris knew better than to expect any of that to continue, though. If he wanted to continue to be able to get cigarettes, the occasional beer, and all the candy bars and sodas he desired at no cost to himself or the elder Higgins, he would have to remember his place.

And that place was under the thumb of Jake Reese.

But this...well, this was just taking things too far. Even for a fairly passive-aggressive sort such as himself, this was getting dangerously close to felonious assault. Hell, it *was* felonious assault. Never mind kidnapping and terroristic threat to life and limb.

"We canda new dis, Shyake!" Chris said, garbling his intended *we can't do this, Jake,* to a hilarity that even Jake Reese seemed to be able to appreciate.

"Shut your cunt, Chris," Jake said through the receiver while laughing. "Don't be such a fag. Meet us out there, got me?"

"Kwhy me?" Chris asked, frustrated. *"Kwhy do jew neet me?"*

Why me? Why do you need me? Goddammit, why the fuck can't I talk straight?

410

Captain Obvious flew in, cape billowing, and explained the situation for Chris, his chiseled and flawless jaw bobbing up and down, one eyebrow raised, a finger bobbing and pointing as his needless points were made. Chris cursed the asshole hero of the overtly explicable and he dismissed the question as Jake responded.

"Because I need both of you there. We're going to teach these punks a lesson they'll never forget! What happened to the four-eyed faggot is *nothing* compared to what we're gonna do to this bitch today! I'm gonna make them wish they'd never crossed our path!"

I'm pretty sure they already wish that, Jake-ass, Chris thought, but didn't say.

And then, he surrendered.

It wasn't as though he was ever ultimately going to say no. It was more that he'd hoped Jake would let him off the hook on his own. Chris wouldn't say no to Jake for virtually *any* reason, none that he could think of, anyway. So his best hope was to not be asked, or for Jake to change his mind.

Which he rarely did.

Besides, he thought after he told Jake he would be there and hung up the phone, *it's not like he's going to kill anyone, is it?*

This question made him pause. He really *didn't* know what Jake was capable of. It was entirely possible that killing them was *exactly* what Jake had in mind, and Chris knew that Bart would dance along like a fat, jolly son of a bitch with any such activity.

He won't, Chris thought, reassuring himself. *He can't...right?*

Chris had made his way to the door to go meet them and paused. His hand was resting on the doorknob. Trembling. Sweat stood out on his forehead.

Suddenly, he wasn't sure of anything. A sick feeling flooded over him, making him forget all about his disaster of a nose.

He stood there several more moments, debating with himself, going back and forth, and finally decided on what to do.

He went back to the phone, picked it up, and dialed information. He asked the operator for the name—he only had the last name—and had them connect him. There were some *beeps* and *boops*, a few clicks, then the phone began to ring.

And it rang again. Then a third time.

Come on! he thought, already feeling his resolve fade. *Come on, answer the fucking phone before I lose my sack!*

A fourth ring buzzed away in his ear. Every time he heard that incessant sound, he felt his heart sink deeper and his bravery retreat. He had no delusions that he was some noble knight by any means, but he did have a conscience. He was at least a human-fucking-being, for Christ's sake! He may not be willing to cross Jake Reese, but when things went this far out of hand, he at least felt he could—and *should*—balance the scales a bit. He had nothing against those poor kids himself. Hell, he'd been their age just a couple of years before, and he hadn't enjoyed getting pushed around by the older kids. So why was he doing it now? Why was he allowing this? Why, even as he was trying to do something decent for once, was he desperately close to slamming the receiver down and running out the door and just forgetting all about—

"Hello?" a weary voice answered in his ear.

He had almost forgotten that he was still holding the phone to his ear, and the sound changing from the buzzing ring to that of a human voice was startling to say the least.

"Dello!" he said, his voice cracking in his nasal register.

"Yes, can I help you?" the weary voice replied. The voice sounded tired, or sad. Maybe both.

"Dyeah," Chris said, trying his best to articulate his words, but still falling short. *"Sowwy to bahdda dew, an dew dond't know me, bud I godda dell hew shumthee, so lissend hup!"*

He told the person on the line everything.

CHAPTER 57

Bart dragged Honey up the stairs to the old, damned house in the woods by her hair. She was kicking and screaming, then begging and pleading in quick succession. Tears streamed her face and her eyes were puffy and red.

"Please!" she screamed at the fat boy who was giggling through the entire ordeal. *"You don't understand! There's something horrible here!"*

But Bart didn't care about anything she said at all. His mind was preoccupied with what her titties and spleen would look like, not with the contents of the house itself. The house was merely a sanctuary wherein he and Jake—and maybe Chris if he could muster up the balls—would partake in the sacrament of dismemberment.

And oh, how he *hoped* they would do just that!

Bart was a cruel boy. There was no getting around that fact. He enjoyed most fervently reliving the time when he'd opened up the family dog. But in Bart's mind, his motivation was not cruelty itself, but mere curiosity. He just wanted to know what was in there. It was more about seeing something than causing pain, though he was aware of that inevitable side-effect. He'd found it fascinating to see the insides of the frog in science class, and he had begun to fancy himself a connoisseur of the art. He dreamed of one day becoming one of those guys he saw on the TV who would do an autopsy after a person died. Of opening up the corpse and digging into the contents therein, sifting through the organs and the guts and the blood.

By Jove, I've found it! he often thought in an Alfred Pennywise—who just so happened to be Batman's butler—voice as he imagined himself standing over a metal slab table with a corpse sitting atop it, the chest and stomach opened and pulled back in a banana-peel fashion, held by metal clamps and hooks.

This chap died of acute explosion of the cardiac muscle tissue, caused by the marriage of nauseating fear and, well, of course, this giant slug from a twelve-gauge shot-gun!

In this fantasy he would look up to a pair of grizzled cops, standing on the other side of his table and holding kerchiefs over their mouths as he performed his work. Their eyes would light up beneath dark fedoras with shock and amazement and the kerchiefs would slowly lower from their faces.

Are ya sure, doc? they always asked. *At the scene we had no idea what had happened!*

Bart would look up through perfectly circular spectacles—even though he had no need of them himself, he always assumed it was as necessary a part of the attire as the white coat and green, rubber apron—and smile broadly.

Quite sure, governors! he would quip in his British accent. *Quite sure, indeed! You can see here—yes, just lean in a bit, old chaps—right here where this pulp of tissue is? Yes, that's it, the one that looks like an exploded hamburger. Well, you see, this was the chap's heart! Moments before his death, it was palpitating rapidly—running quite the race, I assure you, yes quite—and as the slug penetrated his chest, well, the goddamn thing just blew right the fuck up like the fourth of July! Really quite a spectacle it must have been, indeed. So you see, you find the man with the twelve-gauge—I'm quite sure it's a twelve-gauge, because I'm a doctor, you see—and you've got your man!*

Bart was smiling at this fantasy, as he pieced his meager masterpiece together in his mind from all the old TV shows he watched, and some of the more gritty things he'd seen in the movies on HBO after his parents had gone to sleep and he was in search of something to assist him in masturbation.

But, as often as breasts and the furry things below a lady's belly made him get hard enough for the ritual, so did scenes of corpses. Especially when they were opened up on a table in the cop shows and movies when the autopsy was being performed.

He couldn't wait to grow up and become one himself. Then he would have all the spank material a boy could ever dream of. His grades were subpar, but none of that mattered. His father would see to it he got into any school necessary to get into the field, that he knew. So it wouldn't matter.

One day soon, he would have his own table to open people up on. And if providence shined upon him today, well, he'd get a head start.

"Please!" the bitch was screaming at him again. *"You don't understand!"*

"I understand just fine!" he spat back at her as he kicked in the door to the house and threw her inside.

She sprawled to the floor and rolled once, wincing and grabbing at the base of her neck, massaging the area where the roots of her hair had been strained in his efforts to bring her here.

416

He stood over her, looking down at her with a crooked grin. His eyes were on the little nubbins of her budding breasts, which he could see swelling beneath the fabric of her shirt, now soaked in sweat. He loved that smell. The sweat was sweet, because he could smell not only the salt of the excretion, but also her fear. Fear was a wonderful scent, one he'd grown to love that day as he began to open up the family dog. Dogs didn't sweat, he'd learned that much in school, but they still felt fear, and fear had a tangible smell. Be it through the sweat of a person or the panting breaths of a dying dog, it had a scent, and Bart Dyer relished it.

"You need to shut your mouth and stop your bitching, dyke!" he barked at her in a flat tone. "Jake will be here soon, Chris too, and then we'll have some real fun!"

He watched the girl shiver when he said this. It gave him a shiver of his own which snaked down his spine, slithered through his considerable belly, and rested in his groin. He liked that feeling. The exhilaration as the crops of goose-flesh burst forth upon his skin and tingled his nerves. But more than that, he enjoyed watching her sweat.

New streams of the stuff had begun to pour out of her forehead in large beads. They slinked and danced down her face like masters of ballet.

And the smell!

Oh, yes, the smell. The smell of sweat. The smell of fear. The smell of surrender. *That* was the greatest gift of all.

He suddenly wondered—even *hoped*—that she would urinate on herself. That would be a delight all its own. His dog had done that as he'd cut its throat open.

The piss had sprayed from its furry cock just like the blood from its severed neck.

And boy, had that been fucking cool!

It had, indeed! Arcs of yellow and red, spritzing and splashing all around. Was there anything more glorious than the release of the dying body?

He certainly didn't think so. It was so fascinating to him that he felt another shiver streak through him as he thought of it. He really wished he had a knife like Jake had so he could get started early. Have her ready for Jake when he arrived. But he didn't have one with him, and he would have to wait.

The house seemed to groan, then. It was as if the boards and the nails and the shingles and the hinges had all moved at once. Not loud creaks like he heard when he closed the doors in his house, but deep, aching sounds that seemed to come from the pit of the very being of the house itself.

The girl was suddenly looking around, frantic, eyes wide with panic and fear. She scurried over to the wall beneath the staircase, pulled her knees to her chest, and wrapped her arms around them.

She looked at him. Fear, hate, desperation. *All* of these things were evident in her eyes as he met them with his own.

"You're a fool, Bart!" she spat at him like a cobra. "You and your friends! You don't know what you've done!"

Bart looked back at her, his substantial belly beginning a holly and jolly jiggle as giggling gave way to outright laughter. That braying, donkey-esque sound began to burst forth from his lips as they peeled back

418

over yellowing teeth, and his chest began heaving up and down over and over again.

He was laughing so hard that tears began stinging his eyes. He doubled over, putting his hands on his knees to support himself, and wailed in laughter.

"Bitch," he said through his delightful guffaws, "you don't know how lucky you are! Just be glad Jake is the one with the knife and not me!"

She seemed to curl tighter into herself in the fetal position.

"I'd already be exploring your insides by now!" he went on. "But I suppose while we wait, we can check out what's under your shirt!"

Her mouth fell open in a silent scream.

Bart waddled towards her, his donkey-bray laughter cackling and echoing off the halls of the old, damned house.

CHAPTER 58

Honey desperately wished she could fold in upon herself, make herself vanish into the wall, become a *part* of the wall itself.

But she could not.

The fat boy was coming toward her, his belly swaying and bouncing before him as he continued his awful laugh. Tears of—*could they be joy?*—were streaking his face as he came towards her laughing.

You've got to do something! she thought to herself in a panic. *You've got to do something, Honey-bunny!*

She closed her eyes. *Screwed* them shut was more like it. As if by the very act of closing off all light to her neural sensors she could somehow make the boy disappear. Or make *herself* disappear.

Either way was fine with her.

But her ears were another matter. They continued to receive the impulses of his feet as they *clomped* on the floor in his approach. She could hear the scuff and scrape of his shoes on the old, wooden floor, the creaking of the boards as they bowed beneath his ungenerous weight.

Closer and closer and closer.

Though her eyes were screwed tightly shut, she could still sense the sensation of darkness falling upon her. His shadow, to be sure, blocking the ray of sunlight which streamed in through the door.

420

He was just above her now. She could smell him. Smell his sweat. His excitement. His breath, even.

He was leaning down over her, laughing.

She was suddenly thrust into a recent memory, which was, in many ways, just as horrible as the one when she'd seen her mother's swollen and cut face looking back at her over the front seat of their car after the accident. Spitting blood, eyes bulging, gurgling noises.

Control what you see, Honey-bunny!

She opened her eyes. No matter how horrible Bart Dyer was, he was nothing compared to seeing her mother like that, or seeing her drunken father stumbling towards her, pulling his clothes off, mistaking her for his dead wife as she lay terrified and motionless in his bed.

No!

She wouldn't sit here. She wouldn't do nothing this time. She'd barely been able to speak that night to her father, to stop him from God only knew what, and break the spell he was under from the witch's brew of grief and whiskey.

But Bart wouldn't be swayed by mere words. That was obvious. He needed to be dealt with in harsher terms. His intentions were not that of a grieving husband drowning in alcohol, but those of a perfectly lucid—though insane—fourteen-year-old boy, one who had no sense of right and wrong, no sense of conscience for others, and certainly no empathy.

He was nothing like her father, this waddling Cretan. He was a fucked up rich-kid who'd never experienced the word 'no' in his entire life.

But he was about to.

421

She felt his breath lick across her face as another burst of his laughter exploded from his mouth. She could feel hot spittle, which quickly turned cool, speckle her face.

No!

She suddenly lashed out with her right hand, which she had formed into a claw. She was a tomboy to be sure, but she *did* have an affinity for feminine nails, and hers were long and sharp and painted red.

They dug into the side of Bart's jowls and she could feel soft flesh giving way beneath them. His eyes went from portraying delight to anguish in the blink of an eye and she drove them deeper into his face. He began to howl and pull back, swatting at her hand with his.

Still, she dug in deeper. She was aware that her mouth was open now in a snarl and she was hissing deeply like an angry cat as she began to get her feet beneath her, never letting her talons sway from their deepening assault.

His howl turned into a scream as he stumbled backwards, his feet desperately trying to keep from tangling. He stood up suddenly, raising his head as far as he could, and her nails took a large chunk of skin off his face as he did. The flesh dangled from beneath her talons in pinkish-red strings.

Blood was streaking his clawed face now and his scream jumped in pitch as the information from his face finally found its way to his brain and let him know just how bad this fucking hurt.

Honey was on her feet now. She uttered a scream of her own, one which underlined Bart's, and she threw her foot out in a sharp kick squarely into the fat boy's scrotum. The soft flesh gave momentarily under the pointed toes of her foot and then drove into harder stuff.

His scream silenced abruptly, and she was delighted to see a stark paleness wash over his features in a white sheet. His eyes bulged and his bleeding face trembled rapidly. Droplets of blood dripped from his bleeding cheek and speckled his shirt and her face.

She balled her fingers into fists, feeling the loose skin from Bart's face in her nails squish as she did, and her scream rose to a barbarian's bellow.

The house groaned again, seeming to sway ever so slightly, making horrible sounds that would have frightened her to her core had she not been in the heat of battle.

Bart continued to stand and tremble, face white. His mouth was open in an exaggerated *oh*, as though he were trying to scream but simply had forgotten how.

Then she drove her fist into his throat.

The hit was square and true. She felt it bury into him, and the flesh around his throat and his double-chin seemed to try and absorb her fist, as though it were trying to swallow it like a piece of candy.

His eyes bulged again and he began to rock back. But she wasn't through with him. No sir, not by a damn sight.

She unclenched her fists and reached out, grabbing him by the shoulders before he could topple back onto the floor. His expression now was one of panic and fear, the very thing he'd been getting off on in her own expressions just moments before.

He began to make a sound that reminded her of Kermit the Frog from Sesame Street, his throat having undergone a serious trauma. She pulled his face in close to hers. Their noses were almost touching. His face was wide-eyed and bleeding, her own furious and enraged.

"Fuck off, asshole!" she snarled at him.

Then she crushed her knee into his balls with the force of a thousand bullets.

This second barrage on his testicles really did the trick. His eyes bulged to the point she thought they may actually burst from his skull—and that would have been right fine with her if they had—and a horrible, stinking smell followed a deep groan that managed to escape his mouth.

He stumbled back three steps, his hands trying to cradle his damaged jewels, to massage them, reassure them. His mouth continued the throaty groan, and then vomit began to spew from his lips in yellow chunks.

They spattered his shirt and the floor, some of it even getting on her shoes before she could step back. Blood streamed from the wound on his face.

The house groaned again, and this time Honey took notice of it. She could feel the house trying to close in on her, as though the boards themselves were trying to curl out and grab her like wooden arms.

She looked once more to Bart, who was now collapsing to his knees and spewing fresh chunks of puke from his mouth in an explosive manner she would not have thought possible had she not been witnessing it at that moment.

She spat on him, the wad of saliva and snot smacking him squarely on the forehead, and ran for the door. She was free. She'd beaten him. Hell, she'd really fucked him up, for that matter.

But she didn't really care about any of that right now. There would be time enough later to laugh and

424

reminisce about Bart Dyer's squished balls with the boys, but for now, she had to get out. The house seemed to be coming alive, and she meant to be as far from it as possible if it did.

If *it* came.

She was coming through the door, into the sunlight, when the wind was knocked out of her. She folded over something which seemed like an arm, and every ounce of precious breath exploded out of her lungs. She was thrown back into the foyer of the damned house, just a few feet from where Bart was puking his balls out of his mouth.

She folded over on her side and curled back into the fetal position, reaching desperately for breath, seeing black streaks across her vision, and strange rainbow colors in her peripheral.

Then she heard a foot *clomp* on the boards. Entering the house. More *clomps* as they moved in towards her.

She managed to finally pull in a single, gasping breath, and had no time to savor it before her body was forcing her to take in another. The streaks and rainbows began to fade, and she looked up and saw the figure which was casting its shadow over her in the late summer afternoon light.

The house groaned again. But now she could do nothing but look up at the figure over her. And quake.

She heard a terrifying *snick!* sound and saw a glimmer of light dance into her vision. It was reflecting off the blade of a knife. A knife she'd seen before.

"So," a voice she recognized with horrifying surety spoke down to her, "what do we have here?"

Bart vomited a final time behind her. She could smell the bile and could feel the desire to throw up

425

herself wash over her in a tidal wave. But she couldn't do that now. She couldn't let them get to her.

"You trying to run away, you little bitch?" the horrible voice said to her. "There's no running away now, cunt. Not anymore."

The shadowy figure squatted down in front of her, holding the familiar blade out towards her. The light shifted from behind the figure and spread across his terrible, smiling face.

It was Jake.

"She tried to get away!" Bart belched from behind them in a sloppy, wet voice that seemed to be gargling more puke.

"You don't say," Jake said sarcastically, never taking his eyes off of Honey.

She began to cry again. She wished for her mother. Hell, even her father would suffice right now. Her drunken, good-for-nothing father. If only he were here.

Fat chance, Honey-bunny...

Jake's smile was broadening.

"No sense in trying to run away now," he said to her. "We're expecting company!"

The house groaned and ached.

PART SEVEN:

FACE ⊕FF

Thursday, July 5, 1990

CHAPTER 59

Sweetness. It was the only thing that could even begin to approach the sensation Jake was feeling in that moment. Like fresh honey, still dripping from the comb, spreading slowly across his tongue.

The feeling was almost enough to give him an erection. Little actually got his dick in gear, and that was strange for a fourteen-year-old young man, but stranger still was that such a young man could even fathom, much less act upon, the depravity which swirled mercilessly in Jake Reese's mind.

The pictures in magazines of naked women in all sorts of contorted positions, showing their sex and breasts with faces that conveyed desperate pleading, pleading for your hard cock to ram into them over and over and over again, and then some more maybe, and oh, yes, yes *please* shower me with your seed...well, they just didn't *move* him the way they did most boys his age.

In fact, the average boy his age would likely cream his pants after approximately five seconds of staring at pictures such as those, never mind actually racing off to the bathroom or the corner of their room to handle themselves. They wouldn't be able to get their hand on their crank before spewing a geyser.

But not Jake Reese.

No, Jake Reese was another story entirely. For Jake, seeing these things didn't do anything for him at all. He'd had more than one panicked moment in his life where he feared that he might be a faggot like this girl here or her little fairy boyfriends. After seeing the way other boys ogled women with their eyes, he thought he surely must have something wrong with him. Some wires must be crossed somewhere inside of him, the ones which initiated a reaction of focused blood-rush to the loins of a boy when their eyes transmitted these images to the brain, and the brain processed that *yes, yes indeed, this calls for a stubby of the first order, you bet your ass!*

But time and experience had assured him that he was no faggot.

Not only did the same images of men have an equally flaccid effect on him, but he had actually found something that *did* cause the reaction. For most young men, the very hint of cleavage, or even a shirt which formed well around the breasts of a woman, or a nice pair of form-fitting jeans would do the trick. But for Jake, he needed something else. Something a little more...

A little more extreme.

He'd learned that lesson once and for all the day that his mother had tried to whip him with her belt for the last time. He'd learned the lesson *very* well, and more than once. And better still, so had his mother.

A fleeting glimpse of that memory crossed his mind now as he stood over Honey, the little bitch-faggot. She was curled against the wall in the old dilapidated house in the woods, a small trickle of blood drying on the corner of her mouth. And she was shaking. Oh, if there was a best part to all of this ecstasy, it was the shaking. The trembling fear, coursing through her veins so hard her body actually *shook*, was the greatest aphrodisiac in the world.

He twirled the knife around over her head, smiling down at her. There was no empathy in him whatsoever. He wasn't trying to soothe her pain or ease her fear. He was, in fact, hoping to intensify it many times over in the coming minutes and hours.

He thought of fucking her before her fairy-boy bitches got there. Maybe even letting Bart and Chris have a go at her too. Leave her lying there, dripping with blood, sweat, and *them*.

But that would be a mistake. He knew he was sharpest *before* his release, and he needed to be sharp now. Especially today. Especially in this goddamned place. This was, after all, the very place where they had almost beaten him.

Almost.

Though in his mind he hadn't been beaten, he most certainly *had* been embarrassed, and such a sin required recompense. What was it his parents spouted all the time from that baby-book for weaklings? Something from Romans if he recalled correctly...

The wages of sin is death.

That was it! That was the one! Death. Death is the price you pay for sin against their sky-fairy. And death would be what they paid with here, today, and the currency would be in blood.

"Are you scared?" Jake asked, squatting down in front of Honey while Bart giggled incessantly behind them. Chris was there also, having arrived a short time after he had, his face still stuffed with gauze and ribbed with aluminum and tape, but he said nothing.

Did nothing.

She didn't respond. The look in her eyes was one of stark terror, but there was something else in there

431

too. It was more distant, overshadowed by the dominant fear, but Jake still noticed it. He *welcomed* it, actually. It was a similar look to the one his mother had given him when she finally realized that Jake was actually doing what he had been doing to her, no longer denying it or wishing it away.

The look was hate.

"You don't have to talk, Honey," Jake said, tracing the outline of her face with his knife and following the progress with his eyes. "You don't have to say a word, actually. I don't give a fuck what you do, but I *do* expect you to scream. Will you do that for me, Honey? Will you scream for your boyfriends when they get here? Hmm? *WHILE THEY WATCH!*"

His voice had been calm and level, but the last part had risen into a sharp scream, his voice threatening to crack. It *hadn't* cracked however, and he was thankful for that. The last thing he needed was to give this little cunt a reason to laugh. No sir, not here, not now, not *ever*. The moment she laughed at him would be the moment he slit her trembling little throat open and drank her blood from her throbbing artery.

And she did *not* laugh. Perhaps it was something in his eyes which forbade such a reaction in her. Perhaps it was her situation. While Jake himself and the donkey-braying Bart found some humor in all of this, he reasoned this bitch did not.

But even this realization was void of empathy. It was merely an observation.

"Want me to hold her for ya, Jake?" Bart's idiot-laughing voice chortled out from behind them.

Jake didn't turn his head, but he did twist his eyes in Bart's direction ever so slightly. Bart was an annoying fat-ass, but his success today—stupidly accidental as it may have been—*had* earned some semblance of patience from Jake on his behalf. He decided *not* to crush his face in as he had done to Chris the day they had cornered the four-eyed faggot in the alley.

"You won't *have* to hold her down, Bart," Jake said with a slight sigh. Then he turned his eyes back to Honey, addressing her. "Will he?"

The trembling girl looked up at him through the fear and hate-filled eyes. She managed to shake her head slightly, but just enough to get the point across.

You won't have to hold me down, the look conveyed.

Jake smiled broadly and suddenly stabbed the knife into her forearm. It didn't go very deep, but depth wasn't what it took to make a person bleed and feel agony.

She screamed, her eyes bulging from their sockets, her mouth an enormous *oh*. She reached with her other arm to grab at his hand, to pull the knife free, perhaps. But Jake was too quick for her. He snatched the hand and then thrust it and her arm into her own throat, slamming her head against the wall in the process. There was a strangely comic sound as she burped from her mouth and the scream stopped which reminded Jake of Kermit the Frog from Sesame Street, and he felt the knife twist slightly in her arm in the action. Hot tears were pouring from her eyes now, and he could see the hate receding, farther and farther away, as the fear and desperation filled them.

"Good," he hissed into her face, only an inch or two away now. *"Remember what you said? We won't have to hold you down!"*

Bart began to laugh louder, intermittent snorts interrupting his cackles. Chris did nothing, only retreated further from them to the far wall.

He really was worthless. Maybe he would have to dispatch him along with the faggots. Hell, he was acting enough like one.

He decided if it felt right at the time, he'd do it. Then he amended his thought, and decided he *would* do it.

Jake twisted the knife. Honey screamed.

CHAPTER 60

They could all feel something as they turned their bikes onto the old dirt road that led to the damned place.

It was something in the air. Something all around them. Like all the molecules of the universe were thickening, pressing in on them all at once.

There was no strategic plan. No combat logic. Just the sense they absolutely had to move, and to move fast. Jake had their friend, and he had her at that awful place in the woods they had been avoiding, had *planned* to avoid for the rest of their lives. The place they *would* avoid for the rest of their lives if they were able to get Honey and themselves out of there alive.

And it was this realization that was somehow the most haunting.

Would they be able to get out of this alive? To come home in one piece instead of several? They really didn't know. It was evident to them now that the bully they were dealing with—the *real* problem—Jake Reese, was certainly capable of murder. He would cut the meat from their bones with gleeful abandon if he got the chance, and they were beginning to think he just might. What kind of psychopath *kidnapped* a young girl and dragged her to a house in the middle of the forest with the intent of doing anything else?

No kind, that's what.

435

Jimmy had an amazing gift, and Freddie recognized it as something that could be used as a weapon, and rightly so. But when you were twelve years old and scared out of your minds, having a weapon at your disposal didn't mean you'd know how to use it properly. Didn't mean you would be *able* to use it, even if you *did* figure out how.

But the love in their young hearts was overriding all of their logical reservations. They had turned over a thousand things in their minds, even including calling the adults—their parents—into the matter. They would surely know what to do, and more than likely they would get the police involved. The police would *definitely* know what to do. Jake and his scumbag pals would be toast for sure then.

Only, there was this place.

Yes. It was the place, the house in the woods, and the thing that lurked just beyond it. Johnathan Brogan's Glutton. If they brought in their parents or the police, what happened if the thing got out? Might their families and their first line of defense in the police force be knocked out in one fell swoop? And what then? Run screaming back into a town full of defenseless and unbelieving victims who would shake their heads in pitying disbelief all the way up to the point their heads were shorn from their shoulders and their insides pulled from their bowels?

They simply couldn't take the chance, no matter how slim it might be. They would face the bullies and, God forbid, the Glutton, on their own. With Jimmy's gift. With their grit.

And a whole lot of crossed fingers.

They neared the place where they would dismount and proceed on foot. They could see the bikes lying in the grass on the side of the road, those of Jake, Bart, and Chris. There was a fourth bike lying there as well, one which they instantly recognized.

Honey's.

They didn't know what the bastards had done to Honey that would have allowed them to get her out here, and they neither wanted to know nor cared. It was likely too awful to think about, and it ultimately didn't matter in the end. She was their friend. Their newest friend. The smallest. The most vulnerable.

The most beautiful.

There was that too. All of them knew it, even if they wouldn't speak of it. They liked to pretend she was just one of the guys. A Tomboy. Someone to play with. But she was more than that. She was more than that to all of them. Jimmy, certainly, and Freddie too, though with him she shared the most plutonic bond.

Yet, to none of them did she matter more than to Ryan.

Ryan. The coward, the fearful, desperate to run away Ryan Laughton. It was he who loved her the most, and it was something that she would never realize. Though his heart pounded and his gut twisted, he rode on. Though the terrified bucking horse inside of him threatened to tear the barn apart and run away into the night, he rode on.

He rode on.

They dismounted their bikes and looked at one another. There was an element of fear in all of their eyes. But deeper, and in spite of everything, there was something stronger. There was purpose. There was nobility.

And courage.

They said nothing as they dismounted their bikes and let them fall to the grass with metallic squeaks and the rattle of chains. They just nodded all around to one another and made their way to the place in the woods, ready to face their fate.

The air around them continued to press in.

CHAPTER 61

Mommy! she thought, her inner voice was reeling, screaming in terror. *Mommy, I need you so much! I need my picture! Why did you have to die?*

Honey's mind was in a furor of uproar.

There was pain. Quite an exquisite amount of pain, actually, especially in her forearm. But that didn't take away from the throbbing soreness in her throat either, which was wailing away in the midst of everything rather admirably.

There was fear. A phenomenal amount of fear, at that. Not only for her current situation—being held hostage in this awful place by psychopaths—but also for her memories. Memories of her family. Of happiness. Togetherness.

Her mother.

The fat one, Bart, had taken her picture from her in the old garage. That one picture was what embodied her memory of her family. Of happiness. A time before the terrible car wreck which tore them apart and caused joy to exit their lives, right then, stage left. That fat son of a bitch had snatched it from her. Ripped it from her clawing fingers as she desperately and fearfully struggled to hold on to the one thing in her life which granted her respite from the hell of her new life with her father, a man who had withered away in a cloud of alcohol and grief.

He wasn't her father anymore. She had come to terms with that. The man from that photograph, the one with the three happy, smiling faces, had died that day too. As her mother looked over the seat, bug-eyed and bleeding with terror in her eyes, her father had been passing out of this life as well. He had never been the same.

Sure, she and her father had been able to walk away from the crash with relatively minor injuries—a couple of scrapes and cuts, a few bruises that would take weeks to fully heal—but some part of them both had died that day with her mother. While her mother had bled—both from her external wounds and the wounds in her skull which caused her head to balloon up like a basketball—Tom Bascom had been bleeding out as well. His will to live, his will to overcome, his will to father the daughter—their precious little girl—that he and Janie had created in a moment of pure and passionate love, all of it was bleeding out of him as well.

His blood had not been the same red streaks which had flowed from his wife, but rather the salty tears that doused his face as he screamed at the paramedics to do something, *anything*, to save his wife.

"Goddamn it!" he had screamed at them as they struggled to get her out, cautiously trying to move her battered body without causing further damage. *"She's dying, can't you see that? You've got to do something! I can't lose her! We can't lose her!"*

All these terrible, repressed memories came flooding into Honey's young mind like a tidal wave. Memories she would rather forget. Memories she *could* forget, so long as she had that picture to look upon. To long after.

That photograph was her escape.

And now it was in the pocket of that filthy, fat asshole, Bart Dyer. Worse—and it was a damn sight worse—the raging psychopath Jake Reese was torturing her in a place where something even he could never understand or appreciate resided, waiting for them, both inches and worlds away, ready to chew the heads off them all in an instant should it get the chance.

"Please, oh God, stop!" Honey screamed to a smiling Jake Reese as he twisted the knife in her arm once more.

Oh, you're gonna scream, aren't ya? he had said.

She was. She *absolutely* was. There was no shame in her for it, though. No sense of defeat. No worries of ego or pride. She was screaming. Begging him to stop. All she wanted was to be out of there. Out of that terrible place where the Devil lived.

And she wanted her picture.

But as the terrible moment continued to lengthen and get worse, as pain gave way to agony, she began to believe with a growing sense of dread she would never see that picture again. That serene moment, captured in time, which contained all the happiness she believed she would ever experience in her life, was trapped in the grimy pocket of a snorting pig of a person. Imprisoned there.

She believed in that moment she would never see it again. And this, more than anything that Jake had done to her, or *could* do to her, hurt her soul. Only hurt wasn't the right word. It didn't capture the pain she was feeling in that moment. It couldn't begin to encapsulate her horror.

Her soul was being shattered.

Jake was laughing now. His laughter didn't seem to contain the jolliness of a genuine laugh. In his chuckles there seemed to be nothing but malice and hate, sadism and fury. This laugh wasn't conveying humor or joy in the moment at all. It was conveying power, evil, and malice.

All contained within hysterical chortles.

Then there was the fat-ass, Bart. He was cackling away himself, with pig-snorts and the brays of a donkey accenting the diatribe. And then there was the other guy...

Chris, she thought his name was. Chris Higgins. His face was smashed, and she knew this to have been the work of her current torturer from what Freddie had told her and the other guys in the hospital that day he'd been through a similar ordeal. Only Freddie had been able to walk away.

Honey didn't believe she would.

Her tear-clouded eyes fell on Chris, standing behind them all. He wasn't laughing. He wasn't smiling. He wasn't even looking at them.

No, he was looking away, and she got the sense—through all she was experiencing—that he wasn't enjoying this at all. He wasn't interested in hurting people. He almost seemed as trapped as she was, though he lacked the backbone to say so. He was there, and no, he wasn't doing anything to stop it. Yet, he was somehow detached from the events all the same. He was looking down the foyer, out the old door that hung open at the front of the house.

The house made that groaning sound again. Jake didn't seem to notice, and Bart certainly didn't with his cackling brays, but she thought she saw something in

Chris's eyes. He'd heard it too. Perhaps he'd felt it. She couldn't be sure, but she believed she had seen some recognition in him when the house had moaned.

He looked up, just for a second, and his eyes rolled around the foyer, looking to the ceiling and the back wall before returning to the door, looking out.

He was looking for something.

She was suddenly sure of it. He was looking—no, he was *waiting*—for something. Or was it someone? Had this kid done something to defy his ringleader, Jake? Had he called in help? The police, perhaps?

She thought not. Not the police, anyway. But someone.

She began to believe he may have called her friends. Jimmy, Ryan, and Freddie. Were they on the way here? Did they know what was happening?

No.

Now she remembered that Jake had said they were waiting on the little faggots—as he called them—to arrive. Jake had made the call, and it certainly wasn't so they could help her. No, he meant to do them as much harm as he was doing her, and brother, he was just getting warmed up.

So, what? Or who? What was Chris was waiting for?

Another twist of the knife brought all rational thought to a screeching halt and she exulted another cry into the dank air of the house. Tears streaked her face and dirt had begun to settle in dusty tendrils, matting her face with scum.

As soon as she was able, she looked back to the boy with the aluminum brace on his nose and followed his gaze out the door. Just as she did, she noticed

443

something in Chris's eyes. It wasn't much, just a flicker in the eyes, but she caught it.

She looked out the open door and saw her friends coming.

They were hunched over, moving about as tactically as one could expect a trio of twelve-year-olds to move, and they were coming toward the house.

They were carrying sticks. *Big* sticks.

A surge of hope welled up within her, despite her better judgement. She didn't *want* hope anymore. Hope was something that could be dashed, squelched out. Hope could come crashing down, leaving you lower than you had been before it had arrived.

But all the same, she felt it.

Hope. That bastard of horror and the glimpse of possible salvation. It was there. Filling her. *Inside* her.

"How about we see those little titties?" Jake hissed into her ear as he leaned in close after twisting the knife and hearing her cry. *"This place needs some decoration, don't you think? I think they'd look lovely on the wall!"*

But she barely heard this. Her head was turned towards the wall, and she was looking at her friends. The boys she'd only gotten to know this very summer, and who were coming to her rescue, as feeble as their attempt may be. She wasn't concerned anymore with the knife in her forearm, or the pain in her throat. She wasn't worried about her mosquito-bite-sized breasts being relocated from her chest to the wall. She wasn't worried about Jake anymore.

Hope was dashing her fears, as damnable as that hope may be.

There was another groan from the house. This time she *knew* Chris had heard it. And she was still sure that Jake and Bart had not.

Then, she heard something else.

It was a *whooshing* sound, like the air was moving in a strong breeze. Only the air wasn't what moved. Not at all.

Jake Reese's body flew into the air and sailed to the back of the foyer. He slammed into the wall with a loud *thump*, and the wall crumbled around him, sending shards of plaster to the floor in a cloud. His face was dazed and furious all at once, anger welling up in his eyes even as he coughed in pain and dispelled the cloud of dust which enveloped him.

"What the fuck?" he hacked as he shook his head and struggled to his feet.

But Honey was looking out the door, seeing Jimmy standing there, his hands out in front of him and an intent look in his eyes. Ryan and Freddie stood to either side of him and just behind him, holding large sticks in their hands like weapons.

"You leave her alone, Jake!" Jimmy screamed.

Bart was no longer laughing. His chubby face had stilled as the ripples of laughter had faded away from his jowls. Now his jaw hung open in astonished surprise.

Then there was Chris Higgins. His face remained much as it had been. He couldn't create many expressions with the brace across his nose anyway, but his eyes expressed something which caused something very near to joy to leap up within Honey.

It was a look of victory.

Her heart welled with more hope than before, and she cast off all resistance to the feeling at once. Her boys were here, and they had come packing a punch. She began to think—though cautiously—she might get out of this yet.

The house groaned again and she thought she felt it actually move. The angles of the structure seemed to twist and jive ever so slightly.

"You motherfuckers are *dead*!" screamed Jake as he stood to his feet, his knife gleaming in the dimming light.

"Back off, Jake!" Jimmy screamed back at him. "I don't want to hurt you, but if you make me, we will!"

Jake began to laugh at this. The sound began as small giggles, then began to build into overt chuckles, and eventually matured into full-on guffaws of howling laughter. The evolution sent chills down Honey's spine.

"You faggots don't know what you're dealing with!" Jake hissed.

Then he threw his knife, winding up like a major-league pitcher, and hurling it end over end at Jimmy. It sailed through the air, and Honey's eyes followed it in slow motion.

Then she watched in horror as the blade buried itself into the shoulder of her friend, right where the arm and his torso met.

Jimmy howled in pain, jerking to the side, his hand reaching up for the hilt of the blade.

Then something *really* terrifying happened.

The knife ripped out of Jimmy's shoulder, sending a spray of bright blood, and tumbled through the air back toward Jake.

Honey's eyes followed the tumbling knife back the way it had come and watched in horrified awe as it clapped back into Jake's hand.

Jake's eyes were gleaming. Jimmy's were full of astonished terror.

Honey's bulged in horror.

Jake had the same power Jimmy had.

"We're in for a treat, boys!" Jake said with a joyful laugh.

Bart's braying laughter started up again. Chris looked back and forth between them, no discernable emotion in his eyes. Then he looked back to the door, looking over the boy's shoulders.

He was still looking for something. Or someone. It hadn't been the boys he'd been watching for. It was something else.

But what?

"And now," Jake's voice boomed in the foyer of the old house, "it's time for you faggots to understand *no one* fucks with Jake Reese! *No one!*"

CHAPTER 62

He slammed on the brakes of his old car and the tires scraped over the gravel and sand with a rubbery report.

His eyes were focused on the littering of bicycles on the side of the old dirt road, lying askew and forgotten. As though they had been dismissed rather than dismounted. He squinted his eyes.

There was a fog in his head. There were no two ways about it. And it didn't seem to be abating. At least not yet. Maybe not even any time soon. The place just behind his eyes ached and moaned with the strain of focusing. He wanted to close them. To rest them. To forget all about this thing and just sit back and do what he always did. What he always *had* done, at least since the—

No! he screamed to himself as he slammed a determined palm down on the steering wheel. *You're NOT going to shut your eyes! You're NOT going to forget about this thing! You're NOT, God-damn it! You're going to be a fucking man for the first time in God only knows how long, and you're going to do the right fucking thing! You get it?*

He shuddered and nodded to himself. He got it.

There was no real choice, and he knew it. He'd always known it, as a matter of fact, but he'd been running and swimming and diving away from what he knew was right—what he knew *had* to be done—for far too long now. Getting it together. Pulling *himself* together. After all, it wasn't all about him, right? There were other people involved, and he was the one who had to be the adult and set things right.

You can't always control what happens, the voice of his friend drifted to him out of the fog in his mind, *but you can control how you react to it.*

Only he hadn't. Not so far, at least. No, rather than facing life and its unfair nightmares head on, he'd run away, hiding behind grief and excuses and cheap liquor.

But not anymore. It wasn't an option anymore. Something bad had been happening this summer, right under his nose, and rather than recognize it and deal with it, he'd been wallowing in self-pity.

His hand trembled as he reached for the door handle. He seized the handle with all the strength he could muster, determined to put a stop to his trembling, to put a stop to his fear. He was trying to focus through the fog, and for a time he'd thought the strain of it might kill him.

But it hadn't. Not yet, anyway.

He stared down at his hand, the knuckles turning white under the strain they were exerting on the door handle, and he felt tears sting the corners of his eyes. Tears of pain and, yes, misery. Those were always there. Had been since it all happened. But beneath these, and coming on stronger now, threatening to push aside the tears of pain and misery, were another kind of tears. Ones much deeper and infinitely more cutting.

Tears of shame.

Shame for his absence. Shame for his lack of action. And worst of all, shame for his selfishness.

And it really *was* the worst of all. How he could ever have allowed himself to reach such a state was mind-boggling, even in the fog he was straining through. Everything was such a blur, but he saw one thing clearly enough: cowardice.

Yes, *he* was a coward, and nothing else could explain how he'd allowed all this to happen. Not only to himself, but to his family.

I'm NOT going to fail you now! Not anymore! I'm not running away!

As he stared at his left hand which gripped the door handle, he saw the shivers and tremors first begin to settle, then cease altogether. The smallest hint of a grin, one of self-satisfaction, threatened to don his lips.

He looked over to the seat next to him and his eyes fell on the .38 revolver lying there. It was loaded, he was sure of that. He had stuffed the slugs into the cylinder himself only twenty minutes prior after digging around for the gun and the rounds for nearly a half-hour. He remembered faintly that he'd hid it from himself one night over a year ago while in one of his fogs. He had almost used it on himself that night. Had tasted the cold steel in his mouth, the front sight scraping the roof of his mouth. But then he'd pulled it from his mouth with a sob, strings of saliva stretching and then breaking from the barrel. Once he'd realized he didn't have the balls to follow through with it, he'd unloaded the gun, stuffed it into a shoebox, then tossed it deep into the back of the closet.

But not *his* closet.

The bullets he had put in a drawer, loosely rattling around every time the drawer was opened, which was almost never.

450

But not *his* drawer.

He snatched the revolver up and gripped it tightly, much as he was doing with the door handle in his other hand. On impulse—though he already knew beyond doubt that it was loaded—he pushed the mechanism which released the cylinder and let it roll out. He gazed intently for a moment at the dulled backs of the rounds, the primers like blank eyes staring back at him. Then he flicked his wrist and the cylinder swung home with a loud, clicking *snap.*

Time to sprout a sack, mister.

He nodded to himself.

Then, without another thought—much less a plan of any kind—he swung the door to his old car open and stepped out into the growling heat.

As he entered the woods, he thought he could hear—*or did he feel it?*—something else growl.

CHAPTER 63

Jimmy looked down at the bleeding wound on his shoulder in total disbelief.

It wasn't so much that Jake had managed to actually stick him with the knife from a throw—something he had up to this moment fully believed was movie-making magic and wholly void from real-world events outside of a circus act—but that Jake had pulled the knife back out of Jimmy's shoulders from a full twenty feet away. Like it had been on a spring-loaded string or something.

But Jimmy knew better.

No, it hadn't been on a string, and it hadn't bounced off of him either. No, it had been *pulled* back. Not by material or mechanism, but by...by...

The fucking Force.

That was it. All this time, the past few weeks since he'd realized his abilities, he had been using cumbersome language to describe what it was that he possessed. His friends had as well. All the while, *exactly* what it was had been staring them all in the face, blatantly, and yet none of them had seen it.

The *Force* was with him. And apparently, it was with Jake too. Jedi and Sith. Light and dark.

Strong with Jake, the Force is, Yoda spoke in Jimmy's mind.

Oh, shit.

452

"And now it's time for you faggots to realize that *no one* fucks with Jake Reese! *No one!*"

Jake's voice echoed off the foyer walls and smacked Jimmy in his ears. He could feel Freddie and Ryan trembling next to him, the excitement of their fear permeating off them like waves of heat. There was the slightest evidence of tremor in the ends of their sticks, but they continued to stand their ground.

Suddenly, Jimmy was overwhelmed with a sense of dread. Their entire plan had been based around two things, and two things alone: surprise and, well, the Force.

No shred of their plan had accounted for Jake having the same power. None whatsoever. It was such an amazingly unique gift, something they'd only seen little green men, guys with lightsabers, and powerful, black cyborgs use, and even then it was on a screen. Make believe. Movie magic.

But it was real. Oh, God, it was *real!*

Jake was on his feet again, the toss that Jimmy had given him into the wall seemingly doing nothing to injure or even slow him down. His eyes blazed at them, like black fire welling up within his soul of pitch. Honey was crying now. Her momentary hope dashed to shards in the course of a single, horrifying moment. And Jimmy saw then that she knew what he knew.

He was a young, wet-behind-the-ears Luke Skywalker, and Jake was a mad and seasoned Darth Vader.

Jake heaved in breath slowly, and Jimmy almost laughed insanely as it brought to mind the sound of the iconic villain's breathing.

Skeee-coooof.

453

"Just leave us alone, Jake!" Jimmy cried from the doorway to the house. "All we want is her!"

He said this last part as his hand raised up, pointing to Honey.

"We'll stay out of your way, if that's what you want," he said, going on in a calmer voice. "I get it, we fucked with the wrong guy, we embarrassed you, whatever. I'm sorry, okay? None of this is alright, though! It's gone *way* too far! But let's forget it! We'll stay out of your way, and out of your life!"

Jake continued to glare from under his scrunched eyebrows at them for a moment longer, unmoving but for the rise and fall of his chest. Bart Dyer stood stupidly, roughly between them in the hall of the foyer, looking first to Jake, then to Jimmy and his friends. As his eyes swung back and forth, they would fall on Honey, who was huddled and bleeding on the floor beside the staircase. Chris Higgins was closer to the door, and kept fidgeting nervously with his arms, shifting his weight back and forth from one leg to the next as though he had to take a righteous piss, and frequently looking over the boys' shoulders and outside.

What the fuck is he looking for? Jimmy wondered. *Or who?*

But all those questions vanished when Jake spoke again. He began to move toward them in slow, confident strides. The knife in his hand winking light at them as it caught stray beams drifting in from the falling sun.

"You'll stay out of my way, all right," he said, his grin spreading wider. "You'll be out of my way, their way," he pointed to Bart and Chris with the blade of his knife, "and everybody's way. *Forever.*"

The final word of his sentence sent rivers of ice over Jimmy's entire body. Though he was hot and sweating, he actually felt himself begin to shiver, and he literally felt cold. As though the air in the place had suddenly dropped a good ten degrees. Maybe more.

A *lot* more.

A sliver of memory came to him, then, but his mind was racing so fast that he didn't—*couldn't*—dwell on it. Not then. All he managed to grasp from it was that whatever the memory was, it had something to do with the temperature.

The temperature dropping.

"Jake, *listen to me!*" Jimmy spat, his wide, fearful eyes flicking about the room and coming back to Jake's. "I'm *sorry*, okay? Do you understand that? I'm sorry! I take it back, everything we've done to you. We were assholes! We just want her back, okay?"

Then Jimmy turned to Ryan and Freddie who stood on either side of him.

"Tell him, guys, we're sorry, right?"

Jimmy looked back and forth between them, settling first on Ryan. Ryan was looking at Honey on the floor, bleeding and crying and helpless. He began to nod as he looked at Jake.

"I'm sorry," he said in a hollow tone.

"See?" Jimmy said in an almost cracking voice, puberty betraying him. "I told ya, didn't I? Tell him, Freddie! We're sorry, right?"

Jimmy looked to Freddie now. His glasses sat crookedly over his patched eye. There were still cuts, in the later stages of the healing process, littering his face and his arms. But something in his remaining good eye sent a pinprick of panic through Jimmy's heart.

He wasn't sorry at all.

Well, of course he wasn't sorry. None of them were *really* sorry, they were just trying to get out of this terrible situation. They just wanted to get Honey and get the fuck out before something really awful happened. Something none of them could ever take back.

But the look in Freddie's eye told Jimmy he wasn't having any of it.

"Yeah, four-eyes," Jake said, cocking his face towards Freddie with an air of arrogance, "are you sorry? Are you sorry now that your faggot boyfriend here realizes just how royally fucked you all are for messing with me? Hmm?"

Another shiver twisted through Jimmy and, again, the feeling that it really *was* getting cold in the house stunned him. His mind was still racing, and he was unable to fetch the memory.

Why the hell is it so cold?

Shivering, Jimmy glanced down at Honey, crumpled on the floor. Her face was streaked with tears, but it seemed that, for the moment, the flow of them had stopped. He looked at her arm and could see an open wound that was already starting to clot, and he could see the reddened skin which surrounded it outside the smears of blood.

His eyes lifted.

As Jimmy moved his eyes up, fully intending to bring them to hers so he could silently make an attempt to reassure her, to let her know they were doing all they could to help her, his eyes stopped on her small, budding breasts.

Her nipples were popping through the thin material of her shirt.

She's cold too! he thought.

And that brought it all home.

He remembered the day, in this very house, as Jake was coming after him, when he'd gone through the portal to the other place. He remembered how the light was a little different over there. *Everything* was a little different over there. And the air...

It was cooler.

Of course, that day the temperature seemed to be only about ten degrees cooler, and he was sure right now that the temperature had dropped a good deal more than ten degrees. Probably more than twenty degrees. And, following the logic of what little he knew of the other place and how things were just a little different there, who was to say the seasons were the same on the other side? Or the same length of time, even? In Texas, summer heat could last several months, but maybe over there it only lasted a few weeks?

He didn't know, and something else had just caught his attention which caused him not to care either.

There was a sound.

It sounded like a low growl almost, only that wasn't quite right. It wasn't really a growl at all. A growl had a creaturely quality to it, but this sound didn't. It was something else. Something more elemental. Almost mechanical.

But it wasn't really mechanical either.

"You can go fuck yourself, Jake," Freddie finally said in a flat tone. "You and your shit-ass friends here.

If you think you're getting an apology after what you did to me and what you've done to Honey, you've got another thing coming!"

There was a hint of laughter in Freddie's voice as he finished talking to Jake and turned his attention to Jimmy.

"I'm sorry, bud," he said to Jimmy. "I told you these assholes were mine, and I mean to have them!"

Now it was Jake's turn to laugh. It swelled out of him like an ocean wave, coming on subtly at first, then rising to a full-on howl. The volume of his laugh continued to rise and soon Bart began to join in, adding oinks and snorts to the chorus.

"Oh, you mean to have *us*, is that right?" Jake said through his laughter. "Well come on, bitch! Come here and I'll cut your tiny, faggot cock off and feed it to you!"

Jake had spread his arms out wide in what looked like a parody of Jesus on the Cross, the knife winking light at them as it moved.

Jake and Bart laughed some more. Chris Higgins stood silently off to the side, still fidgeting, still looking past them and out the door.

Just what in Christ's name is he waiting for? Jimmy thought passively as another wave of chills struck him.

It was getting cold.

And that sound. The sound was there. A constant underneath the howls and snorts of the bullies. That sound which was somehow mechanical and organic at the same time. A sound that reminded him of...

Of warbling.

That was it. The warbling sound he'd heard when he'd passed between worlds. The sound of the portal that he'd made to the other place. It explained everything. The sound, the cold. And he'd just learned that Jake had powers like he had. Had the fucking Force!

And if he had the Force, he could—

"Jake, listen to me!" Jimmy screamed. This time his voice did crack. "You and me, we can do things. Things with our minds or our wills or whatever! I know you know what I'm talking about!"

The laughs had stopped. Now the bullies were staring at the boys, faces red from their laughter.

Jimmy went on. "There's something else you should know about the Force!"

Fresh wails of laughter rose up now.

"The *Force*?" Jake cackled spitefully. "You faggots must love men in black leather—"

"Shut your fucking hole and listen to me, Jake!" Jimmy cried, and for a wonder, he actually did. Jake's laughing scowl paused, then began to deflate.

"Just listen!" Jimmy went on. "This power can open a portal between worlds. I know this sounds crazy, but it's the damn truth, I promise you! It's how I got away from you in the closet that first day we were here! You remember?"

Jake stared at him, not quite blankly. He nodded slowly.

"But that's not really the point either," Jimmy continued. "There's something there, it's a, it's, well..."

"It's a *what*?" Jake hissed at him.

Jimmy went on, ignoring the venom.

"A monster, Jake. It's a fucking monster. And it almost got us that day. Look, we did some research about this place and there was a family here, long time

459

ago, and the guy who lived here saw this thing! It wants to eat. Like it *needs* to eat, so it can come into this world. Needs the flesh of this world to have flesh of its own! I know it sounds nuts, but it's true!"

Jake and Bart had started laughing again at this point, shaking their heads.

"You fags might get scared of boogeymen hiding under your beds, but not me," Jake said jerking a thumb towards his chest. "I *am* the fucking boogeyman! And none of your fucking campfire stories are going to scare *me*, understand?"

That was when they heard the *thump*.

All of their heads jerked in the direction of the hall behind Jake. The direction of the warbling sound. The direction of the cold.

"The hell was that?" Jake asked no one in particular.

"I'm not lying to you, Jake!" Jimmy said, his voice quieter now for fear of what he almost certainly knew lurked at the end of the hall.

Another *thump*. This one louder.

The warbling sound droned on. The cool air drifted around them and all of them—the boys, Honey, and all three bullies—shivered in unison.

"It's here," Jimmy said in a wavering voice. "God help us, Jake! You opened the portal between worlds!"

"There's no fucking portal, Dalton!" Jake hissed at him. "How stupid do you think I am?"

"I'm telling you it's—"

Thump-Thump-Thump.

Closer. Every second it was getting closer.

Ryan suddenly leaped past Jimmy and Chris and sprinted towards Honey. Just as he was upon her, some force—*the* Force—knocked him back on his ass.

He sprawled out on the floor in front of Jimmy and Freddie, the wind knocked out of him, but otherwise alright. He still had his stick.

Jake's hand was out in front of him and lowering.

"No one's going anywhere, cock-rags! You hear me?"

Thump.

All heads jerked back toward the hallway.

"Jake," Jimmy pleaded. "Have some sense, would ya? You've just opened a doorway to *monsters!*"

"That's the one thing that makes *no* sense!" Jake growled.

Thump.

"I know it sounds crazy, but just look at what we're doing! Throwing each other around like—" *Thump.* "—fucking ragdolls with the power of our *wills!*"

Thump.

"That doesn't mean—" *Thump.* "—there's a goddamned other world full of monsters, moron!"

Thump...Thump.

"There's no time, Jake! You've got to shut the portal!"

"I didn't open any portal!"

"I can try to shut it, but you've got to let me, work with—"

THUMP.

That one was louder. And closer. And there was something more, something much more horrible.

This one, they actually *felt.*

461

It reverberated through the floorboards. Whatever it was, it had just crossed over. Just placed its awful foot in their world, on the same wood they were standing on in this damned house.

It was here.

"Oh, Jesus," Jimmy said. "Oh, sweet Jesus, it's here!"

Honey was crying again. They were *all* shivering. Chris Higgins made another glance out the door past them.

The drone of the warble continued, but another sound came through it, drifting on top of it.

And it was closer.

There was no mistaking it now. What he thought had been a growl before had been the warble of the portal. But what they all heard now was not.

What they heard now was an *actual* growl.

CHAPTER 64

Where the fuck is he? Chris Higgins thought as he looked over the shoulders of the kids. *This is getting out of hand! Oh, God, this has gone WAY too far!*

It had. Things were spiraling out of control. He'd never wanted to be involved in this. Certainly not this deep in it. Push some kids around, laugh at them, whatever. No big deal. But this...

This was too much.

Jake was *really* crazy. Bart was *really* crazy. Out of their fucking minds insane. How had he allowed himself to get mixed up in all of this? How had things gone so far, and just how in the blue fuck was *he* here? Right in the middle of it. Standing aside while Jake and Bart tormented this poor girl, and now in a standoff with a bunch of kids who had never done a damn thing to him or anyone else.

Because you're afraid of Jake Reese, that's why, an inner voice told him. *Because you're too much of a coward to disassociate yourself from him. You're more interested in getting free Snickers bars and Cokes and smokes and the occasional beer than you are in doing the right fucking thing!*

But he'd made the call, hadn't he?

Where the fuck is he?

Yes, he'd made the call. He had bumbled his way through his nearly unrecognizable speech—*thanks for that, Jake!*—to the poor man. It was a wonder the guy had even understood him, much less that the man had agreed to come. Chris honestly didn't even think he would. In fact, he hadn't believed the man would have ever listened to a slurring, nasal-spoken stranger about psychos and murder at the old place in the woods—*you know the one, right?*—from a random phone call in the middle of the afternoon.

Yeah, he had made the call. But not to the police. No, never them. Calling them would put him in a dangerously tight spot, not only with his parents, but with Jake and Bart too. He couldn't have that. Juveniles too often got off with slaps on the wrist, even in crazy situations like this. And then what would have happened?

He'd carve your guts out with a plastic spoon, that's what!

Chris shivered at the thought, still looking over the other kids' heads, out the door, wondering just where in God's name the guy was. He *needed* to be here. Now, not later. This very moment.

He thought he caught movement in the trees outside.

His back stiffened ever so slightly and he rose on the balls of his feet a fraction of an inch. Just the tiniest bit. He didn't need anyone noticing him, what he was doing, while the shit was going down.

It was definitely movement.

And after another moment, he was sure it was a man. *The* man, by God, and just in time.

Jake and Jimmy were screaming back and forth about something. Some boogeyman that Jimmy was convinced was coming, that *lived* here, or some alternate here, anyway.

Then Ryan, the big kid—*my God, he's huge for his age!*—went for the girl. That poor girl. Rushing toward her with singular purpose filling his terrified eyes.

Then more insanity happened. Jake used some...some *power*. Call it that, or ability, call it the goddamn Force, if you liked. But whatever you called it, it was incredible. It was fantastic. It was mind-blowing.

And it was horrifying.

That was the worst part. Witnessing *real* power like that, right in front of him, was as horrifying as it was amazing. Because the one wielding it was Jake Reese. Jake, the terror of their town, even if the town didn't know it yet, was wielding an incredible power. And that incredible power was terrifying because Jake was *evil.*

There. He'd said it. Or, he'd thought it, anyway. He didn't dare say something like that out loud, and certainly not in front of the terror himself. No sir, not him. He meant to live his life in peace. His nose would probably never sit straight again, but at least the damn thing was still on his face. That was something.

A sound.

Jake and Jimmy were talking about portals now, and Chris finally picked up on the sound. It had been there for some time, warbling in the background, but it hadn't taken the front seat until just now. The screaming wails and cries of the poor girl, answered with the mad cackling howls of Jake and Bart had been stealing the show all this time, but now he was hearing it.

And he was hearing the *thumps*.

What fresh hell is this? he thought, growing terror in his mind. He felt as though his heart would burst from his chest and splatter all over the place—all over the kids and Jake—if he didn't get it under control. It was galloping inside his chest. He could almost feel it leaping from one side of his chest cavity to the other in rapid jolts that made his chest rise and fall like lightning-quick breaths.

Why am I here? he moaned inside himself. *Just run! Run away! As fast as you can, just get out of here and let the man deal with it. This isn't your fight! It never was, and it isn't now! You're nothing but Jake's whipping boy, so just get the FUCK OUT!*

He almost did, too. He came within a breath of bolting past the kids and out the front door, running away from Jake, the house, that awful *thumping* sound.

Thump.

What was that, anyway? Was the kid right? Was it really a monster from another world? It couldn't be! There was no such thing as monsters!

But as his eyes fell on Jake Reese, he knew that was wrong. There was a monster right before him, holding a knife its hand. A monster he had just witnessed torturing a little girl whose great crime had been befriending the wrong kids. A little girl whom he had heard about in school. Who'd lost so much. Lost her mother in a terrible accident. Who'd then basically lost her father to alcoholism from what he'd heard through that great bastion of gossip known as public school. A little girl who had the misfortune of being seen by that fat, snorting fuck, Bart, while she was trying to spend some time with her lost parents through a photograph which obviously meant more to her than her own life.

Jake was a monster, alright. And if there was one, it stood to reason there could be more.

Thump.

Something *was* coming. The kid was right. There was no mistaking it now. No chance of reasoning it away. That insistent *thump-thump-thump* was getting louder and louder, pounding its way to all of them, and all they could do was stand around and bitch at each other, at *themselves*, about what it was.

He looked back over the shoulders of the kids and saw the man closing in on the house. He wasn't moving terribly fast, and Chris could now see he looked absolutely horrible. He wasn't even running in a straight line, for crying out loud, and Chris doubted that it had anything to do with tactic.

Oh, Jesus, man, come on!

He was coming. But Chris didn't know what good it would do. He could see something in his hand that looked like a gun, though he couldn't be sure at this distance. But then again, he didn't know just what else it *could* be. If it wasn't a gun, maybe it was a—

THUMP.

Chills froze his body solid for just a moment. He hadn't just *heard* that one. He'd felt it.

Something was here.

"Guys!" he almost shrieked in a voice that harkened back to a time when he'd gotten his first pimples and he'd seen the first sprouting of pubic hair crop up on his crotch. "We should get out of here!"

A growl.

Deep. Guttural. Wet.

Inside the house.

Chris could see even Jake was scared now. Gooseflesh had bloomed all over his arms. It had on his own as well. He could feel the electric tingle of his hair standing on end at the back of his neck like a thousand erect penises ready for action, but void of the excitement.

Another *THUMP*.

He could feel it reverberating through him. Through the boards of the flooring. Through his feet. All around him.

Then there was another growl, but this one was wholly unlike the first. For one thing it was much louder, but it was more than that. *Much* more than that. There were octaves to the growl, like a symphony orchestra playing godless instruments straight out of hell itself were performing the sound, and it was unlike anything he'd ever heard before. It was indescribably horrifying, and he instantly felt warmth flood his crotch as his bladder evacuated itself without his consideration or consent. If *he* wasn't getting out of here, his urine certainly was.

And that was when everything happened.

The big kid, Ryan, was scrambling on his hands and feet toward the bleeding girl. Jake was turning around, facing the back hallway. Bart was looking too, mouth agape, a string of drool rappelling tactically from his lips.

Now the big kid was grabbing the girl up in his hands, trying to get her to her feet, pulling at her roughly. The little kid with the glasses and the braces who Jake had sliced up in the alley the day he'd broken Chris's nose was sprinting toward Jake, raising his big stick over his head and peeling his butchered lips over his orthodontically enhanced teeth in a savage snarl.

Then Jimmy was moving too. As Chris watched this slow-motion frenzy, he realized that Jimmy was moving at *him.*

Jake was noticing Ryan pulling Honey to her feet now and turned toward them, raising his knife, ready to stab down. Chris could see it now, so clearly and so frantically, that Jake meant to murder the big kid. Whatever was coming down the hall, *thumping* and howling—*and it WAS coming, louder and louder as this action played out*—be damned.

"I said no one—" Jake began to scream.

That was when Freddie's stick came down on Jake's arm. Hard. There was a loud *crack* as the stick collided with Jake's flesh and then snapped in two, the broken piece flipping up into the air and down the foyer toward the hall with that incomprehensible, coming *thing.*

The knife dropped to the floor with a *thud* and a clatter. The motion of Freddie's strike had created a momentum he couldn't stop. He was tipping forward now. Ryan and the girl were on their feet, moving away from Jake, and Jimmy was still coming at Chris.

Jake's hand, the one that had been struck by the stick, suddenly snapped up, balled into a fist, and struck Freddie across his metallic mouth. There was a wet crunch as blood slung from the kid's face in a jetting arc and he went down, his momentum now reversed.

"You little faggot!" Jake bellowed as another horrible growl came from the hall, louder than ever now. *"You just signed your death warrant!"*

Jake's hand moved quickly to hover over the place where the knife lay, and the knife flew up and slapped into his hand. He gripped it, the blade pointing down, and raised it over his head, a demonic snarl slashed across his face.

"You're dead, you little shit!"

And that was when the gunshot rang out.

It was deafening in the foyer. Almost all sound was drowned out by the ringing in his ears. Blood spat from Jake's right leg and he went suddenly on his knees, the knife falling carelessly to the floor again.

Jake was howling in pain, but Chris could barely hear it. He looked over Jimmy, who was still charging at him, and saw the man standing there, the smoking barrel of the revolver protruding from his hand, and a look of bewildered excitement on his face.

About time, asshole!

The girl was turning toward him now, her eyes like saucer plates.

Then there was another wet growl from the hallway. The ringing was dying off, much faster than he would have thought possible. The whole house seemed to be shaking now with the force of the growling thing's charge.

Then, just a millisecond before Jimmy crashed into him and they went sailing into the wall, Chris saw a thing come around the corner of the hall which his mind simply couldn't understand or recognize. Some hideous beast that didn't fit the mold of anything he'd ever seen or heard of. It was so out of context to his understanding that he could feel his sanity rushing out of him like blood through a gaping wound. He couldn't understand it. Couldn't describe it. Couldn't categorize it.

It was something from another world.

The Damned Place

The thing screamed at the same time as the girl when her eyes fell on the man holding the gun.

"Daddy?" she howled in confused wonder.

Then Chris and Jimmy hit the wall, pushed through, and were hurled into another world.

CHAPTER 65

Jimmy's mind was racing when he began running for Chris, but it was focused. He knew what was coming around that corner. There was no mistaking those lurking, thundering footsteps. Those snarls.

The cold.

It was here. Johnathan Michael Brogan's Glutton was back, it was in the house, and it was coming for them. For their meat.

Later, he would think that everything he did had been done on pure instinct, and he would be correct. He was in a state of stark terror, but with everything on the line, his presence of mind was acute and tuned to the situation, and he could see it playing out in slow motion several seconds before it happened.

Jake was in the foyer, closest to the hall. Bart was closer to the rest of them, but not by much. Ryan, Freddie, and Honey were on the floor next to the staircase, and Tom Bascom was standing slack-jawed and armed in the mouth of the foyer.

The beast was coming around the corner.

If something didn't change fast, they were all dead. All of them. Jimmy thought that he could perhaps live with Bart and Jake becoming dinner for the thing from another world, but the rest he could not. Not even Chris.

The Damned Place

When Tom had burst onto the scene out of nowhere, Jimmy had intrinsically known in that instant that Chris Higgins, for all his faults and bullshit, had been the one who got him here. Hell, he'd been *watching* for the man for the past several minutes, looking over their shoulders out the door, waiting for him. In hindsight, Jimmy could see desperation on Chris's face as he seemed to have begun to think Tom wouldn't come after all. Chris may have been an asshole, but he wasn't like Jake and Bart. Not by miles.

Jimmy was lowering his shoulder to tackle Chris. As he moved, he willed the wall behind him to open, and there was a sharp warble that went unnoticed by everyone else, their focus on the unnamable thing clamoring around the corner of the hallway, coming for them with a deathly grin full of black fangs and unfinished flesh.

He fleetingly thought, just for a split second, about how different the thing looked as opposed to when he'd seen it with Honey when they'd been on the other side. What seemed a lifetime ago now. The features were basically the same, and it was still huge, but it seemed to have less skin. Less bulk. Like it was still forming.

His brain—as brains can do—put this information and all they had learned from the Brogan journal together and knew that the thing wasn't fully formed in this world yet. It hadn't *eaten* enough here to come through completely, and he also knew then that if it got the rest of them—sitting like fish in a barrel in this foyer—that the thing would then be able to come fully into this version of Earth and destroy it. He doubted even their country's nuclear arsenal could stop it, though he had no reason to believe such a thing. It merely seemed fitting in the moment.

One shot! he thought, a mere millisecond before crashing into Chris's midsection. *I've only got one shot!*

He plowed into Chris, then, the wind rushing out of the older boy's lungs in a wave. Then they were hurling, flying through the air horizontally, passing through the portal that had been a wall just a moment before.

He could hear the monster snarling, growling, teeth snapping as it rounded the hallway corner into the foyer. Everyone else's breath had frozen, and Tom Bascom's loose jaw began to take up the slack for a scream

Now!

They were still flying through the air when Jimmy threw his hand around behind them, towards the others. He would have only one chance to get this right, and the timing had to be perfect or they were all dead. He knew enough to know that the thing couldn't come through on its own, that it *needed* people or creatures such as Cloris and Jake and himself to pass from world to world. At least he knew it couldn't do it at will like they could.

Jimmy willed the floor beneath the others to open.

At once, another warble filled the air as the floor dematerialized into a wavering portal to the cool world beneath them. They all fell through. Jake and Bart. Ryan and Freddie and Honey. Tom Bascom. All of them.

Hands raised up into the air in involuntary acts of exultation as they collapsed through the flooring of the damned house and into the cold space beneath it. Into the other world. He could hear Honey cry out in fright. Someone grunted. Another made a sound which mimicked a squealing pig, and that one he attributed to Bart Dyer.

But they all fell through. The monster was fully around the corner now, its fanged, vertical mouth open in a diamond of damnation, howling octaves of horror as it watched its prey slipping from it a moment before it could sink its ancient teeth into their writhing meat.

Then they were through. Completely through and on the ground beneath. Several *whooshes* of people losing their wind rushed up to his ears. Jimmy saw the monster preparing to leap down on all of them, ready to tear them to a carnage of wet ribbons and quivering bits.

He saw it leap.

At once, Jimmy willed the portal closed. The floor rematerialized a half-second before the beast would have been diving through it, its warble ceasing at once. The Glutton thudded hard against the floor and made a comical *oomph* as it slid across the old, splintered hardwood, claws scraping and gnashing in surprised frustration.

Then Jimmy and Chris hit the floor hard in the other world. More wind escaped Chris, though it couldn't have been much to begin with, and Jimmy could hear him, could *feel* him gasping desperately through his mouth in momentarily futile attempts to wrench breath back into his lungs.

Now Jimmy was rolling off of him and looking back through the wall into his own world where the monster was pushing itself up onto its feet, black eyes glaring through the portal at him. The thing hissed like some demon lizard and he saw a horrific tongue lurch out towards them and snap the air like a whip.

Then it was coming for them. And fast.

Jimmy's face was beaded with sweat, in spite of the chilled air on this side, and his eyes were frantic. But his mind was still aware and functioning. He threw both hands up, willing—*begging*—the portal to close. To close before the thing came through and began to suck his intestines out of his gored belly like shit-soaked spaghetti.

It closed.

And it happened not a moment too soon. The thing had gotten almost to the wall, and would have been through it in just another second had he not acted when he did.

The wall was back, and Jimmy began to breathe. He thought he could hear the thing on the other side, beating against the wall, smashing the plaster to powder, ripping the beams, tearing its way through at them.

But that couldn't be. It was on the other side of the wall, sure, but not in *this* world. It was in the other world, a universe away. There was no way he should be able to hear anyth—

Then a fresh chill coursed over him. He realized he wasn't hearing these sounds through the wall, though he *was* hearing them. It was more distant than that.

He sat up suddenly, scrambling to his feet. Chris was pulling in breath in loud, retching gasps.

"Da fundk bas shat?" Chris managed through breaths and his battered nose.

The fuck was that?

"That's what I was trying to warn y'all about, but your fearless leader wouldn't listen!"

Chris was climbing to his feet now, and looking around, terror and fear and confounded astonishment on his face.

"Hwear dar be?" he muttered through a wavering voice.

Where are we?

"Another world," Jimmy muttered as he rounded out of the room and into the foyer.

He had been prepared for just a moment to come around into the foyer and see the monster there, tearing the wall apart, ready for it to see him and pounce. He could still hear the destruction going on.

But nothing was there.

"Doh, by Gond, ban!"

Oh, my God, man!

Chris was looking around, full horror in his eyes now. He was lost in this new world which seemed so much like his own, yet so different. He was shivering now from the difference in temperature, though Jimmy didn't think that was *all* he was shivering from.

Those tearing sounds continued. Then Jimmy picked up *another* sound. A little quieter, but there. *Always* there. Since they had come into the house on the other side.

A warble.

Jimmy sprinted toward the hallway, barely aware Chris was following him closely, looking around them in bewilderment.

They rounded the hallway and Jimmy made it three more steps before he stopped cold, his feet skidding slightly. He was staring down the hallway at the end. To a place he knew. He knew it all too well. It was the place he'd come through the first time.

The closet door at the end of the hall was standing open.

Not only was it standing open, but he could see the waving shimmer of the portal just beyond it. The same place Jimmy had come through that day Jake had cornered him in this house, or *that* house, or however the hell they were supposed to understand this. The place Jake must have opened by accident.

He had probably been thinking of the closet where Jimmy had escaped that time while he was torturing Honey with his knife and his threats. Jake didn't fully understand the power he possessed, and had been unaware that he'd opened the door for The Glutton to come through.

And it was still open.

"Die cand beveieve dis!" Chris shouted behind him in a nasal abortion of the language.

I can't believe this!

Jimmy's eyes were wide. He could hear the sounds drifting from the portal to the other side, to *his* world. The world where the monster was now. He could also hear shouts and scuffles beneath the house. The others were down there, on this side of the two worlds, safe from the monster for the moment.

But they weren't safe from Jake.

Jimmy didn't have time just now to deal with that yet, however. He had to close this portal, locking the beast in the house on the other side. He somehow knew the thing was too weak yet to move much beyond the house. It needed more meat for that. And if he could lock it there, they would have time to figure out what to do and get everyone home safe.

He lifted his hands and willed the portal to close. He could feel the power coursing through his fingers, could feel the energy of the gift doing its magic. Then he heard the sounds from the other side stop.

There, he thought, his eyes still closed. *Now we have a moment to breathe.* He opened his eyes.

The portal was still there.

Nothing had happened. It hadn't closed. It hadn't even *shrunk.*

What the hell?

He raised his hands again, trying to close the gate to where the monster was, focusing with all his might.

Nothing.

This is Jake's portal, not yours, he suddenly thought. *But why did the sounds—*

His thought broke off when he began to hear the *thump-thump-thump* of the thing's hoofed footfalls drifting from the other world.

It's coming.

"Shit!" Jimmy spat into the hallway.

Then Chris Higgins was screaming behind him.

Jimmy swung around and saw Chris staring at the picture on the wall that he himself had seen when he had come over here an eon ago. The older boy was stumbling back away from the picture of the *other* people, the fur-covered aberrations with the tall ears and the four arms and the nose that looked like a rabbit's and pig's at the same time. The beady eyes.

"*Aaaaggggghhhh!*" he was screaming as he thudded into the wall opposite the picture.

"Chris!" Jimmy yelled at him. "You've got to be quiet! I can't close the—"

Thump. Thump. THUMP.

Jimmy's head jerked back down the hall and he looked through the portal.

The thing was standing at the far end of the hall, smiling at him. At least he *thought* it was a smile. The vertical mouth formed a diamond shape which bore fangs and its black eyes seemed to be full of malevolent joy.

Then it was coming. Coming at them down that hallway, a universe away and right in front of them at the same time.

And it was coming fast.

Jimmy turned and saw Chris was already running. He was still screaming and heading for the door of the house. Jimmy went after him. He didn't think Chris had seen the thing coming, only that he was still reeling from what he'd seen in the picture. The family of Cloris, which Chris knew nothing about.

"Chris!" Jimmy yelled as he went after him. "We have to stay together! It's coming! Do you hear me? *It's coming!*"

But Chris wasn't hearing him at all. He was running out the door now and down the stairs into the fogged landscape of this world, still screaming madly, perhaps thinking this was all a bad dream, that if he just ran home all would be fine. He would wake up from this nightmare and be able to hug his momma and forget about the whole thing.

"You don't know what's out there!" Jimmy tried as he rushed out the door and down the stairs himself.

But Chris paid him no mind, and gave no heed to his words. He continued to run into the mist and vanished, his screams trailing behind him like a macabre, invisible tail.

Jimmy skidded to a stop again on the leaves as he dropped from the last step and onto the ground. To his right, he saw movement and he turned, seeing the others climbing out from under the house. Tom Bascom was already out, his gun still clutched in his hand and Honey in his arms. Ryan and Freddie were crawling out. He could hear Bart and Jake rustling beneath the house to get out.

Tom looked at Jimmy.

"What the hell is this?" he asked, a bitter slur in his voice. "What have you gotten my daughter into?"

Jimmy opened his mouth, but before he could answer, a howling scream halted his words. It wasn't the monster, though. The steady *thump-thump-thump* of its movement was still coming from the house. But the scream had come from the woods, somewhere beyond the cloud of the mist.

The scream had come from Chris Higgins.

Then another howl came, but this time it *was* coming from the house. And it was deeper. It was meaner.

And it was closer.

Jimmy looked back to the group. Jake and Bart were climbing out now, and Jake's face was streaked with grime and pain and hate and murder. He was visibly struggling with the wound in his leg, which was still trickling blood from an ugly hole a couple of inches above his knee-cap. And Jimmy noticed that Jake had

481

somehow managed to get his knife back into his hand at some point.

Jimmy spoke as he began to move.

"We have to move!"

CHAPTER 66

Chris had tripped over a fallen limb and crashed into the ground. For the third time his wind pumped out of his lungs and he could feel the sting of desperation as his mind jumbled, trying to make sense of everything and trying to get his breath back.

What the fuck did I see in there? he thought in terror.

He didn't know. He didn't *want* to know. He just wanted to get home. Get to his parents' house. He'd be happy to work and gruel for his father for a pittance and hug his mother's neck. It may suck to live with his family, but at least there weren't monsters and superpowers and people who looked like animals from the *Island of Dr. Moreau* there. He just wanted normalcy back, and nothing he'd seen in the last three minutes even approached normal.

He had been pushing himself up when he heard something. Something maddeningly close and totally horrible.

Crunch-crunch-crunch.

Leaves. Leaves shattering and pulverizing under the weight of some alien thing. Some monster that was coming for him. Maybe it was one of those four-armed horrors from the picture, with their long ears and terrible, furry bodies.

Crunch-crunch-crunch.

Closer now.

He was aware that his nose was hurting badly and a liquid warmth was pouring over his mouth. In the fall, he had banged his nose again on the ground and damaged it all over again for the third time.

Just fucking great! his mind bellowed.

The *crunching* continued to come closer, and he felt his sphincter tighten along with every muscle in his body.

Then he saw a shadow in the mist. It started like a sphere, coming towards him slowly, menacingly, like a black ball rolling towards him. Then he could see little thin and curled spines protruding out of the sphere, moving forwards and back, carrying the ball closer and closer to him.

Crunch-crunch-crunch.

His spine turned to the hardest ice in all the world. Like titanium ice, if some scientist could figure out a way to forge the hardest metal with the frost of Antarctica. It solidified his back and spread to all his joints, freezing him in place. His eyes were the only thing moving, darting in tiny sweeps to the curled spines on either side of the moving sphere.

Then it came out of the mist. Less than three feet from his face.

It was a whole new world of horror for Chris. The black ball hadn't been black at all, as it turned out, save for its legs. It had a terribly hilarious coat of bright orange fur on its back or abdomen or whatever it was, and an almost neon green skin on its face. Red fangs protruded from purple lips that seemed coated in slime, and diamond shaped eyes which glowed yellow looked dumbly at him. It was making a sound like farts that were getting ready to blow from an upset stomach, horrible wet sounds, and its ten legs carried it over the ground in a terribly slow and menacing pace.

His breath caught. The ice in his body had frozen everything else within him, and now his pulmonary functions were freezing as well. His wide eyes bulged from his head as though on stalks, gazing at the aberration before him that was so much like a spider, but so much *not* like anything his mind could reckon with.

It was much too *big*, for one thing. The thing was probably three feet across, and that wasn't even counting its legs.

Its ten *legs*.

It made another step toward him, seeming to be unaware of his presence. A tinny gasp escaped Chris's lips then, the cold which had frozen him thawing for just a moment.

The spider-thing froze suddenly, and the two front legs shot up as though it was about to scream *Hallelujah*. He noticed the front legs were just a bit shorter than the rest, and its yellow and black eyes seemed to widen and dart about. Slime dripped from the horrible, red fangs.

This is Hell, Chris thought. *I'm in Hell!*

"Fick-a-choo?" the spider-thing said, only it sounded more like a question than a statement.

Chris's eyes flittered ever so slightly.

Did it just talk? Do giant spiders in Hell talk?

But the frozen spider gave no response to his mental inquiries. It just stood there, hands raised to Jesus, its horrible face dripping slime or sweat or goo.

"Fack-a-chut?"

Chris's terror was giving way to comical bewilderment as he stared into the face of this horrible creature before him, and he felt his lungs begin to work again suddenly. He wished they never would have.

Chris actually chuckled a word. It was a single word, and a single laugh. Nothing more. But it was enough.

"Hwhat?" he giggled.

Then the spider's eyes blazed brighter and its mouth opened so wide that physics seemed to legislate their laws out of existence. The bright red fangs raised and what seemed like a thousand red needles appeared all around them in the thing's mouth. And it hissed.

That was when Chris Higgins screamed.

The spider jumped at him then with terrifying speed and sank its teeth into his face. Its now-giant mouth got all the way over his face and the teeth buried into his cheeks and temples, spraying blood in jets as it bit into him.

Chris's final scream was muffled inside the mouth of the monstrous spider. Then it tore his face from his head, leaving nothing but a gore-drenched pit which looked like a piece of fruit that had had a single bite taken out of it and then had been discarded.

The spider then licked its lips free of Chris's blood, judging—so far as giant spiders in Hell can judge—that it had actually been quite tasty, and began to scamper off again in its slow, menacing gait, leaving the teenaged boy's twitching, faceless corpse to bleed in the dirt.

Crunch-crunch-crunch.

CHAPTER 67

Jake could hardly control his fury. The fresh bullet wound in his thigh helped him focus on something other than ritualistically flaying the whole lot of the shits in front of him, but just barely.

His leg throbbed, beat at him like an angry troll with a pickaxe. Putting weight on it hurt, but it wasn't impossible. And he could take it. He was motherfucking Jake Reese, after all. There wasn't a thing in this world that could keep him down.

But this ain't our world.

He had to admit that he'd been rather alarmed to find that the head asshole Jimmy had been right about the thing in the house. The thing he could hear coming after them at this very moment, giant hooves smashing and thumping and clumping their way through the rotting structure of the ancient, secluded home.

"We have to move!" Jimmy was screaming.

Faggot.

Always running, always afraid. Always trying to hide, trying to avoid me and Bart and Chris. Fucking faggot. All of them! Fucking fairy fruits! They couldn't even stand and face me—

But that wasn't true, now, was it? Jimmy had just faced him down in the house. Not only that, but faced him down and then saved his life. Not that saving his life carried even one ounce of weight with Jake. It didn't. But he had to admit that the little fucker had a sack on him, after all. He could almost respect that.

Almost.

Now they were running through the alien woods, around the side of the house. Well, the others were running, anyway. Jake was doing his best impression of running. His leg hurt and had begun to spit fresh jets of blood as he went.

Warbling. He could hear the warble.

Yes, it was somewhere close to them, probably on the other side of the wall in the house. He quickly pictured the interior layout as he could remember it, and he could see the hallway where he had trapped Jimmy—*and from where Jimmy had escaped him*—that first time they'd faced off in the woods was just on the inside of the wall they were passing now on the outside.

Thump-thump-thump!

The thing was still coming. Still charging them. What was it? What wonderful beast could it be, and where had it come from?

He didn't know, but he knew he wanted to know.

The girl. Her throat. Gotta cut her throat.

Thoughts swirled into his mind out of nowhere. Butchering thoughts. The girl was ahead of him. They all were, even the fat-ass, Bart. Little by little, they were all getting away from him, further and further, as he limped and hopped along.

Cut the cunt's throat!

Suddenly he was overwhelmed with a sense of urgency he'd not felt before. Perhaps it was the chase. Perhaps it was his bruised ego, though he wasn't capable of admitting it had been bruised by the cunt's father showing up and shooting him in his goddamned leg like a coward. Couldn't admit that his ego had been bruised further still from Jimmy's acrobatic world jumping when the thing—*the blessed beast*—had come around the corner for them.

Oh, what glorious things he could do with that beast!

He didn't know how, not exactly, he would be able to use the beast, but he knew the thing that was after them—*thump-thump-thump*—was enormously powerful. Enormously *evil.*

A smile spread across Jake's face as he hobbled along, dropping even further back from the group. He was slowing down. Not because he had to. Not because of the pain.

Because he wanted a clear shot.

The *thumps* transformed into *clops* as the thing exited the house and its hooves hit the dirt. It was coming. Oh, yes, it was coming *fast.* In just a few moments—a few *seconds*—it would be rounding the corner again, and this time there was no floor to fall through. This time it would be on top of them and they would have nowhere to go. Nowhere to run.

And nowhere to hide.

The *clops* got louder, and Jake knew without turning that the thing was just behind him, already around the corner, charging him head on. Any moment now, it would sink its claws into him and tear him open with its black fangs. Perhaps it would slurp up his intestines like spaghetti, bloody sauce slinging from them as they whipped in the air on the way down its godless throat.

The little bitch was in plain view, just in front of him, running next to her cock-sucking father. The one who had shot him in the leg.

He dropped to his knees and felt fire in his fingertips as he prepared himself. He focused on the little girl. Focused on the fleshy part of her upper thigh, just below her ass.

The monster was just behind him now. He could feel it. Every hair on him stood on end, tingling in tantalized anticipation.

Now!

He threw his knife.

It tumbled end over end, a well-aimed toss to be sure, but still guided by powers that Jake still couldn't understand. Didn't *care* to understand. He only cared to use them, and that was what he was doing now.

The knife seemed to gain momentum in the air, as though it were accelerating. As a matter of fact, it *was* accelerating. Jake forced it to move faster, to tumble harder, all the while keeping it smooth and on course.

He watched those thighs.

Then the knife struck. It was a perfect shot, debilitating but not mortal. He didn't *want* it to be mortal. That was what the beast was for. This was his way of making sure the beast was at his disposal. Jake's way of making a deal with the monster.

The bitch screamed and fell over as blood streaked out of her leg. She hit the ground with a loud, fleshy tumble, and her father was reaching out to her, not understanding yet what had just happened.

"Honey?" he cried, his blurry eyes wide and more alert than ever. *"What happened, Honey?"*

Jake's momentum had caused him to fall forward after throwing the knife, and now he lay on his knees and his left hand, his right outstretched toward the bitch and her father.

The beast was over him now, moving fast. He could see the thing's shadow casting over him.

Jake turned his head and looked up at the thing. To anyone else, the sight would have been so terrifying, so without frame of reference, that they would most likely have gone mad right then. But not Jake Reese. Jake actually *did* have a frame of reference with which he could associate the thing he was watching leap over him, their eyes meeting for just a moment with an imperceptible nod of understanding. He *knew* this creature.

The thing was what Jake saw every time he looked in the mirror.

Not literally, of course. But in a figurative sense, that was absolutely true. And what was even more frightening was the fact that this not only didn't scare Jake, it didn't even shame him. This thing was Jake's greatest desire. Jake's ultimate goal. His life-long *dream*.

This thing was Death.

Jake snatched at the air for the knife to come back to his hand and it ripped out of Honey's thigh with a spurt of blood. She wailed again, and Jake could see her father was now on his knees, trying to pull her up from the ground and get them going again. Jimmy and Ryan and the four-eyed fuck were turning, trying to get them up, trying to help. Bart Dyer was running with all the jiggling comedy of a fat man on a trampoline in slow motion.

The knife slapped back into Jake's hand with a *clap*, fresh blood dripping from the blade. Jake thoughtlessly licked the blade, tasting the metallic tang of the bitch's blood, and shuddering involuntarily. His eye twitched.

Two shots rang out then, one after the other in quick succession. It was the bitch's daddy, blasting away at the freight-train coming his way.

Pitiful.

Jake managed to struggle to his feet, and somewhere on the other side of the wall, inside the house, the warble stopped. He hadn't consciously closed the portal, but then he hadn't consciously opened it either. Didn't matter now one way or another. The thing was here, it was upon them, upon all the faggots, and was about to tear them apart.

And Jake Reese would be the one to escape.

CHAPTER 68

The Glutton met the boy's eyes as it leaped over him. He understood this young thing with the bleeding leg—*oh, I want it, give me your blood!*—beneath him. This little thing—*humans in their world, yes?*—was making a *deal* with him.

I give you them, you let me be.

Or something very close to that.

The Glutton had no problem whatsoever making deals. Deals were one of the things it had become quite accustomed to in its eons-long life. As it had jumped from world to world, through universes and multiverses, through strange galaxies and through the stars, it had made deals with the indigenous all along its way. It had to, as a matter of fact.

It was able to do many, many wonderful things. It had eaten entire peoples, races, species. It had destroyed entire worlds, time and time again, even a few star systems in the outer reaches of the universe, far beyond where even light seemed able to reach. But the Glutton could reach. Oh, yes, it could reach all these places.

But not without help.

The one thing it could *not* do—at least not very often on its own—was the actual *jump*. The jump seemed to be a rare ability—but one shared across all dimensions and worlds—held by just a few of the creatures who lived in the worlds. In its eating, in its *gluttony*, it always had to hold back on just one. He had to find, identify, and turn one of the creatures so it could move on to the next world.

Sometimes this was more difficult than it needed to be. Often, he would find creatures possessing some sense of *morality* who would try and face it down. *It!* As though the mere mortals could do any such thing!

Oh, but they would try. He'd always turn them in the end, making the jump, from one bad place to another.

And that was another thing. While it considered itself eternal, it really wasn't. It was *ancient*, that was for sure, but not eternal. Not like the Creator. It was old. *Eons* old. Epochs of devastation under its belt.

But it was not eternal.

One eternally true thing, however, was that the specific places of jumping had to be thin. It typically could find these places, places where the morality which seemed ingrained into all sentient beings on some level, had been terribly perverted. These places were thin enough to jump. Thin enough that those rare few who had the gift could open the doorway for the Glutton to jump to the next and begin to grow into their world. Dining on the flesh of the high meat. Birthing into their world to bring about their end.

This was just such a place. Cloris had been here, and she had almost led him through, but that bastard from the other side had ruined everything when he'd killed the witch.

It'd been trapped here for quite some time. Almost a century, though the Glutton did not experience time in the same way other creatures did. But it was still a very *long* time, even for it.

It'd been able to draw in just enough from Cloris to make one jump, and it'd had to save it for just the right time. It'd been too weak to make the jump just after Cloris had died, though it could hear those people on the other side through the thin walls of this world. No, it had been the wrong moment. It needed more strength. More time.

So it had waited. And waited.

Then, decades later, the time had come. And it had been so close. It had managed to get the first man, but the fat one had gotten away. Out of its reach. It hadn't had enough to come all the way in, and it could only project so far.

And the fat man had outrun him.

Then providence had smiled upon it. Some months later, someone had come through. The very boy in front of it at that very moment, as a matter of fact. He and the girl. They had escaped him, though, and had stayed away ever since.

Until now.

Even though it had invaded their nightmares, gotten into their heads, they had not returned. It had hoped the invasion of their dreams might draw them back, might make them think they could somehow come and destroy it. That it might lure them back within its reach so it could devour them and be birthed into their world. But it hadn't worked.

It did not care what had brought them back now, it only cared that they were here. It had planned to use the boy trying to help the girl and the older man up, but it sensed the gift inside the other boy beneath him, and that one would not need to be turned. It was sure of that. It would have a healthy meal on these, nearly enough to make a full jump, then the boy would take him through.

And then he would eat the world's soul.

The older man was using some contraption, spitting stinging projectiles at it. The projectiles did little more than sting, though it found such things a great annoyance.

It roared, its unique, echoing, transcendent bellow. It saw the color rush out of the group in front of it.

Then the shiny thing flew out of the girl's leg and back to the boy behind it. It was sure now. The boy had the gift. This boy would take him through.

Time to eat.

The Glutton came down on all fours and charged faster, and the cluster of people before it began to scream.

PART EIGHT:

SHOWDOWN

Thursday, July 5, 1990

CHAPTER 69

Pain tore through her leg, then bolted all the way up her body as the knife first buried itself in her flesh, then tore out of her and back into the hands of the psychotic boy. Tears seared her eyes with their salt and a scream burst from her as she tumbled to the ground.

"Honey!" her father screamed.

Thumping. Loud, thunderous footfalls. Something big charging.

She gazed up through the pain and tears and saw the thing—the *monster*—charging at them on all fours. It was a fearsome thing, this Glutton from beyond their universe, its wretched, snarling mouth shaped into a diamond, exposing needle fangs and a black snake of a tongue. Foam slung from its jowls in fat gobs, and its black eyes bore into her—into all of them—as it came.

And there was Jake. The insane boy who'd tortured her. Taunted her. *Violated* her. He was smiling, the knife which had just dug into her thigh in his hand now.

He can do what Jimmy does! Oh, God!

The beast was leaping over Jake now, and in abject horror, Honey watched was the boy's eyes met the thing's. His smile never faded. No trace of fear was on his face whatsoever. And did he...*nod?*

Yes. He nodded at the creature. As if some sort of knowing had passed between them. Some terrible agreement reached.

The thing's face turned back to her and it left Jake behind, unharmed. It was charging again now, the thunderous thumping of its feet—its *hooves*—shaking the ground all around her, shaking the bones in her skin. It would be on them soon, tearing the flesh from their bones and slurping their insides through its horrible fangs.

Oh, God! It's going to eat us!

Pain returned now. It had never really left, but her horror at seeing that awful, knowing nod pass between Jake and the Glutton had pushed the pain somewhere to the back of her terrified mind. It was back now, and with a vengeance.

She looked down, even as her hand clutched the fresh wound in her leg, much deeper than the one Jake had made earlier as he teased the blade just under the skin while they had still been in the house. Before Jimmy and Ryan and Freddie had come. Her heroes. Her shining knights.

Before her father had come with the gun.

Her teeth gritted tightly together, her wide eyes still stinging, she looked up to her father. This man who'd loved her so well before her mother had been taken from them. The same man whose only faithfulness now was to a bottle of whiskey. So broken now, so utterly destroyed. The same man who'd come into the bedroom as Honey had been waking from a nightmare, his pulsating manhood pressing through his soiled underwear, so drunk he'd thought it was his dead wife in the bed instead of his grieving daughter. He'd come so close to her. This man whom she loved and hated all at once, the father who'd both pushed her on a swing in the park and nearly deflowered her in a drunken, self-pitying stupor. He was all these things. Father and disappointment. Love of her life and terror of her nights. Yes, all these things, but...

But he's here.

Indeed, this man whom she'd needed more than ever since losing her mother and had disconnected from reality almost entirely, he was *finally* here. For her. His little girl. Not the object of drunken lust, or the forgotten kid who just happened to live in his house. Her father.

Her daddy.

His eyes met hers, and she saw—for the first time since the wreck which had taken her mother and his wife—genuine, fatherly love. His eyes were sober and alert. Self-sacrificing instead of self-loathing. Scared, yes—*who wouldn't be with a beast from beyond worlds bearing down on them?*—but protective.

Brave.

"Honey!" he shouted again, his wide eyes quivering.

"Daddy!" she shrieked back to him, blood pouring through her fingers clutching the wound in her leg. "Oh, daddy!"

The thumping grew louder. Closer.

"Daddy, I love you!" she cried.

For just a moment then, time seemed to still. Someone—maybe God—pushed pause on everything in the world except her. Jimmy was bent over, on his way to help her to her feet. Freddie and Ryan were behind him, mid-stride coming to assist. Bart Dyer, the fat fucker, in what for him might be called a full sprint, his gelatinous boy-breasts floating through the air.

But none of this was her focus. In this one, intimate moment, all her focus was on her father. His eyes softened, and a faint, almost sad smile spread across his whiskered face, creating lines around his eyes. There were tears in those eyes, and one dripped from the corner and left a streak through the grime on his face.

His hand reached out to her, brushing her own tears away with his thumb. She loved how his hand felt on her face, touching her with care and love. The way a father *should* touch his child. Protective, caring, soothing, and loving.

She pressed her face into his hand.

"I love you too, baby," he almost whispered, the thunderous sound of the oncoming beast silent now in their paused, sweet moment. "Now close your eyes, Honey-bunny, and control what you see."

Fresh terror flushed her fragile face as the meaning of his look and his words dawned on her. She wanted to tell him no, tell him he couldn't, not now, not ever. But there was no time. Time itself was restarting, the sounds coming back up to key, motion reentering the world around them.

His face was set now. He was standing and turning, turning towards the monster charging them at a full clip. As he rose, he spoke a single sentence to the boys who'd become her closest friends.

"Get her out of here and keep her safe!"

Then Jimmy's hands were under her arms, helping her to her feet, and her father turned fully to face the Glutton, his small pistol raised, looking pitiful against the giant monster.

He began firing, the pops of the rounds seeming small against the crashing thunder of the thing's giant footfalls. Jimmy was pulling her back, Ryan was grabbing her hand.

The shots ceased and empty clicks replaced the sound. He only pulled a couple of times on the empty chambers. Then her father lowered the gun and ran at the creature, screaming in a primal, fantastic fury.

Close your eyes, Honey-bunny, and control what you see.

She pinched her eyes shut as her father threw his pistol at the thing as the two charged each other. Jimmy and Ryan had her on her feet now, and they were all running, Bart Dyer just ahead of them jiggling and joggling as he ran like a frightened, waddling penguin.

There was a terrible crushing sound, like meat dropping onto concrete. A gust of breath.

Honey's daddy stopped screaming.

CHAPTER 70

Jimmy looked away the same moment Honey did.

He was dragging her, pulling her to her feet, and looping one of her arms over his shoulders. Her leg was hurt, and bad. She had blood all over her from what that sick fuck Jake had done to her. She was trembling as he managed to wrap an arm around her waist and turn away from a screaming Mr. Bascom.

Ryan was there to help too. Between the two of them, her arms looped over their shoulders, Honey wept. But she was moving too.

"Oh shit, oh fuck!" Freddie screamed.

He was the only one watching when the rest heard the meaty smack which ceased Tom's scream.

"Daddy!" Honey screamed into Jimmy's ear, trying to turn her head.

But Freddie was there, snatching her chin and bringing her eyes to meet his.

"Look forward, Honey!" he screamed. "And fucking *run!*"

With that, Freddie turned and began to sprint before them. Jimmy was breathing hard and struggling, even with Ryan's help, to move Honey, but they *were* moving. As fast as they could.

Beyond Freddie, Jimmy could see Bart Dyer vanishing into the mist which hung over everything. The fat boy faded into no more than a jiggling shadow, and then not even that. He was completely gone. Down the hill.

If this hill is on this side...

He really didn't know. The house was the same, the trees and the area around here. Before, when he and Honey had come through the first time Jake, Bart, and Chris had found them, the creek bed had been there. He *thought* it would all be the same, but he just didn't know for sure. There was no way of knowing or understanding *any* of this.

Another roar came from behind them in spine-tingling harmonies of horror. Jimmy thought he heard a grunt too, but he couldn't be sure. Maybe it had been Jake. Jake, shot in the leg, dragging himself to his feet.

As they continued moving, Jimmy dared a glance back and instantly wished he hadn't. The thing was there, where they had all been only moments before. Staring at them, some terrible playfulness in its black eyes. Blood drained from his flesh and all at once he felt cold again, even though he was struggling and sweating.

The thing started to move.

Jimmy didn't wait to see how fast it would be coming on. He knew well and good it would be fast, faster than they were moving, and he didn't have time to watch Death come charging down on them all at once. They had to move, and fast.

Then there was a shriek splitting the air, one of pain and fury. Then the voice of Jake Reese followed.

"*You faggots are dead!*" he screamed to them as they were swallowed by the mist which had just taken Bart Dyer. "*I'm coming for you! I'm gonna finish what we started, and feed you to my new friend here!*"

Ice trickled down Jimmy's spine as Jake spoke of his new 'friend'. He'd seen the glance—the *knowing* glance—which had passed between the Glutton and Jake. Jake had hurt Honey, which had slowed them all down. The Glutton and Jake had made an unspoken deal. The thought of it caused his stomach to knot even further.

The hill *was* there. The decline came on fast and their speed increased. Honey was doing all she could to help, which wasn't a lot, but gravity was doing most of the work now. For one terrifying moment, Jimmy thought they were going to topple over and roll down the hill. He, Ryan, and Honey would all tumble, become human bowling balls, likely taking out Freddie before them as they rolled on their merry way. Then they'd be lined up, bleeding and hurt like some buffet meal for the Glutton.

But—*small mercies*—they managed to stay afoot. They made their way down the hill, the ground leveling out as they went. Jimmy looked around, his eyes squinting through the mist, and shivered.

He knew where they were.

Yes, this was where—on the other side, back home in another galaxy—he and his friends had been chased by Jake and the others from their fort. Only then, they had been going the other direction, toward the house. And, of course, in an altogether different universe.

But it was the same! These worlds, though separated by lightyears or dimensions of space and time—perhaps all these things—they were fundamentally the same! The creatures were different, but not the rock the creatures lived on.

As he squinted and huffed for breath, the mist before them began to thin, revealing new territory. That was when he saw it. In front of him, he could see Freddie had seen it too. A comical, pointing hand shot out before Freddie, pointing stupidly towards it.

"You've got to be kidding me!" Ryan said through heaving breaths. "Am I seeing this, Jimmy?"

Jimmy grunted and nodded. "Yes! Yes! Quick, inside!"

As they continued forward, the mist cleared more, revealing...

...*their fort.*

Well, it wasn't *their* fort. But it was *a* fort. And it was identical to theirs back home. Some person—*or creature*—had put up a fort in these woods just like their own, replete with the jutting sharp sticks facing out, away from the interior of the carved earth within. It was older—*much older*—than their fort back home, but it was the *same*.

I don't know when or how, but thank Christ! Jimmy thought.

They rushed into the fort from the side, dropping Honey down in the back and Jimmy, Ryan, and Freddie turned and peered out into the mist. There was no movement, and no sound other than the distant trickle of the creek. A fresh chill stole over Jimmy, and apparently visited itself upon Ryan and Freddie as they shuddered in turn. The three of them crept forward in unison towards the front of their bunker and the sharp sticks.

"Is it gone?" Ryan asked with a crack in his voice.

"I doubt it," Jimmy said. "It's been here for a long time. It knows this place. It's toying with us."

"Well, fuck that thing!" Freddie blurted as he fetched up one of the sticks and tested its strength. "If it gets me, I'm gonna make that bitch cry first!"

"Jimmy?"

It was Honey. They all turned to her, her hurt leg splayed out before her, her back against the earthen wall at the back of the fort.

"Are you okay?" Ryan asked. "What do you nee—"

"I'm fine," she said, waving him off and turning her attention back to Jimmy. "I've realized something!"

"What is it?" Freddie asked, shoving his thick glasses up on his sweaty nose.

"It's Jimmy," she went on. "This place, it's all the same as home, right?"

"Yeah, yeah?" Jimmy said, urging her along.

"Well," she said, "if it's all the same, then we can jump back, right?"

"Right, but this far from the house?" Jimmy said, gesturing toward the house behind them. "I couldn't do it in town, remember?"

"We're a lot fucking closer here than town was!" Honey barked back. "It has to feed, feed on our flesh, to come through. Otherwise it's just a projection, a shadow! But if we could get it to come through, with *some* flesh..."

Jimmy's eyes blazed as he caught on.

"How the fuck are we going to do that, Honey? You wanna feed it an arm?"

She was shaking her head furiously.

"No, no, no! Not one of *us*!"

It hit him then. Like a brick dropped into a wet paper sack. It tore through the bottom of his gut and settled somewhere around his feet.

"Jake?" he asked shakily.

"Why the fuck not?" Honey replied, a chilling look in her eyes.

The boys all turned to each other, the same ponderous terror in their eyes.

But, why not?

Jake and Bart and Chris had been nothing but assholes to them all summer, terrorizing them at every turn. Beating and torturing Freddie and then Honey. Jake would have already killed them all if not for Tom Bascom's bullet in his leg. And they all knew he was still after them. He still had his knife.

And he still had his power.

"Fuck it, no, we can't do that!" Jimmy started sputtering. "We're not murderers!"

Freddie's hand shot out and grabbed a fistful of Jimmy's shirt, then pulled him face to face with him.

"Jake is!" he hissed and spat in Jimmy's face. "Or at least he will be if we don't stop him!"

"You can't be seri—"

"As a fucking heart attack!" Freddie growled, trying to keep his voice down. "Honey's right! If we can feed it Jake, or fucking Bart or even Chris if he's still around, and get it to follow us back home, it will be in the flesh over there, but it'll still be weak! Remember the journals I found about this place?"

Jimmy nodded and gulped.

"Yeah," Freddie went on. "That's what we've got to do. We need to—"

Grunting huffs cut them off and all eyes turned back to the mist between them and the house. Freddie raised his spear and Jimmy and Ryan both grabbed one.

A shadow started to materialize before them, but they could see it wasn't the Glutton. It was a human. A fat human.

It was Bart Dyer.

He fully materialized before them, huffing for air with snot slinging from his nose in slimy ropes. His cheeks were flushed and his lips were peeled back over his teeth in an exasperated expression of fear and exhaustion. His boy-breasts bounced and swayed before him, out of unison with his belly, and his hands slapped pitifully before him with limp wrists.

Bart saw them and stopped.

"Thank God!" he said. "You!"

He pointed at Jimmy.

"You can get us back home! I'm done with this place!"

Jimmy and the others just stared at him. Coldly.

"Well, come on, man!" Bart said through heaving breaths. "Let's get out of here!"

Indignant anger mixed with fear showed through on the fat boy's face. Jimmy turned to Freddie and Ryan and met their eyes. He glanced back at Honey and met hers.

They all told him the same thing.

He looked back to Bart.

"Okay, Bart...let's go home."

CHAPTER 71

Jake cursed as he tore off a strip of his shirt and yanked it tight around the hole in his leg. The pain was exquisite, causing his teeth to lock and grind together, fully exposed between his curled, snarling lips.

Oh, you faggots are DEAD!

He stumbled to his feet, flicking the blade of his knife in and out, methodically.

They had all vanished. Somewhere into the mist, and he thought he could hear faint voices, though it could have been his imagination. Even the creature was gone now, vanished away into the forest. On the one hand, Jake hoped the thing would shred the little bastards to ribbons. He would relish the sight. Especially the little faggot Jimmy and his bitch.

Oh, baby, thank you very much!

Yet, the thought also created some sort of twisted jealousy to churn inside Jake's gut. *He* wanted to shred them to ribbons. Wanted to cut them to the bone until his knife went dull and drink their blood from a boot. Yes, if deals were to be made with the thing, he'd make them. He already had, he fathomed, though nary a word had been spoken between himself and the beast. And if they had a deal, Jake would make good on it. He wasn't a welsher. He would do what the thing wanted, so long as he got the chance to split the little cunts like ripe avocados.

As he limped along in the direction the faggots had vanished, he heard a low groan. It was deep, strained, and sounded agonized. Jake turned toward the sound, his right eye twitching, and he saw what had made it.

The man who'd shot him was lying near the trunk of a tree, his empty pistol cast aside, glinting in the strange, misty light. He was hurt. Jake remembered him charging the creature as the kids had escaped into the forest. Remembered the loud, meaty slap which had marked the end of his screams.

And here he was. Blood trickled from the corners of his mouth and from his ears. His eyes were open, wide, darting around, and his arms were crossed over his chest as if trying to hold it together. The man trembled and coughed blood, trying to speak but apparently unable, as Jake approached him and knelt beside the man.

Jake winced at the pain in his leg as he dropped to his knee, but otherwise pushed it away. He could hurt later. Now was time for a nice cold dish of comeuppance, fresh out of the freezer.

As he leaned over the man, Jake saw a red chunk of what appeared to be meat in the leaves next to the man's head. Curious, he reached out and picked it up. It was soft and porous, yet had a rough texture on one side. He turned it over in his hand, and began to giggle to himself when he realized what it was.

It was the man's tongue.

Jake barked laughter and looked to the man's wide eyes. No doubt the man had inadvertently bitten off his own tongue when the creature had batted him. Jake leaned over him again, tossing the tongue back to the leaves as casually as one might discard torn cellophane packaging.

"You're the little bitch's daddy, huh?" Jake said with a twisted, delighted grin splitting his face. "Things kind of went left for you, no?"

The man just trembled and shook and coughed more blood. It looked black on his chin in this light, and thousands of tiny stubs of hair poked through it like hands coming up out of tar. He was trying to speak again, and Jake leaned in close, putting his ear next to the man's mouth and cupping his own ear in mockery.

"What's that, sir? I can't quite make it out. It sounds like a cat got your tongue!"

Jake began cackling laughter at the top of his lungs. It was a good joke, and Jake suddenly wished a cat actually *would* come by and pick the tongue up with its mouth. But there were no cats. Not here. Not in this alien place.

The laughter stopped suddenly and Jake spat all over the man's face. Foamy saliva peppered the man's face, and he was trying to blink it away, though his hands never came up to wipe the spittle away. Terror filled those eyes now, and the man began shaking harder, tightly holding his chest.

Jake looked at the man's throat then. He could see the throbbing of the artery, rising and falling as fast as he'd ever seen one do in his life, precious blood moving through the body.

"Does it hurt?" he asked the trembling man. "It sure looks like it hurts. Don't worry, no need to answer me!"

Jake laughed again and picked the tongue back up from its place on the leaves, wagging it in the man's face. It jiggled and made sickening wet sounds as it bobbed back and forth. Then Jake threw it in the man's face, where it made a wet slap, much quieter and smaller than the one the thing had made earlier, but no less satisfying.

"You shot me," Jake stated, his face cold and empty now. "You shouldn't have done that."

The man trembled anew, his eyes so wide they were pushing out of his sockets. He was breathing in harsh rasps, blood running out of his nostrils now as well as his mouth.

"But I'll set it right," Jake went on as he flipped the blade out again. "I like setting shit right!"

Jake leaned in close to the man's face, mere inches away, baring his teeth like a cornered animal.

"And I'll fuck your little bitch right here on your corpse!"

Jake leaned back up and slashed the knife across the man's throat. An exquisite fountain of blood showered Jake's face, and the man made another groan then, weaker than before, his own eyes darting every which way. His legs jerked beneath Jake, kicking at phantoms, writhing in pain and fear. Then, he began to relax. The death grip on his chest began to relax, and Jake could see now why the man had been holding it so tightly. His chest was split open down the middle, and as his arms relaxed, myriad organs began to peek out from behind the curtains of his chest.

The man went still then, his eyes glazed. Jake smiled widely, absently licking his lips. The taste of the man's blood startled him for a moment, but the shock left as he swallowed the coppery stuff, and his smile broadened to its maximum spread.

The Damned Place

It was good.

CHAPTER 72

Jimmy raised his hand in the fort, a concentrated look on his face. His eyes squinted to slits and he felt his hand trembling and radiating heat.

Bart Dyer stood next to him looking stupidly at what he was doing.

"Is it working?" the lardy psychopath asked.

"Shut up, Bart!" Honey hissed venomously. "Just let him do it!"

Bart smirked, snorted piggishly, and shrugged.

Jimmy barely heard any of it. He was focusing hard, trying to open the doorway home. He didn't know if it was the distance from the house or his fear—his *terror*—of what they were attempting to do, but he was having a hard time of it.

He dropped his hand and huffed loudly. A disappointed look fell across his face.

"I can't do it!" he barked. "We gotta get back to the house. Or closer to it, anyway. I-I can't do it here."

"You mean back through the fog with that thing out there?" Ryan's voice cracked, his eyes wide. "Are you out of your fucking mind?"

"Are *you*, Ryan?" Freddie asked, turning to his terrified friend. "You do realize that thing can go anywhere it wants on this side, right? The only place we can for sure get through is the house. Otherwise, we're sitting ducks for that thing."

"He's right, Ryan," Jimmy said, referring to Freddie. "I don't like it either, but we have to. So we can get home and to...to stop it."

His words were dipped in dread. Sure, Bart Dyer was crazy, and a serious asshole to boot, but did he deserve what they were planning to do to him? Did anyone?

Jake, maybe. Jake had lost it. He was out there too, with the thing. He'd made a deal with the monster, and the beast had accepted.

"I'm going," Honey said, struggling to her feet and wincing at the pain.

Ryan's fearful look washed from his face at once as he slid an arm around Honey's waist to help steady her.

"Alright, let's go," he said.

They all turned from the fort, staring into the gray mist before them. It enveloped everything. It was like a living thing, tangible, something you could touch and caress.

Something that could swallow you.

"We have to run," Jimmy said, turning to the others. "Keep up as best you can."

"I don't wanna go back there!" Bart said, his voice cracking.

"Fine then, stay here," Jimmy said coldly.

And he honestly wished Bart would have. It would likely render the same outcome to what they were planning, but it would be Bart's choice, and it would alleviate the growing shame Jimmy was feeling at that very moment. Shame which would swallow him whole if he went through with it. Which would haunt him.

Nothing like a fat-ass ghost to haunt you.

"Naw, I'm coming, you fags," Bart replied casually.

517

"I want my picture back!" Honey said in a sudden burst of emotion. "You give me back my picture, *right now!*"

Bart turned to look at her, his jowly face pinching and spreading into a smug grin.

"I think I'll hang onto it," he said. "At least until we're back home. Give you a good reason not to leave me behind."

A large branch snapped somewhere in the mist and they all snapped to attention. It had been close.

And it had been big.

"We've got to move!" Jimmy said.

They all moved at once, sprinting into, and being swallowed whole by, the mist.

CHAPTER 73

Where are you going?

The Glutton could see them moving through the mist, little more than shadows in the fog. It had been following the fat one, the one which made it salivate in a way it hadn't in eons. His meat would be rich, tender, and *oh,* so juicy. It couldn't wait to sink its teeth into the boy's soft belly and lap his juices with its tongue.

Then it had watched the leader, the little Jimmy boy, trying to break through to the other side. It hadn't worked. The Glutton had known it wouldn't, not this far from the house. The atmosphere was too strong here. No, they would have to be closer. And when they got closer, it would allow Jimmy to open the worlds to one another. That would be when it would pounce. Tear them limb from limb. It would save Jimmy for last, stepping through with him and then dining on his flesh. It would prefer to save the fat one for last, his flesh would be the sweetest, endowed with the rich flavor of all his fat, but he would need Jimmy to go through.

Or the other one...

True. Miracle of miracles, there were *two* who could open the worlds here. The Glutton had never encountered such luck in its near eternal lifetime, and the good fortune of the deal was almost more than the thing could believe. Of course, it seemed the other boy

519

hadn't mastered the art, not yet, but the Glutton could teach him. Could mentor him. Show him the ways. It understood the mechanics, even if it could not itself employ the power but once in a great while. And it had struck a deal with the other one, anyway, as it had done countless times throughout eternity with countless others with the gift.

The Glutton had options.

It lowered itself to all fours and trotted after the kids slowly. It didn't want to overpower them all at once. It wanted to wait for the right moment. The right *second*. Once the doorway was open, *then* it would act, and it would have a whole new world to devour.

Dripping slime fell from its mouth in fist-sized globs.

CHAPTER 74

Jake heard them moving. He got to his feet, grimacing at the throbbing pain in his leg as he did. The knife was clutched in his hand, white knuckles wrapped around its hilt, nails digging into his palm, threatening to break the skin.

The fucks are coming back! he thought with pleasure.

He began limping toward the sounds of their crunching footfalls. Psychotic glee beamed from his eyes and a near-Satanic smile split his face like an awful axe wound. He would carve their throats like Halloween pumpkins, and eat the little bitch's tits right in front of her while she screamed.

Oh, friends and neighbors, Jake Reese was about to feast!

He stopped going in the direction of the approaching kids when a better idea struck him. His smile broadened, the skin stretching taught on his face, threatening to tear. He turned to the house and limped to the steps as fast as he could. He hobbled up, wincing at the pain in his leg, but pushing it away. He would be ready for them.

He reached his hand out and the front door swung open before him. Glass clattered and fell from the door as it smacked the wall. Large shards of stained glass gleamed up in the gloomy light in prisms.

Once inside, he moved to his left into the parlor. A window looked out in the direction where he'd heard the kids moving, and he stumbled over to it, propping his free hand in the frame to steady himself. He peered out, looking into the fog, and felt a chill race up his spine. It was cold here. Much colder than back home. He had a brief moment of contemplation about the seasons between the worlds before he noticed the movement of shadows in the mist.

It was the kids. They were coming—*running*—straight for the house.

That's right, bitches! Come to Jake!

He smiled and turned back into the parlor, hobbling for the entryway to the foyer. He got to the entryway and put his back against the wall, just next to it. He brought the knife up to the side of his face, ready to strike.

Pain exploded once more in his leg and he looked down, groaning. Blood was pouring out of his wound around his blood-soaked strip of shirt he'd used as a bandage.

This could be a problem...

He cut the strip of shirt away with his knife and produced a lighter from his pocket. He flicked it on and stared into the dancing gleam of flame for a moment, mesmerized by it. Then he inched the flame up against the bleeding wound in his leg and bit down on his lip, hard.

Searing pain raced up his leg as first the blood vaporized and then his skin began to burn. To *melt*. Blood trickled from his lip and he released it from his teeth, his lips now peeled back over his gums and his eyes wide with fury and anticipation.

But he held the lighter where it was.

The skin around his wound was blackening now, and a flame leaped up from his pants. He flicked off the lighter and swatted the flame out, almost crying out from the pain as he did so. Thin tendrils of smoke snaked into the air around his leg, which pulsated angrily, but his pants were no longer on fire.

And his leg was no longer bleeding.

Jake smiled and put the lighter back in his pocket, returning his gaze to the entryway to the foyer. His leg was trembling now, and he shot his hand out towards one of the chairs in the parlor. It shifted and scooted before flying through the air to him. He caught the top of the large wing-back and it settled to the floor. He steadied himself on it and sighed. He was able to take some weight off his leg now, and the relief was as exquisite as the pain.

He licked his lips and could again taste the coppery magic of the bitch's daddy's blood, which was only just starting to dry on his face. He licked again, relishing the taste.

Crunching footsteps pulled him out of his ecstasy for a moment as he heard the kids rounding the front of the house, heading for the front door. He glanced back out the parlor window across the room and saw a much larger shadow now, moving through the mist.

It's coming for ya, ya fucks! And uncle Jake's waiting for ya just inside!

Jake wiped his fingers across his face, getting a large amount of the man's blood on them and started licking his fingers clean.

Fuck, that's good!

CHAPTER 75

Ryan bounded up the stairs just behind Honey and Jimmy. Freddie was right on his heels. Despite the chill in the air, he was sweating. From fear, maybe, or perhaps just the exertion of running and scrambling. Likely both.

But another thing had his heartrate up. Something unrelated to the fear and panic, or even the involuntary exercise. Something which crawled under his skin and stayed there like an unwelcome guest. One with malice in its heart. And claws.

Bart. The fat bully who was running with them, even now, bounding a few steps behind them all and panting like a wheezing dog. In all honesty, Bart wasn't their problem. Bart was a creep, there was no doubt about that. But Bart was a follower. Jake was the real problem, the *real* psycho. And of course there was the otherworldly monster after them in this world of horrors. But enough about that for now, his focus was on Bart.

Why?

The why of the matter was what he and the others had discussed doing. The way to get back and stop the monster. The plan had been to use Jake, but then no sooner had they formulated the plan, up trotted the fat bastard who'd always been ever-present with Jake every time they had been tormented.

524

And so, plans had changed.

No one had said anything. No way to do so without Bart hearing them. He was right there, snot and spittle dripping from his face as he had heaved for air. He might be a fat and loathsome son of a bitch, but he wasn't deaf.

Then there was Honey. She'd been cornered by Bart. He was the whole reason she was even brought out here to begin with, which was the only reason the rest of them had come at all. If not for Bart—and by default Honey—they'd never have stepped foot in these woods again. Not in a million years.

But still, it was gnawing at him. Eating at him, just under the skin. There was no love to be lost between *any* of them, and the fat fuck now panting up the first step behind them, but Ryan still didn't know if he could go through with it. Were they really capable of such a thing?

Was *he?*

Jimmy was rushing through the door before them into the gloom of the house. Honey vanished inside a second later, then it was Ryan's turn to go through. The light outside hadn't been bright, but it was much brighter than the interior of the house. He squinted as his eyes adjusted and he came to a stop, breathing deep and steady to catch his breath. Freddie bounded in, followed a moment after by Bart, fresh snot and foam sliming the older boy's face.

"What are you waiting for?" Bart asked between huffing breaths. "Let's get the fuck out of here!"

Ryan's eyes met the others, the silent agreement still in them all. An imperceptible nod seemed to pass amongst them all, though nary a head moved.

All their eyes moved gradually towards Bart, pulses booming in their necks. Ryan's own heart seemed as though it might explode in his chest, right there, bursting out like the Alien in that movie he'd seen a year before on VHS.

Bart's breathing was starting to steady, and his piggish eyes narrowed at them all. Confusion lined his face with a stupidity that matched his sadism.

"What?" he asked, a crack in his voice.

They all raised their pointed sticks, gripping them tighter. A crunching sound issued from outside, beyond the door. It sounded heavy.

"What?" Bart asked again, panic now easing into his voice.

Honey took one step towards Bart, leveling the stick out in front of her.

"Give me back my picture, lard-ass!" she spit, a chilling anger in her voice.

Bart just looked at her a moment, the confusion and panic still etched on his face.

"Fuck you!" he said, finally. "You get it when we're on the other side, I told you—"

Honey yelped, then, her stick falling from her hands and clattering to the rotting floor. All their eyes had been focused on Bart as he made his self-righteous response, which is why they hadn't noticed the figure come up behind them and snatch Honey.

Focus was a shifting thing, however, and now it moved from the piggy lard-ass to something they all found much more terrifying.

Jake was there. His face was specked with blood, and it was smeared around his lips. His eyes were wild and animalistic. They seemed to burn in his sockets, pure insanity and bloodlust fueling the fire within. He had Honey pulled up against him, her back to his chest, his arm across her chest. She was squirming, trying to flail away, but it was no good. He had her tight, and she was pinned.

And he held a gleaming knife, shiny with blood, against her throat.

"Well, well, well," Jake said, a sadistic chuckle in his voice. "Look who decided to come back home!"

Outside, something growled.

CHAPTER 76

Jimmy's soul chilled.

Jake had Honey, knife to her throat. They were in another world, another *universe*. A monster was chasing them, somewhere outside, and they were all trapped between a pair of psychopaths.

Oh shit, oh shit, oh SHIT!

His mind was reeling, screaming. He couldn't think. He couldn't focus. Jake was saying something to them, but Jimmy wasn't hearing it. Not really. It was some chiding remark meant to strike fresh fear into them, he knew that, but he wasn't listening to it. He wasn't even listening to the snorting chuckles of Bart Dyer behind them.

He was focused on the crunching sound outside.

Big crunching sounds, too. Like something massive stalking across the leaves. Stalking the house. Stalking *them*.

Then he heard it growl.

There was no doubt in his mind then. The thing, the *Glutton* from the diary of Johnathan Michael Brogan, was here. It was back. It had stalked them, just as they had planned, but much too soon. Especially now with the damning complication of Jake Reese.

"Is that you out there?" Jake's voice cackled. "I've got 'em here! It's all set! Come on in before dinner gets cold!"

Shrieks of mad laughter burst out of Jake then, and Jimmy turned to look at him, eyes wide and breath panting. Sweat dripped from his brow in the chill.

A fresh trickle of blood was trailing from Honey's throat now, the blade of Jake's knife having nipped her as he laughed. Her eyes were a blur of panic and tears, her chest heaving up and down beneath Jake's pinning arm.

Jimmy heard a loud *thunk* just outside the door. Like a footstep. A very *heavy* footstep.

It's here!

Nothing. Nothing they could do. They were trapped between monsters with no way out. Jake knew they wouldn't sacrifice Honey. She was the reason they had all come. A unifying force.

But what could they do?

Jimmy's eyes then moved to Freddie and Ryan. Ryan's lips were curled up in fury. Jimmy knew Ryan was scared. Terrified, even. If it was an option, he would likely be running and screaming through the forest to whatever this dead world could offer in terms of safety and refuge.

But it wasn't an option. And further, there was Honey.

Their eyes met. All three of them. Another clunking step boomed from outside, closer now. Just outside the front door. Another growl.

Jimmy looked to Ryan and flicked his eyes towards Jake and Honey. He looked then to Freddie and flicked his eyes towards Bart, still snorting laughter in front of the door.

They nodded.

"I'm going to enjoy watching you faggots bleed!" Jake bellowed.

Then things moved fast.

Jimmy shoved his hand out towards Jake and Honey. There was just a split-second for a stupefied look to cross over Jake's face before the knife in his hand—the one pressed against Honey's throat—flew from his grip and slapped into Jimmy's own hand.

Then Ryan was moving, raising the stick over his head, his snarl more furious than ever. Jake's grip loosened on Honey and Jimmy saw her bite down into his forearm a second before Jimmy turned away and toward Bart, the hand holding the knife rising into a throwing position.

Freddie was moving now. He had his stick up and pointed. His own scabbed lips were pulled up over his braces, and his eyes seemed gargantuan behind his thick glasses. Both he and Ryan were screaming now.

Jimmy threw the knife. He also guided it with his Star Wars power, and it flew point first through the air with lightning speed. The tip plunged into Bart's shoulder, hard, and buried up to the hilt. Blood spurted from the wound as Bart's hand went to the knife reflexively.

Then Freddie was there, a half-second later, plunging the pointed end of his stick into Bart's thigh. Bart was squealing now, like the pig he was, high-pitched pain exploding out of him.

Jimmy heard a *thump* then, a fleshy, but also wooden, sound. He turned to see the end of Ryan's stick sailing in an arc past Jake's head and above Honey's. Jake's head was snapping back, strings of blood slinging from his temple, arms flailing. Honey was diving for the ground, clamoring for her own stick, blood smeared all around her mouth.

She was up then, rushing forward toward Bart, screaming in the way only a twelve-year-old girl could do. She crossed the distance to Bart quickly, the point of her stick burying into his gut with an awful plunging sound. More blood spewed from the now staggering fat boy as his screams turned to whimpers and his face streamed with tears, pain etched all across it.

Jimmy heard a moan behind him and turned, seeing Jake starting to stand up, slowly. Ryan was leaned over, the force of the blow he'd delivered having driven him off balance, and he was only just now recovering.

Jimmy reached his hand out again, this time toward Bart, when the door behind him blew in in a shower of glass and splinters. But Jimmy never faltered. The knife in Bart's shoulder returned to his own hand with a slap, then he sent it sailing back toward Jake, burying it into the older boy's right side.

A wince of pain hissed from Jake's lips as he collapsed back to the ground.

"Give me my fucking picture, you pig!" Jimmy heard Honey screaming.

He looked back and saw Honey there in front of Bart, her stick digging deep into his belly, her hand in his pocket. She pulled out a small rectangular piece of paper—her picture, he assumed—then she wrenched back with the stick and a horrible sucking sound came from the fat boy's stomach.

The now disintegrated doorway was cast in shadow then, and Jimmy saw the thing there, its clawed hands gripping either side of the destroyed doorframe, black eyes burning at them.

"Time to eat!" the thing screamed.

It roared then. Freddie and Honey shoved Bart, bleeding and sobbing now, back toward the Glutton, then turned to run.

"Come on!" Jimmy screamed as he began running for the end of the hallway.

He grabbed Ryan's arm on the way and together they leaped over a writhing Jake on the floor. Jimmy threw both hands up and the wall before them opened with a shimmer and a warbling sound. Through it, they could see the house, the hallway, and the front door, but in their own world, the door was still intact over there.

They ran, all four of them, and crossed from that damned world back into their own, the heat hitting them like a ton of bricks.

That was when they heard another growl. Another scream.

Another splash.

CHAPTER 77

No! the Glutton screamed inside its mind. *They're getting away!*

It hadn't had enough meat yet, not enough to enter fully into their world. If it went through now it would be diminished and weak. It wouldn't have the strength or power to begin the process of eating their world.

But, it thought with a hideous grin, *They're only kids. I don't need full strength or power. And after their succulent flesh is devoured, I will have the strength to move on and dine.*

The thing bellowed a roar as it charged through the body of the fat boy it had just torn in two, clawing slinging intestines out of its way as it rampaged through a mist of red hanging in the air. Its awful tongue slurped out, licking up as much as it could on the way, feeling the muscles tighten and grow on its body as it went for the portal into the new world. The fresh world.

Fresh meat.

It leaped over the boy with whom it had a tentative deal, writhing on the floor, and charged all the harder toward the portal.

The kids were through it already, stumbling and dragging themselves toward the door of the house in their universe, but the Glutton charged on. It would not be outdone. Not now. Not when it was so close and it could taste the sweetness of their kind's blood in its mouth from the halved boy behind him, only now thudding to the floor in a pair of fleshy slops.

Something came flying past the thing as it charged on, something small and glinting in the dim light. It flew through the portal ahead of the beast and into the hand of the kids' leader.

An ear-shattering scream—it could not be called a roar this time—exploded from the monster as it saw the boy's hand raise toward the portal. The shimmering wave and the warbling sound—which had always been to the Glutton the sound of dinner time for new worlds—began to diminish. Its eyes grew wide in their black sockets and its tongue lashed out in a furious whip.

It leaped.

It was close enough to jump through, and diving for the portal would cast it into their world. Ideally, it would have devoured the fat boy and the man outside first, just for the added nourishment from this new world it was birthing itself into, but there was no time. It was so close, so *fucking* close! It would have them, and right now.

It sailed through the air, fangs bared in a nightmare picture, claws outstretched, tongue trailing, dripping saliva.

The portal closed.

A second later the beast was crashing not through worlds, but through a wall of old plaster and ancient boards. Dust exploded all around it and fury instantly filled it with nightmarish resolve as it scrambled to find its footing amidst the destroyed plaster and struts. It roared again, but this time it had a whine of frustration to it, something the thing didn't care for at all, yet all the same it spilled from the Glutton unwittingly.

It was not defeated. Who did they think they were dealing with?

I am the eater of worlds! And the eater of worlds uses all cards on the table.

It leaped back into the hallway, hovering over the bleeding, crying boy there. The one it had made the deal with. The one who had been ready to feed them all to the thing.

His new Cloris.

"Time to make good on our deal," the glutton growled to the boy.

The boy's cries stopped at once, though the wincing discomfort remained on his face. Their eyes met, and the Glutton was almost surprised to see the hint of a smile crease the boy's face.

He may be worth keeping around, after all...

The Glutton leaned in close, its rancid breath blowing back the hair on the boy's head. The boy's eyes were mesmerized, not with fear, but with anticipation and...was that *lust?*

"Open the door," the thing said as it searched the boy's mind for something to bind the deal with.

It found it.

"Let's get those faggots."

The boy sat up with a grimace, and with blood leaking from his mouth, he grinned broadly.

It almost caused the Glutton to shudder.

CHAPTER 78

The portal closed a half-second before the Glutton dived through.

"Shit!" Freddie screamed, a tone of relief in his voice.

"That was close!" Ryan added through panting heaves.

It had been. A split-second more and the thing would have been through. On them. Devouring them. And then, onto the rest of the world.

But they'd made it. Chris had disappeared, Bart was gone, and Jake was left with the monster. Jimmy thought perhaps he should feel something for the asshole, the one who'd given them so much grief over the summer and had tortured Honey, but he didn't. He wondered if this was a flaw in his humanity, but dismissed the thought.

Jake is an asshole, he thought. *He...was an asshole.*

Still, though he tried hard to grasp onto some semblance of compassion, a smile began to split his face. The corner of his lip began to curl up in an involuntary snarl of satisfaction, one which both exhilarated and horrified him with equal measure.

Jimmy shuddered and turned to the others.

"Are you all okay?" he asked, his words coming out faster than he'd intended. "Honey? How about you?"

Honey leaned against Ryan, her face and leg bloody, but she nodded.

"I'll be okay, Jimmy," she said.

A sadness settled into her face then, and her eyes drifted to a distant land, somewhere far beyond where they had just been. Jimmy wondered if her mind was on her father, who'd come through for them in the final moments.

"It *will* be okay, Honey," Jimmy said, taking a step toward her. "I know it."

She smiled faintly and lowered her head, zero conviction in the look upon her face. Perhaps it might be okay, but Jimmy felt it would be a very long time before Honey Bascom was close to okay again.

"We should get the hell out of here," Freddie said, his eyes a bulbous parody behind his glasses. "They may be in another universe, but I don't wanna stick around here even one more second.

Jimmy was nodding as his head swiveled and his eyes fell upon Ryan, who was propping up Honey. His eyes were distant, staring at the floor. And Jimmy thought he could see...*tears* in his eyes?

He said, "Ryan? You okay?"

Ryan took several moments before looking up to him, his look remaining distant, but perhaps not quite so distant as they had been a moment before. The tears stood out starkly in his eyes, bulbous globs prepared to fall.

"What did we do, guys?" he asked.

For a moment, no one answered. They *had* no answer. What did they *do*? What the hell was he talking about?

"I don't—" Jimmy started, his head shaking.

"Don't play dumb, guys!" Ryan barked at them. Everyone flinched. "We just sacrificed two people over there to that, that *thing*! Don't tell me you're not feeling anything over that now!"

Jimmy swallowed hard, and he heard Freddie do the same. The fact was, Jimmy hadn't thought about how it might affect the others at all. It hadn't even crossed his mind. Chris, Bart, and Jake were jackasses and deserved whatever they got. Only fleeing the monster had mattered to Jimmy, not a shred of compassion had been spared for the bullies they'd left behind, but now that Ryan was talking, the emotions were all flooding back to him.

What *had* they done? Sure, any one of those boys—with perhaps the exception of Chris Higgins—would have seen any one of them dead as soon as look at them. Yet, that didn't matter now. They had physically participated in murdering a boy—Bart Dyer—and had left another wounded over there to the whims of that thing. And Higgins, well...no one had seen him since he had run off. There had been a single, terrified scream, then nothing. God only knew what had become of him. If, that was, God was still *God* over there.

"W-we did what we h-had t-t-to do," Jimmy managed to mumble in an unconvincing stutter.

"Bullshit!" Ryan screamed suddenly and with such force that both Jimmy and Freddie took a step back. Even Honey seemed to flinch in his arms as he helped support her.

"They were dicks, no argument there, but *we* killed them!" Ryan continued to shout. "I vowed to be nothing like my father, never to hurt people weaker than me. And they *were* weaker! That's why they were after us all summer. Don't you see? It was because they were weak! Not strong, but fucking weak! Only total wimps would ever go after a bunch of kids like that! Sure, they might have hurt Honey worse, or even killed her, but we're supposed to be better than that! Damnit, we're murderers!"

His words hung in the air like a humid fog, touching them and drawing sweat from their pores. Jimmy had nothing to say. Ryan was right. They *had* murdered them, even if it could be justified. They had *killed* those boys.

Jimmy felt sick.

Freddie turned and put a hand against the wall of the hallway, dipped his head, and took a few deep breaths. It was hitting him hard too, Jimmy could see. Freddie hadn't considered it until Ryan spoke up, and now he was distraught, anguish filling his features like a living thing.

Honey limped out from under Ryan's arm, her face incredulous.

"What the fuck do you mean, *we* killed them, Ryan?" she asked in and indignant tone. "Am I the only one who remembers what happened over there? What happened *here*?"

She turned, pointing to a place on the floor of the hallway where her blood lay in a pool, the remnants of those terrible boys' torture.

"Do you see that?" she bellowed at Ryan, but then turned to Freddie and Jimmy to include them. "Do you fucking see that? What do you think they were going to do with me, huh? Let me go? This was physical torture, guys! Not something they could walk away from! They weren't going to let *any* of us out of here alive!"

The three boys all exchanged glances at one another, their eyes wide and mouths agape. Jimmy had believed every word Ryan had said to be true, but now he was believing every word Honey spoke to be even *more* true. Was that possible? To believe diametrically opposed viewpoints to both be the truth? He didn't know, but he was struggling with that very thing now.

"Honey, I—" Ryan started.

She put a hand up to stop him.

"No!" she hissed, her eyes a raging pool now. "No! Fuck those assholes! They *tortured* me! They took the *only* photo of my family I still have and were using it to get me out here without a fight! And Jake was sticking his knife in me! Look!"

She was sobbing as she pointed to the wound on her leg.

"So don't tell me we're no better than them, god-damnit!" she went on, her face beat red now as she began spilling tears. "They were fucking monsters and we left them where they belo—"

As Jimmy watched Honey going on with her monologue, the wall behind her shimmered and he heard that all-too-familiar warble sound.

Jake.

A hand shot out behind Honey and snatched her ankle. She instantly fell face first to the floor with a grunt and whoosh of her breath. Then her eyes were frantic and searching for the boys, her hands made into claws, the fingernails digging into the decaying wood.

"Jimmy?" she whispered hoarsely.

Then she was lurching backward, into another universe, another dimension, and Jimmy and Ryan and Freddie all dived for her, grabbing at her hands.

The Damned Place

"Time to feed the piper, fags!" Jake Reese bellowed to them from the other world, mere feet away from them. They all clutched tightly to Honey's wrists.

CHAPTER 79

Jake pulled at the little bitch, her struggles almost amusing to him. His side hurt, the knife wound still bleeding, but he didn't care. She was in his hands. And his new friend was about to make dinner of all these little fairies, and he was going to get to *watch*!

He was fucking ecstatic.

She screamed and kicked at him as he pulled harder. The boys were pulling on her arms, Jimmy and Ryan on her left arm, the four-eyed Freddie on the right.

But Jake was gaining ground.

She inched towards him, ever so slightly, and behind him he could feel the presence of the monster, its breath hot on his neck causing the hair to stand on end there and his penis to give a Nazi salute.

She'll bleed, he thought, salivating. *They'll all bleed! So much!*

He yanked again on the bitch and gained a few inches. She squirmed beneath him, but to no avail. He was winning. He was overpowering them. They should've known better than to fuck with Jake *FUCKING* Reese! You don't fuck with the baddest fucker in the whole damn town and live to tell the tale, no sir!

His snarl was a vampiric thing, his teeth almost protruding from his gums with his lips pulled so far back. He could smell her. Smell her fear. Her terror. Her pain.

He savored it.

The thing was behind him still, even closer now, its hot breath bringing forth sweat on his back, but Jake didn't care. He had the bitch. The one he was going to fuck on her daddy's corpse, and he meant to savor every second of it. Was there anything better than the writhing terror of a woman beneath you?

Thinking of his mother, her hands bound with the belt she'd tried beating him with, he thought not.

"Time to pay respects to your daddy, cunt!" Jake whispered in her ear.

He raised his hand up to club at the boys, get them to let go for a second or two, enough time for him to pull her over and shut the portal. Once she was out, they could jump through again to claim the little homos.

Only, as his fist came down, Jake Reese saw a very puzzling—*and rather horrifying*—thing.

It was his own knife. The blade was out, shining in the light, and it was rushing up at him. His fist continued to come down in a clubbing motion, and he could see the trajectory in his mind. His fist was going to get raped by his own blade. And not just with the tip. The whole thing was going to plunge into him, violate him like a dirty tramp in an alley, and he could do nothing to stop it.

He tried to pull his hand back, to change its target, but it was too late. The knife in Jimmy's hands, the boy's face a gnarled nightmare of fury, buried into his fist, slicing through bone and sinew and tendon alike and without discrimination.

Jake stared at his now still hand a moment, blood beginning to spurt in giant gouts from him as his throat began to quaver. A strange sound began building, rumbling in his throat. An animal sound. Something made with ingredients of horror, shock, anger, and indignation.

His mouth was opening, the sound within him growing, his eyes nearly popping from his sockets. The bitch was sliding away from him now, from beneath him, but he made no move to stop her. His scream was swimming up from the darkest depths within him, ready to tear free from his throat and shatter the universe around him. The warbling sound began to diminish, and the girl was in the arms of the boys and they were getting up. Two sticks—the ones the assholes had used on Bart—flew past Jake and through the portal even as it began to dim.

The scream finally erupted from his mouth. A harsh, high-pitched noise, wholly disjointed from anything masculine, blew out of his mouth as tears poured down his cheeks. His hand sang to him an awful, ear-piercing tune he did *not* want to hear, and his lungs began to burn.

The portal was fading, and they could see the kids backing up, Ryan and Freddie with the sharp, bloody sticks in their hands. The wall was returning before him, and in moments it would be gone completely. He would be left here with the angry monster, his hand impaled, and nothing to show for it. What would he do?

"Open it!" the thing bellowed an inch from his ear, almost melting the cartilage with its heat. *"Open it now!"*

The Damned Place

Some semblance of sanity returned to Jake then and he focused his energy back on the portal. It cleared at once, the warbling sheen returning.

The beast leaped through, shrinking and emaciating as it went. Jake began to crawl after it.

CHAPTER 80

The thing became almost small when it stepped through. It wasn't nearly as big as it had been on the other side, and its appearance diminished significantly. Skin vanished. Muscles retracted. Its height dropped nearly two feet. It was still much larger than any of them, and fiercely menacing, but it had lost a lot of its stature in the jaunt between worlds.

Jimmy's breath rasped in and out haggardly, sweat falling from his brow in giant gobs.

"Time to be birthed into this world," the Glutton bellowed at them. *"I'll take on your flesh and—"*

Ryan acted first.

He drove the sharp stick into the thing's chest with amazing force, the sharp sound of snapping flesh stinging their ears. Slime began to spill from the wound as the Glutton's face contorted into something which could have been confused or horrified or both. Then Freddie was moving, his braced teeth out in a giant snarl of fury and indignation and flat out terror. The stick was over his head and his eyes were wild and feverish. The thing looked up, screaming a horrible shriek.

The stick went through the side of the thing's face. Right through where a temple might be, through where a brain ought to be. There was a terrible *splat* sound and something akin to a fart as he drove it deeper, his own wail of terrified fury never faltering.

The monster began to wail. It was a terrible sound, one layered in octaves and it seemed to move the very fabric of existence around them, to tear at them with musical claws.

Jimmy rushed forward, kicking his foot out into the thing's abdomen, pushing it back through the portal. As he did this, Ryan and Freddie followed it, twisting their sticks in the thing as it continued to bellow its horror.

Jimmy kicked again.

That was when he noticed Jake behind the Glutton. He was dragging himself through the portal, his face a mask of insanity and pain. Jimmy gasped as he watched Jake rip the knife free of his bloodied fist with nothing more than a wince from the older boy.

"Oh, God," Jimmy muttered as the thing fell through the portal, Freddie and Ryan ripping their sticks out of its body as it went, not willing to give up their weapons.

They all turned to Jake, crawling into their world, half in and half out, the knife in his hand and his face a contorted horror of vengeance and depravity.

"When I said feed the piper," Jake roared with a snarling hiss, "I fucking meant it, you cock-sucking little faggots!"

He raised the knife, readying to stab it down into Freddie's leg, and Jimmy's frozen stance thawed enough for him to move. He pushed Freddie aside, who fell with a grunt and a tumble, and was readying himself to kick Jake in the face with all the force he could muster.

That was when the knife buried in Jimmy's foot.

For a moment, there was no pain, no reaction at all. Only Jake's insane face, grinning up at him with the bloody knife stuck in Jimmy's foot, his bloodied hand clasping the hilt. The insane eyes in Jake's sockets conveyed some sort of victory to him.

Then the pain came, much like a rocket at lift off, the billowing fires of its propelling fuel torching him in place.

Jake ripped the knife free and Jimmy fell, merely a foot away. He had the knife coming into the air again, his teeth snarled out like fangs, his eyes an aberration of normality.

"I'll tear the skin off you, Jimmy Dalton!" Jake roared as the knife reached its apex.

Jimmy's eyes were filled with tears from the pain and the horror, and his body tensed in expectation of the stabbing blow.

But then Jake's eyes took on a different quality. One more like confusion than fury and insanity. A *stupid* look.

Then he was lurching back into the other world, the Glutton yanking him back by the foot.

Jimmy scrambled to his feet then, wincing on his injured foot, and limping to the wall to steady himself. Jake was writhing and screaming obscenities at them from the other world as the Glutton held him down, its own wounds seeming to diminish now.

"I'll get you, Jimmy Dalton!" Jake was screaming insanely beneath the monster. *"I'll get you, you fucking faggot!"*

The beast glared up at them all through the portal, which was even now fading as it held Jake to the ground.

Freddie was on them all, urging them to get out. No, to get the *fuck* out, and right now, before there was another chance to regroup. They began making their way to the door and the hot summer beyond it, Jimmy being helped along by Freddie, Honey helped along by Ryan. Behind them, Jake continued to scream and curse them, and beneath his bellows, they could hear the low rumble of a growl from the monster. The Glutton.

The eater of worlds.

"Soon," an otherworldly voice floated to Jimmy's ears and he stopped, turning back. They all turned back, on the steps of the porch now, peering back through the open front door at the fading portal between the worlds.

"Soon," the thing repeated as the warble faded away and the shimmering portal solidified into the wall. As it faded, Jimmy could see the wounds from the sharp sticks which had penetrated the beast closing before his eyes, and he noticed how much bigger and more fierce the thing was back in the other world. Then it was gone. For a moment, they could still hear the faint screaming of Jake on the floor, flailing around vigorously and insanely, but soon it too was gone.

They all stood there for a long moment, staring at the wall where the portal had been. Where the horror had been left behind. The place where what they had all done would forever remain. Secret from this world, but never from their minds.

They all shuddered in unison. A moment later, they all turned to each other, exchanging fond looks, though they were laden with sadness. They hugged each other. Held each other. Treasured each other. Then they began to make their way back to town.

None of them spoke a word.

CHAPTER 81

There would be questions. *Lots* of questions.

When they had returned to town, the kids made their way to Honey's house, since it was the only sure place to keep away from any adults, a fact which had sent Honey into another sobbing fit for a while. Her three boys comforted her and embraced her, crying tears of their own. Tears for her, for her father, for themselves, for each other. The weight, the *gravity* of it all had finally come crushing down on them, and they were not prepared to cope with it.

They wanted their parents. All of them did. Wanted to run into their arms, tell them everything that had happened and let themselves be comforted and consoled, told they'd done the right thing. They'd literally saved the world. But none of them felt the slightest bit of pride in the triumph. The slightest bit of justification. Not now. Even Honey, as her great sobs escaped her, her breaths heaving and her wails tearing from her, not even she still believed they'd done the right thing. Sacrificing a boy—even a twisted freak like Bart or an outright psychopath like Jake—was simply *wrong*. There was no way around it. They were *kids,* just like themselves. Human beings. And what of Chris Higgins? He hadn't been cruel like the others. Not at all like the others. Yet he was gone as well, and it was their fault. Their doing.

They were murderers.

It was a long time before any of them could pull themselves together, and no one rushed the others. It all came out. The pain, the loss, the relief. All of it poured from them in tears and snot and grief.

Finally—none of them knew how much later—they found all their tears used up, and the four of them sat on the floor at Honey's house, its walls littered with the memories of a once happy family. One now gone entirely. Honey was alone.

She stared at the picture she'd retrieved from Bart Dyer as they had offered him up as a sacrifice to save them precious seconds to escape. She stroked the picture where her mother's face was with two fingers, something she often did with this photograph. But then she did something she hadn't done since her father had fallen into his years-long, drunken despair. She began stroking his face too. Because, in the end, he wasn't a bad man. He had been a broken man, but a good man. And he'd proven his love for Honey in the end. She hadn't given him a chance in these past years since her mother had passed, and not without good reason, but now she wished she could have him back, even for five minutes, to tell him how much she loved him. How proud she was of him. How proud she was to be his daughter.

A final, straggling tear slipped down her cheek.

"What are we going to do?"

They all turned to look at Freddie, who'd asked the question. Their eyes were blank, glazed. None of them had any idea.

"There's going to be questions," Freddie went on. "Three kids go missing, it's going to catch some attention. And there's a good chance they're going to come asking us."

They all turned their gaze to the floor between them, staring at it in wonder.

"We tell the truth," Ryan offered, his voice nearly a whisper. "They'll have to believe us. Jake and his friends were going to kill Honey, and that thing—"

"No," Jimmy cut him off, his eyes remaining focused on the brown carpet. "We can't afford to tell the truth. If we do that, they'll either arrest us for murder or lock us up with your father in the asylum. And we can't let either of those things happen."

"Why not?" Honey asked in a trembling voice.

Jimmy's eyes met hers for a moment, then around the room to the others.

"What if it comes back?"

Silence. No one blinked.

"We're the only ones on the *planet* who even know about this thing. And no one would ever believe us unless they saw it, but by then it would be too late. No. We have to stay vigilant, and keep an eye out for it. If it finds a way back through, and it gets the chance to feed, we're fucked. The whole *world* is fucked. We're the only ones who can stand in the way. So, we can't tell the truth. We can *never* tell the truth."

The others took in his words, considering them. Honey thought about her father, gone now in another universe, and suddenly had an idea.

"I-I have an idea," she said to the others, who all looked at her intently.

"Go on, Honey," Ryan said softly, squeezing her arm gently. "We're all ears."

She smiled at him warmly.

"My parents are both gone now," she started, and stifled a threatening sob. "But I'm also hurt. Bad. I'll need a few days—maybe a couple weeks—to heal up. Daddy was hardly working anyway, so no one will miss him for a while. And there's plenty of food here, the bills are paid up for another month. I can stay here, lay low. Once I'm all healed up, I can come forward and tell the police my father has left. Say it's been a couple days and I haven't seen him or heard from him. It might work. I could live with my aunt. She lives here in town."

Jimmy was nodding.

"Yeah, that could work," he said. "But what about questions about Jake and his gang? What will we say there?"

"Nothing," Freddie offered matter-of-factly. "We don't know, haven't seen them. Stick to that. Keep it simple. The more we add to it, the more we're liable to shit on the whole thing and end up in the crazy house with Chester. No offense, Ryan."

"None taken, fuck that asshole," Ryan responded emptily.

Then they all laughed. It was a long and soothing thing, something which they shared as intimately as lovers. New tears came from their eyes, but the sadness was gone from them now as they guffawed, much harder than the statement had warranted. But this was something they had needed. All of them. A release of sorts.

When the laughs had subsided to nothing more than mild chuckles and, eventually, faded entirely, they all looked about the room at one another. There was genuine love on all their faces as they took each other in, and Honey was compelled to tell them so.

"I love you guys," she said, a faint blush tickling her cheeks. "With all my heart. You're the best friends I've ever had."

They all smiled back at her.

"Love you too, Honey," Freddie said with a brace-filled smile.

"I love you too," Jimmy said sheepishly.

She looked at Ryan, whose face was stricken so serious, she thought something might be wrong for a moment. She leaned forward, intending to ask him what the problem was, but he spoke before she had a chance.

"I love you from the pit of my soul," he said, a tremor in his voice, his eyes cloudy with moisture. "I would do anything in the world for you. I adore you, Honey Bascom."

Her face blossomed into a rose garden and she gasped.

"Ryan, you're so sweet, I—"

"I mean it," he said, laying his hand on her arm and giving it another squeeze.

She smiled warmly at him, placing her hand over his and rubbing his fingers with her thumb.

They stayed like that for a long time, then Freddie broke the moment with another declaration.

"So," he said, clasping his fingers together and sighing harshly. "We're agreed, then. We say nothing of Jake and the others, we give Honey a few weeks to heal up and come out with her story, and we..."

He trailed off for a moment, looking to Jimmy.

"We stay vigilant," Jimmy finished for him. "We stay clear of that place, and make sure others do as well."

"Stay vigilant," Freddie repeated.

"Vigilant," Honey and Ryan said in unison, then looked at each other and laughed softly.

"We keep that damned place off the map," Freddie said, his eyes growing serious and distant.

The others nodded. Jimmy put his hand out between them all.

"It's a pact, then," he said, and the others instinctively put their hands on his. "We saved the world today, guys. But the damned place is still out there, and the Glutton is still on the other side. We do everything we can to keep it there. And if it ever does try and come back, we stop it. Together."

"Together," the others chimed in unison.

Jimmy smiled at them all, and the others returned it. Then they all embraced one another again and held each other for a long time.

"For as long as it takes, to the ends of our lives, we stand watch," Jimmy whispered.

They all agreed. And they all hugged each other tighter.

Epilogue:
October 31, 1996

"I just think it'd be cool to do it one time, you know? Everyone else gets to do it every year, and I'm about to graduate next May. I don't get what the big deal is, Mother."

Though he was questioning her, he wasn't being petulant about it. It was merely a search for knowledge. For understanding. There would be no fit-throwing here, she knew. He was called to so much more, and he was already beginning to answer that call beautifully.

Cherry Reese cocked her head to the left, her wide, phony smile spread cheek to cheek. Norman was such a good boy. Such a sweet boy. But he didn't understand. Perhaps that was her fault. It was certainly her son-of-a-bitch husband George's fault—*and no— no, that's not a curse, his mother really was a bitch.*

George had been pretty detached from them for years now. Ever since Jake had gone missing. Even well before that, actually. But that was another story. Norman needed a father. A *strong* father. A man who would raise him up in the fear and admonition of their Lord like a proper Christian. But George was no strong father. He was hardly even a real man, for that matter. And Cherry reminded him of that fact frequently.

But Norman...

Norman needed guidance, and in the absence of a strong father figure, Cherry would just have to provide him with that guidance herself. And she could do it, yes sir, you better believe it. She didn't need any man to make one out of her son. She could—she *was*—doing that all on her own, and Norman was doing fine. A fine young man, and one called to such greatness as had never been bestowed upon another human being since Christ Himself.

She reached out a hand and cupped it gently on Norman's face. Her thumb caressed his cheekbone just beneath his right eye. His eyelids fluttered closed, but not in annoyance. Not her boy.

Her *man*.

He pressed his face into her palm, rubbing it softly against his cheek. His hand came up and rested gently on her wrist as he kissed her fingers tenderly.

Cherry felt a shuddering heat flush her chest. But now was no time for that.

"Halloween is the devil's birthday, Norman," she said, keeping her voice even in spite of the tremble. "Real Christians don't participate in the celebration of Satan's birth."

His eyes opened from behind her hand, which was now tingling. They were bright and moist, half-lidded, as though he were mulling this over in his mind.

"The devil's birthday?" he asked. "Is that in the Bible?"

She cocked her head the other way and stepped closer to her boy. They were inches apart now.

"Not exactly," she said in a breathy tone. "But it's what we believe."

He nodded slightly, his hand on the back of hers now as he held it to his cheek, still stealing kisses on it every few seconds.

"It's just—and I'm not arguing with you, Mother, I promise—it's just the kids at school, almost all of them are Christians too. Different churches, sure, but Christians all the same. They dress up and—"

She brought her other hand up and covered his lips with a vertical finger.

"They're not *real* Christians, Norman," she said, her voice low and almost seductive. "Not like us. They may not know any better, but that doesn't absolve them. But it's our job to teach them how to follow God properly. It's *your* job to lead them. That's why we have the signs."

They both glanced in unison to the hand-drawn posters on picket sticks. They declared such poignant statements as "HELLOWEEN IS WITCHCRAFT!" and "JESUS DOESN'T REQUIRE COSTUMES!"

"Do you think they'll listen to us, Mother?" Norman asked, returning his gaze to hers. She could feel his breath on her lips, not more than an inch away.

"No," she said, shaking her head slowly, her eyes flitting down to his lips for a moment, then back to his eyes. His beautiful, destined eyes. "But we still have to warn them. We do it because we love them. *Everything* we do should be because we love people, Norman."

He smiled and kissed her palm once more.

"I understand, Mother."

Cherry smiled, placing her other hand on her son's chest, her fingers curling at the tips ever so slightly.

"I knew you would, Norman. You're my big, smart man..."

She paused, her gaze drifting from his eyes, her features hardening.

"I'm glad at least one of my boys was worth something…"

She heard Norman's throat click as he swallowed. His eyes drifted down, looking at the swell of her breasts, but not with longing. It was just somewhere to easily avert his eyes in their strange embrace.

"I miss him sometimes, Mother," he said, his voice betraying a quiver. "He's my big broth—"

"He's *nothing!*" she hissed, her eyes snapping back to his face. He looked up and stumbled back a step, alarmed.

"He's *dead*, and good riddance to that motherfucker!"

She could see the outright horror on her son's face at the use of the curse. But no…no-no, that wasn't a curse. Her eldest offspring had been *exactly* that. A motherfucker.

"M-Mother, I—" he began, but she cut him off with that same vertical finger, cupping his face again and stepping in close, their foreheads touching now.

"Shh-shhhh," she said, her tone softening back to her low, breathy tone.

When Jake and the other boys had gone missing, Mr. Higgins had made quite the uproar around town, demanding they find his son, Chris. He even went to the FBI field office out in Dallas with the worry that the boys may have been kidnapped. But, when no phone calls for ransom or any demands of any kind came, this worry quickly died away and again became a matter for the local authorities. They were utterly worthless, but that was just as well. Cherry had no desire to ever see Jake again. He had violated her and humiliated her and taken the dominant role in the home over her. *No* child should ever have so much power. But she—and of course George, the sackless wonder—had been much too terrified to do anything about it, especially there at the end. Yes, it was a good thing he was gone, and she still prayed every day to the aberration of a god she served that it would stay that way.

There had been some younger kids who'd been of interest to the police during their investigation, which was *technically* still open, though no one had actively investigated it since early '91. There was the Dalton kid, whose drunk of a Catholic Mother disgusted Cherry to her core. The Laughton boy with the psycho father who'd lost his mind in the woods and killed a man while hunting—though no body had ever been discovered. The James boy and the little whore they ran around with whose father had vanished in the weeks after Jake and the others had gone missing.

But without any evidence of wrongdoing—and the kids' adamant assertion they'd not seen her son and his friends for weeks before they'd gone missing—nothing had been done about it.

Still, questions remained.

But Cherry Reese was happy for the matter to remain dormant, if not closed altogether. With Jake gone, she'd been able to reassert control of the house. And since George was all too happy to let her have it, she had been able to start molding Norman. Shaping him into the man God had called him to be. The *mightiest* man of God to ever walk this earth. And he was *her* son. *Her* boy. God had chosen *her* to carry him within her womb, the one He had called to lead Christ back into this filthy world and cleanse it once and for all.

The one *she* had been compelled to lead into manhood.

Heat flushed her anew as she swayed with her son, holding his face and chest. His arms were around her now and she felt her breasts pressing into his chest. Could feel his warmth. His strength.

Her boy.

"I love you, Norman," she whispered, her lips brushing his ever so gently, and she felt him respond against her.

It was her boy, her man, her Norman, who was called by God Himself to save the world through his music and his voice and his charisma. It was his calling, though God had told *her* rather than him. But she'd passed the message on to him. Oh, she'd told him over and over again. And he would be ready. When the time came, when God began to move into the world again, her Norman would be ready.

"We have to meet the others at the church," Norman whispered, their lips still touching, their eyes closed. "They'll be waiting. They're expecting me to lead them in the protest."

"Mmmmm," she moaned against her son and smiled. "And you'll lead them, my sweet, sweet Norman."

Her hands slid up to his head and fisted in his hair.

"But," she said, opening her eyes for just a moment, "they won't start without you."

Their mouths pressed together then, and passion followed. They would wait for Norman, because they knew what she knew. They knew he was God's chosen one. The one to lead God into this godless world where people celebrated the birth of the devil in horrific costumes and called the Pope of Rome the vicar of Christ with a straight face. Yes, they would wait. They would wait for their new prophet.

They would wait for Norman.

About the Author

Chris Miller is an active member of the Horror Writers Association and is a native Texan who has been writing from an early age, though he only started publishing in 2017. He attended North East Texas Community College and LeTourneau University, where he focused on creative writing courses. He is the superintendent of his family-owned water well company and his first novel, A MURDER OF SAINTS, has been met with acclaim from both critics and readers alike, as has his second novel THE HARD GOODBYE and his novella TRESPASS. His short stories–found in numerous anthologies–have likewise been praised. Chris and his wife, Aliana, have three children and live in Winnsboro, Texas.

Website: **http://www.authorchrismiller.com**

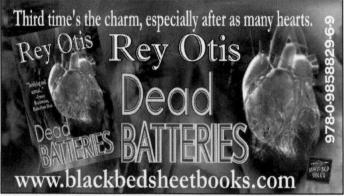

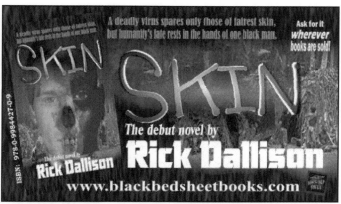

Made in the USA
Columbia, SC
11 July 2024